Formatted with Vellum

A DREAM OF THE FOREST
THE COURT OF THE EARTH
BOOK I

ROSE BITTERLY

A NOTE FROM THE AUTHOR

Thanks so much for picking up A Dream of the Forest! However, I want to be clear: This is a very spicy and very dark MFM horror romance that features potentially upsetting subject matter.

Because a certain online bookseller has a history of removing books with comprehensive content warnings, I have opted to put the full, detailed list of both triggers and sexual content notes on my website, which you can access at rosebitterly.com/content-notes or via the QR code below:

Once you're on the site, just click or tap on the book's title to expand the full list of notes. You'll find this book under the "Devil's Courts" heading.

That said, there are a few triggers that I did want to list here:

- Graphic depictions of sex and violence, including BDSM and other extreme sexual material. Please see the website link for more details
- Morally black MMCs
- Wild animal death (rattlesnake)
- Human sacrifice
- Light blasphemy/religious themes

If you have any questions or would like further clarification, don't hesitate to reach out.

~Rose Bitterly

PS. I would feel remiss if I didn't also mention that this book ends on a cliffhanger. However, the story will resolve with an HEA in Book 2 of the duet.

IVY

It starts with a missed call. I check my phone after lunch and see *Golly* emblazoned on the screen.

That's what we called her, my grandmother on my mother's side. I don't even know why I have her number saved —I haven't spoken to her since I was a child, so long ago I barely remember it.

Something curls in my stomach, seeing the missed call. A vague sense of unease that reminds me of a particular feeling I get when I wake up in the middle of the night, knowing I dreamed but not remembering what I dreamed about.

I take my phone and my laptop out onto my apartment patio, leaving the door cracked in case my cat Gnocchi wants to come out, too. It's a nice day, sunny but cool, and the cactuses down in the apartment courtyard are just starting to bloom. I mean to work—I've got essays to grade—but I keep looking at my phone. Looking at that missed call.

I can vaguely picture Golly: a warm smile, curly dark hair, a brightly colored cotton dress with strappy sleeves. She never felt like a grandmother. My sister Juniper and I stayed with her the summer our parents divorced, when I was eight or so, on her little farmhouse outside Harlan, Texas. On the edge of the Hartshorn estate.

Hartshorn. I don't remember it much, although I was friends with the boy who lived there. Spent the whole summer with him, the two of us swimming in the nearby creek. God, I haven't thought about that in years.

Despite the sun, chills ripple over my skin. I stare at the student essay on my laptop, the words blurring together, and all I can think about is the name *Golly* on my phone. How did I have her number saved? Mom cut off contact with her before I went to high school.

Irritated, I snap my laptop shut and snatch up the phone. Open up the missed call notification. Then I call her back.

It rings twice before a man answers with a breathless, "Hello?"

I frown. Golly wasn't married. She never married, according to Mom. Wouldn't even tell her who Mom's father was, which, from what I gather, is only a small part of their estrangement.

"Hello?" I echo. "Um, you called me? Ivy Myste?"

"Oh, yes! Ms. Myste. Yes, thank you for calling back." He clears his throat. There's a thumping over the phone, the sound of rattling papers. "Sorry, you caught me right as I was about to leave. I was going to try you again from my office, but..." His voice trails off.

"Is my grandmother there?" I ask. "Gloria Arbour?"

The man doesn't answer right away, although I can hear him breathing. Then he says, "I'm afraid I have some bad news."

My body tightens—not with anxiety but with a kind of odd, sparking anticipation, like I'm about to open a locked door.

"Your grandmother passed away last week," the man says. "A sudden stroke. I'm very, very sorry."

"Oh." It's all I can think to say to fill the swell of uncomfortable silence, the only thing that fits the odd, perfunctory sadness I feel at the news. I sink down in my deck chair, staring out at the cactus flowers in the courtyard. There's a little patter of feet and then Gnocchi jumps on my table and blinks at me with his big yellow eyes, like he can sense my discomfort. I scratch him between the ears for his trouble.

"I know she and your mother were estranged," the man continues. "And that you haven't been in contact with her. But—"

"I'm sorry," I interrupt. "But who are you, exactly?"

The man gives an embarrassed laugh. "Oh my god, I didn't —I'm Lee Whitman. Ms. Arbour's lawyer. She put me in charge of her estate shortly before her death."

"So that's why you have her phone."

"No, no, this is a landline. I'm at her house, getting everything ready—well, that's actually why I called you, Ms. Myste." Lee takes a deep breath. "She left everything to you."

I blink, certain I misheard. "Excuse me? Do you mean— like, in her will?"

"Yes." Lee's voice changes, becomes a little less flustered. "A small inheritance of about a hundred thousand dollars—"

I choke. "Did you say a hundred thousand dollars?" *That's small?* I think, although I keep it to myself. I'm an adjunct for the local community college here in Santa Fe. I'm lucky if I clear forty thousand in a year.

"Yes, in stocks and bonds, mostly. She also left you her house, which is appraised at about a quarter of a million dollars. You're welcome to sell it, of course. She didn't leave any stipulations in that regard. But you will need to, ah, clear it out first. Or arrange an estate sale. I can give you the number of a local company that can help with that."

My balcony spins around me, and I brace myself against the chair. Golly's house. I haven't thought about it in years, but memories flash vividly through my head, one after another like dominoes falling.

Like how she kept the house cool during that blazingly hot

summer with an ancient, rattling air conditioner and thick dark curtains she pulled shut during the day. Or the thick tangle of trees that surrounded her property, and the sun-dappled path that led to a swollen creek. I remember the song of cicadas. I remember a wind chime as tall as I was at eight years old, knotted off on an angry, sprawling oak tree, and the way it would bong out at night while I was falling asleep.

"—sign over the estate. In-person, unfortunately. That was the *one* stipulation in your grandmother's will, and—"

"I'm sorry, what?" I stand up, still dizzy, and lean against my balcony. Her house had a screened-in porch, I remember, and I used to sit on a swing with the Hartshorn boy. He had ice-blonde hair and eyes the color of the creek where we would go swimming.

"You'll need to come here to Harlan to sign the paperwork," Lee says. "I know it's a huge inconvenience, but there's language in the will that can allow me to pay for your plane ticket. And of course you can stay in your grandmother's house. It's not a bad deal, really—it'll give you a chance to get a lay of everything and decide what you want to do."

I squeeze my eyes shut and take a deep breath. Mom isn't going to be happy about me going back to East Texas. But I've also not done much in the last several years to keep Mom happy.

"What about the funeral?" The question is out of my mouth before I can stop it. Before I even realized I wanted to ask it, honestly.

Lee goes quiet for a few seconds. "Well, I'm afraid—I'm afraid it's already happened. Two days ago."

My head buzzes.

"I can show you where she's buried. It's nearby. Walking distance from the house, actually." A pause. "At the Hartshorn estate."

The Hartshorn estate. I don't remember it with the vividness that I remember Golly's house. Only that it was a sprawling mansion surrounded by lush, vibrant gardens.

"They have a cemetery?" I ask.

"Yes, a family plot. I'm not sure about the details—I know Ms. Arbour was close with Judith Hartshorn." Lee coughs. "If you give me your email, I can send over the pertinent information, and we can see about scheduling a flight for you to take care of the signing."

I take a deep breath, still trying to process everything. I tap on my laptop and bring up the student essay I was supposed to be grading. "I won't be able to come until the end of the semester," I tell him. "About a month from now."

Lee tuts on the phone. "I really need to get this taken care of," he says. "Maybe you can just come for the weekend? Like I said, you don't have to pay for the plane ticket. Or a rental car, for that matter. The closet airport's a bit of a hike."

A desert wind gusts through the courtyard, making the cactus flowers shiver and dance. Everything's so dry here in New Mexico, but for a moment, I swear I feel a dampness on my skin. It was always so humid at Golly's house, even inside.

"I can maybe make that work." I hardly believe I'm saying it, but at the same time, I'm already working through the logistics. I can give my students a workday on Friday so I can fly out that morning. Fly back Sunday afternoon so I don't have to worry about Monday's class. Juniper would be willing to come over and take care of Gnocchi.

My skin prickles.

"Yeah, email me the details and I'll decide," I say, even though I've already made up my mind.

2

IVY

"I still can't believe you did this," Juniper says, her voice crackly through the rental car's speakers. "Mom is going to kill you."

"Mom doesn't have to know." A sign flashes up ahead: HARLAN, 5 MILES. I'm regretting asking Juniper to feed Gnocchi now. I should have kept it a secret from both of them.

"You don't think she's going to find out?" Juniper says. "How are you going to sell a freaking house without her knowing?"

"We barely talk." I keep my eyes fixed on the road, looking for the turnoff. The little two-lane highway is crowded by dense pine trees and overgrown ferns and grasses, impossibly green compared to Santa Fe. Even the shadows feel green. "How's Gnocchi?"

"He's sleeping on your chair," Juniper says. "And don't change the subject."

"Uh, you're the one who changed the subject. I called to make sure Gnocchi was okay." This isn't really true. I actually called Juniper because some small, worried part of me was afraid I would get lost in all this endless green. I called her because I wanted a tether to the real world.

Juniper huffs. "Whatever. Just—that place always creeped me out, okay?"

"It's only for a few days." Another sign appears up ahead: HARLAN, EXIT 390. "Oh, shit. This is my turnoff. I'll text you when I'm settled, okay?"

"Be *careful*," Juniper says.

"Of what?" I put on my turn signal even though there's no one else on the road and hasn't been for the last fifteen minutes. "It's Golly's house, Junie. Just an old house in the middle of nowhere."

Juniper goes quiet. "I wasn't talking about Golly's house," she says softly, and I know, somehow, that she means the Hartshorn estate. The house I barely remember.

"I'll be *fine*," I tell her. "I've got to pull up the GPS, okay? I'll text you."

I hang up before she can protest or warn me or whatever it is she was gearing up to do. I know Juniper never liked our summer at Golly's the way I did. Probably because she was a couple of years younger and didn't have anything to do while I was running all over the woods with that blond Hartshorn boy.

And his brother, too. I vaguely remember his brother, tall and dark-haired. But he was older. He never spoke to us.

The highway exit weaves me deeper into the woods, although there are signs of civilization: Dusty clapboard houses, their yards blazing with wildflowers. A peeling old billboard for a barbecue restaurant. A white church.

It all stirs up a sense of familiarity that aches in my chest like heartbreak.

I switch on the GPS, and the mechanized voice tells me to turn right and then left, and then, out of nowhere, I'm driving down the main street of Harlan, the battered old storefronts shrouded in the same forest-filtered light as the highway.

Lee Whitman's office is in an old house that sits on the street corner, nestled between a credit union and a faded strip mall. I park on the street and climb out into the thick, humid air and blink at my surroundings. It all looks vaguely familiar, and I have a sudden flash of memory: me pulling my car into that strip mall parking lot and eating at the Mexican restaurant there.

I shake my head. That's impossible. I only came to Harlan with Golly when I was eight years old. I certainly never drove here myself. But as I walk up to Lee's office, I can picture it: sliding into the booth by myself, alternating between the green and red salsas they brought me. My phone buzzing on the table, Golly's name flashing on the screen.

Impossible.

So why *did* I have her number saved in my phone?

I step into Lee's office, the air conditioning frigid. A bell chimes somewhere in the building, and I stand awkwardly in the foyer, which still looks like a house, and try not to dwell on that impossible memory.

"Come on back!" A male voice calls out from deeper in the house. "It's just me today."

I follow the sound of the voice deeper into the tangle of rooms until I find a man with shorn brown hair sitting behind a messy desk, tapping away furiously on a computer. He looks around my age, much younger than I expected.

"Mr. Whitman?" I ask, stepping into the doorway.

He looks up at me, his eyes big behind his glasses.

"It's Ivy Myste." I'm suddenly afraid this is all some ridiculous prank.

"Oh my god! Ms. Myste! I was thinking it would take you longer to get out here." He jumps up and drags out the drawer of a towering filing cabinet. "Thanks again for coming out here like this. I know it's a bit weird."

I step into the office. I've never actually been in a lawyer's office before, but I would imagine it would look like this. Legal books line the wall. Framed diplomas hanging behind the desk. Lots of filing cabinets.

Lee pulls out a file and turns to me with a grin. "Here's everything you need to sign. Won't take but a few minutes." He gestures toward a chair in front of his desk, and I slide into it, still finding this entire situation surreal. I can't believe that I'm sitting in a lawyer's office in Harlan, Texas, preparing to inherit my estranged grandmother's house.

Why do I remember driving here?

Why did I have her number in my phone?

"You ready to begin?" Lee says, jerking me out of my thoughts. "Like I said, it won't take long. I can drive out there with you, get you situated." He hesitates. "I can show you where Ms. Arbour is buried, if you'd like."

"Um, that would be great." *At Hartshorn*, I think, and I can almost picture the house, like it's a word on the tip of my tongue.

Lee's right; it doesn't take long for me to sign all the paperwork. He flips through each document and explains what they are and lets me scan over them, even though I'm too dazed to really decipher the legalese. I initial where he tells me to initial. Sign and date where he tells me to sign and date.

When the last document is flipped over, he taps them all against the table and slides them into the folder. "I'll need to make copies of all this," he says, "And I'll mail the originals back to you for your records. I'll just need to make sure I have your home address—or, I mean, how long are you staying? I could drop them off at the house."

"I'm leaving Sunday."

"Oh, I'll drop them off tomorrow, then." He gives me a sad smile. "I appreciate you coming out here at such short notice. Ms. Arbour was very insistent that you sign in person." He shrugs.

"Do you know why?"

"She didn't say." Lee slides a desk drawer open and pulls out a key ring with three keys and offers it to me. "But, you know. She was always eccentric. That's why I liked her." He smiles.

I take the keys. They look ordinary. They could be the keys to my crappy apartment back in Santa Fe, the keys to the house where I grew up in Las Cruces.

"Did you know her well?" I'm not even sure why I'm asking.

"Nobody really knew her well," he says. "Except for the Hartshorn family, I suppose. But they, uh, they keep to themselves, you know."

The word *Hartshorn* throbs in my ear.

"I don't—I didn't know her well at all." As soon as the words are out, I cringe that I'm telling this to a stranger. But I'm struck with this strange, delirious urge to find out more about her. About why she would leave the house to me, of all people. "My mother and Golly didn't get along."

"Golly." Lee smiles. "That's cute. I remember her telling me that's what you girls called her."

I smile back, thinly, noticing that he sidestepped the whole thing about her and my mother. Which is fair. "Not getting along" is putting it mildly, and I really have no idea how much Golly told him about it.

Although I want to know.

"I guess I'm just—" I pause, looking down at the keys in my hand. "I guess I just don't understand why she willed everything to me."

Lee tilts his head, giving me a sympathetic look.

"I don't expect you to know," I say quickly. "I just—it's a weird situation, like you said."

"She was practically a Hartshorn," Lee says. "And they're weird people. I guess I'm used to it." He leans closer, over the desk. "You're right, I don't know much. Your grandmother was my client, although she wasn't the chatty sort." He smiles a little. "I'll tell you this much. She updated her will about six months before her death. I can't tell you what was in it before that, of course, but I will tell you what she said when she made the change."

I stare at him, my heart thudding. It suddenly feels like there's too little air in the office, and the light shifts in the windows. Turns dark and green, as if the sun went behind a cloud.

"She said you were the only one who would appreciate it," Lee says. 'The only one who really ever belonged at Hartshorn."

3

IVY

It takes twenty minutes to get to Golly's house from the middle of downtown Harlan, almost all of it winding through thick, dense forest. Before I left, Lee scrawled out directions to the house on a piece of notebook paper and told me not to trust the GPS. "It always gets the directions wrong," he said sheepishly. "You'll wind up halfway to Shreveport if you aren't careful."

Left at FM 8931, his directions say, and I nearly miss the sign, which is half-hidden by a spray of dogwood trees. I jerk the car, my suitcase thumping around in the trunk, and barely make it onto the narrow road.

But the road sparks something. Another memory. Me driving again, sunlight flashing over the dashboard of the old Chrysler I drove in college.

But I never came here in college. Mom wouldn't have allowed it, for one.

My car crunches forward over the road. I glance down at the directions: *Look for the painted mailbox.* All I see is trees and greenery, so lush it feels like it's choking me.

But then—a flash of yellow. And with it, another memory,

although one that doesn't feel out of place. It's from the summer I visited with Jumper. I helped Golly paint her mailbox with sunflowers, and it looks like she kept it that way, a blaze of light among all the green.

I slow my car, turning carefully into the driveway beside the mailbox. It's long, twining up through the trees, but I see glimpses of Golly's house up ahead. It looks like what I remember, too. White clapboard siding. Dark blue trim. The wraparound porch. A carport instead of a garage next to a couple of clotheslines.

A well-worn path leading into the woods.

Leading to Hartshorn. The name of the house and of the family that lived there.

I kill my car's engine and, just for a moment, sit without moving, my hands on the steering wheel, staring through the windshield up at Golly's house.

At *my* house.

No, it's not. I can't live here. I'll have to sell it. Use the money to buy my own place in Santa Fe.

The idea should be appealing—how many times have I complained to Juniper about my skyrocketing rent, even if her go-to response is to tell me to get out of academia? But it sits uncomfortably in my stomach.

This is Golly's house. How can I sell it?

You didn't even know her.

The thought sounds like my mother, not me. I get out of the car.

The air is even thicker here in the woods than it was in Harlan, although it feels cooler, laced with the scent of cedar and the moist, musty fragrance of the earth. A breeze blows across the trees, making them rustle around me, sounding like voices.

Lee told me he'd meet me in about an hour and show me where Golly's grave is, but I have the sudden, sharp thought that I don't need him. I can just take the path into the woods. I've walked it before; I know where it'll lead me. I shouldn't remember, but I do.

I grab my purse and suitcase and hold the key ring in my palm as I walk up to the front door. The screen is unlocked and doesn't quite fit in the jam, and I can remember the way it sounded when I'd let it slam after racing home after a day spent at the creek with that blond Hartshorn boy.

What was his name again? Zachary? Zaden? No, none of those sound right.

I wonder, idly, if he still lives at the house. Surely not. The Hartshorn family was wealthy. Someone like that would have gone to college. Moved to a city, even if he stayed close. Houston or Dallas, maybe Austin.

The key fits neatly into the lock, which opens for me with no trouble. When I push the door, an overwhelming scent of gardenias sweeps over me, and suddenly I remember *so much* from that summer, a thousand memories tumbling into place.

Golly grilling hamburgers in the backyard. Catching fireflies with Juniper, the two of us setting up soft glowing jars on the front porch until Golly made us let them go—*You can't trap free things, girls*, she told us, her voice rough from the cigarettes she would smoke. Always outside, though. Sitting on the couch with a glass of iced tea, the smoke trailing up between her fingers.

I remember the ancient mattress I slept on each night, how there was a dip in the center that I would roll into, exhausted from playing all day. I remember Juniper crying over something, and me calling her baby as I took off down the path with—

Xavier. That was his name. Xavier Hartshorn.

I drop my suitcase in the foyer and look into the house. The curtains are pulled open, letting in the sunlight that illuminates the dust I stirred up when I came inside. A staircase to my right. The living room to my left, where Golly would leave the daytime talk shows running even if she wasn't watching them. I know that if I keep walking, I'll wind up in the kitchen, where there's a metal table set up against the wall where we ate breakfast every morning and a window over the sink that looks out at the back yard and the woods behind it.

I follow that path, actually. I walk past the staircases and into the kitchen, and it looks the same as I remembered, with the table and the phone on the wall and the ancient appliances that probably haven't been updated since the '80s. And the back door, its single square window covered with a thin, gauzy curtain. I unlock it and go out on the back porch and look out at the overgrown backyard, the grass turning to a meadow in the drowsy spring heat.

I keep going. I let the door slam shut behind me, the sound ricocheting like a memory around in my head, and step off the porch. I let myself through the metal gate and pass the oak tree with the wind chime, which bongs softly as I walk by. That oak tree marks the start of the woods, and in the woods is the path to Hartshorn.

I stop onto it, the path. It's just packed dirt, a trail where the greenery died from years of people walking back and forth.

Your grandmother was close to the Hartshorn family, Lee said, and I do remember that, now. She was friends with Xavier's grandmother, who would come visiting nearly every day. That was how I met Xavier, actually. She brought him with her right after my sister and I arrived in Texas.

Never his dark-haired brother, though. Him, I met at Hartshorn itself. His name wobbles in the back of my head, though. I can't grasp onto it.

I keep walking, drawn forward on the path by memory or loss or something else—the dark, verdant call of the woods. Once I leave Golly's backyard and enter a tunnel of trees, everything turns still and sticky. I hear the wind overhead, but I can't feel it.

The path is clear, though. And familiar. When I reach a fork, I know instinctively to go left, since going right will take me down to the creek, where there was a rope swing tied to an oak tree and Xavier and I used to take turns swinging out over the water and then letting go. Was that why I called Juniper a baby? Because she refused?

It's all a jumble, and it seems to get worse as I move deeper into the woods. In fact, it only occurs to me, after about five minutes or so of walking, that I left my phone back at the house.

I stop, the forest rustling around me and throwing dappled green light across my feet. I ought to turn around and wait for Lee. I can't just go traipsing around on someone else's property.

But I came this far, didn't I?

So I keep walking. And then, just when I think I made a mistake, that the path doesn't go to the house, the trees fall away, and there's Hartshorn.

It's enormous, so much bigger than I remember. And stranger, too, like two architects designed it around each other. One half of the house has a kind of sharp, midcentury feel to it —all these angles and intersecting lines that almost make me dizzy to look at. But the other half, the half closest to where I am now, sprawls like an English manor house, with three gabled turrets stretching up to the bright blue sky.

I know, suddenly and with a sharp, certain clarity, that if I keep walking, I'll pass through the gardens and by a swimming pool and make it to the front door, and it will be two huge slabs of wood carved with some fin de siècle flourishes.

I don't keep walking, though. The force that drew me forward has vanished, and I don't dare step onto the Hartshorn property. It's been twenty years, and I doubt any of them remember me.

I draw my hand over my forehead, wiping away the sweat

beading there. A bird cries out, another answers. I should go back.

And then a figure moves in the distance, stepping out from behind the big shrubs of azalea, still half-blooming with pink and white blossoms. It's a man with shoulder-length dark hair and a big frame. He lopes across the meadow, heading away from the house. Toward the gardens, I think. I can vaguely picture them, an expansive quilt of blooms on the other side of the mansion.

He doesn't look at me, but I still freeze, my mind babbling up excuses for why I'm here. My heart thumping in my chest feels too loud, and it keeps banging in my head. I can almost hear the banging from outside myself, slow and rhythmic, like it's coming from the house. Coming from the yard. Coming from the past.

The man stops, the wind blowing his hair back from his broad, bare shoulders, revealing a colorful patchwork of tattoos chasing down his muscular arms.

I feel like I've seen him before, exactly like this, except he was covered in blood instead of tattoos.

And then he looks over at me.

Bang.

Bang.

Bang.

And then suddenly everything is black.

✣ 4 ✣

GIDEON

I slam my fist into the sandbag, making it swing back on its chain. Something's got me agitated today, and I don't know why. Xavier's been hanging around the estate more than usual the past month, for reasons that he has not bothered to explain to me. But he got called away yesterday to Houston for some emergency with the Five Courts. Not something I have to worry about, and so the estate is empty the way I'm used to. Just me and Gran.

So why do I feel so fucking aggravated?

I hit the sandbag again and then step back and wipe the sweat off my brow, watching the bag swing back and forth. Whenever I get like this, training usually helps. But today, the sting in my knuckles isn't enough.

Maybe I just need to hit something else. Something harder.

I switch off the music screaming out of the speakers and chug back some water. I shouldn't be hitting anything, really; I've got a match tomorrow night, and the last thing I need is for my knuckles to be too bruised and split open to throw Fabian around. That's his thing, all that flippy shit, and my role is to be a lever for him to bounce off of while the crowd cheers him and boos me.

But I can't shake it, this agitation. It works under my skin and makes it so I can't even stand still. I pace around my patchwork gym, built up over the last ten years, piece by piece. Even brought the practice ring in from outside and set it up like a centerpiece, although that's not what I need right now.

I want to hurt. I want to bleed.

I take another shot of water and stalk out of the gym. Gran let me set up in the old wing since no one ever comes in here, not since Uncle Jack and my quartet of redneck cousins moved out fifteen years ago. I didn't change much of it, though. Just set up the gym and fixed up the biggest bedroom for myself. Everything else is the original furniture, heavy and dark and wooden. And dusty, too, since Gran told her cleaning lady not to bother.

I pace down the hallway and into the cavernous parlor, the stained glass skylights throwing color over me. I still don't know why I feel so damned out of sorts. It's early for another sacrifice—ahead of schedule, even. I only did the last one a few weeks ago, before Xavier showed back up.

But this doesn't feel like sacrifice buzz. It feels like something else. Something—

Something I haven't felt in a long time.

The house is stifling, so I push my way outside and stand for a minute in the courtyard, lemony with spring sunlight. The fountain bubbles softly, and my great-grandmother's wisteria is blooming all over the place, big purple blossoms like cartoon grapes. It smells like honey and makes the bees spin around drunkenly in the sun.

One thing I like about the old wing is that it's made out of dark grey brick, and when I slam my fist into it, the pain shoots through my wrist and into my forearm. I take a deep, shuddery breath, but the agitation is still there, buzzing like the bees. I punch the wall again, hard enough to scrape my knuckles. The split skin helps. The beads of crimson blood. I let some drop on the ground, then lick the rest away. Blood's blood.

Something shifts on the wind, and the hairs on my arm rise. I can feel Him lurking nearby, just for a flash of a second, and I slam my fist into the wall again, harder than before. My blood smears on the brick, and the pain burning in my knuckle is exactly what I need.

"I don't have time for this," I mutter, staring up at the cloudless sky. The pine trees blow back and forth, muttering in their unintelligible language. It's the same language He uses, and sometimes I can understand it. Not today, though. It slips into my ears and turns to tatters.

I lick the blood off my knuckles again, pressing my tongue hard into the scrapes so that the sting brightens.

And then everything goes dead still. The wind stops. The trees freeze. Even the insects shut up.

Interesting.

It only lasts a few seconds, but I know what it means. Something's different. Something's *happening*.

I peel myself away from the wall and head out of the courtyard, trying to see if I can place it. This definitely isn't a sacrifice. It feels more like the day Gloria died. A sign that someone's leaving. Or that someone's coming home.

God, I hope this doesn't mean Xavier's moving back in permanently.

I step out of the courtyard, past the overgrown azaleas—Gran keeps nagging me to trim them back even though they're still half-full of flowers—and into the big sweeping field that rolls down to the forest. Nothing seems amiss, but these kinds of changes, they aren't always obvious. I can still remember how quiet everything went when Gloria died, like the whole world was trying to see how long it could hold its breath. It wasn't until Gran started screaming that it all started up again.

But Gran's not screaming now. No one is. And I can't figure out what the hell is going on until I look across the field and see a woman standing on the path leading to Gloria's house.

And like that, I understand. She came back.

It's been nine years, seven months, and twelve days, and Ivy Myste has finally come back.

All I can do is stare at her, trying to connect the woman on the path with the girl I remember. Her hair's its natural color again, a light, honey-streaked brunette, and she's wearing it in long, loose waves. She's filled out a little, her hips wider and shapelier, and I desperately want to see her how I did the last time she was here, naked and spread out beneath me, her back arching, her full breasts swelling beneath my scabbed, rough hands. The spring sun had melted over both of us as I thrust furiously inside her until she shrieked and trembled and called out my name.

I take a step toward her, my heart hammering against the cage of my ribs. But that one step is too much. She immediately collapses into the grass.

"Ivy!" I take off toward her, thinking only a second too late that I probably shouldn't. But I can't just leave her there, and so I don't stop, not until I fall on my knees beside her limp body.

"Ivy," I whisper, brushing her hair out of her eyes. She doesn't move, and I drop my finger to her neck to find her pulse, strong and sure. Fuck, I don't know why she passed out like this. Was it because she saw me? Saw the house? Why is she even here?

I don't know, but Gran will.

I gather Ivy up in my arms and into a bridal carry. Her honeysuckle scent slams into me, bringing a wash of a dozen memories that I've worn out over the years. Her warm, eager mouth. Her sweet, sparkling laugh. *I've always had a crush on you.*

I squeeze her up close and trudge across the field, half-expecting her to wake up and start screaming. She doesn't, and

I'm reassured by the steady rhythm of her breath, the soft heat of her body.

I head back to the old wing, thinking I can get her settled in my bed and then go find Gran to let her know she's back. But when I come around the side of the azaleas, Gran is waiting for me in the courtyard beside the fountain. The sculpture in its center glares down at both of us.

"It's Ivy," she says flatly.

"Yeah." I stop, not sure what to do. Other than the funeral, Gran hasn't left the house since Gloria died. It's strange seeing her outside.

"Gloria must have left her the house. She'd always talked about it, but I didn't know—" Gran's voice shudders a little, and her eyes gleam like glass. "I didn't know she actually did it."

I didn't either. None of us did. I swallow. "I didn't do anything," I say, a bit of a preemptive defense. "I came and saw her and she just passed out before I could—"

"It was too much for her," Gran says sharply. "Seeing the house like this. Possibly seeing you." Her eyes glint, and I feel a sting of admonishment. "It needs to be gradual. If you show her too much at once, the spells could break, and it could hurt her. Badly."

I squeeze Ivy a little closer to my chest, hardly daring to breathe. Gran walks over to us and gazes down at Ivy, her eyes softening. "Still as pretty as Gloria," she says softly. Then she looks up at me. "We need to get her back to Gloria's house," she says. "That'll be safer for her. I'll get the car. Meet me 'round front."

"Is she gonna be okay?"

"She'll be fine, as long as you keep her away from the chapel." Gran looks up at me, her brow furrowed in concern. "But Gideon, you need to realize—she's not going to remember what you two did. And you can't tell her."

"I know." It comes out defensive, and I have to resist the

urge to pull Ivy closer to my chest. "You made that very clear ten years ago."

Which is true. Gran made me help, made me go out to the woods to gather up larkspur blooms, punishment for breaking my promise to her and Gloria. But I still can't stop myself from adding, "What *will* she remember?"

Gran frowns, and I shift my weight, dropping Ivy into the hook of my arms. "She'll remember visiting when she was a little girl," Gran finally says. "When you all were kids. The rest—"

She looks away, toward the path that leads into the chapel. My skin prickles.

"The longer she stays, the more she'll remember," Gran says, not looking at me. "But it won't be an easy process. God, I wish I'd known she was coming. Wish I'd known—" She stops, and I know better than to keep prying. Ivy Myste was always a sore spot between Gran and Gloria. The only thing I ever saw them argue about, and as far as I can tell, the one thing they never resolved before Gloria died last week. I guess willing the house to Ivy was Gloria's last gift to Gran.

"Come," Gran says. "It's not good for her to be here."

And then she's marching across the courtyard, heading toward the garage. For a minute, I just stand there, cradling Ivy against my chest, breathing in her scent.

Ivy Myste.

The one woman I've ever loved—

And the one woman I thought I'd never see again.

IVY

I dream of the forest, and a hole in the ground in the middle of the forest, a place where the earth cracked and only darkness lives inside. I dream that I'm sitting on its edge, and my feet dangle into the abyss, but I'm not afraid because a man is there, a man with strong arms and long brown hair, and he wraps his arms around my waist and keeps me from falling.

"Ivy," he whispers, his breath warm in my ear. "I want to show you something I'm not supposed to show you."

Then I gasp awake, sucking down thick lungfuls of air, my answer to him dying on my lips—

Yes.

I'm in a dim bedroom, the curtains drawn against the sun, an afghan laid over my legs. I'm still in the shorts and oversized shirt I was wearing when I flew into Texas, but someone took off my shoes and socks.

I sit up, blinking, trying to get a sense of my surroundings. I had been outside, in the woods.

No, not the woods. The edge of Hartshorn.

"Don't strain yourself, dear."

The voice makes me jump, and I look over to see an elegant older woman standing in the doorway. Her hair is the kind of pristine, snowy white that only age can gift you, and she wears it in a pretty braided bun, loose strands curling around her face.

I don't recognize her.

"Who are you?" I press my hand to my temple, where a dull, throbbing headache is already starting to work its way to the surface. "What happened? I was—"

"You had some kind of episode." The woman glides into the room, moving with the grace of a ballet dancer. "My grandson Gideon found you."

Memories come back to me, patchy and strange. Walking down the dappled path. A gangly teenage boy with brown hair falling into his eyes. Me in a swimsuit, jumping into the creek. A man with the same brown hair, blown back by the wind. A steady, rhythmic banging.

"I don't—" I squeeze my eyes shut. "I'm sorry, my head's all confused. That's never happened to me before."

"It may have been the heat," the woman says smoothly, dropping down into a chair that's pulled up beside the bed. "Gideon's fixing you something to drink right now. It'll help."

I keep rubbing my head, looking at her. I feel like I should know her, like I've seen her before, but anytime I think I've remembered her name, it slips away. "I'm sorry," I say. "But I don't—I don't think I know you."

The woman smiles, laugh lines crinkling around her eyes. "Well, it's been a long time since you saw me last," she says. "I'm Judith Hartshorn. I knew your grandmother."

And just like that, I recognize her. Her hair used to be dark and cut in a severe, neat bob, and she was always wearing stylish linen dresses. I remember her sitting on Golly's back porch, the two of them drinking mint juleps and talking about people I didn't know.

"Judith," I whisper, because that's what she told me and her sister to call her.

Judith breaks into a dazzling smile. "You remembered. I hate being Ms. Hartshorn."

Footsteps sound from the hallway, and I sit up a little straighter, feeling some kind of sparking anticipation. Her grandson, she said.

And sure enough, it's the man with long brown hair who steps into the doorway. Up close, I can see how intricate the designs of his tattoos are, a twining, twisting tangle of color and shape, and I can't stop staring. Because he's also extremely handsome, with intense green eyes and high cheekbones and a faint graze of stubble across his chin.

"And there's my grandson now," Judith says.

"Hello," he says, his voice dark and whiskey-rough. "Are you feeling better?"

"I, uh, yes? A little?" Heat creeps into my cheeks. I never know how to act around good-looking men.

He smiles at me as he steps into the room, then holds up a glass filled with pale, creamy liquid. "Fixed you some of Gran's horchata," he says. "It's good for when you—" He stops, just for a second. "Overheat."

"Is that what happened?" I rub my forehead, trying to press the ache away. I don't remember much. Just walking through the woods, coming up to Hartshorn, seeing Gideon.

Gideon. The older Hartshorn boy. He mostly ignored me and Xavier that summer.

Well, not a boy now. He smiles at me again as he hands me the horchata. I can smell the cinnamon and vanilla in it, but also something I can't quite place, something dark and amber. I take a small sip, then a bigger one when the sweetness hits my tongue.

"Oh, this is really good." I haven't had horchata in ages, and

I gulp it down. Maybe I did get overheated, since I'm clearly thirsty as hell.

In more ways than one, too, given that Gideon's closeness is making my heart flutter in my chest.

"Told you it would help." Judith reaches over and pats my arm. "You need to be careful out in the woods. It gets hot in the thicket, without the breeze."

I nod, still sipping at the horchata and trying not to sneak glances at Gideon even though I swear I can feel him staring down at me. Was he this handsome that summer? I barely remember him, honestly. He's four or five years older, which is an immeasurable gulf when you're kids.

Not so much when you're adults, though.

"I'm sorry for causing you trouble." I let myself glance over at him. He jerks his gaze away, and my chest warms from the inside out. "I—I just found out about Golly, I mean, my grandmother, and that she left me the house, and—I don't know, I guess I just wanted to go exploring." No, that's not right. I shake my head. "And her lawyer, Lee Whitman? He told me she was buried on your property."

"Oh, sweetheart." Judith leans forward, her dark eyes kind. "You poor thing. Yes, she is." Her voice sounds strained and cracked, almost like she's about to start crying.

"I can take you to see it," Gideon says suddenly. Judith glances over at him, her eyes narrowed. "When you feel better," he adds.

"I'd like that." My chest is filled with butterflies, especially when Gideon smiles down at me and sweeps his long hair back behind his ear, giving me another quick glimpse of the tattoo sleeve covering his arm. I only see snatches of things—vines and flowers, some dark, twining figures.

"Keep drinking your horchata, dear," Judith says. "It really will help."

"It already is!" I settle back against the headboard and take another drink. And it's true, too. I feel more clearheaded, enough to realize that I'm in Golly's house, in the downstairs bedroom. Her bedroom. I recognize the dark curtains, the antique chest of drawers.

"An old family recipe," Judith says. "Fixes everything. Gideon can attest to that, can't he?"

"Yeah," Gideon says sheepishly. "I always drink it after a match."

"A match?" I look over at him. "Do you—play tennis?"

The question's out of my mouth before I can stop it, and I immediately feel like an idiot. But Gideon grins. God, he's fucking handsome.

"Not exactly," he says.

The doorbell rings, a melodic, rippling chime that echoes through the house. Judith looks over at Gideon again, her expression guarded. I drink more of the horchata.

"Who could that be?" she asks.

"No idea," he says.

"It's probably Mr. Whitman." I drain the rest of my drink and set the glass on the bedside table. I really do feel better. My headache's gone, along with the fogginess from when I first woke up. There's a lingering ache in my limbs that does remind me of the times I've gotten overheated. Even though it wasn't really hot out there, was it? Not like summer in New Mexico. Or summer in East Texas, for that matter.

The doorbell rings again.

"My grandmother's lawyer," I add. "He said he was going to come by and make sure I was settled." I move to get up, but Judith puts her hand out, stopping me.

"No, dear. I'll get it. You keep resting." When she leaves the room, she glances over at Gideon, something unspoken passing between them.

"I don't need to keep resting," I tell him, throwing the afghan off my legs. "I feel fine."

"That's good." He holds out his hand, and when I take it, my palm buzzes. His skin is rough and cool and dry, and I can feel his strength as he pulls me to my feet.

Voices spill from out of the hallway, low and amicable.

"I really am sorry about causing you trouble," I say, wanting to fill the silence. "I've never passed out from the heat before." I look over at Gideon, watching me with his dark green eyes. They're the same color as Xavier's—the color of river water. "I mean, I'm from Santa Fe. It's not like I'm not used to it."

Gideon smiles again. "It's no trouble, really. And I was serious about taking you to see Gloria's grave. My grandma is— well, she's pretty tore up about it. It happened so suddenly, you know? So don't mind her."

"They were close," I say. Not a question. I remember it.

Gideon looks at me strangely. "Yeah," he says. "Very close."

"There she is!" Lee fills up the doorway, Judith lurking behind him. "Heard the heat got to you."

"Yeah, I guess so."

"It'll do that." Lee glances over at Gideon. "Good thing you were out there, huh?"

"Hmm," Gideon says. "Good thing."

They stare at each other for a few seconds. Lee's the first to blink and look away. When he grins at me, there's something strained in his expression. He probably feels put out, driving all the way out here to help me and then finding I don't really need it. But I'm also a little overwhelmed by everything, and honestly, I don't want him here.

"I, uh, I'd really like to rest," I say. "It's been a long day."

Lee holds up his hands. "Hey, I totally get it. I just wanted to make sure you were settled in, maybe take you to see the gravesi—"

"I can do that," Gideon says, quickly enough that the butterflies start flapping furiously around in my chest again.

Lee glances over at him again, and I swear he's nervous until he says, "Sure, of course," and I figure it had to be my imagination. I'm just light-headed from earlier.

Gideon nods, and Lee turns back to me, pulling his wallet out of his pocket. "I did want to give you this, Ms. Myste." He hands me a business card, HUTCHINSON ESTATE SALES emblazoned across the front, a phone number on the back. "Like we discussed."

I can feel Judith staring at us, and suddenly, the idea of selling any of Golly's belongings feels wrong.

"Thanks." I shove the card in my pocket.

"If you need anything," Lee adds. "You've got my number."

He flashes me a smarmy car salesman's smile, which flickers out like a lightbulb when he nods at Gideon. Then he steps back into the hallway. Judith follows him, leaving me and Gideon alone in my grandmother's bedroom again.

"You want us to go?" Gideon says softly.

"I—I don't want to take up any of your time." The truth is, even though I am tired, even though it has been a long day and I feel dazed from being back here, I want him to stay. There's something about his presence that feels right. Like he's meant to be here. "I know you weren't expecting to have to deal with me."

Gideon studies me. "I wasn't doing anything that important."

I look up at him, not knowing what to say. He pushes a hand through his hair, and I notice for the first time the cuts and bruises on his knuckles, like he's been in a fight.

"Maybe I can come back this evening," he says. "Before it gets dark. Take you to visit Gloria's grave. That'll give you some time to get settled. Plus, it won't be so hot."

The butterflies erupt. "I'd like that."

"How long are you going to be here?" he asks. "In Harlan, I mean."

"Oh. Um, I fly back home on Sunday." It suddenly doesn't

feel like enough time, even though, technically, I've already done what I came here to do.

Gideon just nods, though. "Well, I'll see you in a few hours, then. And I'll leave my number in the kitchen, if you need anything, okay? Next to the phone."

"Thanks." I have no idea where my phone is. I'm sure I dropped my purse somewhere when I first came into the house, but I don't remember where. I just remember the pull I felt, dragging me from the front door to the back and then all the way to Hartshorn.

"Great. I'll see you in a few hours, okay?"

Gideon keeps staring at me, and I feel like I could leap into his eyes the way I leapt into the creek when I was a child. I feel like I could drown in him.

"See you soon," he says, with a smile that I know will undo me.

🦋 *6* 🦋

XAVIER

It's been too long since I've gotten my dick sucked properly, but I will say that this woman, Amelia, is doing a damn fine job. She swallows my entire length in a single gulp, her mouth hot and welcoming, and then peers up at me through her eyelashes as she releases my cock in a slow, agonizing tease.

"Keep going," I tell her, and she grins wickedly at me and obeys by sucking hard on my cockhead. I settle back in my seat and let my eyes drift up to the show on stage. One of my favorites is up there, a gorgeous submissive who calls herself Nocturnia and always covers her face with a burgundy mask. She's currently being whipped by a tall, curvy domme, who is not masked but whose face has the fey qualities of a woman who cavorts with demons.

Not unusual here in Lethe.

I don't know the domme's name, although I'm sure I've hired her to tend to my brother's needs on those rare occasions I can drag him into Lethe. He likes hurting, and given that Nocturnia's back is currently streaked with vicious stripes of blood, this domme would be more than capable of delivering what he wants.

The domme stirs up the air with her cat-o'-nine-tails, each tail thin and shiny with Nocturnia's lovely blood. I can smell it on the air, faint and coppery, and every time the tails hit her back, she screams loud enough to drown out the velvety orchestral music playing in the background.

I'm going to spill in Amelia's talented mouth soon, if I'm not careful. I like hurting, too. Except, unlike Gideon, I want to be the one doing it.

Hurting, giving and receiving, is in the Hartshorn blood.

I brace my hand against the back of Amelia's head, holding her in place as she swallows more of my cock. She squeezes the sides of the chair, bracing herself, and I can feel her gag around me. She doesn't tap me to stop, though. Oren Cagot, the club's owner and a fellow Five Courts councillor, knows what I like, and he knows I was put out about having to drive to Houston on such short notice for the council meeting tonight.

I drop my head back, sighing at all the little pleasures swarming around me—Nocturnia's screams, the whip of the tails, the sweet convulsions of Amelia's gag reflex. It's true that I'm not happy to be here, but waiting for the meeting in Lethe does soften the blow.

And then my phone rings.

I drag Amelia off my dick, and she gasps down air, her lips and eyes both shiny. My phone keeps chiming on the table beside me, bright in the moody lighting of the viewing room. I don't need to look at the screen to know who's calling me, though. I'm only allowing one number to go through while I'm in town for the meeting, and he knows damn well only to call me if there's an emergency.

Which means I'm not happy to hear my phone.

Amelia gazes up at me, looking a little worried beneath her

smeared mascara. I smile down at her as my phone falls silent. Nocturnia screams on stage again.

"Did Oren tell you about me?" I ask Amelia. "About what I like?"

She swallows, and the worry on her face flickers with fear and excitement. My cock pulses at the sight of it.

"He said you're a Black Card member."

Oh, Oren *is* buttering me up, bringing me someone who knows what that means.

"And you're all right with that?" I ask, just to be certain. Oren takes those things seriously. Full consent at all times, even for those of us with a Black Card. Always get permission, no matter how dangerous or how depraved.

"Of course." Amelia's eyes gleam with excitement. "It's why I—why I came looking for you."

I stand up, tucking my dick back in my pants, and then gesture for Amelia to do the same. She does, her legs shaky, and I take a good, long look at her. She's wearing a slinky, revealing purple dress that won't do, but her body is the right general shape—lush and curvy, with a nice round ass.

She blinks and casts her eyes downward like a good submissive.

I reach into my pocket and pull out the sleek black key card that proves the extent of my predilections. It offers access to every room in Lethe's sprawling establishment, including places sweet submissive Amelia almost certainly knows not to go. Her eyes go wide when she sees it.

I press the card under her chin and tilt her gaze up to meet mine.

"I have a private room on the third floor," I tell her. "Room 8. Take off this—" I snap the thin strap of her dress. "And put on the item on the vanity. Wipe off your makeup, too. Do you understand?"

Amelia nods. I can sense the excitement wavering off of her, and I suspect she's someone Oren is training for his religious rites. No wonder he sent her to me.

"I won't be long," I say. "I just have to return this call. You can select one of the dildos, whichever one you prefer. I want you fucking yourself when I came in."

"Yes, sir," she says breathlessly.

I slide the keycard into her cleavage and tilt my head toward the door. Amelia scurries away, sneaking one excited glance over her shoulder at me. My cock strains against my pants. If Oren sent her to me this afternoon, knowing I need to blow off steam, then he must think Amelia is capable of handling my desires. I certainly hope so. I suspect I'm going to need someone sturdy after taking this call.

With my entertainment taken care of, I swipe my phone off the table and pull up the screen. One missed call from Lee Whitman. He knows not to bother leaving a message.

I leave Nocturnia and the demon-touched domme to their fun and step out into the quiet, dim hallway. It's early enough that hardly anyone's here, and I call Lee with my back pressed up against the wall, next to a black-and-white photograph of three men fucking in blood.

It rings twice. He knows not to make me wait.

"Hey," he answers, which is what he says when he's nervous. I tighten my fingers around the phone.

"What happened?"

A pause on the other end. The club's music drifts down the hallway, soft and elegant.

"Lee," I say. "Tell me what the fuck happened."

"Your brother got to her." It comes out in a rush. "I'm sorry, Xavier, I don't know how it happened. I told her to wait for me at the house, but she just—went on her own."

Anger bursts in my chest, and I take a long, slow breath. All my careful planning, and I still wasn't able to be at Hartshorn to intercept Ivy before my brother could get to her. All because of this Five Courts bullshit, Cullen Tyloch's greedy brother getting himself killed. I asked Lee to keep an eye on her, but I should have known he'd fuck it up.

"Tell me exactly what happened," I say darkly.

"From what I gathered," Lee says, "She went straight to Hartshorn after getting to the house. Apparently, she passed out on the edge of the woods, and Gideon found her, brought her back with your grandmother."

"Did she go to the chapel?" The question is ashy on my tongue.

"I don't think so," Lee says. "I mean, no, she didn't."

"Which is it?"

"No," Lee says quickly. "No, she didn't. Your grandmother wasn't exactly forthcoming with me, but she said Gideon found her on the walking path, so—"

I take a deep breath. This is still salvageable. I know I'll have some time, anyway. The witchcraft Gran and Gloria used to wipe Ivy's memory will take a while to wear off, and she's supposed to go back to Santa Fe on Sunday. I just hope she actually does. That, I can work with. I need her away from my fucking brother.

"Do not let her stay," I tell Lee. "She's gonna consider it, almost certainly. Make sure she's on that plane on Sunday."

"You sure?" Lee says uncertainly.

"Of course I'm fucking sure. I understand how this works. You don't. She'll be back, and I'll be there when she is. Do you understand?"

"Yeah," he says. "Yes. But—" He stops.

"But what?"

"She wants to see her grandmother's grave."

I roll my eyes. "Because you told her about it, you idiot. You take her. Do *not* let my brother get her anywhere near the chapel."

"Got it," Lee says, and I can sense his nervousness over the phone. Goes straight to my dick. There's nothing better than having power over someone who's used to having the power themselves.

"We'll reconvene when I'm back in town next week," I tell him. "If anything else goes wrong—"

"I'll call you," he says.

"Good boy." Then I hang up before he can respond.

For a moment, all I can do is lean against the wall, trying to steady my anger. I'm not going to lose her again.

Ivy Myste belongs to me. I claimed her first, when we were thirteen. I can feel the magic binding us together.

I shove my phone in my pocket and stalk over to the stairwell, stomping up to the third floor. Amelia kept the door to my room propped open, and my pulse quickens at the angle of light spilling across the dark hallway.

Let's just hope she can follow directions. I'm definitely going to need to work out my frustration with Lee's incompetence before the meeting this evening.

I shove the door open, perhaps more forcefully than necessary. And it seems that Amelia, sweet, eager to please Amelia, *did* follow my instructions.

She's sprawled out on the big king-sized bed in the center of the room, completely naked save for a bright blue wig. She pumps one of the larger dildos in and out of her shaved, glistening pussy, one hand squeezing her breast, her breath soft and panty.

She hasn't noticed me yet.

I kick the door shut, and she snaps up, her eyes dark with lust. She licks her lips.

"Is this what you wanted?" she asks, still slowly fucking herself.

"It is, darling." I unbuckle my belt as I walk toward her, noticing how her eyes follow the movements. "Now give me the dildo and roll onto your belly."

She does exactly as I ask. Exquisite. I toss the dildo aside, let it roll across the floor. That was just to get her warmed up, nothing more.

Then I snap my belt out of the belt loops, the leather dark and sleek in the soft track lighting overhead.

Amelia's breath hitches.

I climb onto the bed, settling myself between her legs. She has two eyes tattooed on her ass cheeks, one green and one brown. I doubt my Ivy has tattoos like that, but I can overlook them. With the wig, Amelia is more than adequate.

"I need to know something before we start," I tell her, folding the belt over on itself. "What do you know of my reputation?"

Amelia twists her head to look at me over her shoulder. Her eyes are the wrong color—blue, not brown. No matter. She'll have them squeezed shut in pain soon enough anyway.

"Mr. Cagot told me what you like."

"And what's that?"

Her eyes blaze hotly. My cock throbs.

"Pain," she says. "You want to see your subs suffer."

I smile, loving how that sounds coming out of her plump lips.

"Did Mr. Cagot tell you the sort of things I do?"

Amelia nods.

"Say it."

"Yes," she says. "He said you leave marks. Bruises. Cuts." She swallows. "That you like blood."

"So you know what you're in for."

"Yes." She hesitates. "Sir, if I may—that's why I'm here."

I lean over her, setting the belt on the bed so that it's in her line of sight. She smells good, powdery and clean, and I nuzzle against her neck. For a moment, I wonder what Ivy smells like. It's been so long that I don't remember.

That'll change soon enough. I just need to have some patience and some faith.

I nip at the flesh beneath Amelia's ear. She barely even flinches.

"What's your safe word?" I whisper.

"Starfish."

I nod and slide off the bed, bringing the belt with me. Amelia watches me over her shoulder, her breath shaky. I can feel her eyes on me as I amble over to the door.

I turn to her, gripping the belt tight in my hand.

"Starfish," I say. "Amelia, I will not let you leave this room until you say that word."

"Understood," she whispers.

It's all the permission I need. I slide the deadbolt shut. Then I introduce my belt to the pristine skin of her back.

It won't be pristine for long, and neither will she.

Neither will my Ivy.

7

IVY

It's eerie being alone in Golly's house after nearly twenty years away. Eerie, because of how familiar it is. How little it's changed.

I drag my suitcase upstairs and set myself up in the bedroom where I stayed as a child because it feels wrong sleeping in Golly's old room. Everything about the guest bedroom is exactly like I remembered. The pink quilt on the bed, the embroidered curtains covering the windows, the scuffed vanity tucked into the corner. There's even a vase I recognize as soon as I see it, bright white ceramic and filled with dusty silk flowers.

The bathroom is the same too: the same buzzing fluorescent light over the streaky mirror, same Pepto-Bismol-pink bathtub tile and frosted glass sliding shower door. I line my toiletries up on the counter and study my reflection. I look tired.

Eventually, I settle down in the living room with my laptop to try and finish up my grading before Gideon comes back. The house *does* have Internet, which was true even when I was here last. I remember Golly's ancient desktop in the office, although that's gone now. She wouldn't let me or my sister use the computer, saying we were too young, but I do remember her working on it.

The WiFi password is written down on a scrap of paper taped to the wall beside the landline phone—and beside a Post-It note with Gideon's name and a phone number scrawled in a spiky, masculine hand. I stare at it for a moment, my breath tight. *If you need anything*, he'd said.

No. I don't want to bother him.

So I connect to the WiFi without trouble and sink into the old couch. The essays are, as usual, mid, and I click listlessly through the rubrics, offering the same feedback it feels like I'm always offering. I was able to nab two extra sessions this semester, giving me a full course load and more money than I'm used to.

Plus, there's the inheritance, whispers a voice in the back of my head, although I shove that aside.

The time passes quickly. I manage to get through two sections' worth of papers by the time my stomach starts grumbling for food.

Food. Fuck. I doubt there's anything in the house.

I snap my laptop shut and go into the kitchen, where I find the remains of the horchata, the glass upturned in the sink, alongside an empty pitcher and a wooden spoon. The refrigerator's empty, save for some water bottles and a few jars of condiments. Same with the pantry.

They must have brought the horchata with them. But that doesn't much help me for dinner tonight, does it?

I eye Gideon's phone number, still posted on the wall. Would it be weird to invite him to dinner? Or should I just drive into Harlan by myself?

The doorbell rings.

My heart leaps at the sound. Gideon already? We didn't decide on a firm meeting time, and it still feels early. But when I go to pull open the front door, he's standing there on the porch, holding plastic take-out bags in each hand.

"It occurred to me you don't have any food here," he says, his grey-green eyes boring into mine. "So I brought over some barbecue."

"I was just thinking about food," I tell him, stepping away from the doorway. "So good timing."

He grins and ducks into the hallway. "I wanted to call to see what you like," he says. "But I realized I didn't have *your* number. Wasn't sure you'd answer the house line." He hoists up the bag. "So if you're vegetarian, we're gonna have to try a do-over."

"I'm happily omnivorous."

"That's good. Because this is the best barbecue in Texas."

"A bold claim." As if I know anything about Texas barbecue.

"Trust me," Gideon says. "You'll see."

He stalks back to the kitchen, moving through the house like he's familiar with it. Like he lives here and not at Hartshorn. "Go on into the dining room," he tells me when I come in after him. "I can get everything."

"You sure?"

But he's already swinging open cabinets and grabbing plates and silverware and napkins. No hesitation. No checking to see where stuff is.

"Did you—spend a lot of time here?" I ask, pressing myself up against the refrigerator.

Gideon glances over at me, tucking a lock of hair behind his ear. "What makes you say that?"

"You know where everything is."

"Oh. Yeah. I guess I do." Gideon opens the takeout boxes, revealing mounds of smoky, dark brisket, a few links of sausage, and a rack of pork ribs. He portions everything out.

"I mean, Gloria was basically our second grandma, you know?"

"I guess that's why she's buried in your cemetery?" I hope it doesn't sound too forward. It's not like I haven't been wondering about it since Lee told me.

Gideon looks over at me, a dark crease between his eyes. Something like panic surges through my chest. I misspoke, somehow. Stumbled across something that these people don't talk about.

But then he says, "You know they were married, right?"

It takes me a beat too long to comprehend who he's talking about.

"What?" I squawk. "Judith and Golly? My grandmother?"

Gideon grins wickedly. "Yeah. Gram told me your mother kept you in the dark, but—"

"They were *married?*" I say. "Like, legally?"

Gideon nods and picks up the two plates and hands them to me, then tilts his head toward the dining room. "Since you insist on hanging around in here, you can help. I'll get the drinks. Wine okay?"

"You brought wine?'

His eyes glitter. "No. But Gloria had a stash. Give me a sec."

I take the plates into the living room as he disappears elsewhere in the house, his footsteps echoing against the walls. The dining room I don't remember as well, probably because we never really ate in here, just at the table in the kitchen. There's something dark and oppressive about it, the floral wallpaper reminding me of the overgrown forest outside.

"Here we go. This one looks good."

Gideon's voice makes me jump; I expected him to come in from the kitchen entrance, but instead, he comes in from the hallway, carrying a bottle of red wine and two glasses.

"I don't know anything about wine," I tell him.

"Neither do I," he says. "I just picked this because of the

label." Then he turns it around to show me: there's an illustration of some dark, smoky demon curling out of a wine bottle like a genie.

"Okay," I laugh. "I don't blame you."

He pours the glasses and settles down in the seat next to me, dragging the plate over. My chest constricts at the idea of being close to him, sharing food and wine like this is a date. Because we're technically related, aren't we? If Golly and Judith were married?

"Cheers," he says, and when our glasses clink, he adds, "Welcome to Harlan."

"Yeah, I'm not staying." I sip at the wine, and it tastes like the demon on the bottle, dark and smoky and whispering of sin.

Which is also what it feels like to be sitting next to Gideon.

"That's a shame," he says. "It sucks to see this house empty."

I look down at my plate, not wanting to tell him that I'm probably going to sell it, along with all of Golly's belongings—

My stomach churns around at the thought.

"Were Golly and your grandmother really married?" I ask, wanting to change the subject away from what I'm going to do with the house. "That's not a joke?"

"Not a joke at all." Gideon saws into his sausage. "They got married down at the Harlan courthouse the day it was legalized." He looks up at me. "My brother and I were witnesses."

My head feels fuzzy. How did I not know this? But then, I didn't know Golly had died until Lee called me. Mom sure as hell didn't see fit to let me know.

Mom has always been weird about Golly, though. Suddenly, I wonder if my mother is more homophobic than I realized.

"Does it bother you?" Gideon asks.

I look up at him, heat blooming in my cheeks. "No, of course not. I just—" I sigh, pushing my brisket around. "My mom and grandmother didn't get along. Like, at all. I just didn't know anything about her."

Gideon gives me a strange, unreadable look. "Well, maybe this is your chance to change that," he says softly. "While you're here."

A pause flickers between us.

"I can tell you anything you want to know," he adds. "Although I'll start with this—Gloria fucking loved Bluebonnet Barbecue." He points his fork at my plate. "So maybe you should try some of their brisket."

I laugh. "Okay, fine. For Golly." Then I take a big bite of the brisket. The meat practically melts on my tongue, tangy and smoky with just a hint of spice. "Goddamn," I say. "That *is* good barbecue."

"Told you," Gideon says. "Best in Texas."

After that, all the tension crackling in the air breaks, and I dig into my food, only realizing as I start eating just how hungry I am. As we eat, Gideon tells me stories about Golly and Judith —how Judith bought this house for Golly when they were younger because they needed to keep up appearances, and how, when 2015 rolled around, Golly was too set in her ways to give it up, even with the marriage certificate. He talks about spending Christmas Eves here when he was a kid, he and his brother sleeping in the same rooms where my sister and I slept, and how they'd wake up and have Christmas at Golly's and then march through the woods to do it again at Hartshorn. He tells me how, whenever he got caught misbehaving, Golly would find out just as fast as his grandmother, and the two of them would team up for punishments. "I'd try to come here to escape being grounded," he tells me, our empty plates pushed aside, the bottle of wine half drunk. "And she'd trick me into doing chores for her."

I laugh, imagining it. I have so few memories of Golly, but hearing Gideon's stories kind of stirs them up. "We would do chores for her, too," I say, swirling my wine around in my glass. "Me and Juniper. She'd pay us for them. Five dollars or something." As I speak, the memories firm up in my head: Juniper and I fighting over the more desirable chores, like sweeping, and me tucking a five-dollar bill into a little silver box. "Your brother and I got ice cream one time," I say, picturing it in my head. "We rode our bikes through the woods and bought ice cream from a guy with a cart."

I remember it. The dirt path. The small, tidy house with roses growing out front. The ice cream melting in the heat. A blond boy grinning at me. Although he seems older than Xavier would have been. Twelve or thirteen, not eight.

Gideon doesn't say anything.

"Where is your brother?" I ask. "If you don't mind me asking."

"Houston," Gideon says. "He's on the—" Gideon stops. "My parents are involved in this business conglomeration. Xavier works with them as a consultant and serves on the, ah, board of directors. He mostly lives in Houston these days."

I don't remember anything about Gideon's parents, other than an image of his mother, a tall, reedy woman who was always drinking martinis out by the pool, reading a book through oversized sunglasses.

"What do you do?" I ask, knowing I'm changing the subject and not really sure why. "Do you work for the conglomeration, too?"

"No." Gideon looks down at his plate, his hair falling into his eyes. "I, uh—I'm a performer, I guess you could say."

"A performer."

Gideon lifts his gaze to meet mine. "Remember how I said I had a match tomorrow?"

I nod, frowning.

"It's a wrestling match."

"Wrestling?" I shriek, nearly spilling my wine in surprise. "Like, Olympic wrestling or WWE wrestling?"

Gideon laughs. "I said I was a performer, didn't I?"

"So WWE wrestling." I'm not sure what to make of any of this, although I suppose he does have the look of the wrestlers I've seen on TV, with his big frame and tattoos and long hair.

When the hell have I ever watched wrestling?

"I mean, not exactly like that, either." Gideon leans back and rakes his fingers through his hair. "I work the indie circuit. There are a couple of promotions here and up in Arkansas. The one I'm doing tomorrow's just a few towns over, in Nacogdoches."

We fall quiet, both of us looking down at our plates. In the back of my head, I hear a strange, repetitive banging, like a memory trying to worm its way out. I force myself to look over at Gideon, my head buzzing. A weird, unfamiliar courage swells up in me."Maybe—" I start. "Maybe I could come check—"

The doorbell bongs through the house, stopping me from embarrassing myself. "I wonder who that is," I say, jumping away from the table, my chair scraping on the hardwood.

Gideon just watches me, his expression guarded.

"Be right back," I blurt out, racing into the hallway. Behind me, he moves to clear the plates.

Was I seriously going to ask if I could go watch his match? I never do shit like that. Never make the first move. I tried once, back in college, a friend urging me to stop wallowing over some boy I had a crush on. I don't even remember his name, but I do remember the sting of his rejection. Ever since then, I leave it to men to do the pursuing. Not that it's really worked out for me. I haven't had a date in two years, not after a disastrous two-week trial run on Tinder.

I fling the door open and am shocked to see Lee standing on the porch, squinting at me from beneath his cowboy hat.

"Hey there," he says. "Hope I'm not imposing."

"Um—" I don't want to tell him that he is, actually, but I also don't push the screen door open, leaving it as a barrier between us.

"Thought we might go see your grandmother's grave," Lee says, sliding off his cowboy hat and holding it up to his chest. "Like we talked about?"

"That won't be necessary."

Gideon's voice startles me; I thought he was still in the kitchen, cleaning up. I'm grateful that he's not, though, because I really don't understand what Lee Whitman is doing here.

Gideon steps up beside me, and I'm suddenly aware of how big and imposing he is. He certainly towers over Lee.

"Gideon," Lee says, his eyes going wide. "Didn't, uh, didn't see your car—"

"I walked," Gideon says. "And I told Ivy I would take her to the gravesite."

Something passes between them, a flicker of darkness that kind of curls the air in on itself. I glance over at Gideon, but his expression is bland and neutral, even though it feels like he's pressing closer to me with an air of protectiveness.

Lee opens his mouth like he wants to protest. But nothing comes out.

"I'm sorry you drove out here," I tell him, "And I appreciate the offer, I really do. But Gideon and I made plans this afternoon."

"Right." Lee nods, looks down at his feet. I hate being rude, and there's a part of me—the people pleaser, the eldest daughter—who wants to invite him along out of obligation. But I don't want him here.

"I have Bluebonnet Barbecue in the kitchen," Gideon says. "I can pack you up a plate for your trouble."

He sounds friendly enough, but Lee still shifts nervously on the porch before smiling and giving a thin, wavering smile. "Appreciate the offer, but I already ate." He stares at us through the screen, his hat still pressed to his chest.

"Thanks again," I finally say. Anything to break up the thick, awkward silence.

Lee nods, his eyes flicking back and forth between me and Gideon. A cold, prickling feeling works over my skin, and I know there's something I'm missing here.

"If you need anything," Lee says. "You know where to reach me."

Then he slides on his hat and steps off the porch—slowly, deliberately, like he thinks I might change my mind.

8

GIDEON

I don't like Lee showing up here like that. Again. I don't care that he put Gloria's will together—the only reason for that is Xavier, I'm sure of it. He and Lee played football together back in high school, and Lee's been his little toadie ever since. After all, Gran had been genuinely surprised to learn Ivy was back. Which means Gloria didn't do the paperwork through the Five Courts lawyers.

I do think that Gloria wanted it to be a surprise. And maybe an apology for everything that happened in the past with Ivy, all the magic they did to erase her memory. But that she went to Lee fucking Whitman of all people—that was Xavier's doing.

I don't say any of this to Ivy. It's risky enough taking her to the cemetery, given what happened this afternoon, but I figure if I keep her away from the house and don't let her near the chapel, she'll be fine. She never spent much time in the cemetery, not with me ten years ago and not with Xavier five years before that.

But just to be safe, when we leave, I tell her I'm taking her on the scenic route.

"The scenic route?" she asks. "You mean the long route."

I laugh. "It's not that much longer. And it's a lot prettier. We'll walk by the creek."

Her eyes gleam a little at that. She remembers the creek, which is why it's fine for her to see it. That first summer here, the summer Gran and Gloria didn't have to erase, she and Xavier spent all their time down there, splashing around in the cold water. I remember wishing I could join them, but summers were for training with Uncle Jack by that point. I didn't exactly get to have the same childhood as my golden boy brother.

None of that matters now, though. He's trapped in Houston, dealing not with a business conglomeration like I told Ivy but acting as our family's liaison with the Five Courts—five families as fucked up as ours, all linked together by magic and other shady interests. He's there, and I've got Ivy at my side, her long, thick hair shining golden in the falling sunlight. We walk side by side down the path, the trees rustling softly around us.

"So how'd you get into wrestling?" she asks suddenly.

My heart pangs. This is not the first time we've had this conversation, and even then, I couldn't tell her the whole truth of it.

"Used to watch it as a kid," I say. "Joined the high school wrestling team, even though, you know, it's not exactly the same."

Ivy laughs, a musical chiming sound that fits right in with the birds and bugs and frogs singing out in the dense Piney Woods.

"Got a scholarship to Texas State," I continue, the words ashy in my mouth. "Wrestled there for four years, then came back home to help with upkeep around Hartshorn."

Lies. Well, most of it. I did get the scholarship, but Dad made me turn it down. The whole fucking family did. My life was laid out for me years ago, and it didn't involve an education.

That was Xavier's path. He's the face of the family. Guess that makes me the heel.

"Upkeep, huh?" she says. "I bet there's a lot. From what I can remember."

"Yeah. Especially since everybody moved out. My cousins used to live with us—" I cut myself off. That was the summer she was thirteen, the summer she doesn't remember. But she and Xavier didn't spend a lot of time around them, and it doesn't seem to spark anything in her. "They moved out," I finish, because she's watching me like she expects me to say something. "Later, my parents did, too. And my brother. So it's just me and Gran."

There's always got to be someone to do the dirty work, Gideon. And you have the strength for it.

We come to the fork in the path, and I veer to the right, taking us down through the dense crowd of sweet gum trees and loblolly pines to Hatchet Creek, which cuts across my family's expansive property like a knife blade.

"God, it's beautiful," Ivy breathes when we step up to the creek bed. I knew it would be; the sun's sinking low in the sky, turning the light hazy so the water glitters like it's full of diamonds.

"Told you. Scenic route."

She takes another deep breath. "All this green," she sighs. "I'd forgotten how lush this place is."

I don't say anything. I know what the lushness conceals.

I let her drink it all in, though. I'm not about to ruin it for her the way it's been ruined for me. When she starts walking along the path again, I start walking, too.

"So how'd you get into wrestling-wrestling?" she asks, glancing over at me.

"You mean like what I'm doing tomorrow night?" I shrug, grateful that I don't have to lie about any of this, at least. "I needed something to keep me busy. It gets a little isolating out here, you know? So I just connected with a wrestling gym up in Arkansas and took it from there."

She nods, her gaze fixed ahead. The last time we had this conversation, we'd been in my old bedroom in the new wing of the house, and she'd been naked because I had just fucked her for the first time. She draped her legs in my lap and peered at me through her bright blue hair, and we made small talk until I could get it up again.

I push the memories aside. It hurts, knowing I have them and she doesn't, and that Gran is the fucking reason.

"What about you?" I say. "What are you doing these days?" I know some of it, mostly from Golly, who would find things out about her two granddaughters somehow. I know she went to graduate school, like Xavier, although I don't know much more than that.

"Teaching," Ivy says. "College. I have an almost-PhD in comp lit."

Holy shit. I didn't know she'd had that much graduate school. "An almost-PhD?"

"ABD." She laughs a little, like she's embarrassed. "All but dissertation. I've got all my coursework done, and I took some time off to work on the stupid fucking thing. But then I started adjunct teaching at the community college and got all caught up in that—" She waves her hand around. "The academic job market is shit. I don't know if it's worth finishing."

"Of course it is," I tell her. "Don't you want to be Dr. Myste?"

Ivy laughs. "No one will call me that."

"I would."

Ivy stops and looks over at me. Her eyes gleam in the falling sunlight, and it takes every ounce of my willpower not to kiss her like I did ten years ago.

"Well, I appreciate that," she says softly.

We take up walking again. "So what's your dissertation about?"

Ivy gives another embarrassed laugh. "Twentieth-century gothic literature." She glances over at me. "There was a revival of it in the '70s. All these stories about girls marrying mysterious rich men and finding out they're killers and such."

For a second, all I can hear is the blood rushing in my ears.

"I was fascinated by those books when I was a teenager," she continues. "So I kind of looked at the history of those kinds of storylines." She shrugs. "I know, nerdy stuff."

"I think it's cool," I manage to choke out, my heart hammering.

We walk in silence for a few minutes longer, our feet crunching over the fallen leaves. Then we fall into a new conversation about Ivy's teaching career. Well, she talks, and I mostly listen. I'm afraid if I say anything, it'll be the wrong fucking thing.

By the time we get to the edge of my family's property, it's nearly twilight proper, and all the color has started to leach out of the surrounding woods. Little sparks of light blink on and off in the shrubbery. Fireflies, even though it's still early for them.

I shiver. Feels like a message, especially when they swarm up around us, and Ivy lets out an excited little gasp.

"Are those fireflies?" she cries, stopping on the path.

"Sure are." I shift my weight back and forth as the swirl of floating light heads in the direction of the cemetery. I know what that means—He wants us to keep going. I can feel it, too, an insistent tugging in my belly, trying to drag me out of the woods. Not to the cemetery, though. He doesn't care about that. He wants us in the chapel.

I want us in the chapel, truth be told, but Gran told me it was too dangerous.

"We don't have them in New Mexico," Ivy breathes. She pushes forward, a little too quickly, and I know she feels His call too, although I doubt she recognizes it for what it is. The fireflies blink too quickly, shimmering like stars and drawing together like the Milky Way. "God, there are so many! Are there usually this many?"

"No," I say stiffly. "But it's warm this year. I guess that's why."

"They're so pretty. It's like a movie."

Ivy trails after them, following to the clearing, and I keep close behind. When we step out of the woods, the fireflies disperse, soaring overhead until they disappear against the violet sky.

I can feel the presence of the chapel, buzzing and hot. That's the real reason I brought Ivy to the cemetery this way. Because you can't see the chapel from here. I just hope she can't feel it pulsing in the background like I can.

"Is that the cemetery?" Ivy asks. "Where that sculpture is?"

I force myself to focus. "Yep."

Ivy frowns and steps forward. The Hartshorn family cemetery doesn't look like much, especially in the fading light. The entrance is marked by a massive twisting oak tree that, according to Gran, grew out of a seed tucked into my great-great-grandmother's hand when she died. The rest of the family graves are scattered around it, marked with moss-covered headstones.

"Where's Golly?" Ivy asks softly.

"I'll show you." I want to take her hand, the way I did the last time she and I were here. The cemetery was covered in wildflowers then, so thick that they hid most of the stones. The air had smelled like honey. Ivy had tasted like honey when I kissed her, right before I led her to the chapel hidden behind the hedge I work diligently once a week to maintain.

But I don't take her hand, because Ivy doesn't remember any of that. She barely remembers me.

Gloria's grave is on the outer edge of the cemetery, next to the plot that's reserved for Gran. I take Ivy the long way around, hoping she doesn't notice the hedge in the bad light. Because He's definitely calling to us. I can feel it coursing through my bloodstream.

Fortunately, the grave's easy to spot. The soil is still dark and upturned, and the gravestone glows in the near-dark. Ivy sees it before I have to say anything, and she drifts over and kneels in the grass, her hair falling over her shoulders.

"She changed her name," Ivy says, brushing her fingers over the place where *Gloria Arbour-Hartshorn* is carved into the stone.

"I told you. They got married." I kneel beside her, and the wind picks up, bringing the sense of Him with it.

Ivy smiles a little. "That's still so strange to think about it." She looks over at me. "I guess that makes me a Hartshorn, doesn't it?"

"Makes us cousins, I think."

Ivy gives me a strange look, although it's getting hard to see her face. "I'm not sure I want to be your cousin."

My heart nearly bursts out of my chest. I know exactly what she means.

"Just by marriage," I say carefully. "Step-cousins."

"Right."

We look at each other.

The wind blows harder, rustling the leaves of the oak tree. Ivy sucks in her breath and tilts her gaze up, as if she's trying to see where the sound's coming from.

I don't like this.

"I feel like I've been here before." She stands up, and I *really* don't like that, especially when she turns in the direction of the chapel. I can just barely make out the hedge, all that tangle of undergrowth that my great-great-grandfather cultivated to hide the chapel from the outside world.

"I doubt it," I say, standing up behind her, my thoughts whirring wildly.

"No, I think I came here when I was a kid." She looks over at me, the fierce, shivery wind blowing her hair across her face. "With Xavier, maybe? I just remember—there was like an old building or something—"

Alarms ring in my head. She did come here with Xavier. Not when she was eight, like I know she's thinking, but when she was thirteen. He tried to claim her even though he was too young to know what it meant.

And of course, she's been here with me. When I really did claim her.

"Yeah," Ivy picks up her pace, weaving through the gravestones. "I do remember it. There was an old church. Xavier told me it had burned down." She glances back at me over her shoulder. "Could we go see it? I remember it being cool as hell."

My body throbs with the need to say yes, to pick her up and throw her over my shoulder and carry her into the chapel for the second time. But I can't. Not with her memory wiped of that place twice.

But Ivy doesn't wait for any answer. She's still picking her way toward the hedge. Once she hits that, she'll see the chapel, and it'll be over.

"Wait!" I jog after her, and she stops and turns to face me— her hair wild, her eyes bright. She looks up at me expectantly.

Do not let her see that chapel, Gran told me right before I left to pick up the barbecue. *I don't know how it will affect her. The bindings are still in place, and you're pushing your luck taking her to the gravesite.*

"Is it still there?" Ivy asks. "Or did I totally make it up?"

The wind howls furiously around us, whipping up leaves and day-old blossoms. The insect song rises, thick and lilting. Fireflies flicker on the edge of my vision.

He's calling for us, but I can't let her go. I also can't lie to her.

"Yeah, it's still there."

"Then let's check it out." She turns to move toward the hedge, and I grab her hand without thinking.

"Wait."

She looks at me.

And then I do the only thing I can think of to stop her from descending into the darkness.

I drag her into my chest, and I kiss her.

9

IVY

Gideon's mouth is warm and gentle against mine, almost chaste, even as his tongue parts my lips and he brings his free hand up to cup my face, tilting my head every so slightly to deepen the kiss. For a split second, I'm too stunned to move.

And then I don't want to do anything but kiss him.

I wrap my arms around his shoulders, surprised by the size of them. The *firmness* of them. Gideon catches me by the waist and tugs me closer, bending me back a little, his hand trailing gently to the sensitive skin behind my ear. Electric shivers work down my spine, as if he knows exactly where to touch me.

He breaks the kiss just enough to gaze down at me—lips parted, eyes glazed. I slide one hand around to press again his chest, feeling the muscles beneath the thin fabric of his tank top.

"Was that okay?" he says huskily.

I study the tattoo peeking out of the top of his shirt's neckline. In the dim light, I can't really make out what it is. Just a swirl of thick dark lines, a splash of red.

"More than okay." I force myself to look at his eyes.

He smiles.

Then he kisses me again, and it's more forceful this time. Harder. Hungrier. I'm so caught up in the intensity of the kiss that I almost don't realize my feet are no longer touching the ground. Gideon has picked me up by the waist, and he swings me around and leans me up against one of the many eerie statues that guard the graves here. The marble is cool through the fabric of my shirt.

I slump back against it as Gideon moves his mouth along my jawline and down to that spot on my neck, which he nibbles and licks until I'm gasping and bucking against him. He grabs my hips, pinning me against the statue, and kisses my mouth again. Our tongues grapple together, and it feels like we're devouring each other.

The kiss breaks, both of us gasping for air. An eerie, damp wind stirs around us, and Gideon cups my face, runs his thumb over my lips.

"Keep going," I whisper hoarsely.

He grins. And then he does, drawing me into another hungry kiss. This time, I hike up one leg around his hip, grinding against him until I feel the thick ridge of his erection.

A *very* thick ridge.

He knows I feel it, too, because he stiffens a little against me, his kiss slowing. And I worry I've crossed some line I didn't know not to cross.

But then he slips his arms beneath my legs and hoists me up so that I'm straddling him and pressed between his strong body and the cool touch of the statue. I roll my hips, as if I can wear away the fabric separating us until I get to him.

Gideon groans softly and thrusts his hips up against me, wedging me into the statue. Even with our clothes still on, he manages to slot his cock up against my pussy, and I grind down on him, panting and desperate.

"God, I want to fuck you so bad," he rasps, his thrusts quickening.

His words shoot fire straight through my core. No one's ever said anything like that to me, and I hardly know how to respond.

"I-I want that, too," I whisper, my breath panty.

Gideon groans and nuzzles the side of my neck. "Fuck," he whispers. "I can't. Not out here. Not—"

Before I can respond, he sucks hard on the spot below my ear, making my whole body shudder. I moan softly as he drops one hand down to gently massage my breast over my shirt, his palm rubbing up against my nipple as I keep grinding against his thick cock. I understand why he wouldn't want to fuck in a cemetery. I do, even if, in this moment, I don't care. I don't care that Golly's grave is just a few feet away, that we're surrounded by the graves of Gideon's ancestors. I'd let him rip my clothes off my body and fuck me down into the dirt on top of any of them.

I don't say that to him, although I do manage to gasp out, "Do you want to come back to the house?

He moans softly and bites at my neck. "More than fucking anything," he growls. "But I can't."

The rejection hits harder than I would expect. I jerk away from him on instinct, suddenly aware that I've made a complete fool of myself, and scrabble to find footing back on the ground.

But Gideon grabs my waist and stops me from fleeing completely. He yanks me up to him, my back pressed into his chest.

"Ivy." He says my name sharply enough that I jerk my gaze over my shoulder toward him, feeling almost like I'm being reprimanded. "I didn't mean it like that."

I stare at the statue he pressed me against. An angel, I think, although it looks strange in the purplish light. The face is mocking, almost cruel, with a mouth twisted in a grimace.

Gideon shifts his hips a little, and I can feel his undeniable erection again, this time against my ass. I let out a sharp, fluttery breath.

"Do you have a girlfriend or something?" I mutter.

Gideon whips me around and grabs my chin with his hand, forcing me to look at him. His roughness leaves me breathless. And exhilarated.

"No, I don't have a girlfriend." His eyes search mine, his pupils blown out with lust. "Gran needs me back at the house," he says softly. "And when I fuck you, I want to take my time with it."

My breath lodges in my throat, and I search Gideon's face, looking for some sign that he's joking.

There is none.

"I'm leaving on Sunday," I say weakly.

Gideon catches my mouth with one of those slow, perfect kisses. I melt into his body, my hips rolling against him of their own accord.

"Then that gives us tomorrow," he rasps into my ear. "Come with me to Nacogdoches."

He kisses along my neck and squeezes one breast, making me moan softly.

"Won't you be, um, busy?" I ask the question into the thick tangle of his hair, not sure why I'm even arguing with him. Wasn't I going to ask if I could watch his match, not even an hour ago?

It's because this all feels like a joke. Like it can't be real.

Gideon chuckles softly. "In the evening, yeah. But we'll have time before—" He gives me a long, deep kiss on my mouth. "And after." Another kiss on that spot on my neck. I moan, slumping back against the statue.

"What do you say?" Gideon tucks his fingers under my chin, his gaze boring into me. I feel trapped by him, in the best possible way—trapped by his strong arms, his intense eyes. "Come with me."

I nod. I'm afraid that if I speak, I'll say the wrong thing. Like *no*.

"Perfect." He gives another long, lingering kiss, his hands running lightly down my arms, over the curve of my waist, around the side of my neck.

It's like he knows exactly where to touch me. Like he's been touching me our entire lives.

"Do you really have to go back home?" I ask as he drops kisses down my jaw.

He stops, his breath warm on my skin, his fingers digging into my hips. For a moment, I feel him hesitating. But then he says, "Yeah, unfortunately. Gran's not as, um, independent as she seems. Especially after..."

His voice trails off, and he looks away from me. Across the meadow. Toward Hartshorn.

"Right." I flush, suddenly embarrassed that I let myself get carried away. I'm suddenly very aware that we're in a graveyard, that my own grandmother's grave is just a few feet away. How did I not care about that? "Well, if you need to get back—"

"I'll walk you home," he says quickly. "It's getting dark."

It already *is* dark, honestly. And I'm grateful that I don't have to navigate that path by myself.

Gideon doesn't move, though. Just keeps himself pressed against me, the eerie wind blowing his hair across his face, his eyes burning through me.

And I'm fine with that.

I'm fine with being trapped by him, surrounded by the night and the dead.

10

GIDEON

I brace my back against a pine tree, squeezing my cock so hard it hurts. It's nearly pitch black here in the woods, but I couldn't wait until I got home. Not with Ivy's sweet, fresh scent clinging to my clothes, trailing behind me as I walked away from the house.

God, I wish I were buried in her cunt right now. I wish she were dragging her nails down my back, splitting me open in her ecstasy. I dig my free hand in my thigh, trying to pierce the skin, but of course my nails aren't long enough.

"Fuck," I pant, strangling my dick a little harder. I thrust into the darkness, imagining that Ivy's kneeling in front of me, gazing up at me as she waits for my cum. My frantic breath drowns out the croaks and insect song crowding in around me. Tension tightens in my belly, and I dig deeper into my thigh, chasing the high that only pain can bring. I'm close, and when I squeeze my eyes shut and imagine Ivy dragging a knife blade down my back, the blood blooming over my tattoos, I finally peak. My cum arcs out, splattering across the ferns, and I shout through my pleasure.

Then I slump back against the tree, sucking down breaths.

It was agony stopping things back in the cemetery, but I couldn't fuck her there. *He* was there, my family's fucked-up god, calling out to both of us. If I had done anything, we would have wound up in the chapel, and I would have risked shattering Ivy's mind into a thousand pieces.

But fuck, it hurt seeing the disappointment in her face when I said I couldn't go to her house. I wanted to do that, too —it would have been safer, certainly. But He wasn't the only one calling out to me.

There's a sacrifice nearby, the air buzzing for blood. And, as has been made abundantly clear to me over the years, I've got one role in this family. One fucking job.

I tuck my dick back into my shorts and take a deep breath. The buzz is louder now, thick and insistent. I don't know where the hell the sacrifice came from. They usually build up. You can sense them coming like a thunderstorm.

This feels different. I don't know if it's because Ivy's here, or because of that Five Courts shit my brother's dealing with, or if it's something else entirely. But I won't stop feeling it until I get it taken care of. Which means I need to do it tonight if I don't want to miss my match.

Or my date with Ivy.

I lope through the dark woods mostly on memory, moving quickly back to the house. A few of the windows in the old wing are lit up, including my little makeshift den. I frown. Someone's here.

My heart hammers as I make my way into the courtyard. The door leading into the old wing is unlocked, and when I step into the foyer, the air feels hot and still. "Hello?" I shout, anxiety knotting in my stomach. "Gran? Is that you?"

The ruddy, shaggy-haired head of my cousin Vincent pops out from the door leading to the den. I stop in my tracks, my anxiety replaced with irritation.

"Motherfucker," I sigh.

"Hey, Gideon." He gives me a sheepish smile as he slinks into the hallway. His oversized T-shirt is soaked with drying blood. "Gonna need your help."

"No." I cross my arms over my chest and glare down at him. We're the same age, but I'm bigger and taller than he is. "I gotta go to sleep. I have a match tomorrow."

Vincent gives me a look of absolute desperation. "I really need this one, man," he says. "We all do. Dad pissed the money away again, and we gotta catch a break. I've been planning it for ages." He stares up at me, eyes big. "Please? We're overdue on the property taxes again and—"

"Okay, stop." I shove my hands through my hair. We're all Hartshorns, of course. Uncle Jack, Vincent's dad, is my dad's brother. But that whole branch of the family has always been more feral than mine. Dad says they're closer to our god, that they're part of the darkness of the earth. Which is fine, until you remember that we live in the twenty-first fucking century. You can't just live in a hovel in the woods anymore. "What exactly do you need from me?"

Vincent takes a deep breath. "The sacrifice escaped," he says quickly, shoving it all out at once. I bite back a groan of annoyance. "He's hurt. Bad. It won't be much to take him down."

"We just have to find him," I say flatly.

Vincent's cheeks darken. "Yeah," he mutters. "Look, I know this isn't your business, really, but you're so much better at this than—"

"Where did you see him last?" I don't like hearing about it, how good I am at death. Especially not when Ivy's back, and I want to pretend, for as long as I can, that I'm normal. That I didn't spend my entire childhood training with Vincent for exactly what we're about to do.

"I had him in a trap near the treehouse," Vincent says. "He managed to pry it open."

I nod. That's in the deep part of the woods, on the other

side of the creek. The Hartshorn estate wasn't isolated enough for Uncle Jack. "I can feel him," I say. "He's close. Ish."

Vincent lets out a long, relieved sigh and grins up at me. "So you'll help me, then?"

I glance over at the big grandfather clock pressed against the wall, the one I dutifully wind up every Sunday like Gran taught me. It's nearly 9:45. If we can wrap this up in a few hours, I can be in bed by midnight. That'll be fine.

And it's not like I have a choice. Not really.

"Yeah," I say grimly. "Yeah, I'll help you."

WE DON'T FIND the sacrifice until nearly five in the goddamn morning.

All night, Vincent and I scour the woods, moving as quickly as we can through the dark. The only sign of the sacrifice is the persistent buzzing on the air, and that's the one reason I don't tell Vincent to go fuck himself and head back to the house. That, and twenty-five years' worth of training that beat into me one cardinal rule:

You never let a sacrifice escape.

I'm the one who finally finds him, after Vincent and I split up around three. It's happenstance that I stumble across a slick trail of blood staining a patch of ferns in the deep part of the woods, out near Uncle Jack's place. The sacrifice must have circled back around and nearly wound up where he started, and I know that means he's confused and desperate and hiding. They don't all try to make a stand.

I follow the blood trail, muscle aching, my thoughts foggy from lack of sleep. All night, Ivy's been in the back of my mind. I can't let her see me like this, exhausted after a night of hunting a human in the woods. I need to sleep anyway. I need to sleep, and then play-fight, and then maybe I can be myself around her, two hours from this fucking hellhole.

Meet her there, I think, trudging through the woods. I'll tell her something came up, I can't drive her into Nacogdoches like I planned. But I can meet her after the match. It'll be fine. I can salvage this.

The blood trail leads me to a swampy area, the ground moist beneath my feet and stinking of rotting vegetable matter. I stop and listen. It's quiet out here, and I can hear the forest breathing, soft and shuddery.

I hear someone else breathing, too.

Relief surges through my sore body. *Fucking finally*. Vincent is family, and family comes first. That's what Dad taught me. Gran, too. Uncle Jack. All of them. Because our whole family descends from a nightmare, so who can we trust but ourselves?

I creep forward through the underbrush, moving slowly. It doesn't take long before I hear the first whimper of fear, and somehow I draw up the strength to attack. I lunge toward the sound, not caring that the underbrush rustles thunderously around me. Let him hear. Maybe it'll flush him out, and I can finally go to bed.

The sacrifice screams, a shrill, piercing sound, and then tries to run. He doesn't get far because his left leg collapses under him, and he splashes into the shallow, stagnant water pooling beside a rotting old log. I leap on him and get him in a bear hug and drag him backward.

He's young. College-aged, the way they usually are. My family's god likes youth. The sacrifice screams and thrashes against me, but I'm a lot stronger than he is.

"Give it up," I say softly. "You've lost."

"Fuck you!" he sobs, trying to wrench himself around. He's covered in filth—mud, old leaves, piss, blood. His left foot looks mangled, presumably from Vincent's trap, and when I heave him backward, it drags at a painful-looking angle.

Once I'm on solid footing, I heave him up over my shoulder, which sets him to screaming again, his little fists pounding into the muscles of my back. It's nothing like the sort of pain I crave. Just a steady, rhythmic thudding.

I put two fingers in my mouth and whistle. The sound bursts through the dark woods and makes the insects go silent, just for a second. A wind stirs around, parting the trees to send streams of silvery moonlight flowing into the clearing. It's Him, our family's god, ready to accept His gift.

"Why are you doing this?" the sacrifice screams, squirming against my shoulder.

I sigh. It's not the first time I've been asked it, and it won't be the last. The first sacrifice I ever helped hunt, when I was eight years old, she asked it, screaming it up at Dad and Uncle Jack right before Dad drew the saw blade across her throat.

Even then, I didn't like the suffering. Not like Xavier does. Which is why Dad chose me to do the killing for our family.

"Why?" the sacrifice screams, sobbing and desperate. But beneath that, I can hear Vincent's crashing jog through the underbrush.

"You'll have to ask him," I say wearily. "You aren't my sacrifice."

"Sacrifice?" There's a kind of panic in the way he says it, but an understanding, too. Then he starts screaming just as Vincent bursts out of the trees. He looks almost as beat-up as the sacrifice does. I'm sure I'm not much better.

"Finally," Vincent breathes, his relief clear.

"Let's get this shit over with." I throw the sacrifice onto the ground, hard enough to stun him. He blinks up at me dazedly, and I know what he sees. A monster.

Vincent crouches beside him and does it quick, slicing his throat open with his father's big hunting knife. The blade glows like a star in the moonlight, but the blood that spills over the sacrifice's chest looks black. I watch it flow out, rushing like Hatchet Creek, as He comes alive around us, pulsing through the leaves and branches of the surrounding woods, singing out with the voices of frogs and insects and nightbirds. The racket is like a hymn.

Vincent mutters in the old language, asking for wealth and good fortune and the usual shit we ask for. The wind picks up, and the trees thrash around, almost like a hurricane is blowing in. But it's not a hurricane.

It's the god my family has worshipped for five generations. The one we call the Shadow Thorn.

And like always, He accepts His gift.

IVY

The phone in Golly's kitchen jangles as I'm scrounging around for coffee in the pantry, and I nearly leap out of my skin. I haven't heard a landline in years, and I've forgotten how loud they are.

I'm not sure why, but I answer it—I guess I figure anyone calling this early in the morning has to be calling for me. I half-expect to hear Lee on the other end, but instead it's a low, gravelly voice that says, "Sorry for calling so early." A beat. "This is Gideon, by the way."

"Oh, hey." I slump against the wall, my heart fluttering around in my chest. Last night, as I lay in bed, I kept thinking about his mouth on mine to the point of distraction. I eventually had to snake my hand between my thighs, my thoughts flooding with images of him fucking me in a field of wildflowers, his big arms pinning me down by the wrists as he thrust into me.

I'm not sure where that fantasy came from, but it felt right. And it feels embarrassing, now, thinking about it while he's speaking to me on the phone. Apologizing again.

"I hate to do this, I really do." Gideon sounds tired. "I

wanted to drive you into Nacogdoches this morning, maybe show you around a bit. But something came up, and now I've got to take care of some shit outside of town."

Disappointment surges through me, as sickening as nausea. I'm sure he's lying, trying to let me down easily. I tell myself it doesn't matter, that this is what I get for opening myself up, even just a little. It was the fireflies, I think, and the balmy night air. It might as well have gotten me drunk.

I fumble around, not sure what to say, and eventually settle on, "Oh."

The line crackles. "I was hoping you'd be okay with meeting me there."

It takes a minute to register. "Wait, you still want me to come watch you?"

"Yeah, of course." Gideon's voice seems to lighten, like he's smiling. "I'd drive you, but this shit I have to do, I'll be halfway to Nacogdoches by the time I'm done, and I won't be able to pick you up. But—" His voice falters for a moment. "But it'd mean a lot to me if you could make the drive. I get it if you don't want to, but I can get you in for free if that sweetens the deal at all."

I blink, my disappointment immediately replaced with the same girlish churning from last night. I wrap my finger around the phone cord and try to steady my breath. "It's not like I have anything better to do," I tell him, hoping I don't sound overeager. I'm not good with men. I've never been good with men. And when I like one, I'm always afraid to let them know.

"Well, I'd love for you to come," Gideon says. "Again, I'm so sorry—this is kind of dirty work, what I have to do. You don't want to mess with it."

"Yeah, I can imagine." I can't, actually, although I assume anything related to an estate in rural Texas would get messy. "No, I'll drive myself."

"Awesome." He sounds genuinely happy, and that makes

butterflies flap around in my belly. "Gloria's notepad should still be by the phone if you want to take down the venue address."

There is, in fact, a notepad by the phone, and a pen on a string taped to the wall. It's like I'm trapped in the 1980s. But I am able to scribble down the information for the Nacogdoches VFW hall, and my chest gets all full when Gideon says, "I'm really looking forward to seeing you again. Seven PM sharp."

"Got it."

While my coffee brews, I google the venue, and it only takes a second to find a website advertising something called Chaos Clash Wrestling for tonight. There's even a picture of Gideon on the homepage, although he's wearing a dark, leathery mask that covers the bottom of his face like a muzzle, and the name emblazoned beneath him is BORUTA. But I recognize his eyes and hair right away. And the thick-lined swirl of tattoos on his shoulders.

It's a weirdly hot picture, though.

I check the drive time, and it's a little under two hours, which leaves me with most of today to myself. I suppose I should do something useful and sort through Golly's things like I told myself I would. After all, I have to decide what I'm going to do with all of this stuff that now, apparently, belongs to me.

Golly's house feels homey and lived-in, which makes the furniture feel homey and lived-in, too, at least at first glance. But as I'm having my breakfast at the dining room table, I keep rubbing my hand over the polished wood. It absolutely does not feel like the particle board table I have at home. It's sleek and heavy, and there's an intricate design carved into the edge that I hadn't noticed last night. Arabesques, I think, although the more I look at them, the more they seem to form a face, dark eyes and a severe mouth peering out of a tangle of leaves, like the leaves outside.

As I start poking around the house, I realize the same is true of all of Golly's household goods: The thick, fluffy blankets in the bathroom hamper. The silky cotton bedsheets on her bed. The china in the cupboards. Like the furniture, it looks ordinary at first. It's only when I look at it closely, when I weigh it in my hands, that I realize it's very old or very expensive or both.

The china in particular catches my eye, because it has the same designs as the table, painting around the rim in a very pale gold that I almost don't notice at first. It's not until I tilt one of the plates sideways that I see it, a face peering out at me.

Did she have all these things when I was here as a kid? I can't remember. But then, you don't really notice things like fine china as a kid unless someone yells at you to be careful with it. And Golly never did that. I don't think.

When I'm putting my breakfast dishes away, I find the business card for Hutchinson Estate Sales lying on the side table in the foyer. I don't remember putting it there, but maybe Lee did while I was recovering from my heat stroke, or whatever it was.

I study the card, anxiety knotting weirdly in my stomach. Mom's voice rattles in the back of my head. *You barely knew her. She just took care of you one summer twenty years ago. Sell it. You need the money.*

I do need the money. However much the house itself is worth, plus all of this heavy, expensive furniture—I wouldn't have to live in my crappy one-room apartment anymore, that's for damn sure.

But the knot in my stomach tightens at the thought, and the house seems to crowd in around me, like it's got a message of its own. Golly wanted *me* to have the house and all her belongings, not a bunch of random strangers. This is my birthright.

It's an odd word to pop into my head like that. Who has birthrights in the twenty-first century?

I slap the business card back down on the table. I don't have to make a decision right this second.

I've still got a couple of hours to kill before I have to drive to Nacogdoches, and I'm not sure what to do with myself. Like yesterday, I feel an odd, persistent tug into the backyard, and more than once, I step out onto the porch and stare out at the meadow that rolls into the woods while the oversized wind chime bongs softly. It would be easy to just keep walking. Follow the trail back to Hartshorn.

And do what, exactly? Gideon said he's doing something off the estate, and I don't want to impose on Judith. It's warm, too, the sun bright overhead. I definitely don't want to pass out again.

So every time, I resist the call, or urge, or whatever it is. I step out on the porch, squint into the wind for a few minutes, and then force myself back inside to poke around in Golly's things. That I do it over and over feels like it should be alarming, but it feels strangely ordinary. Certainly more reasonable than selling all her stuff.

Which is why I'm not sure I keep digging around in everything. I feel like I'm searching for something, although I don't know what—especially when I find myself in her bedroom. Even in the bright morning light, it feels vaguely transgressive to be in here, like Golly is just in town for a few hours and there's a good chance she'll catch me in the act of snooping.

But I want to know—something. Anything. It's like a wire has become disconnected, like if I can put it back into place, I'll understand something important, even if I don't know what it is.

So when I find a bulky old laptop tucked in the drawer of Golly's desk, I plug it in and open it up, the little chime singing through the quiet room. It's not locked, either. After it boots up, the desktop flutters to life, crammed with a bunch of folders, half of them unnamed. But it's the desktop photo that catches my eye.

It's a family portrait, with Golly and Judith side by side in the center.

Gideon stands unsmiling in the back, taller and broader than the rest, his hair pulled back in a ponytail. A couple of bigger older men stand beside him, their expressions severe. His father and uncle, maybe. They look like him. A guy around his age and some teenagers, all almost certainly his cousins. There's also a thin, elegant older woman—that's definitely his mother. I remember her, suddenly and clearly, lifting her gaze to meet mine as I walked by, as beautiful as a fashion model. Here, she's still beautiful, just older. She looks bored.

And then there's Xavier.

My heart palpitates a little when I see him, because he looks nothing at all like the boy I remember, even though I recognize him immediately. His white-blonde hair has darkened with age, but only a little, and he's become the kind of lean, good-looking man I'm used to only seeing on TV. He also has the air of haughtiness I'd expect from someone who knows he's handsome: his chin lifted, his smile bright but also tinged with a faint hint of cruelty.

I stare at the picture, my breath tightening a little in my chest. They're all strangers, even Golly. Even Gideon, despite our desperate kissing last night and the fact that I'm about to drive two hours in a rental car just to go on... a date, I guess you'd call it.

The laptop screen goes dark, jarring me out of my reverie. It's just a family portrait, I tell myself. It's not like Hartshorn froze in time just because I wasn't here.

I wiggle the cursor and open up a bunch of folders so I can cover up the faces of the Hartshorn family. Snooping has lost some of its lustre, but opening the folders just reveals more photographs—rolls and rolls of them. Pictures from Christmas, with tree lights in the background and wrapping paper on the floor. Pictures of the woods and nothing else. Pictures of a cat and some chickens. Pictures of bones.

That one stops me. I almost don't even realize what I'm looking at. It takes me a moment to recognize that the grey tangle isn't some accidental shot, but a stack of bleached bones all in a pile.

My heartbeat quickens.

I click through to the next picture, and it's clearer. The bones are laid out in the grass—the meadow in the backyard? No, this is a lawn, the grass shorn nearly to the quick and vividly green. There's a grey wall rising in the background.

Hartshorn.

I click to the next picture, and the bones have been arranged in the grass, not just laid out side by side. Laid out in the shape of a person.

The air in the house suddenly feels stifling and oppressive. Too still. Too warm. I stare at the picture, trying to understand what I'm looking at—

A human skeleton it's a human skeleton Golly was taking pictures of a skeleton—

But it's not entirely human. There are extra bones jutting out from behind the shoulder blades, long and fine and delicate, as if they might be the scaffolding for wings. And the skull doesn't look quite right, either. The mouth is too big, I think. Or the teeth are too sharp. Or—

I catch a sharp curl of ozone right before white sparks fly out of the side of the laptop. Black, foul-smelling smoke pours upward, and I shriek and jump back as the sparks turn into an honest-to-god fire that quickly crawls across the laptop's keyboard.

"What the fuck?" I whip my head around, a million grade-school fire safety lessons going through my head. Does Golly even have a fire extinguisher?

I don't want to go looking for it, especially as the fire swells, melting the laptop into a black, twisted lump. Isn't there something about laptop batteries that turns them into bombs if they catch fire?

So I wrench the comforter off the bed and beat it over the laptop, smothering the fire and filling the room with that thick, awful black smoke. As soon as I'm sure the fire's out, I race into the hallway, choking and sputtering. The smoke follows, drifting like a storm cloud. A few seconds later, the smoke alarm goes off.

I have no idea where the stupid thing is, so I just flap my arms around as I stumble to the front door and fling it open, hoping that will clear the house out. I push out onto the porch and breathe in the fresh, piney air. It doesn't do much to cover up the toxic stink from the laptop smoke, though.

I turn around, leaning up against the banister. The screen door darkens the entrance to the house, like it's trying to conceal the inside from me.

I keep seeing that last picture in my head, the skeleton lying in the grass. The weird skull. Now that I'm outside, it feels absurd. It had to have been a Halloween decoration or something, as normal as the rest of the pictures I clicked through.

I tell myself that, but I don't really believe it.

12

IVY

The dirt parking lot for the Nacogdoches VFW hall is more crowded than I expect, and rock music throbs through the dusky twilight as I slam my rental car door shut.

I can not believe that I'm doing this. That I drove two hours for a man I barely know, even if he kissed me like he's known me our entire lives.

What else did you have to do? Burn down the rest of Golly's house?

I toy with my hair, trying to arrange it around my shoulders. People drift toward the hall's entrance in groups of twos and threes, their voices laughing and jovial. I'm too nervous to share their excitement. This isn't exactly a date, but it sort of is, and my hands were shaking for nearly the entire drive here.

There's a big, burly man scanning people's tickets as they head into the building. "Hi," I say, when it's my turn. "My, uh, my friend told me he'd get me free tickets?"

"Name?"

I swallow, feeling like I'm holding up the line. "Um, mine or his?"

The man stares at me. "Yours."

"Ivy Myste."

He scrolls through his tablet, finds what he's looking for, and gives me a nod. "There you are," he says, tapping on the screen. "You get to sit in the reserved section."

I have no idea what to say to this, or what it means that Gideon put me there. The man gives me a plastic bracelet and directs me inside, where everything is dark and loud and smells of beer and decades-old cigarette smoke. I never watched wrestling as a kid, although I have memories of it somehow. I remember how it looked on TV, the way the cameras would turn the spotlights into stars while comic book characters flung each other around in a boxing ring. It was always on during summer afternoons, and I guess I would pass it by as I channel-surfed.

The VFW hall doesn't look anything like that, though. There are no spotlights, and the ring itself seems smaller and less imposing. The rows of folding chairs are already almost completely full, and voices buzz excitedly over the music pouring out of some tinny, invisible speakers.

I find the reserved section easily—it's the only one that's still mostly empty—and I slide into a chair on the second row and squeeze my purse into my lap. I'm still waiting for something to go wrong. For this to be a joke somehow. For another big, muscular man to appear out of the crowd and tell me I'm not supposed to be here.

It doesn't happen. A few more people sit down in the reserved section, and they ignore me. The lights dim a little, and the crowd gets more excited. A big screen over the walkway switches on, CHAOS CLASH WRESTLING emblazoned in neon letters.

I feel a hand on my shoulder. "Ivy Myste?"

It's not a muscular man, but a middle-aged woman, her voice thick with Texas twang and her hair teased halfway to heaven.

"Um, yes?"

"Gideon wanted me to pass on a message." She smiles indulgently. "He said to tell you he's going on second to last, and that he'd love it if you could meet him backstage after the show."

My heart flutters. I tell myself not to get my hopes up, but it's getting harder and harder to listen. I keep thinking about how he kissed me in the graveyard. How I would have let him strip me down and take me right there, out in the open.

"Am I allowed back there?" I spit out, the first thing I think to say. "Won't they be—changing, or whatever?" Naked, is what I mean. Won't they be naked.

The woman laughs. "Yeah, you're allowed. They know to keep to the locker room." She straightens up and gives me a wink. "Enjoy the show. I know Gideon's excited as hell you're here."

He told this woman about me? He told *anyone* about me?

I can't respond, though, because the lights go down completely, plunging us into darkness, and the crowd's excited chatter swells into a literal roar. I wouldn't have expected it, the crowd being so small. But they're fucking loud.

The woman slips away in the chaos, and I turn my attention to the ring, where an announcer is doing everything he can to get the crowd even more riled up. He announces the first wrestler, who comes out to boos, and then his opponent, who comes out to cheers. It's a story that everyone knows but me.

Still, by the time the first bell rings, I've relaxed into it. The wrestlers alternate between throwing punches and flipping each other around, their bodies making the entire ring shake with a loud, resounding *bang* that echoes in the back of my skull. *Bang. Bang. Bang.* Over and over, until the crowd's excitement swallows it up.

The next match is between two women, who smile prettily and blow kisses to the crowd and then flip around like cheerleaders. I have no idea what's going on, but it's fun, and it distracts me from everything that's happened over the last few days. For a few hours, I don't have to think about what I'm going to do with Golly's house or how I'm going to tell my mom that I spent the weekend in Texas, in a place I know she doesn't want me to go. I even manage to stop feeling nervous, a little, about meeting up with Gideon.

Well, until the announcer steps into the ring with a malicious glint in his eye. "Our next match," he says when the crowd quiets down, "with no holds barred, is between Guerrero Fantasmo and the monster of mayhem himself, Boruta!"

The crowd loses it, cheering and stomping so loudly that my chair rattles. I recognize Gideon's stage name from the website, and my heart flutters in my chest. I wonder if they're cheering for him or Guerrero Fantasmo. Or both.

I get my answer a few minutes later, when dark, heavy music pipes into the hall, and dark, swirling images flash on a flat-screen TV hanging above the entranceway.

"Hailing from parts unknown," the announcer cries, "It's Boruuuuuuutttttttaaaaaaaa!"

The place erupts with good-natured boos as Gideon steps out onto the ramp, although it doesn't look like Gideon. He lurches forward, his hair wet and hanging into his eyes, which are dark and intense above the dark leather of his mask.

He's also shirtless, and my breath catches again at the way the overhead lights gleam on his big shoulders and the soft taper of his belly. For the first time, I see the extent of his tattoos, thick and dense and colorful across his skin. They cover his entire torso and wind down his forearms, accentuating the swell of his muscles. They're so thickly layered I can't tell what I'm looking at, but they sort of remind me of the design on Golly's furniture. I swear I can see a face in the lines, staring at me.

But then Gideon stalks forward, and it's gone.

Last night, I had felt Gideon's strength, but tonight I actually see it, thick and powerful as he stomps into the ring, flipping his hair back with a dramatic flourish. When he jumps onto the ropes, the crowd roars again—Cheers? Boos? I can't tell, but I clap politely like I'm at the symphony, just to be on the safe side.

Gideon leans forward over the ropes, eyes gleaming above his mask. He sweeps his head toward the reserved section, and his gaze lands on me. It's hard to see his mouth beneath the mask—there's just a small slit for it—but his eyes crinkle like he's smiling.

I give him a shy little wave, and I swear he winks. Just once. Then he lifts his hands overhead, clenching his fists up tight.

"And his opponent," the announcer says, "from Brownsville, Texas—Guerrrrrerrrooooooo Faaaaaantaaaasmoooooo !"

It's clear Guerrero Fantasmo is the good guy in this scenario, because the crowd cheers in earnest as he runs out from backstage, lithe and dressed in bright superhero's clothes, his face covered in a satiny mask. He's also got to weigh fifty pounds less than Gideon, but I suppose that doesn't matter when it's all fixed.

Gideon hurls himself over the top rope and tackles poor Fantasmo to the ground, and the bell rings a second later. The crowd jumps to their feet, urging them on as they brawl on the ramp. It doesn't exactly look fake, especially when Fantasmo grabs hold of Gideon's hair and slams him against the floor. Gideon stumbles backward, and my throat constricts because I'm certain, just for a moment, that he's really hurt. But then he lunges forward, grabs Fantasmo around the neck, and drags him through the ropes and into the ring.

At that point, it starts to look a little more like the other matches I watched. Fantasmo does a bunch of acrobats off the rope—and off Gideon—and Gideon picks him up and hurls him around, and I kind of understand why the promotion put the two of them together.

At one point, Gideon bodyslams Fantasmo down onto the ring, making it rattle, and then leaps to his feet and towers over him, his body gleaming with sweat beneath the bright overhead lights.

I squeeze my thighs together. I think about his mouth on mine.

Fantasmo isn't deterred, though. He drags himself up and kicks Gideon in the face—or pretends to, I guess. I *hope*. Gideon flies back and slams against the ropes, sending electric shouts through the crowd. Then he slumps forward.

I tense up, jumping to my feet. He's hurt for real this time. I'm sure of it. But then I see his hand move, slow and sneaky. Something gleams in his palm.

Fantasmo pulls out a folding chair. The crowd loses its shit.

I've seen this kind of thing before, flipping through TV. Or on a movie. Absorbed through cultural osmosis. Gideon flips onto his back, and I see the thin cut across his forehead right as he draws up his arms and Fantasmo brings down the chair, driving Gideon to the ground.

When he gets up again, the part of his face above his mask is covered in blood.

I know he cut himself. I saw him do it. But the lights make his blood more vivid than I think it should be, and everything feels too heightened. Too real.

Gideon snarls and flings himself at Fantasmo, somehow grabbing the chair in the turmoil. Fantasmo wrenches it away. They wrestle like fighting cats, rolling around, Gideon's blood smearing on the ring. Gideon pins Fantasmo; Fantasmo breaks free at the last second and climbs on the ropes and goes flying. Before I realize what's happening, Gideon is pressed on the mat and the bell dings. It's over. Fantasmo is the winner.

I slump back in my chair as the crowd cheers around me, sucking down breaths. There was something exhilarating about watching that. About watching Gideon. All that gleaming flesh. All the bright blood.

Fantasmo holds up his arms in victory, and Gideon rolls out of the ring, stumbling backstage. And I know there's one more match, but I grab my purse and bolt out of my chair to follow him.

13

GIDEON

I press up against the wall in the narrow hallway outside the main room, the slick paint on the cinderblocks cool against my bare back, and unlatch my mask. As soon as the AC hits my sweat- and blood-drenched face, I let out a relieved sigh. The mask is uncomfortable as hell, but it was the only reason my family agreed to let me do any of this. Dad, Gran, Mom, Uncle Jack, even Xavier—the mask was the compromise. Hide my face, and I can do whatever I want.

The mantra of our whole fucking family, really.

Fabian bursts into the hall. "Good show, man," he says, holding up his hand for a high-five. I deliver it. "You need to get that cut bandaged up. You're dripping all over the place."

"I'll be in there in a second." He's right, of course, but I want to sit with the sting of it for a few seconds longer. I cut deeper than we'd talked about, mostly because of the bullshit with Vincent last night. I need the adrenaline and the pain to make me feel human again.

Also, I was hoping to impress Ivy. At least a little.

I press my hand against the cut, and my palm comes away

bloody. There's an EMT around here somewhere who can get me cleaned up. But I also just like blood.

The sounds of the crowd filter in through the thin walls. The announcer's gearing them up for the main event, and I wonder what Ivy's doing right now. I have no idea if Gladys, who runs the promotion, actually told her to meet me backstage when the show's over. Maybe I can go sit with her once I'm patched up. Buy her a beer from the concession stand. See if I can talk her into staying with me overnight at the room I booked at the motel across the street. Presumptuous, I know. But I want to fuck her before she goes back to New Mexico, and it's a hell of a lot safer to do it here in Nacogdoches, two hours from the Hartshorn chapel.

That, more than anything, convinces me to peel myself away from the wall. My whole body aches. I went harder than I intended tonight, and I'm still exhausted from last night.

"Gideon?"

I recognize Ivy's voice immediately, and my heart starts pounding furiously. I guess Gladys did pass my message along.

I turn around just as Ivy stops in the middle of the corridor, her face twisted with concern. She's dressed up a little, in a lacy-edged sundress and ankle-high black boots, and my heart twists up, that she did that for me.

"Jesus Christ," she says. "Are you okay?"

I grin at her. "It's nothing. Barely a scratch. Face wounds just bleed a lot."

"I saw you do it while you were on stage." She shakes her head, blushing a little. "Or in the ring. Whatever. I mean, I saw you cut yourself."

"Yeah, that's how it works." We keep staring at each other, at least two feet between us. "I was actually gonna go get it cleaned up if you want to come with me."

"Can I do that?" Her eyes gleam. I'm so glad she's here. So glad I can pretend this thing we have is normal.

Normal the way she thinks it is.

"You can do whatever you want." I tilt my head. "It's this way. Won't take long."

Ivy nods and follows me down the hallway, her boots tapping softly against the tile. The EMT is waiting in a little office in the back of the hall, just like Gladys said he'd be. He grins when I walk in, and I know immediately he recognizes me. I'm not sure how I feel about that, with Ivy here.

"That was fucking awesome," he tells me as I sit down on the ripped pleather chair in the corner. "It's always a treat to see Boruta work." He says this to Ivy, who stands by the door, still looking concerned.

"It's a lot of blood," she says.

I cringe inwardly.

"There's always a lot of blood with Boruta, isn't there?" The EMT dabs at my cut. The sharp sting of astringent doesn't offer the same surge of adrenaline as the cut itself did, but everything's heightened with Ivy so close by.

"Is there?" Ivy says. "I've never seen him wrestle before."

The EMT laughs. "She doesn't know who you are?"

I shake my head as he wipes the blood away. "She, uh, she knows me from my civilian life."

"I feel like I'm getting left out of this conversation." Ivy smiles.

My face heats. Fortunately, the EMT answers for me.

"Boruta here is known for getting beat up," he says. "It's his whole thing. Usually it's a hell of a lot worse than this."

Ivy gapes at me. "You're covered in blood!" she says. "How's that possible?"

"This is not covered in blood," the EMT says. "Trust me."

Ivy looks at me, his eyes big and disbelieving. But interested, too. I see it, that spark in her expression—the same spark that makes drivers slow down for traffic accidents, or for people to crowd close when they see DEATH MATCH on a wrestling card.

"I do a lot of extreme stuff," I tell her, feeling sheepish. "Let guys beat me with barbed wire and that sort of thing." As if that's the worst fucking thing I've done in my life.

"Jesus."

"That's why guys like me are backstage," the EMT says, digging around in his First Aid kit. "At least you won't need stitches tonight, eh?"

Honestly, I could have used the pain of it after what happened last night. A good scourging. But I sure as shit don't say that out loud.

"Yeah." I smile at Ivy, and she smiles back at me. "Yeah, thank god for that."

The EMT finishes up, pressing some butterfly tape to my cut and then sending me on my way.

"Do you need to change?" Ivy asks.

"Yeah, but I've got all my shit across the street." I lead her out through the back door, into the little alley between the VFW hall and a tall wooden fence. It's quiet out here, and the only sound comes from the night insects buzzing in the shadows. And it feels good to be in the cool night wind.

"Across the street?"

"At the motel there."

Ivy looks at me when I say *motel*, and something changes in the air around us. Everything gets hot and electric.

"You didn't tell me you were getting a hotel." She stares at me, the yellow lamplight carving her face into shadows.

"I usually do," I say carefully. "More privacy to shower and get cleaned up." And sleep, although right now, sleep's the farthest thing from my mind.

Ivy steps closer to me, and my body buzzes. My blood's up after the match. After the violence last night, too. Being around the EMT, I held it back, but out here, just the two of us—

I swear I can hear Him on the wind, even two hours away.

"Do you want to shower?" she asks.

"Yeah." I take a step toward her, and she doesn't pull back, even though I know there's still dried blood on my forehead. "Yeah, I was hoping I could take you out for drinks or something."

"I'd like that." Ivy moves closer. The wind picks up, and I *know* He's watching, traveling on the shadows. And I can feel it, the claim I made on her all those years ago, throbbing through my veins.

"It's a nice night." Ivy's voice is low and throaty.

"Yeah, it is." I clear the space between us, my hard cock uncomfortable in my tights. If she looks down, she'll see it. But she doesn't look down. She looks at my chest.

The air is ionized, ribbons of destiny swirling around us, pulling us together.

It's safer here, I tell myself, because it nearly killed me last night to stop, and I know I won't be able to do it tonight.

Ivy reaches up one hand and touches my chest, right above the sigil that marks my heart. My body jumps, and I curl my hands up, letting her take the lead. She traces the lines of the sigil, following them until they flow into the design across my belly. Two decades' worth of agony seared into my skin.

"I want to see your tattoos in the light," she whispers.

I grab her wrist, and she looks up at me, her eyes gleaming in the dark.

"I'll show you all of them," I murmur, hoping I'm not about to make a massive mistake. But god, I want to show her. I want to feel her lust throbbing through the air.

So I guide her hand down to my waistband, my eyes on her face. If she wants to stop, I'll stop. But she doesn't resist. Doesn't protest. Even when I hook her fingers around the top of my tights and pull down.

Her eyes widen. She makes a startled noise in the back of

her throat, and that one motion reveals my secret: The tattoos keep going, past my belly and around the full length of my cock. Every single one was an act of magic and pain.

Ivy doesn't see all of it now, though. She pulls down just enough to see the base, then yanks her hand away.

"On your—" she whispers, looking up at me. "You have a tattoo on your dick?"

I nod. I don't tell her I want to watch it disappear down her throat.

Ivy looks at me, her lips glossy and parted. The wicked wind blows her hair around.

"Why?" she asks.

I cup my hand around her neck, pulling her up to me. She twines her hand around my waist, never breaking eye contact.

"The tattoos are a long story," I tell her. "And I'm not really in the mood for talking."

Then I kiss her because I can't stand it anymore.

She moans against me, our tongues grappling, and I know I'm going to fuck her out here in the alley. Then I'm going to take her back to the motel and I'm going to fuck her there, too. I'm going to fuck her as many times as I can because I don't know if I'll ever get to do it again.

"Gideon," she breathes against me, running her hands over the map work of tattoos that lay out every single one of my family's secrets in a language only we can speak. A language I would love to teach her, although I know I can't. "You were so hot up there."

"In the ring?" I push her backward, a little roughly, until she's pressed against the fence. She nods, her chest rising and falling with her rapid breaths, pushing her full, gorgeous tits up toward the neckline of her dress.

"It was hot seeing you in the audience." I run my hands over her breasts, squeezing and kneading them. She moans again, slumping her head back against the fence. "Never had a girl come see me wrestle before."

"Really?"

I kiss her so she doesn't try to ask any more questions. Because, yeah, it's true. It's not like women haven't tried. But she's the only one that matters.

For ten years, I've been starving. And now, I finally get to eat.

14

IVY

Gideon is as devouring as he was last night, and for a moment, I'm sure we're back in the cemetery. The night has the same damp, windswept quality, as if the shadows themselves have come alive.

But then Gideon hikes my dress up to my waist, and I'm not thinking about the wind anymore.

"Here?" I pant against him, his firm body pressing me up against the fence.

"Yeah," he rasps into my ear, his fingers already hooking around the hem of my panties. "Right fucking here."

Then he jerks them down and kneels in front of me, his mouth and tongue exploring along my thighs. I gasp, bracing my spine against the fence, and press my hand against the top of his head as he lifts my leg and props it on his shoulder and kisses the inside of my thigh, forging a trail to my cunt. I stare at the back of the VFW hall. I can hear music thumping inside, the occasional burst of voices. The big metal door stays closed, but I keep expecting it to swing open, for someone to walk out and catch us.

The idea sends hot jolts of desire through my body.

Gideon's tongue finally finds my pussy, and when I moan, it's as loud as an explosion. I slap my hand over my mouth, trying to trap my whimpers. But Gideon licks me harder until soft wet sounds fill up the alley.

"Someone's going to catch us," I gasp through my fingers.

"Don't care," Gideon growls against my pussy.

I close my eyes so I can't see the door and try to just give myself over to the pleasure. It's not hard. Gideon eats me out like he's done it before, like he knows exactly how much pressure to apply to my clit that's enough but not too much, like he knows instinctively to shove his tongue up into my pussy right when I'm on the precipice of tipping over, dragging out my pleasure.

"How are you so good at this?" I pant out.

He doesn't answer, and I presume it's because his mouth is full. I braid my fingers through his hair, pressing him up against me, and he grunts.

"Harder," he rasps.

"W-what?"

Gideon peers up at me, past the soft swell of my belly and the voluminous fabric of my skirt. "Pull my hair harder," he orders—and it *is* an order. There's nothing shy about it. Nothing that makes it feel like a request.

I think about his tattooed cock, about what the EMT told me. *He likes pain.*

I yank on his hair, and his eyes glitter.

"Harder," he snarls, in a way that suggests I won't like it if I disobey him.

So I don't, and instead pull on the hair knotted up in my fist with as much might as I dare. He grins, his teeth gleaming in the dark. "Perfect," he says, right before he dives into my pussy again.

I drag back on his hair, and he fights me to keep licking my clit in slow, languorous circles. I thrust up against him, my thighs trembling. I'm going to come, even though it feels preposterous—we're out in the open, someone could walk out at any moment and catch us and *why* does that idea just make me thrust harder against Gideon's face?

Then, just as I'm about to spill, he jerks away, leaving me desperate and panting up against the fence. He rises to standing in the pool of golden light from the industrial sodium lamps affixed to the building, his eyes never leaving mine. I wait for him to say something, to explain himself, but he only pushes down the band of his pants and pulls out his cock.

I didn't really see it earlier. Just an inch or so, enough to know that it was tattooed. And even then, it was hard to make anything out in the dark. But now he's standing in the light, and I can see the full glory of it.

He's big. Like, *really* big. But more than that, the tattoo I caught a glimpse of earlier wraps around his entire length. Roses. His cock is wrapped in roses, thorns and all, from base to head. In the lamplight, the colors are bright and garish, the red of the petals almost as red as his blood.

"Holy shit," I breathe.

Gideon squeezes himself at the base. "That's why I had to make sure you were ready."

I force myself to meet his dark, glinting gaze. The wind picks up, hot and damp. As hot and damp as I am, even.

The metal door stays closed.

Gideon drops his cock and turns me around so my breasts press up against the fence. He flips my skirt up and runs his hands over my bare ass, making me shiver. Then, with a rough jerk, he tilts my hips toward him and spreads my legs. I sigh into it, the sense of being thrown around. Manhandled. It makes desire spark in my blood.

"Breathe," he whispers, the word hot on my ear.

He nudges his cockhead against my slit and then rubs it

back and forth, like he's slowly working it in. I moan softly, arch my back into him.

"You're wet," he murmurs into the back of my neck. "You're so fucking wet."

Then he slides himself into my pussy.

It hurts. Even as turned on as I am, even as much as I want him, the stretch of him is intense, and I cry out and brace my arms against the fence. Gideon kisses the side of my neck. "You've got this, baby," he murmurs, his thrusts slow and exper-imental. "I'm going to make sure you come, okay?"

I whimper. All the words have fled out of me, especially as the initial burst of pain melts into a hot, molten pleasure. Gideon keeps his thrusts slow and measured, his breath ragged against the back of my neck. At first, it's perfect. But then it's too slow. Too gentle.

I shove back on him, impaling myself on his cock. It hits something deep inside me that makes the pain flare again.

And I have a wild, unfamiliar need for more of it, that pain. I thrust back again, shrieking as it slams through me. But Gideon grabs my hips and holds me still.

"No, baby," he rasps, snaking his hand around to stroke my clit. "No, we're going to do it slow right now."

I whimper, not sure what came over me. Because Gideon does feel so fucking good. I press my cheek against the fence as he fucks me with long, careful strokes, angling himself so he presses up against my G-spot, his finger deftly toying with my clit. He doesn't go deep enough to stab my cervix again, but his slow, rolling rhythm is agonizing in its own way. Agonizing in its pleasure.

My whole body trembles uncontrollably, and soft, wordless pants fall out of my lips. I'm aware of the music from inside the building, and I swear I can feel it thumping through the fence as Gideon keeps drawing me closer and closer to my orgasm.

He brushes his lips across my cheek, pulling me into him as

his cock keeps stroking my walls and his hand keeps rubbing my clit. "You're gonna come for me," he mutters. "I can feel it."

"Y-yes," I pant, pressing my palms into the fence. I'm so close, and Gideon just keeps dragging it out until I think I can't stand another fucking second—

And that's when I come. The pleasure quakes through my entire core and sends shockwaves into my body. I can't stop myself from crying out. I scream into the fence, trying to dig my nails into the wood. Gideon grunts and keeps fucking me until I think I might never stop coming.

"That's it," he groans, and I don't think he's even talking to me. "That's what I fucking needed."

He quickens his pace, which sends a rippling electric aftershock along my nerves. Then his hands dig into my thighs, and he tilts my hips back as his thrusts harden until they're rough and pounding. It's the sort of rhythm that would never make me come, but it feels fucking amazing after my orgasm. I love how desperate and ragged Gideon's breath gets as he slams into me. I love the starburst of pain as he shoves himself deeper into my cunt. And I love how he pins me in place as he uses me.

"Fuck, Ivy," he growls. "You have no *idea* how much I fucking needed this."

I cry out at his words, rolling my hips back against him, matching his pace. Then he slams deep inside me, deep enough that a dizzying, exciting pain explodes through me. It almost feels like an orgasm itself.

Gideon makes a strangled, throaty sound and jerks roughly. A second later, I feel something warm and wet sliding down my thigh, and I'm just grateful I've had an IUD since college.

"Ivy." Gideon whispers my name into the ridge of my spine like it's a prayer. He wraps his arms around my torso, drawing me close as his cock softens inside my pussy. "Ivy. Ivy. Ivy."

I fall back into his embrace, lifting my gaze upward to the faint swell of stars overhead. The wind gusts, blowing my hair and my skirt both, and I can smell something sweet on it. Honey and wildflowers and sugar water. Roses.

Gideon kisses me along my neck and the top of my shoulders with sharp, hungry little bites. "Come back to the motel with me," he murmurs. "Stay the night."

I turn around to face him, my heart thudding. It's absurd that I'm even considering it. I have to fly back to Santa Fe tomorrow afternoon, which means I have to make sure the house is secure before I leave. I have to decide what I'm going to do *with* it, the house and Golly's stuff. I have a million responsibilities.

And I'm going to ignore all of them.

"Okay." I'm still breathless. "I'll stay."

Gideon grins against my shoulder. "Then I'll get to fuck you properly this time."

And it feels like my whole body unravels.

15

GIDEON

The Lone Star Motel isn't much to look at, but that doesn't matter, because it has a bed and a shower and, most importantly, it's two hours from the chapel and all the dark magic I want to protect Ivy from.

My room is right next to the big vacancy sign, which means the light in the room has a faint pink tinge even with the curtains drawn. When we come in, I crank up the AC, trying to drown out the remnants of the night. We may be two hours from the chapel, but He's still here, drawn by our lust. But there's nothing He can do besides watch us, not out here. He's tied to the Hartshorn property, same as me. Same as all of us.

I put those thoughts aside, though. None of it matters. What *does* matter is actually making the most of this last night together. Getting to taste Ivy again, to sink into her, to trace my tongue over every inch of her body. I need new memories. All the ones from ten years ago have gone stale after a decade's worth of jacking off.

Ivy throws her purse on the bed and turns around, taking in the room.

"Sorry, I know it's not the greatest," I say, sliding the deadbolt into place.

"It's just fine." She looks at me, her hair falling in thick, tousled waves around her shoulders, all mussed up from the eldritch wind outside. At least that can't make its way into the room.

"I gotta shower." I'm already undressing, standing one-legged to pluck the laces out of my boots. "You're going to join me."

Ivy tilts her head, a smile dancing on her lips. "Not going to ask me? Just order me around?"

I pull off my boot and throw it on top of my suitcase. "I like ordering you around."

Her cheeks darken. Her eyes glitter. "What else are you going to order me to do?"

"Get in the shower, and you'll find out."

Ivy grins, wicked and salacious. She liked submitting last time, too, although it took a couple of rounds of fucking before I worked up the nerve to start ordering her around. I was still new at it then, still figuring out what I like. Now I know *exactly* what I need, thanks to a decade of chasing the high Ivy gave me that afternoon in the chapel, the hot sunlight pouring around us. I never quite caught it, but I know I will tonight.

The wind gusts outside, loud enough that I can hear it over the AC.

Fuck off, I think, pulling off my other boot. Not that He's gonna listen.

I make myself focus on what matters. Ivy.

"You can't get in the shower with your clothes on." I peel my tights down around my thighs. Ivy stares at me, her eyes big. Taking in my tattoos. This is a new experience: I'd only just started getting them last time, and I certainly didn't have the dick tattoo yet.

"How long did it take you to do all of that?"

I walk up to her and wrap my fingers lightly around her throat, smiling when I feel her pulse quicken against my palm. She sucks in her breath, her eyes never leaving mine.

"We're not going to talk about my tattoos." I rub my thumb against the little conclave of her throat until her lips part. "You're going to undress and get in the shower with me."

Then I squeeze lightly on the sides of her neck, making her eyelashes flutter. I pull her toward me and kiss her, dark and hungry, and she runs her hands up my arms. I wish she'd dig her nails into my skin, deep enough to make me bleed.

Later. I'll tell her to do that to me later.

"Undress." I drop her throat and step backward and watch her, waiting for her to obey.

"Jesus," she breathes, fumbling around at her side for the zipper. "You really know what you're doing."

I smile at that. "I've learned some things over the years."

Ivy drags the zipper down and peels out of the dress, letting it fall in a puddle around her feet. Even in the motel's cheap fluorescent light, she looks as beautiful as I remember, with her round hips and thick thighs and wild tangle of hair. I step backward, moving toward the bathroom without taking my eyes off her, and she shrugs out of her bra and pushes down her panties.

Outside, the wind howls and batters at the window like it's trying to get inside.

I hook my finger at her, drawing her closer to me. She moves the way I remember, the way I've dreamt about for ten years—that soft sway, her full breasts trembling with every step.

When she reaches me, I wrap my arms around her waist and drag her up to my chest. Then I kiss her, deep and probing. I don't ever want to stop kissing her. Because she's *mine*, not my brother's. I'm the one who claimed her in the chapel all those years ago, and I'm the one who claimed her behind the VFW hall tonight, and I'm about to claim her as many more times in this motel room as I can before she leaves for good

Not for good, I tell myself as I pull her into the bathroom and turn the water on. *She'll be back.*

I can feel it, a certainty deep in my bones.

As the water heats up, Ivy presses herself against my side, tracing her fingers over the tattoos on my arm, following the patterns like she wants to decipher them.

"In," I tell her before she can start asking questions about the designs. Then I switch on the shower head, the water glinting in the too-bright bathroom lights. Ivy tilts her head up at me, expression coy.

"Don't disobey me," I say softly, twining her hair around my fingers. "I want to make you come again."

A shadow flickers across her face, although she steps under the showerfall, the water turning to diamonds along her gorgeous tits. "You can try," she says ruefully. "But I'm usually a one-and-done."

"We'll see about that." I drag the shower curtain closed and pull her into another kiss, wrapping my fingers around her neck to hold her head in place. When I pull back from her, Ivy's eyes gleam with arousal, and it takes all my willpower not to bend her over and fuck her again. My cock's already starting to get hard thanks to the steam and the warmth and her big, adoring gaze.

"I'll make you a deal." I run my thumb along her bottom lip. "If I can't make you come again, here in the shower, I'll give you a hundred bucks out of the door pay from the show."

Ivy laughs, sharp and surprised. "Sounds good to me."

"Not so fast." I trail my hand down her throat to squeeze one of her breasts. Ivy gasps softly, her nipple hardening against my palm. "But if you do come in the shower, you have to do whatever I say once we're back out there." I tilt my head toward the motel room.

Ivy gazes up at me. "And what if you want to do something really fucked up?"

Oh, she has no idea the depravity I'm capable of. The things I've done over the years—usually at Xavier's urging and always at Lethe, where depravity is the only thing that matters. I bite back my tongue.

"Pick a safe word," I say. "Other than that, anything's fair game."

She grins, and there's a darkness there that shoots straight to my cock. I know that Xavier thinks our family's god made her for us—well, made her to him, anyway. But he's not fucking here, is he? I am. And my cock is still coated with her pleasure.

Which is why I think he might be right.

"Fine," she says. "Safe word. That's my safe word."

I roll my eyes. "Whatever you say, darling. But first, you're going to help me get clean."

Then I kiss her again, long and slow beneath the water, taking my time. When I pull away, I grab the bar of complimentary soap from the dish and unwrap it, then press it into her hands.

"Wash me," I order.

Ivy's eyes flash with lust, and she lathers the soap up between her hands and then rubs it over my shoulders, a slow, careful massage that's a balm against my sore muscles. I close my eyes and drop my head back as Ivy works the soap down across my pecs and onto my belly, her hands tracing the path of my tattoos.

"This really is beautiful work," she says softly.

"It took a long time."

"What do they mean?" She's working her way lower. Almost to my cock. I grab her wrist and slide her hand around to my hip.

"You do that last," I tell her.

She grins. God, I love the way she smiles at me like that, like she's thinking of all the wicked things we've done.

She doesn't remember them, idiot.

"Get your mind out of the gutter." She works the soap into my hips and then down to my thighs. "You're supposed to make *me* come."

"Don't worry. I will."

Ivy looks up at me through her wet eyelashes, the water streaming over her face. She doesn't say anything, although I can tell she still doubts me. Well. She might not remember it, but I do: the last time I had her like this, I got her up to four orgasms in a single session.

She keeps cleaning me, winding around to scrub my back with soap. That feels really good after getting thrown around in the ring, and I groan as she kneads my muscles.

"You didn't answer my question," she says. "About the tattoos."

"Because it'll take too long to answer." I turn around to face her, my cock jutting up between us. She looks down at it expectantly, but I shake my head. "Gotta clean my legs before you can touch that."

Ivy fixes me with a look of pure lust. Taunting me, I think. Let her. I know how to be in control.

Then she kneels in front of me, as supple as ever. And she does wash my legs, although it's agony, having her face that close to my cock. I want to slap her across the face with it, want to feel that sharp jolt of pain deep in my core. I want to thrust it down her throat. Want to watch her worship me.

I don't do any of that, though, just brace my hand against her wet hair as she scrubs me with soap, all the way down to my feet. Then she sits back on her heels and looks up at me.

"May I clean your cock now?" she asks. The primness in her voice, the obedience—

Xavier's wrong. She's absolutely fucking made for *me*.

"Yeah," I tell her, and she smiles and lathers up the soap between her palms. I suck in my breath and grunt when she wraps her fingers around my shaft, one fist stacked on top of the other.

Then she strokes.

I groan, rocking my hips into her hands. She's gentle with me, much more gentle than I like, but that doesn't matter. I'll show her how to do it proper once we're out of the shower.

She pulls her hands away and waits, still kneeling, as the water washes off the soap.

Then, without me even having to prompt her, she pulls my cock into her mouth.

Her warm, silky tongue is as good as I remember. She takes as much of me as she can and sucks gently, her mouth sliding up and down my length. Then she releases me and traces my full length with her tongue until she gets to my balls, and she sucks on those, too. At the same time, her hand slowly jerks me with a tenderness that's much too sweet for my taste.

"Harder," I growl, tangling my hands up in her wet hair. "Squeeze harder."

She does. Better, although still not hard enough. Her sweet mouth on my balls is heaven, though, and I let her work me for a few seconds longer.

Then I grab her by the hair, drag her to her feet, and kiss her.

"You ready to come?" I growl against her lips.

"You ready to pay me a hundred dollars?"

In response, I shove her up against the shower tile. Ivy gazes up at me, her tits wet and trembling, her cheeks flushed.

"It turned you on, didn't it?" I slide my hand down between her thighs, and she gives a soft, shuddery sigh as I massage her pussy. "Sucking my cock?"

"It's an impressive cock." Her voice is strained.

I can't help but grin at that as I grind my palm against her clit. It's not the first time I've heard it, but coming from Ivy, it might as well be, the way it swells up my ego. "You'll get to suck it again, if you want." I slip a finger into wet, waiting pussy, and she jerks a little.

"Before or after you pay me the hundred bucks?" She's trying to stay still. I can tell. I can feel her muscles straining with the effort.

"Oh, I'm not paying you anything." I slide another finger inside her and stroke her walls. This little trick I learned ten years ago, the two of us exploring each other's bodies up in my old bedroom for hours, the window open to let in the spring sunlight.

She came three times that day. It really is a shame she doesn't remember it. Although apparently I'm the only one who's ever been able to do it to her, which also swells my ego.

I cage her with my free arm, bowing my head to press our foreheads together. The whole time, I keep stroking her pussy, angling my fingers against that soft, spongy spot I remember like it was yesterday.

Ivy's fighting me. Her whole body trembles with the effort, and she keeps biting her lip and curling her hands into fists.

"Come on, baby," I mutter, adding some little nipping kisses to the mix. "I know you're close."

"It's not... not gonna happen," she gasps, even as her hips roll up against my hand.

"Oh, I think it is." I move my thumb so I brush against her clit, and she cries out, her body slapping against the tile. "Look at that. Look at you shaking for me."

The water pours around us, hot and steamy. My cock is throbbing with the need to be inside her again, but I know my restraint will be rewarded when I win this bet and I have Ivy at my command, at least for one night.

"Gideon," she gasps out, hips rolling like I'm fucking her. Then my name dissolves into a low, soft keening, and Ivy clutches at my wrist, her fingers digging into my skin. I groan against her.

"Come for me," I rasp into her ear. "Right fucking now."

And she does, her whole body spasming against mine. She shrieks and bucks, and I press her up against the tile, still plunging my fingers in and out of her, drawing her orgasm out as long as I can.

It's perfect.

"Oh my god." She slumps forward, falling onto me, and I wrap my arms around her waist and bury my nose in her neck, as the water pours and steams around us. "I can't believe you— that's never happened before."

Yes, it has. But I don't say that. I just hold her underneath the spray of water.

"Now what?" She tilts her head, trying to look at me. I brush a strand of damp hair out of her eyes. And smile.

"Now?" I say. "Now the fun can really begin."

☙ 16 ❧

IVY

My legs are shaking so badly when I step out of the shower that I worry I might tilt forward and crash into the wall. But Gideon keeps me steady, one strong arm wrapped around my waist as he grabs a pair of towels and then dries me off.

I let him. I'm reeling from what just happened. Orgasms don't always come easily to me—that's why it shocked me how well he ate me out in the alley. But I *never* come more than once. I've tried, once with an insistent boyfriend (that ended in tears) and a few times by myself, with a vibrator. It never happened.

But Gideon, it seems, knows exactly how to touch my body.

"Come on," he says, throwing the towels onto the counter. I don't know what he means until he hoists me up onto his shoulder like he did Guerrero Fantasmo a few hours earlier.

"What the hell!"

"Told you." He marches us both into the room, where the AC chills my still-damp body. "You're gonna do whatever I want."

Then he tosses me onto the bed, and I shriek as I bounce

on the cheap mattress. Gideon grabs me by the waist and flips me onto my back and then spreads my legs on either side of his hips so I'm staring up at him—his long, wet hair curling around his shoulder, the bright tangle of his tattoos, his heavy erection.

"And what do you want?" I breathe out.

He drops down, stopping himself just before he pins me to the mattress. His cock presses into my thigh, and I desperately want it inside me again, which surprises me. Like I told him, I'm usually a one-and-done girl.

"There's something I like," he rasps, his arms caging me in place, his breath warm on my skin. "And you're going to do it to me."

"What is it?" For the first time, fear worms through my system. *He asked for a safe word*, I tell myself. As if I have experience with safe words. Every man I've ever dated has been painfully vanilla.

Gideon kisses me, his hand curling around my throat. I moan into his mouth, shivering at his touch—it's not enough to cut off my air, but it teases the sensitive skin along my pulse.

Gideon pulls away, just enough to speak.

"I like to bleed," he says darkly.

"What?" My fear blooms again. "You're going to make me bleed?"

"Not you." He kisses a line across my jaw and down my neck until he pulls one of my breasts between his lips. Pleasure surges through my core as he sucks hard on my nipple. Almost hard enough to hurt.

"You— mean—" My words come out jagged. "You mean *you* want to bleed?"

He releases me and nuzzles between my breasts. "Yes," he growls into my skin. "Now don't fucking move."

He peels away from me, leaving me sprawled and breathless on the bed. I don't know what to make of any of this. I feel like

I should be disgusted or horrified, like I should spit out *safe word* and be done with it.

But I don't want to. I think back to the match, to the mask of blood coating his face.

It was hot, wasn't it?

You can't possibly think that's true.

Gideon is digging around in a suitcase, giving me a clear view of his strong back and muscular ass. The tattoos are just as dense here as they are on his chest. A snake tracing the path of his spine. Thick greenery dotted with red eyes.

He stands up and turns to me. Silver flashes in his hand.

"A razor blade," I whisper.

"Got a whole pack of them in my suitcase." He settles between my legs again, jerking me up so his cock rests across the bottom of my belly, the tattoos vivid in the lurid motel lights. Red and greens, just like his back. A rosebud on his cockhead.

"I've never done this before," I say in a rush.

He gives me an odd look at that, almost sad. I don't know how to read it.

"I'll walk you through it." He presses the razor blade into my hand. It's one of those old-fashioned kind, sharpened on both ends. I hold my breath.

"Sit up," he barks.

I like it when he talks to me like that. When he orders me around. I push myself up, my legs still wrapped around his hips. Gideon stares down at me, his intensity hot and pulsing.

"Start on my chest," he says. "Keep it small. You're gonna have to press harder than you think you do."

The razor blade pinched between my fingers looks like a shard of moonlight.

"What if I don't?" I force myself to meet his gaze.

"Use your safe word, and it stops," he says. "But if you just refuse..."

He wraps both his hands around my throat, and I freeze, staring up at him. *Squeeze*, whispers some dark voice in the back of my head.

"I don't like hurting as much as I like to be hurt," he says, soft and dangerous. My clit throbs. My wetness soaks into the bedsheets. "But I can turn the tables if I need to."

And then he tightens his grip, just enough to make me gasp. Just enough to make heat course up into my womb.

A knowing light flashes through his eyes. "Are you going to refuse, Ivy? What do you want to be? The victim or the perpetrator? The predator or the prey?"

I shiver; words like those don't seem like they should belong in a moment like this, our naked bodies all intertwined together on a bed. But then, neither should a razor blade.

And the deep ache in my pussy says otherwise, especially as Gideon tightens his fingers around my throat. Part of me wants to stay exactly like this, wants to feel the blood flowing to my brain cut off so stars crowd around the edge of my vision. But part of me wants to see him bleed again.

All of it is terrifying and unfamiliar and utterly exhilarating.

I push up to my knees, breaking Gideon's grip on my throat, although his face stretches into a feral grin that makes me breath catch. I'm still pinching the razor blade between my fingers. It weighs nothing, but it feels like a weapon.

I shift around on the bed so I'm the one with the upper hand. I'm the one looking down at him as he looks up at me.

"I was hoping you'd choose that," he says, his voice low and throaty. "Now, do you remember what I said to do?"

"Start at your chest," I whisper, resting the razor blade just below his collarbone. "Keep the cut small." There's a pattern in his tattoos on his right pec, a kind of lopsided, fizzing spiral. "Anywhere?"

"Anywhere," he breathes.

I move the blade down and press it into the center of the spiral. Gideon doesn't even flinch.

"Do it," he says, sharp and commanding. I don't actually know which of us is in control here. "Cut me, Ivy. Now."

I suck in my breath and drag the blade sideways about half an inch. For a second, nothing happens.

Then bright crimson drops bead along his skin. I take a deep, shuddery breath, and my clit pulses.

"Again," Gideon orders. "Deeper."

"Are you sure?" The blood is already starting to drip down, marring his tattoos.

"I'm sure," he growls. "Do it, Ivy."

So I dig the blade into his skin again, this time piercing a tattoo of what looks like a long, twining blade of grass, or maybe an animal tail. I drag the blade down slowly enough that I can see his flesh part around the silver. This time, there's much more blood. A hot gush of it.

"Fuck, that's perfect." Gideon's eyes roll back, his eyelashes fluttering. The blood pours down his chest and streaks over his belly. I have the sudden, delirious thought that I want it *on* me, and to fight against the urge, I cut him again, on the right side of his chest this time. He groans and grabs my wrist, keeping the blade lodged into the skin. Looks right at me.

"Follow the tattoo," he says hoarsely.

I nod, trying to ignore the furious, distracting heat between my legs, as I trace the blade down a long, twining morning glory vine that runs from just below his heart to just above his belly button. He gasps with pleasure, his head thrown back, his Adam's apple bobbing. Blood pours out of the wound, and this time, I can't stop myself. I run my fingers through it, shuddering at its heat, its stickiness.

Gideon looks at me through heavy-lidded eyes. "More," he gasps.

It's not an order, like it was earlier. It's a plea.

Do you want to be the victim or the perpetrator?

I cup his face with my bloody fingers, leaving streaks of crimson in their wake. "More," he says, more forcefully this time. "Make it fucking hurt."

"Yes, sir," I murmur, feeling almost coquettish. Then I slice at his belly, sharp and fast enough that a few drops splatter across my own belly. The heat is searing.

Gideon shouts and grabs the back of my head and pulls me into him. Somehow, our mouths find each other, the kisses so hungry and desperate that they're barely kisses at all. But I don't think he wants kisses. I think he wants my body to press into his wounds. To make them burn.

I don't feel that hurt, of course. But I feel his blood, hot and slippery. And I'm so turned on I can barely think straight. I did this to him. I carved that pain into his skin.

"Ivy," he groans against my lips. "More."

I shove him backward and crawl on top of him, straddling him at the waist. The blood almost completely covers his tattoos, and I dig the blade into his belly again. When more blood spills out, both of us moan.

His cock jumps against me, searing me like a rod of fire, and I smear my free hand with more blood and reach down to grab him. He groans, thrusting into my fist.

"Put me in your cunt," he says. "I need to fuck you right now."

"No," I say, guiding him toward my wet, dripping pussy. "I'm going to fuck *you*."

And then I impale myself on him. A blinding, exquisite agony tears up through my core—as wet as I am, he's still huge, and his tattooed cockhead just slammed into my cervix with a brilliant burst of pain. I scream and cut him, blindly slicing across his chest, wanting more. He grabs my hips and thrusts himself up inside me, slamming against my cervix again.

I can't tell the difference between pain and pleasure anymore.

I hurl the blade away, watch it smack against the wall and leave a splatter of blood. Then I brace myself against his shoulders and ride him, bouncing hard and fast on his bloody cock, making myself hurt every time I slam down on him. Gideon moans beneath me, his blood shining in the lights. I have a distant, stupid thought—*we'll have to take a shower again*—and then it's overwhelmed by a fiery surge of power. Because Gideon is bigger than me, stronger than me, but I'm the one who has him pinned to the bed.

Acting on some dark, primeval instinct, I dig my nails into his shoulder as hard as I can. Gideon howls and thrusts up into my pussy, and I just dig harder until his eyes fall open and we lock gazes.

"Harder," he snarls.

I rake my nails across his chest, and splatters of blood fly up between us. Gideon roars and thrusts faster, jackhammering up into me as I grind my clit against his pelvic bone, hot and dizzy with the syrupy hurt of his thrusts. When my orgasm tears through me, I don't expect it, and I slash at him with my nails again. He grins, eyes feral and manic.

"I knew this would make you come," he growls. Then he wraps his arms around my thighs, pinning me up against him, and empties himself inside me with a roar.

I slump forward onto his bloody chest and tangle my hands up in his damp hair as I kiss him the way he kissed me earlier. Dark, hungry. Like I'm claiming him. Like we're two wild animals fucking in the woods.

Gideon wraps his arms around my waist, holding me still. As my breath calms, I drape myself over him and settle my head beside his on the pillow, feeling the rhythm of his breath beneath me.

And then it hits all at once—we're not wild animals. We're humans. We're in a motel.

'The sheets," I whisper. "Oh my god, we ruined the sheets—"

"Don't worry about it." Gideon rolls me over, swapping our places. I settle into the ruined mattress as he cages me again, and I'm suddenly struck with the coppery, overwhelming scent of blood.

It doesn't disgust me the way I think it should.

"They're going to think we killed someone in here," I mutter.

Gideon smiles. Brushes a strand of hair away from my face. "I said not to worry about it."

I look up at him, suddenly struck with a quivering anxiety. What the fuck did we just do?

Has he done this before?

Of course he has, a voice whispers in the back of my head. *You can't think you're his first.*

"That was good," Gideon says softly, stroking my cheek with his thumb. "Real good."

My doubts waver. In my limited experience, no man has ever said anything like that to me before. And—

And I agree with him.

"Yeah," I say. "It was."

"Not too much?" He keeps petting my hair, soft and gentle, and his tenderness is shocking after all the violence we just did to each other.

I'm not sure how to answer that, though, so I just say, "I didn't use my safe word, did I?"

"Guess not." He brushes his lips against my forehead. Then my cheek. Then, finally, my lips. And this kiss is slow and gentle and sweet.

"Are you going to come back?" he murmurs, so softly I'm not sure if I even heard him.

"Here?" I say shakily.

"To Hartshorn."

The name throbs in the back of my head Of course he's not worried about blood in a motel bedroom. His family lives in a house with a name instead of an address.

God, what have I gotten myself into?

"Well?" He keeps kissing me, but I also feel the brief flicker of his tongue against my skin, as if he's cleaning up the blood he left behind. "Are you?"

"I didn't even go to Hartshorn this time."

He stops, nuzzles against my neck. "Well, then, will you come back to me?"

As soon as he says it, I know there's only one answer. I wind my hand in his hair, and I nod, and I whisper, "Yes."

17

XAVIER

I tear into the driveway and slam my BMW right up next to Gideon's ugly-ass Honda Civic. Home sweet home.

Ivy's not here, Lee told me that much. Flew back to New Mexico earlier this morning just like she said she would. Months of planning and I still fucking missed her.

That's how it is, though, when you worship the Shadow Thorn and all the other capricious gods of the dark.

At least I have Lee. I already got his full report last night, after I finished up my bullshit with the Five Courts. I called him in the comfort of my condo in downtown Houston, the room dark so I could look out over the city lights, and listened to his rundown while I sipped a glass of Cognac. Gideon took her to see Gloria's grave, but they didn't go to the chapel. And that's what really matters.

Plus, even just the two days she was here will be enough for her memories to start jostling loose, opening up the pathways I need. When she comes back again, I'll be waiting. Hartshorn has its hooks in her now, and I think next time will be an extended stay.

Especially if I have anything to say about it.

I saunter into the house through the front door, tossing my keys on the antique table next to a big spray of blood-red roses from the garden. Gran's doing, no doubt. She's always bringing flowers in from inside.

The house is quiet, which took some getting used to when I first came back a month ago to get everything ready. Growing up, my family lived in the new wing, and Uncle Jack's lived in the old wing. But these days, everyone's scattered to the wind. Mom and Dad retired to the Outer Banks, and Uncle Jack moved his wife and brood of hooligans out into the deep part of the woods. I don't blame any of them. I certainly prefer my condo, with its view of the city skyline and its five-minute walk to Lethe.

Well, *preferred*, I should say. Because this ugly, sprawling house is how I'm going to get what's mine.

I just have to be patient.

I head up toward my suite of rooms on the third floor, intending to change so I can get down to work on the next part of my plan. But I'm halfway up the stairs when I hear a dull buzzing from the direction of the library. I know what that means. My cousin Vincent's here. And if Vincent's here, it means Gideon must have prepared another sacrifice while I was gone.

Funny. I just missed the last one he did, too. And I don't mean funny in a *fun* way, either. I don't actually like it one damn bit.

I amble down the hallway, following the sound of the tattoo gun and the underlying shriek of some edgelord black metal album. Vincent and his redneck dad take this family's fucked up religion even more seriously than Gran does. He's the reason Gideon's torso looks like a goddamn Picasso painting, if Picasso worshipped the Shadow Thorn. They started doing the tattoos when Gideon was a teenager. One sacrifice, and Vincent adds another tattoo. Eventually, he's gonna run out of room, regardless of how big my brother is.

I step into the library doorway, completely unsurprised by what I find: Gideon sitting in the big leather chair by the window with his leg propped up on one of the tasseled ottomans. Vincent's hunched over his thigh, bobbing his head to the music despite the fact that it sounds like TV static recorded in a gas station bathroom. Gideon has his head thrown back, enjoying this more than he should. I know how he is.

I announce myself by unplugging the speaker and saying, "Looks like someone had fun while I was away."

"Oh, fuck me, you said he wasn't here," Vincent grumbles, his eyes fixed on Gideon's new tattoo.

Gideon lifts his head and looks over at me, his pupils blown out. He's almost certainly got a boner hidden in those baggy shorts, but Vincent's always been a brave man and not one to be freaked out by a little masochism. "He wasn't," Gideon says flatly. "He's supposed to be in Houston for Five Courts business."

"That 'business' was taken care of, dipshits." I slide down into the other armchair, hooking my knee over the armrest. "Because, unlike the two of you, I have an actual job. Actual responsibilities."

Vincent snorts, his eyes on Gideon's new tattoo. "We both know you didn't do shit to resolve anything. It was probably Cullen Tyloch, like always."

I scowl, annoyed that Vincent is a hundred percent correct.

"Cullen's brother was the one murdered, so yeah, he took the lead on this one."

Vincent rolls his eyes. "Like that matters. You don't do shit on that council."

I resist every urge in my body to slap Vincent across his unshaven mouth and instead watch him work for a few moments, tracing dark lines over Gideon's skin. Gideon, of course, is desperately trying to enjoy himself. "What brought this on?"

Gideon's eyes flutter open, and Vincent looks up at him, their gazes meeting halfway. I frown, irritation bubbling in my belly. Because what was it Lee had told me? Nothing happened save for a trip to the graveyard?

Vincent's the one to break the silence. "There was a problem over the weekend," he says stiffly. "Gideon helped me handle it."

My skin prickles. "This weekend?" I say lightly, looking over at my brother. "Don't tell me you sacrificed Gloria's granddaughter."

Immediately, the air in the room shifts. Vincent bites back a chuckle. And Gideon looks far too pleased with himself.

"Yeah, that's not what he did with her," Vincent says with a smirk.

A hot, blinding fury slams through my chest, sudden and unexpected. The conversation with Lee runs through my head: *"Yeah, I followed them to the cemetery, but they came home after about twenty minutes. That was on Friday. Things were quiet on Saturday."*

If that stupid motherfucker lied to me, I'm going to kill him myself.

"Vincent had some difficulty with a sacrifice," Gideon says. "He escaped, I had to help catch him."

My rage quiets a little. At least it was Vincent's sacrifice, not Gideon's.

"Ivy—" Gideon gives me a smarmy smile, which I *really* don't like. "Let's just say we reconnected."

Vincent smothers another laugh.

"Reconnected how?" I say slowly. Cautiously. As if I don't know exactly what the fuck he's getting at. The blood pounds in my ears. Heat scorches my face. *They just went to the cemetery.*

Gideon looks over at me, a half smile on his lips.

"Vincent," I say. "Time to take a break."

The tattoo gun keeps buzzing, sounding like a drill boring into my brain.

"I'm fucking serious." I march over to him and reach out to slap the tattoo gun out of his hand, but he's quicker than me, jerking it back with a glare.

"The fuck are you doing?" he snaps.

"Out."

We stare at each other over, Vincent's eyes narrowed.

"It's fine," Gideon says. "I can handle him."

He really does sound pleased with himself, the motherfucker.

Vincent sets the tattoo gun aside and stands up. "You're not winning this one," he mutters, and my anger flares again. It takes every ounce of my willpower not to haul back and slap him, especially when he gives me that devious grin of his before slinking out into the hallway, leaving me alone with my traitor of a brother.

Who's currently just staring up at me, waiting for me to make my first move.

There are a hundred different things I would normally do in this circumstance, and not a single one will work on Gideon, given that he lets grown men beat him with chairs and tubes of lighting every weekend. He can certainly take one of my punches. As for anything more creative—

Well, we both know he enjoys pain too much for that sort of thing to be effective.

So instead, I sit down in Vincent's chair, directly in front of Gideon's new tattoo. It's mostly an outline right now, but that's enough for me to see that it's not a sacrifice tattoo. It's a woman with long, wavy hair and a sly smile.

"Is that supposed to be Ivy?" My anger surges up again, hot and bright. Or maybe it's not anger. Maybe it's jealousy. I don't know; that's an unfamiliar emotion for me to have, and one I really shouldn't be feeling about my redneck loser of a brother.

Lee. This is Lee's fucking fault. He was supposed to keep Ivy away from him.

"Yes," Gideon finally says. "I told you, we reconnected."

"In the chapel?"

The question comes out before I can stop it. I curl my hands around the chair's armrest, burning with fury.

Gideon's smile widens. "I didn't need to fuck her in the chapel, Zave. Because I already did that, didn't I?"

I lunge at him, going for his throat. He reacts the way he always does, rolling out of my grasp with an annoying quickness and then landing in a crouch, his hair hanging in his eyes.

"Wanna fight?" he says. "I'll fight."

"Where'd you fuck her?" I throw myself at him again, and this time, I manage to catch him square in the chest. The two of us fall backward into one of the bookshelves. Our great-grandfather's occult book collection promptly avalanches over us, and I grab the heaviest of the bunch and swing it at Gideon's head. He catches it, wrenches it out of my hands, and slams it into my temple.

"You motherfucker!" I howl, scrabbling over the sludge of books to claw at the half-formed tattoo on his leg. I manage to get one good scratch in before he shoves his foot in my chest, and I fly backward, gasping for breath. At least Gideon is sprawled on his side, clutching at his leg.

The library door slams open, but it's not Vincent. It's Gran.

"What the *hell* is going on in here?" she shouts, stomping into the room. When she sees the pile of her father's books, she lets out a loud, exasperated sigh. "Who started this?" She whips between me and Gideon, eyes sharp and angry. "I can't believe I'm asking that. You two are *adults*."

"He started it." I use one of the big leather chairs to drag myself up to standing. Gideon death-glares me from between the dark strands of his hair. "Because he fucked Ivy Myste."

Gran sighs, shoves her fingers through her hair. "You can't be serious," she says. "That happened ten years ago."

"It happened last weekend," I snarl. "He did it again. He has no *right*."

"Neither of you has any *right*," Gran spits back. "Not then. Certainly not now." She turns her angry gaze away from me and over to Gideon, who's sitting with his arms draped over his knees. "I told you to keep her away from the chapel. You have no idea how lucky—"

"I did," Gideon says darkly. "But she went to see my match in Nacogdoches. We spent the night at a motel there."

Suddenly, the pieces fall into place. No wonder Lee's reports felt underdeveloped. Ivy wasn't even here for half the weekend, and he didn't see fit to fucking tell me about it.

Gran shakes her head. "It's too soon for me to deal with this," she murmurs, shuffling over to pick up the fallen books. "You boys couldn't have waited a little longer to start up this pissing contest again?"

I scowl at her, arms crossed over my chest. "Gloria left the house to her," I say. "She had to come back to execute the will. That's not *our* fault."

"It's your fault that you can't let this go," Gran snaps at me. "*Yours*, Xavier, specifically." She shoves the book back on the shelf with enough force that the wall shakes, and I feel sheepish enough that I pick up one of the books and dolefully slide it back into place. Gideon's still glaring at me, though.

"You convinced Gloria to hire Lee Whitman before she died," he says snidely. "I wonder why."

"She wanted someone she could trust," I snap back. "And she wanted it to be a surprise for Gran, that the house is staying in the family." None of this is a lie, by the way.

"Shut up, both of you." Gran keeps reshelving the books,

not looking at either of us. "Not a day goes by that I don't think about what Gloria and I had to do to that girl. Twice."

I don't say anything. Neither does Gideon. Just for a second, I wonder if he remembers it the way I do, the magic Gran and Gloria worked together out in the shed, their voices weaving together, storm clouds drawing in so thick that they blotted out the sun. Ivy was laid out on the workbench, ethered into oblivion. Because that's what they were doing. Casting her memories into oblivion.

I didn't see it the second time, because I was away at college. But the first time, Gran made me watch, because it was my kiss she was wiping from Ivy's memory. The kiss at the front of the chapel, in front of the statue of the Shadow Thorn. I was only thirteen, and I thought a kiss would be enough. It wasn't, and Gideon stepped in and stole her from me five years later.

At least Gran wiped that memory from her, too. Now, Ivy Myste is a blank slate, and one I fully intend to take advantage of, regardless of what my brother thinks he might have accomplished in some shitty motel in Nacogdoches.

"I won't have you fighting in my house," Gran says, still shoving the books into place. "And I certainly won't have you fighting over Gloria's granddaughter like she's a prize belt. Do you understand?"

She looks at me when she says it, eyes burning. And just for a moment, I'm thirteen again, getting the tongue-lashing of a lifetime from her and Gloria both.

"He's the fighter," I say, tilting my head toward Gideon.

"Do you understand?" Gran says, more sharply.

"I understand," Gideon says primly, which is probably the most irritating thing he could have done in this particular moment. I glare at him, but he doesn't take the bait. And why would he? He won this round. And not because he's more handsome than me, or more charming, because he's sure as shit neither. But because he was *here* and I wasn't.

Just like ten years ago.

Well, I won't make that mistake again.

"Do you understand?" Gran says for the third time, and I know I'm on shaky ground.

"I understand." I whip around and stalk out of the library. Vincent's made himself scarce, thank god. I didn't want to see his weaselly little face again.

My brain whirs as I go up to my suite. I knew I would probably need witchcraft to bring Ivy back, but it's clear now that I'll need the darkest kind of witchcraft to make this work. Blood magic. Death magic.

Because I'm not missing my chance again. I'll do whatever it takes to drag Ivy back to me.

This time, for good.

18

IVY

I push open the door to my apartment and hurl in my suitcase, sighing at the familiarity of my living room, with its cheap, shabby furniture and mismatched decor. My flight out of Houston was delayed, and it's nearly midnight, six hours after I was supposed to arrive in Santa Fe. When I was stranded in the airport, grading student papers on the shared WiFi, I couldn't shake the feeling that something wanted me to stay in Texas.

That *I* wanted to stay in Texas.

But now that I'm back home, the feeling has faded. Especially when I switch on the lamp and immediately hear the patter of kitty feet on the laminate flooring. Gnocchi trundles in to greet me, his fluffy tail lifted in an inquiring question mark.

"Gnocchi! My little potato. I missed you." I scoop him up and bury my nose in his cream-colored fluff. He mews and nudges at me, purrs filling up the living room. "I best Juniper didn't play with you the way she said she would."

Gnocchi leaps out of my arms and trots into the tiny galley kitchen and sits next to his empty food bowl, which I dutifully fill with kibble. There's a note next to it from Juniper: **CALL ME WHEN YOU GET IN** in big block letters. I stare at it while Gnocchi munches down, foreboding clawing at my chest. Why didn't she just text me? I texted her when I landed.

Didn't I?

Actually, now I can't remember. I swore I had been sending her text updates all weekend, but now that I think about it—I barely looked at my phone. I'd been so distracted. I'm not sure I even texted her that my flight was going to be late.

I go back into the living room, where my purse is lying on the floor right next to my suitcase, and dig out my phone.

Twenty-five missed messages. Five missed phone calls. Three voicemails.

"What the fuck?" I stare at my phone as I slump down on the sofa, scrolling through the messages. Almost all of them are from Juniper, but the phone calls, save for one, are from Mom. And they aren't from today, either. They're from the entire weekend.

FRIDAY

How's it going? What's the house like?

FRIDAY

Text me back when you get a chance.

SATURDAY

U ok? Call me. I'm really worried.

SATURDAY

Did you get my voicemail? If you don't call me back, I'm telling Mom where you are.

SUNDAY

I told her. Ivy, I'm really fucking worried.

I slump back on my flimsy couch cushions, too exhausted to

deal with this. Too exhausted, even, to be angry that Juniper told Mom I went to Texas. Honestly, it's kind of a relief. Now I don't have to do it, although I will have to listen to her yell at me for going behind her back.

I must not have had reception at Golly's. But then why didn't the messages show up while I was in the Houston airport? I know I looked at my phone, doomscrolling while I ate a ten-dollar bag of candied pecans from the Hudson's kiosk, waiting for updates on my flight.

"Fucking Verizon," I mutter, tapping off a message to Juniper.

> Something went wrong with my signal, I guess. I'm fine. Back in Santa Fe. How mad is Mom?

I don't expect her to answer, it being midnight on Sunday, and Juniper having to get up early for her daily Pilates class before work. She's always in bed by ten on weeknights. But as I'm peeling myself off the bed so I can at least change into my nightgown, my phone starts chiming. I sigh and force myself to answer.

"What the fuck?" Juniper shouts. "We were freaking out!"

"I'm fine," I tell her. "Jesus, calm down. My flight was just delayed."

"And you ignored my messages all weekend!"

I collapse on my bed and stare at the strands of cobweb fluttering from the light fixture in my ceiling fan. "I didn't get them," I say. "Something must have been wrong with my reception. They all came through when I was driving back from the airport. My flight was delayed by like six hours, by the way, so that was part of the problem."

"Mom was about to file a missing person's report."

I squeeze my eyes shut and rub my temple, feeling jittery. "Did she?"

"No, I talked her out of it. But she—she is not happy about you going back to Harlan."

Hartshorn, I think, a sense memory of warm sun on my shoulders.

"Well, I don't know what she expected me to do. I had to sign the paperwork."

Juniper lets out a loud, exasperated sigh. "Did you?"

"I'm not talking about this right now."

"Well, Mom's freaking out. You need to call her."

"I'll text her and tell her I'm safe," I say. "And then I'll talk to her about this tomorrow."

I don't even want to do that much, truth be told, but as much as Mom and I clash, I don't want her fretting herself into a heart attack.

"You need to sell that house," Juniper says. "And don't go back to Texas."

Well, then, will you come back to me?

"Good night, Juniper." I hang up before she can argue with me any further, then I fire off a quick text to my mom. Then I shut my whole phone down and toss it across the room.

Tomorrow. I'll deal with all of this tomorrow.

Gnocchi jumps on the bed and nudges up against my hand, trying to curl himself up beside me. I let him, rolling onto my side so he can tuck up next to my chest the way he likes. "Yeah, I missed you, too," I mutter, although my thoughts are back in Texas. Not even Harlan *or* Hartshorn, but that motel in Nacogdoches, where twenty-four hours ago I sliced open Gideon's chest and rode his cock until both of us came.

I haven't stopped thinking about it, not once.

And I'm still thinking about it as I drift off to sleep, my dreams as crimson as his blood.

"Sell it," Mom says. "Sell the whole goddamned thing."

I suck my iced latte up through its flimsy paper straw, staring at her from across the rickety wrought-iron table. We are, much to my annoyance, sitting at the coffee shop on the Santa Fe Community College campus because Mom thought it was appropriate to wait outside my classroom while I taught my morning comp and rhet class. How she got the classroom number, I have no idea. Probably bullied it out of the registrar.

"What else would I do?" I ask, although I can feel the doubt like a cough in the back of my throat. Selling the house is the obvious answer.

So why does the idea make my skin crawl?

Mom huffs and shakes her head. "I don't know, Ivy. Why did you fly out to Texas without telling anyone?"

"I told Juniper," I say evenly, knowing I'm in dangerous territory. "I told my department head."

"You just didn't tell me," Mom snaps.

"And do you blame me?" I set my latte aside and press myself forward onto the table. Students drift past us, their voices rising and falling, and I just hope one of *my* students doesn't see me sitting here arguing with my mother. "You're freaking out. I'm twenty-eight years old. People have fucking children at my age, and you're acting like—"

"Language," she snaps.

I roll my eyes. "You only say that when you know I'm right. Golly left the house to me, and I took care of it like a responsible adult."

"And you don't think it's strange that you *had* to sign the paperwork in person?"

"Not really. Juniper and Brian had to sign the paperwork for their house in person. How is this any different?"

"Because you're not going to live there!" Mom shouts.

I freeze as her voice carries across the campus courtyard. I swear that half the students look over at us, and I wish I could melt into the uncomfortable metal chair.

"I'm sorry." Mom pushes her hands through her hair, shakes her head. "I just—I didn't want you going back there. To that place."

I sip on my latte, watching our hot, dry wind stir my mom's hair around. It's nothing like the wind back at Hartshorn, as damp and silky as a tongue.

I force myself to focus. "Why not?" I say carefully, although I don't expect her to answer. Mom has made her feelings about the place she grew up very clear over the years, but she's never explained why. She always changes the subject or gives a look of disgust.

But today, she does neither. She doesn't say anything. Just sits there, staring down at her cardboard coffee cup.

"It's not—" She stops, gnawing on her lip, her brow furrowed. I lean forward. This is new. This is interesting.

"There's nothing there for you," she finally says, looking up at me.

I rub my thumb over the condensation dripping down my cup. The thing is, I can see what she means. It's in the middle of nowhere. Not even a small town, really, and I've always liked the bustle of cities. There's certainly not a freaking college out there.

But to say there's *nothing* for me there, when Gideon's there—

Gideon. He didn't even ask for my goddamn phone number, although I do have his, saved like a secret. I haven't worked up the nerve to text him yet.

"And it's just not a good place," Mom continues quickly,

jarring me back into the present. "It's in Texas, Ivy. Do you want to live in Texas?"

"You've never really explained it. Why you hate Hartshorn so much. Why you hate *Golly* so much."

Mom jerks her gaze up, and honestly, I can't believe I said that myself.

"Excuse me?" she says.

"I'm serious. You've never given us a straight answer." Now that I've started, I can't stop. "The closest you ever came was telling me and Juniper you shouldn't have sent us there when we were kids—"

"Well, that's certainly true," she mutters.

"But why not?" I scrape my chair forward. "Nothing freaking happened. I spent the whole summer down at the creek with Gideon—" No, that's not right. Not Gideon. "Xavier," I correct myself, but Mom's already worked up again, anger marching across her face.

"Did you see him?" she asks.

"Xavier? No, he wasn't there."

"Not Xavier." She hisses the name. "The other one."

"Gideon?"

She blanches like I just swore in front of her again.

"Why?" I ask. "Why would it matter if I did?"

Mom stares at me, her gaze sharp and piercing. "Did you see him?"

The skin on the back of my neck prickles. I have to answer, but it's clear to me, even if I don't know why, that *yes* is the wrong thing to say. I mean, why would Mom care about Gideon? The last time I saw him before this past weekend was when I was eight years old.

"No." The lie feels ashy on my tongue, but Mom's relief is immediate, the way her shoulders slump and she gives a small, quiet sigh.

"I met with Golly's lawyer," I continue. "Lee Whitman.

Signed the paperwork. Spent the weekend inventorying the house so I can—" I only hesitate for a moment. "Sell it."

"What about the rest of the family?" Mom says. "Henry? Jack?" A pause long enough for me to notice. "Judith?"

"Judith stopped by," I say carefully, watching Mom's face darken. "On Saturday. She, um—she took me to see Golly's grave. At the Harlan cemetery," I add in a rush, thinking that will keep Mom from losing her shit again. Something tells me she wouldn't be happy to know her mother was buried on Hartshorn property.

"Judith," Mom spits out. "You shouldn't have spoken to her, either."

"She's an old woman, Mom."

"She's dangerous." My mother reaches across the table and grabs my wrist, startling me enough that I meet her gaze. "That whole family is dangerous."

"How?"

"They're rich," Mom says sharply. "They have a lot of power in that area. They can hide a lot of wrongdoing."

Suddenly, I think of the motel room, the bedsheets soaked in Gideon's blood. *I can take care of it.*

A chill ripples over my skin.

"Just sell the house." Mom tightens her grip on my arm. "Promise me, Ivy. Tell me you'll sell the house. You can use the money to buy a house anywhere you want. Something better. Promise."

My tongue feels heavy in my mouth. Nothing she says is unreasonable. Wasn't I even thinking the same thing, drifting through the rooms, looking at Golly's expensive furniture? But the idea feels wrong somehow. A mistake I'll spend the rest of my life regretting.

I don't tell that to Mom, though. I just nod. "Yeah," I tell her, pulling my arm away. "Yeah, I promise."

Mom doesn't look like she believes me. But she doesn't say anything.

"I have to get to my next class," I say, which is a lie. My next class isn't for another hour. But I don't want to sit here anymore. I don't want to keep having this conversation.

"Promise me, Ivy," Mom whispers. "Don't ever go back there."

It takes me a long time to nod my head yes. But I don't say a word.

19

XAVIER

I unlock the door to Gloria's house and step inside, letting my eyes fall closed as I take a deep, shuddery breath. Ivy's been gone for three days, but the air in here still smells like her. As sweet as honeysuckle and wisteria. As sweet as sex.

I kick the door closed and drop my bag of supplies on the kitchen table. It's not quite full dark yet, although the shadows are long and creeping, and I can feel the Shadow Thorn's presence in them. Watching with an air of approval.

I told Lee to meet me at nightfall, which means I don't have much time. I wanted to get here earlier, but Gideon was up in the living room talking to Gran about some shit with the gardens—sucking up to her, most likely, so she won't be as angry with him about fucking around with Ivy. The last thing I wanted was for him to see me leave and come sniffing around.

Eventually, though, I just took the old servant's hallway, part of the endless, confusing labyrinth of the house my great-grandfather designed in an act of worship to the Shadow Thorn. The hallway dumped me unceremoniously out by the swimming pool, and I stole away in the night like a thief.

Or like a witch, which I suppose is what I am.

I go into the living room, which offers the most space for my spell. The first thing I do is tuck one of the knives Gideon uses for sacrifices between the couch cushions, hiding it just out of view. Then I shove the couch back across the floor, clearing space in the middle of the room. I do the same with the big oversized armchairs, then bring my supplies in from the kitchen. They're all things I pilfered out of the room Gran *thinks* she keeps locked away from us: black candles anointed with oils and herbs, a jar of rabbit hearts floating in formaldehyde, a plastic baggy of dried devil's weed. White chalk, which I use to draw a big circle on the hardwood floor.

The doorbell chimes, making me jump. Lee's here. The final, and most crucial, element to my spell.

When I open the front door, Lee's staring out at the yard, running his hand over his jeans. He's nervous.

"Feels weird out here," he says, glancing over at me. "How long is this gonna take? I don't want to get caught up in a thunderstorm."

"Not long," I say, which is true for him but not for me. "Come on in."

Lee steps through the threshold, his eyes dancing around the room. He's not part of my family's world, except for what I've shown him over the years. Glimpses, here and there. Promises of power. He might be doing bullshit legal work now, but what he really wants is to move into politics. That's why he helps me. Because he thinks I can help him.

And I could, if I wanted to. But he fucked up this past weekend, didn't he?

The thing about Lee, though, is he's seen enough of what my family does, of what I can do, that he can sense when something's off. And I can tell he senses it now, because he stops in the foyer, his arms crossed over his chest. When he looks at me, I practically see the fear rising off of him, just for a second.

"Why'd you want to meet out here again?" he says, making

his voice overly light. "Told you we could get two-dollar well drinks down at the Silver Bull."

"Why the fuck would I want a well drink?" I tilt my head toward the living room. "Besides, I need your help with my Ivy Myste problem."

This time, I see the fear flash through his pale eyes, as sudden as lightning.

"I thought I did that already," he mumbles.

"Did you?" I step toward him, and he takes a shuffling step backward.

"I did everything you asked me to," he says, the words coming out too fast. "I made sure they didn't go to the chapel."

"I *told* you to keep them apart." I take another step, pushing Lee toward the living room. Toward the white circle. Toward the sacrifice blade hidden in the sofa. "So imagine my surprise when I learn from Gideon that they went to Nacogdoches together on Saturday."

Lee's eyes widen. He shakes his head. "That can't be right," he says. "I had eyes on the house. He never came over here on Saturday."

"But she left, didn't she?" I keep stepping toward him, keep corralling him into the living room.

"Well, yeah, but not with—" Lee swallows. "She was by herself, man! I figured she just went to Houston early or something!"

"So why the *fuck* didn't you tell me that in your report?"

For a second, Lee stares at me. Then he tries to run.

Tries, of course, is the operative word. I stop him by hooking my arm around his throat, a move I learned from Uncle Jack one night when I got him drunk enough to train me in the hunt. Dad forbade it around the time I turned ten, said it was Gideon's job to prepare the sacrifices. But I'm not one to take no for an answer.

I drag Lee forward, bracing all my strength against his

squirming body. Then I slam his head against the wall hard enough to leave a faint dent in the plaster. It dazes him; I can tell by the way he slumps against me, his weight turning heavier.

"Why?" he mumbles as I drag him into the living room. "I did everything you asked."

"Did you?" I heave him into the circle, although he's too frightened to notice the chalk on the ground. The darkness helps, too, and I think that's the Shadow Thorn, showing his approval. "I asked for one simple thing, Lee. I asked you to keep Ivy away from Gideon. And he went and *fucked* her."

Lee stands in the circle, still unsteady on his feet.

"Not at the chapel," he slurs. "He never took her to the chapel."

I ignore him as I stalk over to the couch. Hiding the knife now seems like it was an unnecessary step, but better safe than sorry. I yank it out and whirl around to face him. Lee blinks at me. Then he blinks at the knife, which I hold loosely at my side.

It takes him a second. Then he runs.

He runs, but he doesn't get far. I leap across the room and shove the blade into his shoulder, sinking it in all the way to the hilt. Lee screams and staggers forward, slamming his shin into the easy chair. I grab him by the collar of his shirt and drag him backward. Last thing I need is blood on the chair's fabric.

"Fuck!" Lee howls as I drag him back into the chalk circle. When I let go, I immediately pull out the knife, and his blood gushes hotly over my hand. Between his screams and his fear and that rich, thick blood, my cock is rock-hard.

"Sorry, Lee." I slam the knife into his back again, relishing the wet, slapping sound the blade makes, a sound that reminds me of fucking. "But your blood's more useful to me than you are."

He sobs, trying to wrench himself around to grab at the

knife. I get it before he does and slash the blade across the side of his belly, deep enough that his intestines bulge out, pink and shiny in the dim light. That's not strictly necessary, but I've always liked it, bringing the inside of a body out.

There's a howling in the fireplace that sounds like wind, but I know it's the Shadow Thorn, arriving to collect his payment.

"Fuck you!" Lee sobs, pressing his hands against the cut on his belly. I kick him hard in the back of his knee, the same knee that he injured when we played football together in high school and had to have surgery on. He crumples like a rag doll into the middle of the circle. More of his intestines spill out, and for a minute, I watch him try to gather them up, tears streaking over his face.

Suffering. There's nothing in this world so sweet.

I stomp down on Lee's knee again, hard enough that something cracks inside of him. He screams in agony, his body wrenching upward at an interesting, unusual angle. My cock strains hard against my pants, tight and uncomfortable, and I give it a slow, teasing stroke as I adjust it. Normally, I'd jack off while Lee dies in the ever-widening pool of his own blood, but tonight, I want to save my seed for something else.

"You just wait right there," I tell him, sliding the knife into the waistband of my pants. Then I take my time as I arrange the candles at the circle's compass points and light them, their flames pale and eerie. Wind gusts in through the fireplace, bringing bits of the surrounding woods with it: pine needles and dead azalea blooms, curls of fern fronds, a sparkle of dust. Cicada shells. It blows in a tornado around a still-screaming Lee, a sound as sweet as music.

I slip off my shoes and socks, swallow a handful of the devil's weed, and dig out one of the rabbit hearts, which I hold in my hand as I recite a prayer in the secret language of my family—a dusty, ancient tongue that tastes like ash. By then, Lee's screams have softened into wet, choking sobs, and when I step into the circle, his blood squelches up between my toes like wet sand on a beach. I squat beside him, and he's able to lift his head just enough to meet my gaze. His skin is deathly pale, his eyes wild.

"You *promised*," he rasps. "You said—you'd help—"

"I lied." I squeeze the rabbit heart as hard as I can until it turns to a wet mush in my palm. Then I streak it across Lee's forehead. He thrashes, splattering blood up between us.

I look at the fireplace. Well, I look at the darkness in the fireplace, at the absence of light coiling there like a rattlesnake about to strike.

I look at the Shadow Thorn.

"I want to go into her dreams," I say in the secret language of my family, my voice husky with need. "I want to shape them to my will until she comes back to me."

A voice forms on the wind. *Give me a life, and I'll grant you entrance for a month.*

A month. More than enough time.

"You hear that, Lee?" I look down at him, and he howls when I say his name. "This is how you're going to help me now."

"Go fuck yourself!" he sputters.

I shove his chin back, revealing the frantic line of his neck. This is a cleaner death than I prefer, but it is meant to be utilitarian.

With one quick motion, I split his throat open and turn it into a fountain of blood.

I FALL asleep in Lee's cooling blood and wake up back at home. Well, not home. Ivy's fragmented memory of home.

She's dreaming of Hartshorn.

I find her standing at the base of the big spiral staircase in the old wing of the house, beneath the enormous crystal chandelier my great-great-grandmother brought with her from Europe. She's an adult, but she's dressed in the clothes she wore as a kid. That won't do at all, and I whisper a few soft words, and then she's naked.

Ivy turns to me, and I drink her in, this dream version of her body. It seems close to the real thing—not that I would know, a thought that fills me with a tight knot of jealousy.

Focus, I think. *You'll get to fuck her for real soon enough.*

"Xavier?" she says, her voice distorted from the dreaming. "You look so different."

"It's because I'm not a little boy anymore." I walk over to her and grab her by the waist. She looks down and cries out, trying to cover her nudity.

"Don't do that." I pull her hands away from her breasts, which are full and firm with large, lovely nipples. "You're too pretty to cover up, cicada."

"Cicada," she breathes. "Didn't you call me that once?"

"Mmm." It seems she remembers more when she's in her dreams. Gran and Gloria's memory wipe didn't go quite deep enough, did it? "Right before I did this."

I kiss this dream version of her. It's like eating cotton candy—sweet enough, but mostly air. Still, it's better than nothing, especially when she melts her naked body up against my clothed one, her hips rolling with lust.

"Greedy, aren't you?" I murmur against her lips. "What would my brother say?"

That was a fucking mistake, because as soon as I plant the idea of Gideon into her dreamscape, he shows up. Well, a dream version of him, anyway. The real Gideon is still lodged away back at Hartshorn.

But this dream-Gideon presses up behind Ivy, sandwiching

her between us. He ignores me in favor of kissing along her bare shoulder, his hand scooping up to squeeze her breasts. Ivy moans, leaning her head back against him.

"Away," I whisper, and the dream-Gideon vanishes into mist. I laugh, delighted at the power. I've never shaped dreams before, although I know it's possible. Gran and Uncle Jack would do it to us cousins whenever we misbehaved as children, sending us nightmares as punishment.

Ivy looks up at me, her eyes dark with lust. I'm definitely not interested in giving her a nightmare, though.

"You're going to fuck me tonight," I tell her, and to my delight, she moans at that, too. I wrap the dream around my thoughts, pulling on it like wet clay, until we're in my old childhood bedroom. I'd love to take her to the dungeon in my condo, or to my private room at Lethe, but this is Ivy's dream, and I have to work with the memories locked away in her pretty head.

I throw her onto the bed and conjure up ropes to bind her to the posts, dragging her legs apart to reveal a pussy too glossy and perfect to be hers. It's not hers. This is a dream. But you can still come in a dream.

"I can't move," she moans, writhing around on my bedsheets. My lust is feeding into her dream, I think, heightening everything, making her impossibly horny.

"I don't want you to move," I say, pulling out my cock. It's as idealized as her cunt, big and veiny and glistening with precum. At least there aren't tattoos on it, so I know she's not trying to dream of Gideon.

I don't warm her up any more than I already have; I'm about to spill as it is. I shove my big porno-dream cock into her tight porno-dream pussy without any fanfare, and Ivy arches her back and groans and pulls on the ropes I used to bind her. I fuck her hard, pouring all my jealousy and frustration into my thrusts. In real life, it would hurt her, an idea that makes excitement spark in my blood. In the dream world, she comes almost instantly.

"Knew you wanted me," I mutter before I bite at her breasts, which makes her dream-self come again, her whole body shaking so hard the bed trembles. I fuck her harder, thrusting deeper into her cunt than I could reasonably go in real life. I imagine I'm shredding her insides to ribbons, and Ivy screams like she's in pain. Or like she's coming again.

That does it. My cum erupts out—in the dream, but out in the waking world, too. I can feel it, distantly, my seed mixing with Lee's spilled blood. I can feel how it pleases the Shadow Thorn.

I look down at the dream version of Ivy. Her cheeks are streaked with tears, and her lips are red from coming. I'm still hard inside her. It's a dream, after all. Anything can happen.

"Where do you want me to fuck you next?" I murmur, and I wrap my fingers tight around her throat.

❦   20   ❦

IVY

Three nights after I get home from my trip to Texas, I slam awake in the middle of the night, drenched in sweat with the sound of cicadas ringing in my ears. I was dreaming of Hartshorn.

The dream fades fast, lingering in snatches and fragments: a grand entranceway, with a spiral staircase winding up around a glittering chandelier. A maze of dark hallways lined with sullen-faced portraits. A boy's bedroom, shelves of books against the wall.

I know it's all Hartshorn, even if I don't remember ever going inside the house. But I must have, at some point that summer when I was eight years old.

After that, I dream of Hartshorn every night.

At first, it's easy to ignore the dreams, even though they always wake me up during the witching hour with the sheets twisted around my ankles and my skin flushed. But I never remember them beyond a few hazy, lingering images. And when I get up in the morning, I've forgotten them completely.

Besides, the end of the semester is approaching quickly, which means I have five classes' worth of research papers to grade and enough anxiety to fuel the kind of dreams that will drag you out of sleep. And that they're centered around Hartshorn isn't that strange, either. That place is always lingering in my thoughts during the day, because of Gideon.

I'm too chicken-shit to text him, of course. I want him to text me first, even though I never actually gave him my number in return. But he could find it, if he really wanted it, right? He could ask Golly's lawyer.

That he hasn't—well, that's how men are, isn't it? They say anything to get you into bed.

So I have my crush on Gideon strangling me throughout the day, and I still have to deal with Golly's house, another weight hanging over my head. The business card for Hutchinson Estate Sales is currently magneted to my refrigerator, not so much a reminder for myself but to stave off any questions from Mom or Juniper when they swing by to visit.

Because both of them ask about it constantly—have I looked into selling the house? Have I hired cleaners to clear out the property? Within a week of being back, it's clear to me that Mom actively roped Juniper into nagging duties, too.

"It's the end of the semester," I tell them when they bring it up. "Can I *please* just focus on surviving until summer? Please?"

It shuts them up for a few days, at least.

I do throw myself into my work, partially because I don't have a choice and partially so I don't get that sick knotted-stomach feeling about Gideon, how I promised him I'd come back even though he can't even be bothered to text me.

I tell myself that means it wasn't a real promise. It was just… sexy talk. Heat of the moment. That's why I don't text him. Because in the glaring New Mexico sun, it's clear that night was a fling. Not a mistake, not exactly, but not anything serious. Not anything *real*.

Of course, that doesn't stop me from googling him one hot afternoon when I need to take a break from grading. I type in his name, *Gideon Hartshorn,* and nothing comes up, not even an abandoned Facebook page. But when I type in *Boruta wrestler,* my hands shaking against my phone, I find him. Pictures on some Instagram account advertising THE BEST INDEPENDENT WRESTLING IN ARKANSAS! A handful of YouTube videos, which I watch on my living room couch, Gnocchi kneading his little claws into my thigh.

The videos aren't exactly well-made. They're clearly shot on someone's cell phone from the audience, with people moving around and blocking my view of him. In one of the videos, Gideon's opponent goes out of the way to make him bleed. It seems to be the entire point of the match, in fact, with barbed wire and broken glass lying around the ring. By the end, when the referee holds his hand up in victory, Gideon's entire upper body is drenched in blood.

Just like the night in the motel.

I press my thighs together, a sudden, distracting pressure flaring up between my thighs. Gideon glares out from above his mask, his hair stringy with sweat and blood, and it feels like he's looking straight at me. I bite my lip, my head flooding with the memories of everything we did that night. The power I felt as I slashed open his skin and rode him to orgasm.

I start the video over, kick Gnocchi off the couch, and slip my fingers into my underwear, where I find I'm already drenched. And then I touch my clit until a shuddery, shameful orgasm surges through my core. The video isn't even over yet. I let the phone drop out of my hands, still playing, the audio tinny and distant.

It was just a one-night stand, I tell myself, my fingers still toying with my clit. *He hasn't even called me.*

That night, my dreams are more intense than usual. More vivid. We're in a courtyard, the grass lush and impossibly green, and there's a fountain bubbling with blood instead of water.

Gideon stands naked in it, his erection as big as I remember. Bigger.

"Worship me," he says in a rough, strained voice, and I drop to my knees and lick the blood off him, slow and methodical.

"Will you come back to me?" he says.

"Yes," I murmur against his skin, salty with blood.

"When?"

"When do you want me?"

"Now." His fingers tangle in my hair, sharp and painful. "Now. Now!"

Then he jerks my head back, and it's not Gideon towering over me, but a man with hair the color of sunlight. His brother, grown up like he was in the photograph I saw on Golly's laptop.

I wake up on my belly, humping my bed, aching with need. I slide my fingers in and out of my drenched pussy, still in a kind of half-dreaming state. As my orgasm builds, I swear I see Xavier Hartshorn at the foot of my bed, stroking his cock and watching me pleasure myself.

Which, of course, is absurd, and as soon as I come, I see the truth: it's just my dresser and some shadows and a mirror reflecting the safety lamp outside. I kick my blanket off and stumble into my bathroom and splash water on my face, then slink back into my bed. Gnocchi stirs beside me, grumbling a little in his sleep, and I reach over and stroke his silky fur, staring up at the dark ceiling.

I wonder if I'll ever stop dreaming of Hartshorn.

During finals week, an email comes through from my department head.

Ivy,

What would you say to a couple of asynchronous online classes this summer? One per
session?

I'm on campus when I get it, sitting at the coffee shop and waiting for my next exam to start, and it sends a little flutter of excitement through my chest. Asynchronous online classes are the holy grail of adjuncting, especially in the summer. You don't have to come on campus. You don't have to sit on endless Zoom calls. You get a paycheck without a fixed work schedule.

Usually, the full-time faculty snatch them up. That I got two in one summer?

Well, someone's watching out for me.

I email back right away, tapping off my I'd love that! with a sense of freedom. I always set aside a little money during the school year to see me through summer, so these classes are just a bonus. Plus, there's the money from Golly's house—

I stop, my coffee straw still tucked between my lips. My summer is open now. I can teach from anywhere.

Even in the middle of nowhere, Texas.

When do you want me?

Now. Now. Now.

It's an idea I can't shake for the rest of the morning. The whole time I'm sitting in the overly air-conditioned classroom, watching my students scribble out their final exam, the more excited I become. I can drive out there with Gnocchi as soon as my final grades are in. My apartment is close enough to campus that I can sublet it to a student for the summer. And I can finally get Mom and Juniper off my back because the whole reason I'm going to is to clean out the house to sell it.

Isn't it?

I shove that thought aside. Of course that's why I'm going—

it'll save me quite a bit of money, not having to pay for someone else to do it. It's not like I'm exactly rolling in dough at the moment.

And I'm certainly not going back for *Gideon*, who still hasn't bothered to reach out to me.

When my last student has turned in their final, and I'm walking out to my car with a bag full of blue books, I'm still rolling the idea around, looking for problems with it and coming up short. That afternoon, as I sit at my rickety kitchen table marking up my students' essays, my thoughts keep wandering over to the promise of a summer trip to Texas, just like when I was eight years old.

The thought simmers in the back of my mind all day. And that night, I dream of Hartshorn, the way I always do.

It feels different, though. More vivid, as if the thought of returning has infused my imagination with color.

In the dream, I wander the twisty, labyrinthine hallways in a long, pale dress, looking for Gideon. I swing open doors and only find dusty, empty rooms until I open one door and hot, white sunlight pours in, along with the scent of wildflowers and the soft, lulling buzz of insects. I step through the doorway, and like that, I'm outside, standing in a field of blood-red flowers that ripple and roll up to the burned remains of a stone building.

It scares me, that building, but it also sends heat shooting through my body, and I float toward it like I'm drawn on some invisible line. Because Gideon's in there. I'm certain of it.

And sure enough, he is, standing naked in front of a circle of stained glass. The glass filters colored light over his skin, making his tattoos shift and dance as he turns toward me. He holds out his hand, and although I'm a dozen feet away, I'm also sliding my palm over his. He lays me down in a patch of silky grass sprouting up through the floorboards, setting himself between my spread legs.

And then he's fucking me with slow, rolling strokes.

"You have to come for me," he breathes raggedly in my ear. "You have to come."

I moan and latch my legs around his strong hips. My dress is in tatters on the ground, splattered with crimson flower petals. Or blood. I don't know which.

"Come to me," Gideon grunts. "Come for me. Come to me."

I arch into him, bending my spine at an angle I could never manage in real life. We aren't on the ground anymore, either, but floating above it, Gideon's thick cock stretching me to my limits. I flutter my eyes open and see the world upside down.

Xavier watches us, dark-eyed and sullen.

"Are you going to come back to me, Ivy Myste?" he asks. I know it's him speaking, even though his lips don't move. His voice echoes in my head like a recording.

"Are you going to come for me?" Gideon growls into my breasts, his teeth biting at my nipples. Each burst of pain feels like a star.

"Yes!" I scream, shuddering furiously as Gideon and I swirl up toward the violent blade of sunlight slicing through the destroyed roof, his cock still buried deep in my cunt. "Yes! I'm coming! I'm coming!"

Then I'm in an unfamiliar bed, swimming in dark, satiny sheets, and it's not Gideon who's inside me, but his brother. He leers down at me and wraps his long, elegant fingers around my throat, pinning me down as he fucks me. My vision darkens at the edges.

"Harder," I rasp, as if oblivion were the same as orgasm.

"Oh, you like this, do you?" Xavier says, slamming his hips against mine. "You're wasted on my brother. He doesn't know how to hurt like I do."

I let out a strangled moan, bucking against him.

"He doesn't like to draw out the pain," Xavier sighs. "He wants to keep it all to himself."

Shadows crowd around us. The silk glides against my bare back, impossibly luxurious. It's the only thing that feels real, aside from Xavier's fingers constricting around my neck, cutting off my air.

"I'll see you soon, cicada," he purrs into my ear.

And then I slam awake, choking and clawing my throat. I can still feel the phantom press of hands around my neck, and I suck down breaths, filling my lungs as I fumble around on the nightstand until I can flick on my lamp. Warm, dim light shines across my bed, revealing my twisted, sweat-soaked sheets and half-naked body. Somehow, the oversized T-shirt I sleep in got twisted up around my shoulders, baring my breasts. Maybe that's what was strangling me.

My panties are soaked.

I slump back on my pillow, the AC's cool air brushing across my exposed nipples, and play back the dream in my head as best I can. It's already starting to fragment, the way they always do, although I remember certain things. Gideon holding out his hand to me. The blond man, his brother, watching us fuck with dark eyes. Xavier.

For a long time, I just lay on my back, staring up at the pale blur of my fan. I lay there long enough that the dream slips away from me, although not Gideon. Nor my desire to see him again, as foolish as I know it is—it's been a month and he's made no effort to track me down, no effort to reach out to me.

Of course, I haven't tried to reach out to him, either. But it's different. When a man wants you, you'll know—that's what my mother taught me, anyway, as old-fashioned as it sounds. Maybe it's not true. I honestly don't have the experience to know for sure.

I roll onto my side and switch off the lamp, the darkness sudden and startling. But I still can't fall asleep. I keep thinking about how easy it would be for me to go back to Golly's house, to stay there for the summer. It's not even permanent. Just a few months. Just like when I was a kid. I don't even have to see Gideon if I don't want to. But it's my house. I have a right to go there.

By the time I slip back off to sleep, light is starting to creep around my curtains, and I've made my decision.

I'm going back.

IVY

For the second time in as many months, I find myself pulling up to Golly's house.

This time, however, I'm not in a rental car but my decade-old Camry, a suitcase and a couple of banker's boxes worth of clothes and other odds and ends stacked in the trunk and backseat. I also have Gnocchi with me, curled up in his little carrying case on the passenger seat.

It took two days of nonstop driving to get here. I spent last night in a Holiday Inn in Wichita Falls, where I dreamed of another motel in Texas. Then I drove across the vast, sweltering state, watching the landscape change from desert to forest.

"Here we are," I tell Gnocchi, who mews pitifully from his carrier. "Home sweet home. At least for the next two and a half months."

I step out of the car, gasping at the thick, oppressive heat. It's still shocking, this heat. The whole way here, it would melt into me every time I got out of my car to use a rest stop or fill up on gas. And now, nearly five in the evening, it feels more miserable than it did when I stopped for lunch at noon.

I take Gnocchi into the house first, fumbling with the key

in the lock. There's a moment where I think it won't work, that it was all some fever dream and this house isn't actually mine. But the door swings open, and hot, stagnant air billows out.

"Motherfucker," I mutter, setting down Gnocchi's carrying case in the foyer and then making a beeline to the AC thermostat. I called to have the electricity turned back on a few days ago, but forgot that I'd switched the AC off completely the last time I was here. I drop it down to 68, holding my breath until it kicks on with a groan and a rattle. Cold air blows out of the vent.

Thank god for that.

I open Gnocchi's carrier, and he takes off like a shot, disappearing down the hallway. I leave him to it; he did the exact same thing when I moved into my apartment three years ago. He'll hide for a few hours, then creep out, smelling everything in sight until he feels comfortable.

I drag in the rest of my stuff and stack it in the foyer, then collapse on the couch in the living room, my body sheened with sweat. It's cooler in here, but still hot, and I stretch out on the couch to try to maximize the amount of cold air touching my skin. The living room feels nice, too. Like it's cleaner than the rest of the house.

As I'm lying there, the enormity of what I've just done sweeps over me. The past week was a flurry of preparation—getting my grades in, arranging a sublet, packing up my stuff, having my car checked out for the long drive.

Avoiding Mom's phone calls.

It all came shockingly easy, as if randomly deciding to flee town for a few months is something I've done on the regular. There were no real hiccups, other than fielding the constant protests from my Mom and Juniper, and once I got in the habit of keeping my phone on Do Not Disturb, even that felt easy. There was so much to do, though, that I never really thought about it. I just did it, and then loaded up my car and drove here, and now—

"What the fuck did I do?" I say out loud to the empty living room. I shove up to sitting, looking around at the elegant furniture and darkened television above the fireplace.

I peel myself off the sofa and head into the kitchen. I mean to get a drink of water, hoping it'll ground me, but I get hung up when I see the landline phone. Well, not the phone itself, but the ancient, brittle sheet of paper taped to the wall beside it. The paper filled with phone numbers.

Someone's added to it.

X, it says in black ink, darker than the others on the paper, which have all faded with time. Then a phone number beside it, without an area code. It must be local.

Fear twists in my belly. Someone was in the house while I was away.

It had to be one of the Hartshorns, I'm sure of it. If Golly and Judith Hartshorn were married, then someone in that family must have keys. I have the quick, distant thought that I should change the locks, although it flitters out of my head faster than it came on, replaced by a soft, fluttery sense of hope.

Did Gideon leave this? Why didn't he write out his name?

Images flash through my head. A blond man with dark eyes. *You're wasted on him*.

Goosebumps ripple over my skin. X.

X for Xavier?

Why would *Xavier* leave his phone number? I doubt he even remembers me—

Although Gideon did

—And Gideon said he doesn't live at Hartshorn anymore. But my curiosity is overwhelming. That it's intertwined with a dark, coiling fear just makes it more exciting.

I snatch the phone out of the receiver and punch in the number before I can talk myself out of it. The phone rings twice, jangly and mechanical, and the plastic receiver feels cool and unfamiliar against my ear. The whole situation is anachronistic, like I've stepped out of time.

The third ring is cut off short. "Ivy," the voice on the other end says, as smooth as soft butter. "I see you got my message."

"Who is this?" I demand, wrapping the phone's coiled cord around my finger.

The voice chuckles softly. "It's Xavier. Don't you remember me?"

Blond hair flashing in the sun. Cold river water. The heat bearing down on my shoulders as lips, rough and dry, brush against mine—

No, he never kissed me. We were only eight years old, and my first kiss was with Danny Tafoya when I was fifteen, a late bloomer whose first kiss came from a game of Spin the Bottle my friends dragged me into.

So why do I remember it? Xavier's breath on my skin? His glittering eyes? We were in the woods, someplace cool and shady. Not in a cramped bedroom with a six-pack of beer that my friend Alicia bribed a homeless man to buy for us.

You're losing your mind.

"Did you break into my house?" I say, hoping that will force the thoughts aside.

Xavier laughs, the sound soft and buzzy over the phone. "My brother and I were always welcome at Gloria's house, even if she wasn't home."

I squeeze the receiver more tightly. "It's not her house anymore," I say sharply. "It's mine. You need to give me your key."

It feels futile, saying it, and when Xavier laughs, my face heats up.

"I don't think I'll be doing that."

"Then I'll change the locks."

He laughs again. It sounds like a challenge.

"What do you want?" I spit out. "Why'd you leave your number?"

"I wanted you to call me," he says smoothly. "And you did, good girl that you are."

My skin prickles when he says *good girl*. I focus instead on the million questions I have for him, starting with how he knew I was coming back here.

I don't get to ask it, though. Xavier speaks first.

"You're supposed to say, 'Why did you want me to call you?'"

"I'm not supposed to say anything," I snap. "And I don't care why you wanted me to call you."

"Oh, darling, we both know that's not true."

Darling. I immediately think of Gideon, our naked bodies intertwined in that motel shower. Why couldn't he have been the one to leave his phone number?

Why the fuck am I even here?

"Say it," Xavier orders, and that reminds me of Gideon, too, enough so that I feel a traitorous flare of heat between my thighs.

"Are you at Hartshorn?" I ask instead. "Is your brother there?"

Immediately, a dark, overwhelming silence floods the phone line. Then: "That's not what you're supposed to say."

I consider my options. Part of me wants to hang up the phone because this conversation is weird and deeply unsettling and clearly going nowhere. I need to get dinner and call a locksmith, clearly.

The other part of me, though, wants to stay on the line. Wants to keep playing this game. It feels dangerous, but it also keeps cajoling heat from out between my thighs.

"Ivy." Xavier draws my name out like a warning. "I'm waiting. Do you need to be reminded what you're supposed to say?"

"Why don't you just tell me if you want to know so bad?"

He clicks his tongue, three sharp *tsks* that crackle over the phone. "You think I won't punish you?"

"Punish me?" I laugh. "Xavier, I haven't seen you in twenty years. I barely remember you. Your brother—"

"We're not talking about him," he says sharply. Angrily. The hairs on my arm stand on end. The only time it doesn't feel like a game, albeit a fucked-up one, is when I bring up his brother.

"We're talking about me leaving my phone number for you to find," Xavier continues. "Me. Xavier Hartshorn. Now, you have one more chance to get this right, or I'll have to come to Gloria's house and punish you for your disobedience. Don't worry, though." I can practically hear him grinning over the line. "You'll enjoy yourself."

"You don't even know me!" I laugh, not because it's funny but because of the sheer audacity of him to say that to me. I'm completely baffled by this entire conversation. Maybe even afraid, although the fear is like the night I spent with Gideon, warming my blood like alcohol. Loosening up my heart. Amplifying everything.

"We were fast friends as kids," Xavier says. "Remember? I took you out to the creek? Showed you how to use the rope swing? *Gideon* didn't do that."

He spits out his brother's name.

"No offense, Xavier," I say. "But you're making me uncomfortable."

"That's not what you're supposed to say." It comes out in a sing-song, almost like he's mocking me.

I lean against the wall, my fear quivering more deeply through my spine. This isn't normal. I shouldn't be going along with it. I should be calling a locksmith right this fucking minute.

But instead I say, "Why did you want me to call you?"

"There she is!" Xavier cries. "There's my good girl."

My clit throbs once again. Stupid. This is *stupid*.

On the other hand, Gideon certainly didn't put much effort into reaching out to me. Even if this weird little game from Xavier makes zero sense.

"Was that so hard?" Xavier coos, as if I'm a child.

"Are you going to answer or not?"

"Of course I'm going to answer. Ivy, I left my number because you and I have unfinished business."

My fear spikes, drowning out any of the lingering sense of playfulness I'd allowed myself. "Excuse me?" I mean for it to sound strong, but it comes out barely above a whisper.

"From fifteen years ago."

"You know what?" My voice shakes a little, but I swallow back my fear. "This conversation is over. You're being weird."

"Am I?"

"Yes. Real fucking weird. And if you show up tonight, to punish me or whatever, I'll call the cops."

"I'll keep that in mi—"

I hang up, slamming the phone down with a jangle. For a minute, I just stare at it, waiting for it to ring again, the tension coiling hot and thick in the kitchen. Then I reach over and yank the connector out of the wall.

Let him call back now.

I go back into the hallway, my body hot and agitated and vaguely turned on. Who the hell does he think he is, talking to me like that?

I snatch up my cell phone, which feels safe and familiar compared to the old landline phone. There are several new texts from my mom, which I ignore, although I catch a few words of them first: *worried* and *we can talk* and *home*. Her hatred of Golly, of this place, always felt absurd to me. But after that conversation with Xavier, I can almost see where she was coming from.

Almost.

I search for a local locksmith. There's only one in Harlan, but they offer same-day service. Thank god for that.

Unfortunately, while I do have Internet, I don't have any service bars to make a phone call. I groan and look down at the end of the hallway, into the dim light of the kitchen.

No wonder Golly still had a landline.

I plug the stupid thing back in and punch in the number for the locksmith. While I wait to speak to them, the on-call music fluttering in the background, my thoughts keep going to the conversation with Xavier. We have unfinished business, he said. From fifteen years ago.

But that timing isn't right. Fifteen years ago, I was thirteen.

But the only summer I spent here, I was eight.

22

GIDEON

Something's got the Shadow Thorn riled up. I feel it when I go out this evening to take care of the chores in my workshop. There's a damp, hot wind sweeping through the trees that makes the sunlight seem to glint on the grass. A tricky wind. A wind that's like an exhalation.

It reminds me a little of that night a month ago, as I made Ivy come against that fence behind the Nacogdoches VFW hall. But then, these days, *everything* reminds me of that night. The only thing keeping me going is the way she whispered *yes* when I told her to come back to me and the hope that she's going to keep that promise. I'm reassured by the fact that there's no For Sale sign on Gloria's house—not that Gran would let that happen. She'll snatch it up to keep the property in the family, where it belongs.

But Ivy hasn't even *tried* to sell it. And that means something.

I run a damp cloth over my tools, polishing them and making sure they're clean. Blood will rust metal, and these tools have been in my family for five generations. So, just like Dad taught me, I come out twice a week, regardless of whether or not there's been a sacrifice, to keep them looking nice. I've got my routine down, and it doesn't take long. It's so hot outside, though, even with the devilish wind curling through the trees, that I have to switch on the big metal fan I keep in the corner just to stir the air around while I finish up.

I'm working on the last chore on my list—sweeping up the workshop so that it'll be easier to mop up when the time comes —when someone knocks on the door. That the door doesn't immediately slam open tells me it's not Xavier, who has apparently decided he's moving back to the estate. Vincent wouldn't be up this early. That just leaves Gran.

"Come in," I call out, sweeping a little pile of dust into the broom pan. The door cracks open, letting in heat and bright golden-hour sunlight. Gran steps into the doorway.

"I knew I'd find you out here," she says warmly.

"Well, it's Wednesday."

"Just like your daddy taught you."

I sweep up the last of the dust and carry it over to the door to toss it out into the woods that grow wild around the structure. Uncle Jack and Dad built it when they were in their early twenties, after the old barn got pummeled by remnants from Hurricane Bret. They put it out in the woods at Gran's request, away from the house. Away from prying eyes.

"Yeah." I don't want to talk about Dad. Don't want to talk about the training he put me through when I was a kid. Gran knows it, too.

Which makes me wonder why she's here.

I can feel her watching me as I put away the broom and do my final check: that the tools are in the right place, that the chains and rope are coiled and put away, that the workshop's sole window is locked and covered.

"You really are just like your dad," she says softly. "So methodical."

The only reason I work like Dad is because he taught me

how to do all this, regardless of what I wanted. It's been baked into me since I was five years old, and I saw someone else's blood for the first time.

"Well, I'm all done now." I turn to Gran, crossing my arms over my chest. I know she's here for a reason, and I want her to get it over with. I need to go work out.

Gran smiles thinly. "I need to tell you something."

No one likes hearing those particular words. "What happened?" It could be a new sacrifice, although I haven't felt any of the signs. No, it probably has something to do with Xavier and whatever he's planning. I know he killed Lee Whitman a few weeks back. There was a story on the news about it, although they just said he disappeared. I'm sure Xavier paid off everyone he needed to so he could sweep his wrongdoing under the rug. He always does.

And then Gran says it.

"Ivy Myste is back at Gloria's house."

"What?" I whip my head over to her, my heart suddenly thudding furiously. *She came back to me.* "When?"

"I'm not sure," she says. "Earlier today, most like. There was a car parked in front of the house when I went for my walk just now. Wasn't one yesterday."

"How do you know it's her?" My head buzzes. I need to get over there before Xavier does. I hate that I didn't have a way of reaching out to her. I never got her phone number, but we have shit reception out here anyway, and I rarely keep my phone turned on.

Besides, we're bonded. I claimed her. I knew we'd pick up where we started when she came back.

"Well?" I prompt. Gran's taking too long to answer.

"I don't know who else it could be," she says. "But I wanted to let you—" She stops, looking me dead in the eye. "Your brother is not going to let this go, our traditions be damned."

Our *traditions*. Yes, by my family's traditions, Ivy's mine.

Except Gran and Gloria erased when it happened. Gloria's daughter, Ivy's mother, completely lost her shit. That's why Ivy doesn't remember.

Although I do.

I remember all of it.

"Does he know she's here?" I demand.

"I don't know," Gran says. "But I wanted to—I thought you deserved to know."

I lunge past her, flinging the workshop door open. Gran sighs.

"Be careful!" she says. "Do not bring her to the chapel!"

"I know," I snap, shoving out into the dense, humid woods. Gran trails after me.

"You have to go slowly, Gideon. I'm serious. If she's exposed to too much—"

"I remember the last time she was here." I stomp down the trail, my heart pounding with adrenaline. Gran follows after me with her warnings.

"That magic we did, it's not stable," she calls out. "You can not expose her to too much. I don't want to risk driving the poor girl mad—"

"Well, you shouldn't have erased her memory!" I shout, whirling around to face Gran. She stops, hitches her shoulders.

"I know," she says softly. "But I didn't have a choice."

This is a decade-old argument, and not one I feel like rehashing right now. Because I need to get to Ivy before my brother does.

"I'll be safe!" I take off in a jog, weaving through the overgrown path I know by memory more than anything else. It winds me around the western side of our property, opposite the chapel, but I still feel His presence, His dark eyes watching me from the trees. Every time the wind gusts, I know it's Him.

By the time I make it to the meadow behind Gloria's house, I'm beaded with sweat, and the sun is at that point in the sky where all the shadows stretch out like taffy. The house looks like it has for the past month, sullen and isolated. The only reason the yard's not an overgrown mess is because I came out here and mowed it. Xavier certainly couldn't be bothered.

I jog up to the back porch and push my damp hair out of my eyes. There's a light on inside, which makes my heart seize up.

I always knew she'd come back. She had to, because that's how it works. When I claimed her in the chapel ten years ago, I brought her into the family, brought her into our world, even if she doesn't remember it.

I bang on the door's window, the way I would whenever I'd come to see Gloria. Then I step back, smoothing my palms down over my cut-off shorts. The tattoo that shares her face is safely hidden, thank god. I don't want to have to explain that, although I guess if I'm lucky, she's gonna see it.

Footsteps echo inside the house. A shadow moves behind the window. It's her. I don't have to see her to know. I can just feel her, the way the air lights up with electricity.

She's my mate. My girl. *Mine.*

The back door swings open, and finally seeing her pretty face breaks all the tension of the last month. For a minute, she just stares at me through the screen, and I catch a whiff of something like fear.

But then she breaks into a smile. "Gideon," she says. "Wow. I didn't—I was going to—"

She pushes the screen door open, and the cold air from inside wafts over my skin.

"Hey," I say, and it clangs around stupidly in my head.

She looks beautiful, as beautiful as on our last night together. Her hair's piled up on top of her head in a messy bun, and she's wearing shorts cut high enough to shove off the faint swell of muscles in her thighs. I force myself to look up at her face.

"Gran said she saw a car at the house," I add, hoping to offer some kind of explanation. "I figured—hoped it was you."

Her smile brightens, although I can still sense that faint sense of fear in the tightness around her eyes.

I step up to her, and she steps back, letting me inside. I want to ask her what's wrong, but I also don't really want her knowing how adept I am at sniffing out fear.

"Yeah," she says, letting the screen door slam shut. "I, um, I'm actually going to be staying here for the summer."

My heart soars at that. She's back. She's *back*.

"I was hoping we could, you know." She swallows. "Hang out."

"Of course." I move closer to her and put my hands on her waist. Immediately, she melts into my touch, her hands coming up to run along my arms, tracing the lines of my tattoos.

"I hadn't heard from you," she says shyly, peering up at me. "So I wasn't sure if you were, you know—"

I kiss her. She makes a muffled shout of surprise and then gives herself into my kiss, as supple as I remember. I walk her backward until she bumps against the wall, and I've got her pinned in place, right where I want her—where I've dreamed of having her. And then I run my hands over her body, massaging her breasts through her flimsy T-shirt until I feel her nipples harden beneath her bra. Then I drop my hands lower to trace along her hips.

"Gideon," she breathes against me.

"I'm going to fuck you." I kiss along her throat, and she moans and tilts her head back, showing me her pulse. "If you don't tell me otherwise, I'll do it right here."

"Why didn't you *call* me?" she gasps.

I yank her shirt over her head and throw it into the kitchen. "Didn't have your number. Shit reception out here anyway." I slide my fingers up beneath her bra strap and snap it open, then fling that aside, too. Ivy gazes up at me, her lips swollen from my kisses, her eyes dark with lust.

"I wasn't sure," she whispers. "If you were still interest—"

I suck her right breast into my mouth, hard enough that her words dissolve into a moan. "Does that answer your question?" I growl, and then I zip down her shorts. Before I can slide them off and get to the treasure underneath, though, Ivy yelps and grabs my wrist.

"Wait!"

"What?" I look at her, fire coursing through my body. Outside, the screen door slams in the frame, like the wind is trying to get inside.

Ivy takes a breath deep enough that it makes her tits tremble. There's that fear again, dark and curdling.

"I have a locksmith coming," she says breathlessly. "He's supposed to be here in an hour."

"A locksmith?"

Ivy nods, pushing her hands through her hair. "Yeah. Your brother—"

All that fire in my blood turns to ice.

"He has a key. He left his phone number, and I called it, and he said he was going to—" Her cheeks turn bright pink with embarrassment, and a dark, flinty strike of possessiveness flares in my heart.

Ivy is *mine*.

"Punish me?" she finishes, tilting the sentence up like a question. "And I got freaked out and called the locksmith and—"

I grab her by the waist, cutting her words short. "You said he'd be here in an hour?" I rasp.

"Yes, but—"

"This won't take an hour."

Ivy's eyes widen. Her lips part. And when I shove her shorts down, she doesn't try to stop me. Which is good, because I have no intention of stopping. I want my cum dripping out of her cunt and down her leg, marking her as mine. Xavier has no fucking right to break into her house or scare her like that. He certainly doesn't have the right to *punish* her. I know what his punishments look like. And if anyone's doing that kind of shit to her, it's me.

I yank her up to me and kiss her, holding her in place by her throat. I love her like this, stripped naked and me still fully dressed. Her vulnerable. Me the protector. Because I'll protect her from anything.

"I won't let him hurt you," I snarl into her lips, and I don't know if I'm talking about my brother or the Shadow Thorn, who is undeniably here, with the way the wind is rattling around the house.

Then I fling Ivy around and bend her over the kitchen table, spread her legs, and slide two fingers into her soaking wet cunt.

23

IVY

I cry out as Gideon's fingers slide against my G-spot. He grunts and presses his other hand against the small of my back, crushing me down onto the table. Its worn metal is cool against my scorching skin.

"Stay right there," he says softly. "I need you warmed up first."

"The locksmith," I gasp out, my cheek pressed against the table. "What if he—"

"Don't worry, darling." Gideon brushes his thumb over my clit, and I scream and buck against his hand. "You're halfway there already. This won't take long."

He isn't wrong. Seeing him standing there on the porch, his tattooed skin gleaming with sweat like he ran here to see me, was probably enough on its own. But then he said he would protect me...

I moan at his touch, giving myself over to the pleasure. Gideon works me without saying anything, stroking me inside and out until I'm shuddering and panting and moisture slicks between my thighs.

"How do you want to come?" Gideon asks, leaning over me so his mouth is on my ear. "On my fingers? Or on my cock?"

I'm too unravelled to answer right away, and at first all that comes out is a low, keening moan. This is all happening so *fast*. I spent a month never hearing from him, and now I haven't been back an hour and already his fingers are inside me.

"Your cock," I spit out.

He chuckles softly. "Good girl. That's exactly what I wanted to hear."

Good girl. I swear I hear it in his brother's voice, and my clit surges with a sudden, overwhelming rush of heat.

"Oh, you liked that, huh?"

Did I?

"Well, don't come for me yet." Gideon slides his fingers out of me, and any traces of his brother are gone. All I can focus on is the sudden emptiness between my legs.

"Stay right fucking there." There's a rustle of clothes behind me: the whine of a zipper, the whisper of fabric.

And then Gideon presses his cockhead into my pussy, slow and careful.

I moan, bracing myself down on the table. For all the times I've touched myself in the past month, thinking of him, I'd forgotten just how big he is. Just how much he stretches me open, how much I have to fight through an initial burst of pain before the pleasure.

"Good girl," Gideon purrs again, and I whimper at that, too. "I know it hurts, baby. But you're taking me so well. You always take me so well."

The praise makes me want to melt across the table. I spread my legs wider and tilt up my pelvis, trying to accommodate him. Gideon pins me in place, though, both hands digging into my hips.

"Right there," he rasps. "Don't fucking move, okay? I've got you."

Then he thrusts into me, deep enough that a startling, shuddery pain rolls through my body. It's blinding. It's also beautiful.

But when Gideon starts to thrust—slowly, carefully—his cock is exactly where it needs to be, gliding easily over my G-spot so that the pain melts into pure, candied pleasure. I still don't understand how he knows my body so well, a thought that shimmers wildly and then dissolves as a small, initial pulse of ecstasy flares up through my core. I shriek and roll my hips against him, chasing myself to the precipice.

"You're close, aren't you?" he grunts, folding himself over me so that his lips brush against my shoulder. "Told you it wouldn't take an hour."

"How?" I gasp out. "How are you so good—"

Gideon laughs and jerks me backward and buries himself inside me. "Good at what, baby girl? Making you come?"

I nod, my cheek pressed against the table. I try to speak, but all that comes out is a tangle of keening and whimpering. Another spark of orgasm flares between my legs. I feel like I'm standing on the edge of a cliff, and all I need is for Gideon to push me.

"Right there," I manage to get out. "Don't—don't stop. I'm so close—"

Gideon tightens his grip on my thighs. I love it, the stab of pain. It makes the pounding stretch of his cock feel that much better.

"So am I, baby," he growls. "Now. Come for me."

He says it like an order, harsh and unyielding, and it's the push I need. All my ecstasy crests up inside me and spills over, flooding my body with heat. I scream out my orgasm, thrashing up against him, and he just chuckles and fucks me through it, each thrust hard and firm and calculating. And I keep coming, surge after surge of pent-up pleasure. All my frantic masturbating this month, all those delirious, feverish sex dreams, and this is what I needed—

Gideon's cock plunging deep inside me.

"Fuck, I missed that," Gideon pants, his pace quickening so that the table thumps against the wall. As he speaks, each word is punctuated by one of his thrusts. "The way your pussy contracts around my cock?" He slams into me, and I cry out, arching my back in pain or pleasure or both. "Nothing fucking compares."

He starts fucking me again, harder and faster than before, and all I can do is press myself into the table and let myself be used by him.. As he fucks me, he runs his hand up my spine until he reaches the back of my neck, and he holds me like that, pinning me down like I only exist for his pleasure.

It's unbelievably hot.

"Almost there," he grunts, tightening his fingers around my neck. "Don't move, baby. I need my cum inside you right. Fucking. No—"

The last word transforms into a deep, throaty roar. That's the only word for it: a roar, hungry and animalistic. His hips shudder against mine, and then he slumps over me, his cotton T-shirt soft against my bare back.

We breathe together. I can feel everything softening: him, inside me. My breath. My doubts.

I'm the first to move, tilting my head to look at him over my shoulder. His eyes are closed, his long dark lashes fluttering against his high cheekbone. When I shift beneath him, pushing myself to standing, he moves with me until we're both upright. Then he wraps his big arms around my back and holds me up to him, kissing along my shoulders until he gets to my neck. I'm glad for it, too, because my legs are wobbly and weak.

"The locksmith," I say, my words slurred. "I need to get dressed."

"I know, baby." Gideon doesn't let me go, though. He just keeps kissing along my neck, one hand gently massaging my breast. "But give me another minute. I fucking missed you."

"You could have called. Or something." It comes out before I can stop it, and I hate how accusatory it sounds. But Gideon only sighs.

"We don't have good reception at my place," he says softly. "And I never got your number."

"Whose fault is that?" I turn around to face him, and he runs his hand over my hair and smiles a little.

"Mine," he says. "But you're here now."

I'm not sure what to say. Then it doesn't matter, because he cups my face and kisses me with a slow, sweet tenderness that's such a contrast to how he fucks. "You're here now," he whispers again. "And I'm not going to let anything happen to you."

A shiver ripples down my spine, and I pull away from him. "What would happen to me?" I say, something dark and hard forming in my chest. Suspicion. This whole situation is weird, isn't it? It's not normal.

"Nothing, not while I'm around." Gideon gives me an affable, charming grin as he buttons up his shorts. "Especially not from Xavier."

His brother's name thuds around in my head. "Why did he do that, anyway?" I ask, fumbling around the kitchen to gather up my clothes. I catch sight of the clock on the microwave—fifteen minutes after six. He's right. We have plenty of time before the locksmith is supposed to arrive.

"What exactly did he do?" Something in Gideon's demeanor has changed. Turned harder.

I tell him as I get dressed, although I leave out how weirdly sexual it all was, and I *certainly* don't tell him about the way his brother's velvety voice flooded me with heat. I barely even want to admit it to myself. "It freaked me out," I say when I'm done, which is true enough. Certainly more true than me liking it. "Like, I haven't seen him in twenty years?" I say. "And Xavier just—"

Gideon throws his arm over my shoulder and pulls me into

him. "My brother is used to getting what he wants," he says stiffly. "Because our parents always gave it to him."

I hear something like bitterness in Gideon's voice, although I don't say anything about it.

"He's not really going to show up here in the middle of the night, is he?" I wind my arm around Gideon's waist, falling into the crook of his shoulder. It feels good here. Safe.

But then Gideon hesitates, and coldness crawls over my skin.

"I don't know," he finally says. "Maybe. It's good that you called a locksmith, actually."

Fear spikes in my chest.

"What would he *do?*" I twist around to look up at Gideon. He's gazing straight ahead, at the back door. The screen door didn't latch, and it keeps banging in the frame.

"Nothing," Gideon says, pulling me closer. "I won't let him."

My breath lodges in my throat.

"I mean it," Gideon adds, turning to look down at me. His hair curls into his green eyes, and I think he might be the most handsome man I've ever seen. "But I'm going to stay here with you tonight, okay? Just in case he shows up."

As soon as he says it, I realize how badly I wanted to ask him. How badly I didn't want to be alone in this rattling old farmhouse. "Thank you," I breathe out. "Although—I hope you aren't allergic to cats. I brought my cat Gnocchi with me."

Gideon smiles. "I love cats."

"He's hiding now. But he'll come out in a few hours." I fidget with a hangnail on my thumb, my thoughts still on Xavier. "Your brother won't be able to get in with the new locks, right?"

"No," Gideon says quickly. "But I don't want to leave you alone anyway." Then he smiles, and heat curls in my belly. "Besides, we've got a month's worth of fucking to do."

Now the heat rises right up to my cheeks. "You could have *called,*" I mutter, although I'm also squeezing my thighs together, my clit aching at the thought of having him inside me again.

"You said that already." Gideon tilts my chin up to meet his eye. "I could say the same to you, by the way. And you actually had my number."

I blush.

"But you're here now, and that's what matters. Now." He presses his forehead against mine. "How long 'til that locksmith gets here? Because I want to make sure you're well fed before we get down to it."

I laugh, despite everything. "About half an hour."

"That's plenty of time to pick up something from Bluebonnet Barbecue," he says. "My treat. Consider it a welcome home dinner."

Then he pulls me into another kiss, and the word *home* echoes around in my head.

24

XAVIER

I didn't let myself jerk off after that enticing phone conversation with Ivy, as much as I wanted to. The waiting is sweet sometimes, and she needs to be punished anyway. Personally, I like the idea of easing into her dark, quiet bedroom and covering her sleeping face with my cum.

I wait as long as I can stand it, and I manage to make it to almost midnight before I slip out of the house to visit her. I was holed up in my third-floor suite, working on Five Courts business, and neither Gran nor Gideon came up to bother me. When I finally creep out into the hallway, everything is dark and silent. Gran's bedroom is on the other end of the hallway and easy to avoid, and since Gideon's living in the old wing now, I don't have to worry about him hearing me, either. He's the only one I'm really worried about anyway.

The night is alive, stirring with a damp wind that blows from the direction of the chapel, pressing me along the path between the two houses. I switch on my phone flashlight out of habit more than anything else; I don't really need it. I've travelled this path so many times in my life, this artery that connects the Hartshorn family to the Arbour family. Ivy might have her father's name, Myste, but she's an Arbour through and through, and that's why she belongs to me.

It's also why she belongs to Gideon, whispers a traitor of a voice in the back of my head. I shove it aside. She does not belong to Gideon because I claimed her first. I took her to the chapel in the woods and kissed her in front of the Shadow Thorn's altar when we were thirteen years old.

True, I didn't understand the full extent of the ritual. I'd heard bits and pieces of it from my parents, who called it a wedding. I'd seen weddings on TV. I knew they involved a bride, a bridegroom, an altar, and a kiss.

How the hell was I supposed to know that this particular ritual required *fucking?*

Still. The intention was always there. I claimed Ivy first. Gideon should have understood that when he decided to steal what was mine a few years later.

Well, I'm going to steal her right back. I don't care that she's spent the last month conjuring him up in her decadent, luxurious dreams. They're always in Technicolor, her dreams, everything saturated and soft at the edges. And Lee's blood must have been a good gift for the Shadow Thorn, because it's been easy for me to take root inside all that luxury.

I've fucked her every night since then. Sometimes as myself, the way I did that first night. Other times, I put on different costumes so she'd spread her legs for me in the dreamscape, pulling bits and pieces from the memories of men still lurking in her head. Anything to get her to turn away from Gideon.

It hasn't been as good as fucking her for real, of course; it always feels like a dream to me, too. But more nights than not, I would snap back into reality with cum stains on my boxers.

Tonight will be different, though. Tonight, I'll finally feel her body for real. And it's going to be very, very satisfying.

When I arrive at the edge of the woods, I switch off my flashlight before stepping into the meadow. The wind is stronger here, damp and blistering, and it howls like a woman in pain across the sweep of grass and makes the big wind chime at the edge of the woods bong arrhythmically. The house—once Gloria's, now Ivy's—is dark against the starry sky.

Well, except for one window.

I frown. It's upstairs, probably one of the guest bedrooms. I thought for sure she'd be in bed by now.

I creep closer, moving through the damp wind. The Shadow Thorn is here—I can feel Him crawling on my skin, urging me forward. He wants this as much as I do, because He knows I claimed her first. He witnessed it, how eager she was to kiss me when we were thirteen.

I'm nearly to the fence that wraps around the yard proper when someone moves in front of the window. A female silhouette.

I crouch down on instinct, even though I know if she looks outside, she won't be able to see me in the dark. For a moment, she just stands there, nothing but a voluptuous shadow. I'm fairly certain she's naked, which gets my cock's attention.

But then another shadow moves behind her. Bigger. Taller. Undeniably male.

Jealous rage fires through my veins.

The wind gusts furiously, and the rustle of the surrounding trees sounds like the ocean. On the back porch, the screen door slams in its frame. The wind chime rings out like a church bell.

The two shadows blur together.

"Gideon," I whisper, even though it can't be. How the fuck did he know she was here? I only knew because I left my phone number so she'd call me first thing when she arrived. More magic, of course. I mixed the ink with my blood.

I grip the fence, hard enough that my knuckles turn white. The two shadows pull apart, and then Ivy's shadow kneels, and Gideon's shadow rests his hand on the top of her head, and I know when she starts bobbing back and forth that she's sucking his hideous, coloring-book donkey cock.

"You *motherfucker*," I snarl, even as my own cock hardens. Because it's supposed to be me up there, towering over her while she worships my dick.

The wind blusters again, and I can feel the Shadow Thorn everywhere. I can feel Him in my blood, making it hot and sparking.

Ivy keeps working Gideon, clearly not remotely intimidated by his size. I'd be impressed if I wasn't so fucking pissed off. And the fact that my own cock is straining at my jeans, well, that just pisses me off more.

Watching her try to fuck a dream version of Gideon night after night had been bad enough, but at least I knew it wasn't real. This shit is.

The shadows in the window shift around, separating and then coming back together until they're moving in a steady, rhythmic way that I know means he's fucking her. Again.

"She's mine," I snarl out to the night, to the wind. The Shadow Thorn blows around me, and the dampness against my skin makes me even hornier. Horny enough to rub myself over my clothes as I watch them in the window. I think he's fucking her from behind.

It's supposed to be *me*.

I yank down my zipper and fist my cock, squeezing my shaft so hard that it hurts. Punishing myself because I can't punish her, although I imagine it, all the ways I would hurt her for her betrayal. Tying her to my bed for hours so I can fuck her whenever I feel like it. Bringing her to the precipice of orgasm only to deny her over and over again. Or the opposite: forcing her to come so many times she loses count, so many times that she's begging me to stop.

Squeezing her throat until she passes out, all while I'm inside her, so I can feel the spasm of her body around my cock.

I grunt as I stroke myself, still watching the shadows in the window and imagining it's me up there, the way it's supposed to be. But I don't want to spill my cum out here at the fence. I don't want to fucking waste it.

So even though it's agony, I shove myself back in my pants and creep up to the back porch. The grass is neatly shorn, the porch swept clear of leaves—Gideon's doing, no doubt. I wonder, briefly, if he worked his own magic on her, but I dismiss the thought. Gideon never learned magic. He learned other things.

I *did* learn magic, though, and I'm going to fucking use it. So once I'm on the porch, I split open my palm with one of the hooks holding up the porch swing, sucking air through my teeth as the blood oozes out. Then I pull my cock out again.

This time, I fuck my bloody hand with purpose, my jaw clenched. One image after another flashes through my head, but all of them are Ivy, my Ivy, spread out and naked and worshipful. Moaning in pleasure. Screaming in pain. Covered in blood.

I come with a strangled cry, tamping down on it so there's no chance that they hear me, even upstairs. My cum arcs out and splatters across the back door, dripping like moonlight-colored paint. *Fuck,* it would have looked pretty on Ivy's pale skin. I step up to the door and run my cut palm across it, smearing the door with my blood.

The air sparks with magic, ready to work my intention.

I'm not done, though. Marking the house with my blood and my cum is one thing, but I want my scent, my essence, to permeate her home. I want to make sure she dreams of me tonight, even if she's tucked in my brother's arms.

So I step closer to the door, still holding my softening cock. And then I empty my bladder, sighing as my piss streams out and darkens her doorway. She'd look pretty wearing that, too.

By the time I'm finished, there's a small, glimmering puddle between the doorframe and the doormat, and I can smell the faint tang of ammonia on the air. I wonder if she'll recognize it when she comes out tomorrow morning. I know Gideon will, and he'll know it was me, too.

"Motherfucker," I mutter, finally tucking my cock away for the night. He thinks he's won because he's taking her upstairs right now. But I know the intricacies of witchcraft, and when it comes to getting what I want, I'm patient. I waited this long—fifteen goddamn years since I kissed her in the chapel when we were both thirteen.

A few more weeks is nothing.

Ivy is here, at Hartshorn, because of me. I burrowed into her dreams. I marked her house with my magic.

She'll be mine by the time all of this is through.

25

GIDEON

I always wake up with the sun. Dad trained me to do it since I was a kid, the way Gran trained him and the way her father trained her and her siblings back in the fifties. Wake with the sun, sleep lightly, listen for sacrifices.

Ivy is not a sacrifice, thank god.

She's still asleep beside me, naked atop the tangled bedsheets, her hair streaming across her pillow. I'm not sure when we finally fell asleep, but it was late. I couldn't stop touching her. Couldn't stop kissing her. Especially when she raked her nails down my back without me even asking, hard enough to draw streaks of blood that left dots of crimson on the bedsheets.

I kiss her forehead, and she stirs, rolling toward me, her eyes fluttering beneath her lids. I don't want to leave her, but I have chores to do and a piece of shit brother to confront.

"Ivy," I murmur, relishing the way her name rolls around on my tongue. She blinks, her gaze soft for a few seconds as she focuses on me.

"Good morning, baby." I kiss before she can say anything,

and she melts into me, drawing her arms and legs up around my body to pull me into her. My cock throbs.

"Good morning," she says sleepily, and I sort of wish I hadn't woken her up, that I just started licking along her slit until she was moaning.

But no. I have to stay focused.

"I'm sorry to wake you up," I say, "But I have some shit to do on the estate. Can we meet up this afternoon?"

"What do you have to do?" She stretches, arching her back and lifting her arm overhead. There's a red bruise on her neck. My doing, of course, from when I latched my mouth to her skin and sucked until she was grinding against my upper thigh.

I brush my fingers against her cheek. *Yell at my brother* is the correct answer, but not one I want to tell her. I don't want her thinking about him. "I gotta clear some brush," I say. "Clean up the gardens a bit. Boring stuff, really."

Ivy smiles, incandescent in the morning light. "Don't you want to stay for breakfast?"

"You don't have any breakfast here."

"I thought we could drive into Harlan."

My heart tugs at that. The truth is, I'd love to go have breakfast with her. There's a little diner on the edge of town run by a Guatemalan family that moved here five years ago and doesn't have a few generations' worth of fear of the Hartshorns, like most of the people around here do. But I need to take care of this shit with my brother. I need to nip it in the bud before either of us lets it get out of hand.

"It'll be too hot to work by the time we're done," I tell Ivy instead, still stroking my fingers over her hair. "But maybe I can take you to dinner."

"Or maybe I'll cook something for us," she says. "I need to get groceries anyway."

"It's a date." I brush my lips against her forehead and crawl backward out of bed, not wanting to take my gaze off her. She settles into her pillows, watching me with sleepy eyes.

"Are you just going to show up again?" she says coyly. "Or will you call me this time?"

"I told you, we get shit reception." How Xavier was able to take her call yesterday is beyond me. He certainly didn't have her call the house line—that would risk Gran answering. "But I can call you here at the house. Oh, and leave you the number to Hartshorn."

"Wait." Ivy sits up, her hair shimmering in the sunlight as she moves. She crawls across the bed toward me, and for a moment, all I can think about is last night, when she did the exact same thing as I stood waiting for her with my cock in my fist like an offering. That was also when she noticed the tattoo on my thigh for the first time. The tattoo that wears her face.

She swallowed me to the hilt when she realized what it was, moaning with pleasure.

This time, though, she slides off the bed and digs around in the little writing table tucked up beside the window, all her naked flesh glowing in the sun.

Fuck, I don't want to leave.

"Here." She turns around and hands me an ancient Post-It note on which she scribbled a phone number with an unfamiliar area code. "That's my cell. Try it first, okay? Then you can call the land line."

"Got it." I grab her hand and the note itself, pull her up to me, and kiss her one last time before I leave. She moans against my lips, eyelashes fluttering.

"Stop making this so hard," I murmur.

"That's not the only thing that's hard," she murmurs back.

She's right, and she presses her thigh up against my cock to prove it. I grin at her.

"Didn't get enough last night?"

"No." Her eyes flash, and I feel a hot, primal urge to throw her on the bed and fuck her again. I refrain, though. I can't let myself get distracted.

"Well, you'll just have to be patient, won't you?" I cup her chin and tilt her head up toward me. "And you better be patient. I don't want you getting off until I'm here, do you understand?"

"How will you know?"

I squeeze her chin a little harder. "I'll know."

She grins wickedly, and I release her, knowing full well she's probably going to touch herself as soon as I'm gone. I don't care, though. Bossing her around is a fun game, but I don't demand obedience. Not the way Xavier does.

I scribble out the phone number to the house line at Hartshorn and then get dressed, pulling on yesterday's clothes as she stretches out on the bed, still naked, one hand trailing around her breasts. I can feel her eyes burning through me. I can feel the ancient, terrifying magic that links us together.

"Behave," I say, one last warning before I slip out of the bedroom and down the stairs.

I go out through the back door, having been trained to since I was a kid. But as soon as I step onto the porch, I know something is wrong. I feel the lingering spark of witchcraft, as scratchy and thick as pollen.

Then I smell piss.

"You *motherfucker*," I snarl, whirling around to examine the door. The first thing I see is a smear of dried blood. Then, to my disgust, I discover the splatter of pale stains against the wood. Xavier was here.

I don't know much about magic. I never learned. And frankly, I think Gran and Uncle Jack only taught Xavier as a consolation prize since they didn't want him to make the sacrifices. Then, when he showed some aptitude in it—along with politicking—they let him be our family's liaison to the Five

Courts, along with Mom. Lord knows no one else wants to do it.

But just because I'm not well-versed in witchcraft doesn't mean I can't tell that he did something on this porch. Marked this house in some way. Instigated a literal pissing contest.

"It doesn't fucking work like that," I mutter, stalking around to the water hose Gloria kept on the side of the porch. It's half-buried beneath a spray of red bougainvillea—had these been here when I mowed the yard last? I don't remember, but then, bougainvillea grows fast.

I drag the hose through the flowers and spray down the door and the porch, hoping that'll at least wash the scent away. Whatever malice Xavier left behind, though—that won't wash away easily.

I claimed her, I tell myself as I wind the hose back up and then stalk across the meadow, my whole body raging. Xavier can use all the stupid magic tricks he wants; it doesn't change the fact that I'm the one who claimed Ivy in the chapel, not him. He's delusional if he thinks his schoolboy kiss is enough. I'm the one who laid her down in the wildflowers growing through the chapel's burned-out floorboards and shattered her until her soul merged with mine.

And I *know* that's what happened because I feel it every time she and I are together, the way the air kind of unravels and then ties us up close to each other. The link is there, and it's undeniable.

Xavier can't break it, no matter how fucking hard he tries.

By the time I'm back at Hartshorn, my anger has my whole body stirred up. I slam into the new wing of the house, not caring if I'm tracking mud or grass onto the polished wood. "Xavier!" I bellow. "Get your worthless ass down here!"

I stomp upstairs, banging my fist against the wall. "Xavier!" I roar. "You motherfucker! Come out here and talk to me!"

The house is silent in return, but when I come to the third-floor room he's settled in since moving back, the door is locked. I don't even bother to knock; he won't answer. I hoist up my leg and slam my foot into the knob with every ounce of my strength, and it's enough that the wood splinters and the door flies open.

"What the fuck?" Xavier jumps from his desk, his laptop open behind him. He's dressed, although his clothes look rumpled.

"Didn't sleep after you jacked off all over Ivy's door?" I snarl, hurling myself across the room. Xavier, to his credit, darts out of the way, shoving his rolling chair at me. I catch it and fling it aside, hard enough that it slams against the wall.

"Calm down," Xavier says. "Before you tear the whole damn room apart."

"Stay the *fuck* away from her." I lunge at him again, and this time he throws out a punch that lands on my shoulder, although the pain is laughable. I catch his wrist and twist it back. Xavier howls, face twisting. "What the fuck did you do last night?" I growl, forcing him down to his knees. "And what the fuck did you do to get her to call you so you could threaten her—"

"Uncle!" Xavier shouts.

"This isn't a goddamn game." I twist his arm back further, and he flops against me, trying to squirm free. If I wanted to, I could break his forearm. "Tell me what the fuck you're doing."

"I'm doing exactly what you're doing!" Xavier hisses, his eyes furious. "I'm taking what's mine."

I keep his arm clamped against me. "So you admit she's mine?"

"Fuck off."

I twist his arm back just a centimeter more. Then I release it—and him, throwing him backward on his bed. He curls his wounded arm up to his chest and glares at me. But he's smiling, too.

"That's the only way you know how to do anything," he says mockingly. "Violence."

His words make my stomach coil around. "What did you *do?*" I say in response, my voice low and dangerous.

Xavier's eyes bore into mine, and his mouth curls up, cold and cruel. "Just a little witchcraft," he says in a lilting sing-song. "Like the witchcraft I did to get her to come back here." He winks. "You can thank me whenever you'd like."

Blood pounds in my ears. "She came back for me."

"Did she?" Xavier's grin widens, distorting his features. "Or did she come back because I stepped into her dreams and told her to?"

Dread rattles through my body. I already guessed he killed Lee Whitman, and suddenly I understand why. A sacrifice. "You didn't."

"I did." Xavier sits up and smooths down his shirt. "There are benefits to being the brains instead of the brawn."

He's plunging his fingers into an old wound, although it's old enough now that I can mostly ignore it. "Stay away from her," I tell him. "I don't care what the fuck you did in her dreams. She's here for me. That shit you pulled, leaving your phone number, that scared her."

Xavier's eyes glint devilishly, and I know it was the wrong thing to say. He likes his women scared.

"She doesn't want you," I snap. "Magic or not."

A shadow of doubt flickers across Xavier's face. Anyone other than me would have missed it, but I've known him his entire life, and he's not the only one who knows how to reopen wounds. I step closer to him, my chest heaving, my hair hanging into my eyes.

"She never wanted you," I say softly. "She chose me ten years ago, and she chose me this time around, too. So stay the *fuck* away from her."

Xavier doesn't move. Doesn't say anything, either, which means I've needled him deeply enough.

"If you scare her again," I say, "I'll kill you myself."

Xavier scoffs. "No, you won't. You're too much of a coward to break family tradition."

I lean closer to him, rage coursing through my veins, and he pulls back, just a little. He's masking it, but he's afraid. He's always been afraid of me, deep down, because I am the weapon at the end of our family's arm, the blade that spills the blood for the Shadow Thorn.

"It's tradition that family can't be a sacrifice," I say with slow, careful precision. "But you wouldn't be a sacrifice."

Xavier glares at me, but his fear is brighter than ever.

"I'll kill you for fun."

Then I whirl away from him before he can shoot back some smart-ass comment. The air conditioning kicks on when I stop into the hallway, as if it knows I need something, anything, that can cool my rage.

26

IVY

After Gideon leaves, I drag myself out of bed and into the upstairs shower. There's no blood to wash off this time. Well, very little. Just a few specks beneath my fingernails from where I raked his skin while he slammed into me, begging for pain. The memory makes me shudder beneath the shower fall, but I refrain from touching myself. I mean, he did ask.

And I rather like doing what he asks.

After I'm clean, I pull on a loose, flowy tank top and some cut-off shorts and head downstairs. Gnocchi has finally decided to reappear after hiding all night, and he meows when he sees me, tail twitching.

"You hungry, buddy?" His food is one of the only things I've actually unpacked, and I dish him up a bowl of pate. He munches contentedly on it.

I find my phone balanced on the kitchen counter next to my wallet, which I'd pulled out to pay the locksmith after he finished with everything. Not that I was really scared at that point. Not with Gideon here.

Still, he's not here now, so I turn the brand-new deadbolt in the back door and scoop up my phone to see where the closest grocery store is. More messages from Mom and Juniper, of course. A missed call from this morning. At least they're coming through now, even if I wish they weren't.

I know I should call at least one of them back and let them vent to me about how terrible my life choices are. But I just don't feel like it.

Because, despite the weirdness with Xavier, I do like it here. I like the quiet and the way the sunlight pours in hot and white through the little window above the kitchen sink. I like all of Golly's antique furniture and the weird sense of history that seems to hang around this house like cobwebs. I like—

I like Hartshorn.

My few memories of the house buzz around in my head. I want to see it again. *Really* see it. Go inside it. See if it matches the odd, insistent dreams I've been having for the last month—

And that I didn't have last night.

It hits me at once that this was the first night I woke up without the sense, however vague, that I had dreamed of Hartshorn. The dreams I did have were darker and stranger, though. I can remember vague fragments of them: A mouth on my mouth. A bed of black silk. My naked body wrapped in thorned brambles that cut my skin and made me moan with pleasure.

But not Hartshorn.

This is where I'm supposed to be, I think, leaning over the sink so I can look out at the rippling meadow and the dark green woods beyond it. I've never felt like I was supposed to be anywhere.

My stomach grumbles, bringing me out of the clouds. I can't just rattle around in here all day, waiting for Gideon to be done with his chores like a lovestruck teenage girl.

The promise of food gives me focus, and half an hour later I'm pushing a cart through the HEB in Harlan, nibbling on a sausage roll from the bakery. The grocery store is new—the one we visited with Golly had been small and cramped and kind of faded. This one feels like a magazine cover, the lights too bright and the colors too saturated.

By the time I get back to the house, it's nearly noon, and the heat is unbearable. It feels like I'm breathing in sunlight as I cart my bags in, and even that little bit of effort has my skin sheened with sweat. At least Golly's AC works well, so I don't completely melt.

I take my time putting the groceries away and learning where everything is. When I'm finished, I pour a glass of iced coffee and then drink it in front of the sink, staring out at the meadow. It just *looks* hot, with the way the sun scorches the pale, rippling grass and the wind chime hangs perfectly still, but I can't stop batting around the thought that I need to be outside, walking to Hartshorn. I went to California a few years back with Juniper and her husband, and I got caught in a minor riptide when we were at the beach. It dragged me sideways along the shore, and it took every ounce of strength in my legs to kick free.

That's what this feels like. Like there's a riptide in the air, desperately trying to drag me to Hartshorn.

I sigh, brush my hand through my hair. I need to work on class prep before my first summer session starts in a week. *Just a few minutes on the porch*, I tell myself. *Then you can settle in to work.*

So I turn my new deadbolt and pull open the back door. And freeze.

The back porch is overgrown with thick, crawling vines.

For a moment, all I can do is stare at them. I think they're bougainvillea, with their red, papery blossoms and dark green leaves. But red bougainvillea is always pink or magenta, not this dark crimson color. In the shadows, these blossoms are almost purplish-black, and it gives a kind of creeping feeling over my skin.

I dreamed this.

The thought's fleeting, replaced by a more urgent one: that these flowers were not on my porch last night. Not when Gideon knocked on the back door, and not when the locksmith was out there working.

But now, twelve hours later, they're everywhere: twining around the balcony, smothering the rusty old porch swing, crawling up around the doorframe to the point that they barely leave room for me to pass through. I don't know how Gideon got out. He must have used the front door.

Except no, he didn't. The deadbolt wasn't locked.

The wind gusts, hot and dry, and makes the leaves rustle. I think I smell cedar.

"What the fuck?" My hands shake, and I take a stumbling step backward, coffee sloshing over onto the floor. The vines are still there, beautiful but mocking.

I set my coffee on the table and grab at them, shrieking as thorns cut in my palm. I forgot that bougainvillea was thorned, and I jerk my hand back to see a smear of blood on my skin.

Memories from a month ago flash through my head. Digging the razor blade into Gideon's skin as he fucked me, his Adam's apple bobbing with his moans.

I jerk my gaze up to the bougainvillea again. They aren't so thick across the door that I can't see the meadow on the other side, or the woods and the wind chime, or the path that will take me back to him. That riptide feeling washes over me again, and I drift forward, not even carrying that I'm dripping blood on the tile. Maybe Gideon will like it when he sees it later.

The bougainvillea rustles softly and then seems to part and peel away from the doorway. Or maybe they just weren't as thick as I thought.

I step through, ducking underneath without scraping myself on the thorns. The bougainvillea is everywhere, trailing off the porch and into the yard. When I walk, I step on it, crushing its blossom under my sneakers and releasing that scent. It's not cedar, I decide, but something muskier. I didn't know bougainvillea even had a smell.

I step off the porch and turn to look back at the house. The bougainvillea is mostly centered around the porch, although it's crawled over the porch's roof and started climbing up toward one of the second-floor windows. My bedroom window, in fact. Or at least, the bedroom where I slept last night with Gideon.

A weird, buzzy feeling rolls around in my chest. The bougainvillea blossoms almost look like blood pouring out of my bedroom window and draining over my porch.

And they weren't there last night. They *weren't*.

Acting on some deep, feral instinct, I turn and run toward Hartshorn, and it feels, just for a moment, as if the wind is chasing me. I duck as I slam into the woods, all the tree branches reaching out to scrape at my hair and clothes. The wind roars through the leaves, and now I'm *certain* something is chasing me. I can feel it, hot and hungry and closing in, and it's both terrifying and exciting.

Like Gideon.

Like my dreams.

Like—

An image floods my head. I'm twelve or thirteen, and I'm in some kind of outdoor shed, surrounded by shining knives. And Golly is there with Judith, the two of them holding hands and praying. Or at least I think they're praying. They're not speaking English. Not speaking a language I recognize at all.

I'm laid out on a worktable and I can't move, but I smell flowers and copper, and it feels like something's worming through my head—

I trip on an exposed tree root and go flying, landing hard on my hands and knees. The image is gone, mostly. It feels the way my dreams do, distant and tattered.

The creek glimmers up ahead.

I frown, falling back on my heels. How did I get turned around? I meant to go to Hartshorn. To Gideon. And I never came to the split in the trail.

Didn't I?

But I'm definitely at the creek. I rub at my palms, now scraped from my fall as well as from the bougainvillea thorns. The creek babbles by, throwing off dots of sunlight.

It's peaceful.

But then something snaps behind me. A gentle rustling. The soft thud of footsteps.

And then a low, unctuous male voice:

"Now, what do we have here?"

27

IVY

I scramble up to standing and whip around to find a tall, thin man leaning rakishly against one of the nearby dogwood trees. His pale, white-blonde hair is neatly swept back from his sharp, angled face, and he smiles at me with a smile I only ever remember seeing on a little boy.

"Xavier," I whisper, hating that it comes out sounding breathless.

It's not a question. I know it's him, as if the last time I saw him was a few days ago, not when I was thirteen—

No, eight. I was eight.

And you dreamed of him.

"In the flesh." Xavier pulls away from the tree to spread out his arms in invitation. He's wearing the kind of clothes that look casual but expensive—a pair of dark shorts and a loose, cottony shirt unbuttoned enough to reveal the hollow of his throat. "I was wondering when you were going to come by the creek."

I blink, feeling hot and disoriented. Why am I even here? I'm supposed to be at the house, building up my online class before the semester starts. Why didn't I just call Gideon, especially after he gave me the number to Hartshorn?

"What are you doing here?" I say, which feels like the only question safe enough to ask.

Xavier steps toward me, his dark green eyes boring into mine. The two brothers don't really look alike except for their eyes. It was like that even when we were kids.

"I was going for a walk." Xavier moves closer to me, and I feel like I should run, but I don't. "I heard my old friend Ivy was back in town, and I wanted to come see her."

"Wanted to punish me, you mean?" I step backward and bump against a tree trunk, our conversation from yesterday thumping in my thoughts.

Xavier chuckles. "My brother made sure that didn't happen, didn't he?"

Ice ripples over my skin despite the thick, crushing heat of the woods. The trees crowd around, and it almost feels as if they're bowing their heads toward us. Or toward Xavier.

"How do you know what he did?" I say shakily.

Xavier smiles and moves closer. I press my back against the tree, my torn palms scraping against the rough bark. I don't understand how the boy I went swimming with as a child became such a menacing man. He's like the blade of a knife.

Xavier tilts his head, studying me. "Because I saw him fucking you," he says plainly.

Heat flares up through my cheeks, and I remember last night, how Gideon dragged the curtains open and said he wanted to look at the night while he was inside me. It had been exciting to be put on display. But I didn't think for a second we had an audience.

Or that said audience was his *brother*.

"Why would you—" The words lodge in my throat. "Why would you watch that?"

Xavier doesn't say anything, just keeps searching me with

his dark green eyes. The way he looks at me, it's like he's holding me hostage there against the tree.

"I've watched a lot more than you realize," Xavier says in a low, velvet purr. "But don't worry, cicada. I'll have my turn soon enough."

"*Excuse* me?" I want to sound defiant, but it comes out soft and whimpery.

"You heard me." Xavier takes another step closer, and this time, I tear myself away from him and try to dart sideways into the underbrush. But Xavier catches me by the arm and shoves me up against the tree and then pins me there by the throat, his fingers long and grasping.

And thin, compared to Gideon's fingers when Gideon holds my neck like this. But Xavier squeezes me much tighter, enough that the air stalls in my lungs.

"Let me—" I rasp. "Let me go—"

"Not yet." Xavier presses against me, angling his hips so I feel the thick ridge of his erection. I have a fleeting, shameful thought—*big dicks must be hereditary*—and then I tamp it down, back in the dark where it belongs.

"There's something I want," Xavier says softly, his breath brushing against my lips. "You gave it to me once before, although you don't remember."

I squirm against him, trying to fight my way free. But he's strong, stronger than he looks, and he squeezes my throat hard. Hard enough to scare me.

"I know you like this," he says, tilting his head so his lips brush my cheek. "This pain."

I close my eyes, not wanting to give any hint that it's true. Because it *can't* be true. Terror thuds through my core, as hot as lust.

"I like pain, too," Xavier continues, and his words become kisses, soft and fluttering. I tense my entire body and clench my jaw so I don't cry out, especially as he nips sharply at my earlobe. "I like giving it. I know that's what you want." He bites my ear again, harder, and this time I do cry out, my voice drowned out by the rushing, furious wind. "My brother will only ever take pain, but I suspect you know that already."

"Don't talk about him," I snarl, or try to. It comes out frightened.

Xavier laughs and finally releases my neck, but only so he can bury his nose there. "He did this to you, didn't he?" he says, kissing softly against the hickey that Gideon left behind. "Marked you? That's not usually his style. He's jealous."

"Let me go!" I try to squirm away, but Xavier shoves me back against the tree by the arms, his eyes flashing angrily.

"Not yet," he growls. "Not until I've taken what I came here for."

And then he smashes his lips against mine, forcing his tongue into my mouth. At first, I don't know what to do. He kisses like his brother—hungry, devouring. But angrier, somehow, his teeth nipping and scraping at my bottom lip, giving me little bursts of pain.

And fuck me, but—

But I like it. He's fucking right.

Xavier shoves his thigh between my legs and saws it back and forth, teasing my clit through my shorts. He also runs his hands down my arms and then grabs my wrists and hoists them overhead, pressing me up against the tree.

That's when I relent.

I don't know why. Maybe it's all too much—his angry mouth, the pressure of his leg against my inflamed clit. Or maybe it's like the force that draws me to Hartshorn. It feels the same. Like something inevitable.

The first sign of my submission is a moan, a low throaty sound that Xavier seems to swallow whole. But then I kiss him back, even as horror gnaws at my chest.

I do it desperately, hungrily, like I'm trying to match his

force. Through the wet, sloppy noise of our kisses, he makes a soft approving sound, a kind of chuckle in the back of his throat.

Then he pulls away with a gasp and drops my arms. I'm too dazed to do anything but stare at him as he reaches down and adjusts his erection beneath his shorts. Which, to my embarrassment, he notices.

"Like what you see?" He grins, his lips red and glossy from our kiss. "I know I'm not as big as my brother, but trust me, you won't be complaining."

"Fuck you," I spit out, furious with myself for giving in to him.

Xavier laughs. "Is that what you want? I'll take you right here, but I figured you'd need more time to get used to the idea."

"There's no idea to get used to!" I shout, even if the suggestion sends heat coursing through me. "I'm not going to—Gideon's my boyfriend."

The words come out before I can stop them, and I realize I don't know if they're even true.

Worse, they make Xavier laugh. "Oh, Ivy," he says, shaking his head. "My little cicada—"

"Stop calling me that."

Xavier's eyes bore into me, and for a moment, I'm terrified he's going to do something worse than a kiss. "Don't fucking interrupt me."

I suck down a deep breath, wary as I watch him. His anger flares and then melts into a cold, mocking smile. "As I was saying," he purrs. "Do you have any idea how many women Gideon and I have shared?"

I stare at him, my throat suddenly dry. His eyes glitter wickedly.

"Yes, I'm sure Gideon won't have told you about that," he

says slyly. "But trust me. There's a reason I know what my brother's cock looks like."

My face is hot. He's lying. He's trying to disgust me. Or turn me against Gideon.

"Don't look so shocked." Xavier slides his fingers back through his hair, letting each golden, shimmery strand fall one after another. He fixes his gaze straight on me. "If it makes you feel any better, he only does it with women who look like you."

I have absolutely no idea what to say to that, and I don't want to dwell on the weird, warm feeling it gives me. "Fuck you," I say again, voice shaky.

Xavier raises an eyebrow. "That's the second time you've said that," he says. "Shall we get down to it?"

"No!" I shove him hard in the chest, and he actually stumbles back a little, although he grins up at me as I take off running down the path, away from the creek. Away from him.

I intend to go back to my house, to lock the door and jump in the shower and scrub my skin clean.

But that's not where my feet take me.

The oddest thing is, I don't even realize it until I spill out of the woods and Hartshorn rises up like a prison wall.

28

GIDEON

I'm digging in the garden when the wind picks up, hot and blustery, and just for a second, I smell Ivy.

I try to shake it off, tossing another layer of rich, dark soil beneath the azalea shrubs, already spindly for the summer. I've been daydreaming about her all morning, and now that it's nearly noon, the heat is starting to get to me. I need to finish this shit up and get inside.

But then the wind stirs again, blowing from the east. From the direction of the chapel.

I stop, my skin prickling like there's someone nearby that the Shadow Thorn wants for a sacrifice. Fuck. I don't want to deal with this right now. Burying the bones from the last one was enough Hartshorn work for me this morning.

But I don't think it's a sacrifice. There isn't that dark, coppery scent that always accompanies them, and I don't feel the surge of bloodlust roiling around in my belly. This is something else.

Ivy, I think distractedly, just as I hear my name on the wind. "Gideon!"

I hear it again, louder this time, and I recognize the voice.

Panic seizes through me, even though, thank god, all the bones are safely tucked under ground where they're supposed to be.

Because it *is* Ivy. She's here, on the estate.

I toss the shovel into the grass and take off in the direction of her voice, wanting to intercept her before she gets too close. Her mind's still wrapped up tight from that magic Gran and Gloria did ten years ago, and I don't want it coming unravelled.

"Ivy!" I call out, jogging through the heat. I pass the swimming pool, which is as still and bright as diamonds, and then duck through the garden gate.

That's when I spot her, running across the big meadow. The Shadow Thorn lurks nearby, watching us from the dark green shadows of the woods. Orchestrating this?

I have the thought, sudden and sharp, that I need to take her to the chapel and fuck her until she remembers everything.

No. No, I can't. Gran said it could split her mind in two.

"Gideon!" Ivy's voice drags me out of my thoughts. She sounds relieved.

I jog over to her as she slows down her own pace, and she stares up at me, her face flushed red and her hair wild. "Oh, thank god, you're here. I—" She pauses to take a deep breath, her breasts rising and falling beneath the thin fabric of her top.

"What's wrong?" I smooth her damp hair away from her face while she catches her breath. Gran said to keep her away from the house, but she needs to get out of the heat. As long as I keep her from the chapel, she should be fine.

But then she gasps, "Your brother," and my whole body goes cold.

"What about him?" I manage to keep my voice measured and calm, even as panic thumps through my chest. If he hurt her—

"I saw him in the woods," Ivy says dazedly. When she looks up at me, her eyes are pained.

Immediately, I look over her shoulder, at the army of trees that stand sentinel between Ivy's house and Hartshorn proper.

"Let's get you inside," I say, deciding almost on a whim. I circle my arm around her shoulder, and she leans into me, her skin hot from exertion. "You need some water."

"I need to tell you something," she pants out.

"Once we're inside." My chest feels tight. Fuck, I wish I knew how to stop Xavier from doing this bullshit meddling.

"No, I need to tell you now." Ivy shakes her head. "Xavier—he was in the woods—and he—" She blinks, her eyes big and sorrowful. "He kissed me."

She says it like a confession, like she did wrong. I suppose I should feel jealous, but jealousy isn't the emotion coiling in my stomach. It's something more primal. An urge to protect her from whatever he's planning.

"Inside," I say. "Then you can tell me everything that happened, okay?"

She nods at that, and I guide her back toward the house, moving her along quickly. I just hope she doesn't notice me glancing back over my shoulder, looking to see if Xavier has followed us.

He hasn't. But the Shadow Thorn is still here, like a single patch of dark cloud in the hot, sunny sky.

I relax once we're inside. The old wing is dark and cool, a balm after being out in the heat, and His presence isn't so strong here. Ivy blinks at the entranceway like she's seeing the house for the first time. She's not, of course, but I imagine it feels like she is.

But then she says, softly, "I remember all this."

"Hasn't changed much, has it?" I try to act normal, not wanting to trigger some memory she's not supposed to have anymore.

"Not really." She drifts forward, and I wonder if she remembers how to navigate this place, all its twisty, sideways hallways and sudden rooms. The new wing is even worse for that sort of thing, because my great-grandfather wove magic into its walls. The whole house is meant to be a sigil of power. A prayer to a nightmare.

"This way," I tell her, tugging her gently toward me. I take her into my den, which hasn't been updated since Uncle Jack moved his family out, save for a new flatscreen TV that I mounted on the wall. Same ratty old furniture and scuffed hardwood floors.

Ivy sinks down on the sofa, staring listlessly ahead at the unused fireplace. "Are you angry with me?" she asks softly.

Her question brings me up short. "No," I answer truthfully. I sit on the couch beside her. "But I am angry with Xavier. Have been since you told me he snuck into your house."

And did fucking magic so he could invade your dreams. But I keep that part to myself.

Ivy stares straight ahead, her arms draped over her knees, her back hunched. "I told him to stop," she says numbly. "I told him—" She cuts herself off and then tilts her head to look at me. "He said you shared women."

My whole body freezes, save for a sick coiling in the pit of my stomach. That *motherfucker.* We had a goddamn agreement not to talk about that shit. It was all his idea anyway, dragging me to that stupid Five Courts club in Houston. Introducing me to one woman after another, each one looking more and more like Ivy until I couldn't say no.

Ivy's still staring at me, waiting for an answer. I take a deep, shuddery breath. I don't want to lie to her any more than I already have to.

But then she says, "It's true."

I look down at my hands because I can't look at her. "It's complicated," I finally mutter. "But yeah, it's true."

"Are you going to share me?"

The question comes out very quiet. I jerk my gaze over to her.

"No," I say darkly. "Absolutely not."

An emotion flickers across her face. Relief? Disappointment?

Something slams against one of the den's windows, making Ivy jump.

"It's just the crepe myrtle," I tell her, putting my hand on her shoulder. She doesn't pull away. "I need to cut it back."

Ivy nods, wraps her arms around her chest. "I'm sorry," she says. "I just—I'm a little shook up."

"I'll tell Xavier to stay away from you."

"It's not just that."

There's that coiling again. My skin prickles.

"I mean, you can still tell him to…" Ivy's voice trails off, and she looks over at me, her face unreadable. "He forced himself on me, so yeah, definitely, if you can talk to him…"

She liked it, I think, with a sudden, chilling clarity. She liked that Xavier wrung a kiss out of her.

Something hot and black surges up inside me, but it's not jealousy and it's not anger.

"Then what else is it?" I lean close to her, mostly because I have a sudden urge to *be* closer to her, to feel her warm skin against mine.

"You won't believe me," she says weakly. "But I can show you. These flowers—they grew all over my porch. Overnight."

This time, the chill that freezes me in my place goes straight to the marrow of my bones. "What kind of flowers?"

"Bougainvillea, I think." She stares at me, eyes searching my face. "So you didn't see it when you left?"

I shake my head numbly. Except—

No, that's not true. I saw it by the garden hose. It must have taken over when I left.

I know what it means when plants appear suddenly in one

place, when they take over like a virus. This is Xavier's fucking magic.

"I went out through the front door," I say stiffly, because I don't know what else to say.

"Oh." She looks down at her hands. "The deadbolt was open, so I thought—" She shakes her head. "I know bougainvillea can grow fast, but it can't cover an entire porch overnight."

"I'll clear it for you," I say, cupping her face. Anything to stop talking about this.

"But how did they grow so fast?" she asks. "And there have been other things. Like Golly's computer, the last time I was here—did I tell you about that? How it caught on fire?"

"No." My body vibrates. That sounds like the Shadow Thorn's handiwork. He uses the elements to send his messages. But I don't know what He could be telling her.

"It was so strange. I was just looking at old pictures—" Ivy's eyes glaze a little. "I don't even remember what they were. Pictures of the house—or the yard—"

"It doesn't matter." I need to ground her back to me. She shouldn't be here, in the house. She's too fucking close to the chapel, and I think the house is affecting her, like it's tightening those two spells into a vise around her mind.

"Why is everything so strange?" Ivy whispers, tears glimmering in her lashes.

"Because," I murmur, running my thumb over her lips. "Because you're at Hartshorn."

And then I kiss her, because that grounded her before, in the cemetery. And it works here, too. Ivy makes a low, hungry moan and collapses into me, her tongue plunging through my lips. I pull her on top of me, and she notches into place immediately, spreading her legs on either side of my hips and then grinding down on my quickly hardening cock.

"Gideon," she murmurs against my lips. "You're the one I want. Not—"

"Shhh." I kiss her more deeply and run my hands over her breasts. As much as it swells my ego to hear her confirm that, what I really need right now is to be inside her, to fuck away whatever spells Xavier thinks he's working on her.

"God, you feel so good," she moans between kisses, her hips rocking furiously against me. I wrap my arms around her waist and flip her onto her back, the sofa scraping against the floor with the force of the maneuver. Ivy moans and arches her back as I yank up her shirt to reveal her soft, smooth stomach.

"I'm going to fuck you right here," I tell her, unbuttoning the fly of her shorts. My fury at my brother is calcifying inside me, turning to hard, cold determination. I'm not just going to the fuck his magic out of her. I'm going to wash it out of her.

I yank her shorts down over her hips and then bow down to kiss her lower belly. "I'm gonna make you come," I mutter into her skin, moving my lips up to her tits, which I free by shoving her bra up around her neck. "And I'm gonna mark you so my brother knows you belong to me."

The words are out of my lips before I even realize I was going to say them. Ivy moans and gyrates against me. She likes the sound of it, even though I'm not sure she one hundred percent understands what I mean.

Because Xavier might think he's so clever, working his magic all over her back door and marking her porch up like a fucking dog. But if that's how he wants to play, I'll play. I might not know magic, but I can mark *her* just fine.

I've already smeared her with my blood; might as well complete the trifecta. Shoot my load on her tits. Piss on her pretty clit. Whatever it takes to let Xavier know who Ivy Myste really belongs to.

Beneath me, Ivy moans and bucks her hips, already spreading her legs for me.

And outside, the Shadow Thorn's dark wind batters at the windows.

29

IVY

Gideon rips my clothes away with a furious urgency that makes me feel completely out of control. His nails scrape against my skin as he wrenches off my bra, leaving little stinging streaks in their wake, and I think of what Xavier said to me, about how Gideon keeps all the pain for himself.

Do not think of Xavier, I tell myself, and it's an easy enough instruction to follow, especially when Gideon rocks back on his heels and peels his T-shirt over his head to reveal his thick, muscular chest and the map of tattoos wrapping around his skin.

"You belong to me," he growls, shoving his shorts down over his hips just low enough to yank out his cock, already heavy with need. "Not my brother. Do you understand?"

A weird, hot thrill ripples through my body, and I don't answer right away. For some delirious reason, I want to see what happens if I stay quiet.

"Do you understand?" Gideon roars, pressing me down into the sofa cushions. His eyes are wild and feral, and liquid heat immediately floods into my core. I don't think I've ever been so wet.

"Yes," I croak out, bucking my hips up toward him.

Gideon grins. "Then you won't mind if I mark my property, will you?"

Electricity shoots through me when he says *property*, and I can't believe how much I like it, the way he talks about me like I'm a valuable patch of land, an inheritance the two brothers are squabbling over.

"No," I gasp.

"Good fucking girl," he snarls, yanking down my panties and flinging them over his shoulder. He shoves my legs apart, his movements rough and calculated. Cool air blows across my soaked pussy.

"That got you wet, didn't it?" he murmurs, rubbing his massive cockhead over my slit, his eyes on mine the whole time. "The idea of me marking you? Proving you belong to me?"

"Yes," I whimper, grinding against him like I can draw his cock into my cunt.

Gideon's grin widens. He looks like a madman, with his long hair sticking out in wild curls around his face and the points of his canines digging into his lower lip.

"That's what I want to hear."

Then he thrusts his hips and shoves his cock home.

I'm wet for him, but it still hurts, having him go in so suddenly. I shriek and jerk on reflex, but Gideon pins me down with his weight, settling his length inside me. He pushes my hair away from my face and leans in close.

"You're mine," he purrs. "You're exactly where you need to be."

"Underneath you," I murmur.

His eyes flash. "Exactly."

Then he starts to piston his hips, slamming so deeply inside me the pain blooms like pleasure. And I think, just for a second, that Xavier is wrong. Gideon is more than happy to give me the pain I apparently crave so much.

Then Gideon kisses me without breaking his steady, pounding rhythm, and I'm not thinking about Xavier at all anymore. He plunges his tongue into my mouth, his hair falling like a curtain around us. I moan into his mouth, the pain of his thrusts melting away into a wet, liquid arousal.

But then he breaks the kiss and jerks back and says, "Slap me."

"What?" I blink, so distracted from the pleasure and pain of his fucking that I'm sure I misheard.

"Slap me," Gideon growls, "in my fucking face."

Something hot and unfamiliar surges up in me, a winding cyclone of lust that feels like the hot, wet wind that's always blustering through the woods.

"Do it," he snarls, driving his cock deep enough into me that it strikes my cervix.

Agony tears through my core, and then, almost on instinct, my palm strikes against his cheek.

"Harder," he growls, jackhammering into me again. "I know you can do it, baby girl. Make me fucking hurt."

Lust surges in me again, and I slap him a second time, this time with every ounce of my strength. It's hard enough that Gideon's head jerks sideways and his thrusts slow. For a moment, he rolls against me, his chest heaving, and I'm afraid I went too far.

He turns his gaze back to me, eyes wild beneath the tangle of his hair, and I feel a sudden, wild sense of fear—

What are you doing this is fucking crazy this isn't how you're supposed to—

"Again," he snarls. "Just like that."

And I do as he says, striking him hard enough that there's a loud cracking sound as his head jerks sideways. Gideon moans and ruts against me like an animal. He doesn't have to ask me to slap him again, though. Because I do it on my own. I hit him with my left hand, not quite as hard, and he grins and chuckles and keeps fucking me, his cock a rod of fire sliding through my wetness. I don't know what I'm feeling—if it's lust or power or both. But I want to keep hurting him.

So I do. As Gideon fucks me, I keep slapping him, my hips rolling in time with his thrusts. I slap him across his face, across his chest. He groans each time my palm makes impact, and I love the wet, angry sound of it. I love the way my hand stings afterward, my own gift of the pain I crave as much as him.

"That's it, baby," he gasps, red marks already appearing on his skin. "Keep going until I piss in this perfect fucking pussy."

I don't register what he says at first. Then it hits me with as much force as one of my slaps. And it gives me the same feeling, too: lust and fear and confusion all wrapped up together.

"What?" I shriek.

Gideon stills inside me and twines his hand up in my hair, pressing me down against the couch. "I told you," he says, eyes boring straight into mine. "I want to mark my property."

He rolls his hips, just a little, just enough to put pressure on my clit. I gasp out and grab his big arms, squeezing the muscles and softness there.

"And this cunt is mine," he breathes.

It feels good, what he's doing—this slow, rhythmic grinding against my clit. I was already halfway to coming, and now he's dragging me even closer.

"What about the couch?" I whimper.

"Fuck the couch," he says. "Claiming you is more important."

Lust surges through me. Because all I want in this moment is to be claimed. To be *his*.

"Last chance to tell me to stop," he says through strained teeth.

I drop my head back against the sofa, distantly aware that

I'm grinding up against him, heat swelling in my core. I know he'd honor it if I told him no. He's not like his brother.

And that, I realize with a whole-body shudder, is why I want this as badly as I do.

"Do it," I spit out, my legs shaking uncontrollably. I'm so close to coming.

Gideon grins. "That's my good girl," he growls. Then his eyes flutter closed, and he goes still. For a second, he looks like he's concentrating hard on something.

Then I feel it. A hot gush of liquid deep inside me. And it feels fucking *good*. Like running a shower head over my pussy and having a finger shoved up my cunt at the same time.

I shriek, digging my nails into Gideon's skin as his piss fills me to bursting. I can feel myself tipping over from the pressure.

"That's it, babygirl," he purrs, his mouth on my throat. "That's it. You're mine now."

I have a single, frantic thought: *Oh my god, I'm going to come from this*, and then I do, my entire body contracting with intense, hot waves of pleasure. I scream through the ecstasy, slamming my fists down on the couch.

Distantly, I'm aware of Gideon sliding his cock out of me. Then his hot, strong piss hits right on my clit, and a second smaller orgasm ripples through me, making me arch and thrash beneath Gideon's stream.

"You like that?" Gideon growls, his stream still steady against my throbbing clit. He hunches over me, his gaze inches from mine, pinning me in place. "You like knowing you belong to me?"

I'm too lightheaded to do anything but nod.

Gideon's stream fades away to a dribble, and I gasp softly with a shuddery disappointment. But Gideon shoves his cock inside me again with a wet squelch, and I cry out as he fucks me again with those hard, jackhammer strokes from earlier. I don't even care that the couch is drenched beneath us, or that my entire lower body is soaked.

He marked me. I'm his. I belong to him.

Gideon grabs my hair and forces me to look up at him.

"Tell me," he says. "Tell me how much you like coming from my piss."

Something's changed in him. That feral wildness in his expression is overwhelming, and he slams into me, using me for his pleasure in a quickly cooling pool of filth—

And *god*, I fucking love it.

"Yes," I gasp out. "Yes, I loved it."

"So did I, babygirl." Gideon drags me up by the hair to kiss me with a hungry, animalistic force. "You have no idea how fucking hot you looked. Just completely at my mercy."

Pleasure courses through me, making me tremble. I *was* at his mercy. Pinned down. Degraded.

"It— felt— incredible." My words come out jostled and panty, each one punctured by another of his violent thrusts. My legs tremble. I'm going to have a third orgasm. But by now, with Gideon, I'm used to it.

"Too bad I emptied everything out," he says with a smirk. "Or I'd piss on those pretty tits, too. But I've got something else they can have." He tightens his grip on my hair. "You ready for my cum?"

Lust coils in my belly. "I'm close to— to coming again. If you could just hold out—"

"Sorry, baby." Gideon rises to kneeling, still slamming into me. "You feel too fucking good."

He yanks his cock out with a roar, just in time for his cum to fall across my breasts and belly in thick, warm ropes. I moan at the contact.

"Rub it into your tits for me," Gideon orders, his fingers already on my pussy. "While I finish you off."

I do exactly as he says, gathering up his thick, hot cum and working it into my skin like a lotion. Gideon fingers my sensitive clit with his expert touch, his eyes boring into me the whole time, his gaze like a predator watching me in the woods.

What do you want to be? The victim or the perpetrator? The predator or the prey?

With that thought, my orgasm shudders through my center. Gideon milks it out of me, sliding two fingers into my pussy to press up against my G-spot. I groan and roll into his hand, not caring that I'm writhing around in his filth.

"Perfect," Gideon says. "That's what I want to see. My property melting for me."

My body gives one last violent shudder, and Gideon slides his hand away from my pussy and up over my belly, between my breasts, and then around my throat. He keeps his touch gentle, though. Not choking. It feels protective.

I flutter my gaze up to him, and for a moment, we just stay like that. The wildness has gone out of Gideon's expression, and his eyes search my face, looking almost worried.

"Are you okay?" he whispers.

He's Gideon again, sweet Gideon, who brings me barbecue and acts nervous about inviting me on a date.

I nod, and relief passes over his face. He pulls me up, holding me against his sweat-damp chest. I kiss over his tattoos, soft and fluttery until I reach his neck, and then I just nuzzle against him, breathing in the woodsy scent of his skin rather than the lingering tang of ammonia rising around us.

"Although I need a shower," I murmur into his neck. "And we ruined the couch."

"Don't worry about the couch," he says. "We've got plenty of furniture in this house, and destroying a forty-year-old couch was more than fucking worth it to do that to you."

I blush. "That's weirdly flattering."

"I meant for it to be flattering. Now, as for the shower—"

Gideon sweeps me up into a bridal carry. I cling to him, giggling at the dizzying feeling of being lifted in his arms.

"We'll take care of that right now," he says.

I squeeze him around the neck, settling up against his chest so that I can feel the soft fluttery beat of his heart as he carries me out to the hall and into a large bathroom, the window over the tub letting in streams of bright sunlight.

He sets me down on the counter and kisses me, twining his hands through my hair, and I can hear the wind outside, like it's trying to tear down the walls to get to us.

30

XAVIER

I can't fucking breathe.

I lean against the hot stone of the house, rage pounding in my head like a migraine. Fucking Gideon. How the *fuck* did he have that in him?

Shaking, I peel away from the wall so I can peer in through the window again. They're gone. My rage courses even hotter, and I wonder what he's doing to her now that I can't see. Tying her to his bed and flogging her until his dick's hard again so he can fuck her a second time? No, that's what I would do. He'll probably have her flog him.

I whip away from the window, my hands curled up into fists. After our kiss, I followed Ivy out of the woods, although I hung back when I realized she was talking to Gideon. He had been in the garden, burying a bunch of old sacrifice bones, but he met her out in the courtyard so she wouldn't see what he was up to. If she had, there's no way she would have let him do all that filth to her.

My cock throbs, straining against my clothes. I despise that it's hard, that it got hard while I watched them through the window. And yeah, I saw *all* of it. I watched my unworthy brother tear Ivy's clothes off her body and watched as she slapped him—with strength, with *vigor*. I'd be lying if I didn't feel a swell of pride that she has that sadistic streak in her. That's why she's meant to be *mine*.

But he one-upped me, that fucking bastard. I marked her door, so he marked her cunt. And she let him. I heard her screaming in pleasure while he did it, too, even if her voice was muffled through the thick glass of the windows.

I rub my cock distractedly, loathing myself but wanting to relieve some of the tension. This is not how this is supposed to happen. I have magic on my side, and what does Gideon have? An oversized dick?

My thoughts roil around as I stalk past the swimming pool and into the gardens. I hardly realize where I'm going until I'm at the cemetery, the gravestones gleaming like bones in the sunlight. I stare at them, sullen and jealous, my cock so hard it's painful.

Part of me wants to turn around and slam back into the house and interrupt whatever filthy things they're doing right now. Hundreds of furious, lustful images fill my head—Ivy bound up in shibari ropes, Ivy hanging from hooks in the ceiling, Ivy screaming as Gideon lashes her with a steel-tipped flogger.

Except none of those things are Gideon's style, are they? And frankly, he only conjured up the will to degrade her on that ugly old sofa because of the magical territory marking I did last night.

But god, I could make Ivy hurt so beautifully. She would be exquisite wrapped in my ropes, the binds pulled so tight that her lush, perfect tits turn purple. I got my first real glimpse of them earlier, bouncing up under her chin as Gideon rutted into her like a goddamn animal, and I focus on that memory of them now. Not bouncing but still, held in place by my handiwork, nipples swollen with blood. In my mind, I flick them with my nail and relish the sound of Ivy's pained screams.

The wind gusts with a violent surge, and I smell decay on the air, sweet and heady. It's coming from the chapel.

"Fuck off," I mutter. "You aren't getting shit from me. Not when you couldn't uphold your end of the bargain."

I immediately regret saying that; the hot sun overhead suddenly seems to pour all of its heat directly onto me, as if I'm an ant and the Shadow Thorn is holding some eldritch magnifying glass over my head. I screech, falling hard onto my hands and knees as my skin burns like I'm wreathed in fire.

"I'm sorry!" I scream. A few heartbeats later, it stops. The wind rustles; the insects sing. The heat is gone, and my skin's untouched save for a prickle of discomfort that reminds me of who my family serves. Of who I serve.

"I'm sorry," I say again, staring out at the graveyard. No crosses on our markers, that's for damn sure. Just white statues of the Shadow Thorn, carved to look like other things. Trees. Vines. An angel with bat wings and a broken halo and a cruel, stern expression.

That's Orpheus Hartshorn's grave, the one who burned the chapel and built the house. My great-great-grandfather. The Shadow Thorn chose him when he was a boy, a preacher's son, and told him he was destined for something more.

That statue seems to stare at me from the shadows beneath the oak tree, tugging me forward. I push back up to standing, feeling agitated more than angry now. Listless.

If Gideon wants to escalate, then I'll fucking escalate.

I cut through the cemetery, moving with a heavy determination. I haven't been to the chapel in ages. I usually skip out on the yearly rituals these days. Make sure I'm in Houston when the time comes, claiming some Five Courts business. I never had much use for religion. Magic's one thing—that can get me what I want. But my family's endless blood-soaked rituals always felt like a waste of time.

Now, though, I question that attitude. Because who *does* go to every one of those goddamned things? Gideon.

And look what it's got him.

The hedge appears up ahead, as thick and thorny as I remember. Gideon maintains it now that Uncle Jack has moved out to the middle of nowhere, and it looks like he takes the work seriously. He's cultivated the yaupon holly and lantana and rockrose so they braid together into a wall of greenery and flowers—a barrier between our world and the world of the Shadow Thorn.

The chapel itself looks how I remembered, its charred walls peeking up over the hedge. The oak trees grow low here, their heavy branches forming a new roof since the original burned over a century ago.

It feels like I remember, too. Dead silent. No insects or twittering birds. No wind rustling through that cathedral of oak branches. But the air is all sparking like the molecules are on fire, and He's here, watching from the green shadows.

"This is what you want?" I say, and my voice is muffled, swallowed up by the enormity of this place.

There's no answer, although the hairs on my arms stand on end, and my cock, which had softened a little in the walk over here, turns to granite again. I'm not thinking about Gideon desecrating my Ivy, though. I'm thinking about the time I brought her here when we were thirteen. I decided that summer that she was going to be mine. That I was going to bring her into the family, the way my father did my mother.

I walk over to the chapel entrance, a narrow gap in the hedge guarded by a stone statue like the one marking Orpheus Hartshorn's grave. Its carved stone eyes bore into me, goading me on.

And then I pass through the boundary, and I'm in the

chapel itself, the only holy place my family can ever go. The sound is even stranger inside the hedge—that odd, eerie buzzing that comes from everywhere and nowhere. I stare up at the burned remains of the church, and I feel the Shadow Thorn pass through me and over me.

After I kissed Ivy when we were thirteen, Gloria's daughter lost her shit over it. I remember sitting next to the AC vent so I could eavesdrop while she screamed at Gloria and Gran. She didn't *want* Ivy in the family, she kept saying. She said the Hartshorns were fucking monsters.

And Gran relented. I don't know if she decided on her own or if Gloria had to convince her, but it doesn't matter. They took the memory away and denied me my prize.

Well, they aren't the only ones who can work magic.

"Give it back," I say, my voice echoing inside my head. "Make Ivy remember what we did." Power surges in me, as hot as arousal. "Make her remember that she's mine."

A cyclone wind scorches around the chapel, hot and blustery and laced with black magic. It blows me up to the church's carcass and through the broken doorframe until I'm inside. The chapel has been open to the elements for decades, and everything is wild and overgrown with honeysuckle and sunflowers and thick, feathery ferns. Half the pews are rotted away, giving themselves over to the earth.

The only unnatural thing in the entire chapel is a statue of the Shadow Thorn, rising in the place where the altar was, when this was a Baptist church and Orpheus Hartshorn burned it all down.

Sacrifice.

The word materializes in my head, and excitement prickles over my skin.

"Who do you want?" I say breathlessly. "Or can I choose some—"

I'm cut off by a low, ominous rattle. I glance sideways

toward the pews, where a timber rattlesnake moves in on itself into a coil.

"A snake?" I say, watching it warily. "That's all?"

It must suffer for her, or she will suffer instead. I hear the voice on the wind and in the rhythm of the snake's rattle. *And you have no weapon.*

I frown at that, the snake getting tighter and tighter, preparing to strike. Fear ripples through my chest. This is harder than killing a human, to be honest. I like snakes.

I move closer to the rattler. It hisses, the pink forked tongue vibrating. But every step closer to it reminds me of bringing Ivy here when we were kids. She'd been nervous, her voice breathy and soft, and she had peered around the chapel with wide, terrified eyes. *Is it safe?* she asked, looking up at the lattice work of three ancient ceiling beams caught between the snare of the oak's branches.

Of course it is, I told her, taking her hand in my own. Her palm had been damp from the summer's warmth, and when I finally kissed her, right in front of the statue on the altar, she had tasted of salt, like the sea.

The snake's rattle tears through the memory. It hisses again, and I'm close enough that I can see its pale, hollow teeth.

"Fuck," I mutter, leaning close—

The snake strikes, moving as fast as lightning. But the Shadow Thorn guides my hand, and I catch it behind the head so it can't get its teeth into me. Its tail whips out and then wraps around my forearm and tightens like a vise.

If it doesn't suffer, she will lose her mind.

"Fuck!" I shout, slamming the snake down on the pew. It hisses and loosens around my arm, and I fling it hard against the charred stone. It hits with a thump and slides down, leaving a smear of blood in its wake.

I take a deep, shuddery breath. "Was that enough?" I ask, keeping my eyes on the snake. It doesn't move.

It was enough.

I make my way over to the wall and pick up the snake. Its head hangs crooked, its eyes glossy. It feels limp in my hand as I carry it over to the altar.

The statue glares down at me. It's a hideous thing—carved out of some kind of hard black stone, a swarm of limbs and tentacles twisted around a single, monstrous face. According to the family lore, Orpheus burned the church down to cleanse the land, and when the fire died away, this statue was waiting in the wreckage.

I kneel in front of it and drape the snake's body at its feet. Whatever floorboards had been here rotted away decades ago, and all that's left is thick, spongy forest floor. I clear the leaves and ferns away until there's a patch of dirt. Then I use an old stick to trace out words in a language I learned a long time ago, a language every Hartshorn learns, even the ones who marry into it, like my mother. Uncle Jack told me once it's the language of Hell. Sounds about right.

In English, the words I carve into the floor would say, *Release the first binding.*

The character for *first* looks like an eye wreathed in flame, and I gouge my stick hard into the earth for emphasis. Because Ivy has two bindings. One to hide what I did, and one to hide what Gideon did. And the last thing I want is her remembering what she did with Gideon.

I toss the stick aside and peer up at the statue. The air buzzes and sparks, and I can feel the energy of the place working across my skin like static electricity. *When you want something,* Uncle Jack taught me, *you just go to the chapel, you kneel in front of the Shadow Thorn, and you ask for it in His tongue.*

That's why I brought Ivy here when we were thirteen. Because even then, I knew I wanted to keep her forever. And now I'm going to make sure it fucking happens.

I stand up, step around my plea in the dirt, and run my palm over one of the statue's many jagged edges. It cuts me as easily as Gideon's precious knives, the ones he keeps out in his workshop.

Blood pours out of my cut, hot and thick. I step back and pull my throbbing cock out of my pants. The chapel's energy isn't just static electricity and weird, electronic buzzing. It's blood and sex, violence and cruelty and deep, thick pleasure. Sadism has always been my birthright.

I wrap my cut hand around my dick, sighing as the blood squelches up between my fingers. Blood doesn't make the best lube; it dries too quickly and turns sticky. But I'm so worked up right now, it doesn't matter. I stroke myself, angling my cock so the blood splatters across the plea I carved into the dirt, across the snake I killed to take on Ivy's madness.

While I touch my cock, I think of Ivy. I think of all the things I'm going to do to her when she remembers that she belongs to me. I'll tie her up in one of the spare rooms in the house, naked and spread-eagle on the floor, so I can make her come over and over until she's begging me to stop. I'll whip her back until she's bleeding, then fuck her from behind so I can admire the wounds. I'll dose a bottle of wine with sleeping pills until she's knocked out, then play with her limp body. I'll choke her until she passes out.

I'll hurt her once for every year she denied me. And then she'll beg for more. Because she's fucking mine.

My balls draw up tight to my body. Heat courses through my erection. Blood pulses out of the cut on my hand.

Then I groan, throwing my head back as my cum arcs out and splatters across my plea. Immediately, the air in the chapel changes. It becomes hard to breathe, and my lungs are tight and choking. I drop down to my knees, watching the statue of the Shadow Thorn. It looks the same as it did when I started, at least superficially. But there's a spark there in those carved black eyes, cruel and glinting.

The scales of the dead snake darken, like it's filling with ink.

"Do it," I whisper, shaking my hand so more blood splatters across the words in the dirt. This time, it sizzles a little, and curls of acrid black smoke drift up and waft around me. "Do it. Make her remember."

The statue glowers at me. The dead snake, now solid black, stirs and slithers around the base of the statue, its rattle still. It belongs to the Shadow Thorn now.

And then my blood and my seed sizzle and pop and suck into the soil with a wet, slurping sound.

I gasp in relief and fall to my knees, my bloody cock flopping against my shorts. The air clears; a breeze rustles the oak branches, making the shadows move.

It's done.

I fall backward, lying out on the damp, soft ground. I can breathe again, but I feel exhausted. Drained. But that's the price of making a deal with the Shadow Thorn.

It's done. Ivy will remember. And there's nothing Gideon can do about it.

Now, I just have to wait.

IVY

I get dressed in Gideon's bedroom after the shower, my body still buzzing from what we did. He's in the next room, his voice a soft murmur as he talks on the phone. An actual landline phone, so I guess he wasn't lying about there being no reception out here. Although he did get a text while we were... indisposed.

"Sorry, gotta call this guy back real quick," he told me when he saw it, then kissed me on the forehead. "It's about a show. This won't take long."

He did bring me my clothes before he called, though. I pull on my shirt and go over to the window, which looks out over the garden. Dots of color bloom amid the green.

In the next room, Gideon laughs. I like it, his laughter. It's warm and rumbly and makes me feel safe, even in this rambling, creepy old house. And knowing the sort of filthy things he's willing to do—the sort of things I'm willing to *let* him do—

I press my thighs together at the memory. God, that had no right being as hot as it was. It should have been disgusting, and I guess it was. But it felt so unbelievably good, too. Just like our first night together, when he pressed that razor blade into my fingers and told me to cut.

Outside, something flickers through the rose bushes. It's a flick of a shadow, but it makes the hair on my arms stand on end. I frown, pressing closer against the glass.

There it is again. A movement in the greenery. But I can't see what it is.

Just a bird, I tell myself. Or a rabbit. A snake. Some other animal. We're basically in the woods.

There's another spark of movement, like something's darting through the garden. Except there's nothing there. It's just the sense of a presence.

It reminds me of something.

I step away from the window, my heart thudding. Gideon's still on the phone, but the walls are thick and I can't make out what he's saying. He laughs again.

"It's nothing," I whisper, although I *know* it's not. Where did I feel that weird, prickling sensation before? It was—

Images flash through my head, one after another. Xavier, but he's a teenage boy. Thirteen or so. We're sitting on a couch together, a horror movie playing in the background. *I need to show you something. It's a surprise.*

The two of us walking through a narrow, dark hallway. It was part of Hartshorn. A servant's hallway, Xavier told me. A secret passageway.

Then we're outside. The images come faster, all in a jumble. A hot, sunny meadow. The heavy, humid woods. The cemetery.

A burned church.

I stumble backward until my legs hit Gideon's bed, and then I collapse down on the edge of it, taking deep, sucking breaths. Gideon sounds a million miles away. That's where I felt that sensation before. Xavier took me to see the ruins of an old church in the woods, and the whole time I felt like something was in the trees, watching us.

But we weren't eight years old. We were thirteen. Mom had sent me and Juniper back to Golly's house the summer before I started high school. I *remember* it now, all the memories surging through my head like a flood. She had just gotten that new job and had to do two weeks of training in Chicago. She flew us into Houston. Golly picked us up and bought us snow cones on the drive into Harlan. I spent the whole time with Xavier. It had been hot, hotter than normal. He took me to his weird, burned-out church—

He kissed me.

My chest gets tight, and I can't move. That can't be right. I didn't have my first kiss until I was fifteen years old, at Danny Tafoya's party. I never kissed Xavier—

Except I did. The memory plays like a movie in my head. We were inside that burned-out church. He told me it was his family's church, and that I was practically a Hartshorn, so it was my church, too. Then he asked me if I wanted to pray, and I had no idea what he was talking about until he kissed me. I'd been so excited that someone like him would want to kiss me—

Gideon's footsteps fall heavy outside the bedroom. I jerk my head up just as he pushes the door open, his damp hair falling into his eyes.

I kissed his brother when I was thirteen years old. How could I have ever forgotten that? How could I have ever forgotten that I came here at all?

"Sorry," he says with a rueful smile. "That was a promoter out in Alabama. They want me to do a show this weekend..."

His voice trails off, and his sweet smile melts into a frown. "Ivy? Are you okay?"

I shake my head, but he's already rushing over to me. He pulls me into a hug. "I'm sorry if it was too much earlier. I-I got carried away, and—"

"No!" I kind of blurt it out because there's this two-second delay where I think he's talking about kissing me in the burned-out husk of an old church.

"Ivy?" Gideon tucks his fingers in my chin and tilts my head up, his green eyes brimming with concern. And I just melt for him. I don't want to tell him that I'm suddenly convinced I kissed Xavier fifteen years ago. Because it makes no damn sense. In all the times I've talked to Juniper and Mom about Hartshorn, we've only talked about that summer when I was eight.

"I think I just—I think the heat's getting to me."

Gideon's frown deepens.

"I was looking at the garden and started to feel woozy. I'm fine." I force a smile, although Gideon still looks doubtful. "Really," I add.

"Well, I'll drive you home, just to be safe."

The word *home* buzzes weirdly in my chest.

"Thanks." I give him another smile, and this one feels less forced. Gideon's shoulders seem to relax a little. "You can look at that bougainvillea I told you about."

"Yeah, of course. I probably won't get to cut it down til after my match, though." Something darkens in his face. A sense of hesitancy. "I'm going to be spending this weekend in Huntsville. You should come with me."

He says it casually enough, but I still sense the urgency between his words, almost like he's giving an order. *You* should *come with me*. As if something might happen if I don't.

But a queasy feeling worms around in my belly. I don't want to leave Texas. I don't even want to stray too far from Golly's house. "I probably shouldn't," I say. "My first class starts on Monday, and I still haven't gotten the course built out."

"Right." Gideon reaches over and squeezes my hand, and something about his fingers on mine flares the weird, alien memory of Xavier's kiss, how we had been standing up, and he put his hands on my hips and neither of us moved except for our mouths.

Do you like it, cicada? he asked when he finally pulled away. *Praying?*

"—could you work at the hotel?"

Gideon's voice drags me back into the present. I blink at him, working backward through the conversation. He was asking if I could work on my class at the hotel before the match.

He watches me, and the air feels heavy between us. My skin crawls with something like dread.

"I'll just miss you, that's all," he finally says, brushing his hand over my hair.

Affection surges in my chest, and all the weirdness of today leaches away. I throw my arms around Gideon's shoulders, and he makes a kind of surprised noise before he returns the hug, burying his nose in my damp hair.

"I'll miss you, too," I say softly. "But I have a lot to get done, and it'll be easier if I can work at home."

Gideon nods against me.

"I'll be fine," I tell him. "Really."

I just hope it's true.

I LEFT the back door open when I fled the house earlier. I find it after Gideon drops me off, revealing the vine-covered porch outside. Worse, though, the screen door had caught on that weird bougainvillea, so the house was open the whole time I was away. Leaves and blood-red blossoms spill across the kitchen tile.

"Fuck!" I shout, my heart twisting up in a panic. "Gnocchi?

Gnocchi, where are you?" I slam the door shut, trapping the plants outside where they belong. Then I run into the hallway, my heart pounding. I can't deal with Gnocchi getting lost out in the woods. Not with everything else that's going on.

Thankfully, I find him curled up in the armchair in the living room, snoozing peacefully.

"Good boy," I breathe out. "You know how to stay."

Gnocchi opens one eye, studies me, then closes it again.

I stroke his soft fur, then go back into the kitchen. I'd meant for Gideon to come in and look at the vines when he dropped me off, but I was so wrapped up in that memory of Xavier that I completely forgot. I don't call him back, though. I just sweep the leaves and blossoms up and drop them in the trash.

I know I need to deal with the bougainvillea, but I'm too shaken up from the pounding, insistent memory that I kissed Xavier Hartshorn when I was thirteen years old. It keeps ricocheting around in my head, worse now that Gideon's gone, and it feels too real and vivid to be from fifteen years ago.

I read somewhere once that we don't actually remember events; we remember memories of those events, and that's why things fade over time. They're like when you make a photocopy of a photocopy. The memory wears out, and you aren't remembering what happened, but what you think happened.

This memory of kissing Xavier, though—it's as strong and vibrant as my memory of surrendering to Gideon this afternoon.

I stare out the kitchen window, replaying the memory. In my head, I see Xavier as a teenage boy, his face still soft and childlike, his eyes dark, watching me in the dappled sunlight. It's the same dappled sunlight that now floods the kitchen. The bougainvillea has grown over the window.

That snaps me out of my head, just for a second. It wasn't

on the window this morning. But it's here now, blocking the sun and scraping against the glass.

I flee the kitchen and wind up in the dark living room. My phone's sitting on the table where I left it this morning, and I snatch it up, my heart pounding. More messages from Mom and Juniper.

Juniper. Juniper can let me know if I'm losing my mind or not. If she doesn't remember coming here a second time—

Well, I don't know what I'll do. Because I remember it. Clearly.

I pull up her number with shaking hands. She answers on the first ring.

"Ivy? Oh my god, tell me you're okay. Mom is freaking out."

Hearing her voice grounds me. "Why? Because I haven't responded to any of her messages?"

"Um, exactly? What the hell, Ivy?"

"I don't feel like being chastised."

"Chastised?" Juniper's voice pitches up an octave. "Are you shitting me? You announced out of nowhere that you're moving to Texas for the summer and that you don't want to sell that fucked-up house, then you just—ignore us?"

"I'm not ignoring you," I say primly. "I'm literally talking to you right now."

"Yeah, well, why?"

The question feels like a slap.

"What do you mean?" I say carefully, although I know.

"You're not calling to check in," she says sharply. "You would have done that already. So what's wrong? Did something happen? Something with the Hartshorns?"

I swear the phone crackles and buzzes when she says their name. "No," I say. And then, for reasons I don't totally understand, I lie. "I haven't seen any of them."

Juniper makes a scoffing sound. "That's for the best. They were always off. Weird redneck freaks."

Redneck isn't exactly how I'd describe Judith or the two brothers, but I keep my mouth shut.

"So why are you calling?" Juniper says. "Decided living in the middle of nowhere sucks, so you want to come back home? You need a place to stay?"

"No," I snap. "I need to ask you something."

Juniper goes quiet. I take a deep breath. I'm going to hear no end of shit for asking this, but I have to know.

"We only came here once, right?"

A long pause. Then: "What do you mean?"

"When we were kids," I say slowly. "We only came here that one summer, right? When I was eight and you were six?"

"Yeah, of course," Juniper says.

My skin feels cold and clammy. The memory whispers at the edge of my thoughts.

"You're sure?" I say, a little bit of panic curdling my voice. "We only came here once? Not when I was thirteen?"

"Why the fuck would we have gone back there?" Juniper says. "Mom hated that place. She told me once that one of her biggest regrets was sending us there when we were kids. She would *never* have sent us back."

My skin prickles. I feel vaguely lightheaded. "Mom never told me that."

"Yeah, because you would have freaked out." Juniper laughs a little, kind of sharp and bitter. "You were always going on about how much you loved Golly's house, and Hartshorn, and how you wanted to visit again. Don't you remember that?"

I frown. As if I can trust my memory. "Sort of. I guess."

"You kept nagging Mom to let us go back there one Christmas, I remember—we were in high school, I think? Anyway, Mom told me later that she wished she'd never sent us there in the first place."

I push my hand through my hair, not sure what to do with

this information. I know Mom hates Hartshorn. I know she never really spoke to Golly, either. But I didn't realize it went *that* deep.

"But why?" I say. "It's not like anything happened."

Juniper laughs again. "Not to *you*. You were off running around with the weird blond boy—"

He flashes through my head. Eight years old. Thirteen. An adult.

"—But *I* had nightmares every night we were there. I could barely sleep."

I sink into the couch, staring at the blank TV fixed to the wall. I remember Juniper crying that summer. Coming into my room with her little stuffed rabbit, her eyes big and wet. Me telling her to go back to bed.

That memory, I can trust. But this other, with Xavier—

I don't know what to think.

"I didn't know that," I finally say. "Sorry."

"Yeah, well, now you do." Juniper pauses again. "Why are you asking about this? What made you think we went there twice?"

"Nothing," I say, too quickly. "Or just—being here's bringing back a bunch of memories. I was just curious."

Juniper gets quiet again, and I squirm around, trying to figure out what to say to fill the silence. But then she says, "Be careful."

"Of what?" I say, too sharply again.

"Of that *house*, Ivy." Juniper's voice sounds strained. Shaky. "Of that place. Stay away from the Hartshorn family at least, okay?"

"Fine." The lie comes out even easier this time. "I promise."

"And call Mom," Juniper adds. "Tell her you're safe. And—" She cuts herself off.

"And what?" I prompt, my heart thudding around.

"Be careful," she finally says, after another long, staticky pause. "That place—I think that place drives people crazy. And I don't want it to happen to you."

XAVIER

It's funny how well things can work out even when you aren't orchestrating them in the shadows. For example, I had *nothing* to do with Gideon getting invited to wrestle in Alabama this weekend, a nearly ten-hour drive from Hartshorn. But it couldn't have happened at a better time, could it?

I find out about it that evening, after their little betrayal in his living room and my spell-working in the chapel. We're all having dinner, me and Gran and Gideon. She insists on it, one of those old-fashioned Hartshorn things. Family dinner every night, even when it's not a sacrifice meal.

Tonight is not a sacrifice meal. We're having pork chops and mashed potatoes and a green salad. Nice, normal food for a nice, normal family.

"I'm gonna be gone a few days starting tomorrow," Gideon says out of nowhere. "Got to drive to Alabama."

Gran looks over at him, her eyes glinting from the chandelier light. "That's fine," she says. "But you need to hurry back. Another sacrifice is coming."

Gideon lifts his gaze from his plate, his dark hair hanging in his eyes.

Just like it was when he fucked my Ivy on his couch.

"I don't feel anything," he says flatly.

Gran smiles indulgently. "Because you're young," she says. "And you've been distracted. It'll probably be another week, maybe less. But it's coming."

Gideon's shoulders hitch, and he twitches his gaze over to me. I know what he's thinking, because there was a time, right after he took over the sacrifice duties from Dad, that he would say the same thing whenever a sacrifice was imminent.

Why can't Xavier do it?

He doesn't say anything now, of course. No point. It was decided a long, long time ago, a compromise between Mom and Dad. One child would follow in Dad's footsteps and take care of Hartshorn business here on the estate. The other would go into the city and keep up our connections with the Five Courts, per Mom's request. Her family is part of the Occult Underground, a loose assortment of sorcerers and demon-worshippers. It was a big deal for her to marry a Five Courts family like mine. She didn't want us to slip away from our duties.

"I'll be back before then," Gideon finally responds. "Monday at the latest."

Gran nods. "That'll give you plenty of time," she says, sawing at a pork chop.

"Is Ivy going with you?" I can't stop myself from asking. I know the answer, though. I can feel it crackling in the air around us.

"No," Gideon says. "She needs to work."

"A college professor," Gran says cheerfully. "Can you imagine? Teaching classes from all the way out here?"

"Miracle of the Internet," I say dryly, reaching for my wine. "She's lucky Dad had that fiber line put in." Hartshorn—and by extension, Gloria's farmhouse—had been without Internet until the early 2000s. And we still barely have cell service.

"We're all lucky," Gran says. "If it means that house doesn't have to sit empty." Her voice is thin, the way it gets when she's sad. "It's not right, you know. It needs someone in it."

It needs a Hartshorn in it, whether by blood or by magic. We all know that. Gloria was Hartshorn by marriage and magic both. Which I suppose makes Ivy a Hartshorn by blood, technically. But the link is weak. My magic will seal the deal.

Not Gideon's.

The air crackles, and when I look up from my plate, Gideon's watching me from across the table, his eyes cold and dark. Suspicious. I meet his gaze and pick up the red wine, daring him to say something. He doesn't, just glowers at me, and I take a long, satisfying drink.

Because there's nothing he can do. He's not going to give up a chance to go to one of his silly little wrestling matches—it's his one way of pretending he's not a part of this family, that he hasn't done all the dark, fucked-up shit we do right along with the rest of us. Even if that means leaving Ivy alone at Hartshorn.

With me.

I MAKE myself scarce after dinner, slipping up to the little servant's room on the third floor, where I've stashed the various magic books and assorted supplies I've filched from around the house the last few weeks. If Gideon leaves tomorrow morning, that means I'll have four days to make Ivy mine for good.

It'll be tricky, though, even with magic on my side. Love spells are bullshit; they'll make someone obsessed with you but not *want* you, not for real. Which means I have to do this the old-fashioned way. Good thing I have plenty of experience in seduction, although I'm not above calling on the Shadow Thorn to amplify Ivy's lust. It won't be hard. I felt it earlier in the woods. Tasted it on her lips as I kissed her. Some part of her wants me.

And that was even before I gave her back the memory of our childhood kiss. A perfect seed I can nurture and grow over the next few days.

I'm sitting at my desk, trying to work out the details, when I hear heavy footsteps out in the hall. I freeze, pen hovering above the paper, and listen.

It's Gideon. I know those stomping steps anywhere.

But does *he* know I'm in here? That's the real question. He's obviously looking for me; there'd be no reason for him to be sniffing around in the new wing of the house. The old wing's his domain these days.

The footsteps stop outside my door.

"Open the fuck up, Xavier."

I roll my eyes. He can't think it'll be that easy, that I'll just listen to him.

The doorknob rattles. He sighs, clearly annoyed, and I spin around in my chair so I'm facing the door, waiting for him when he busts in here like he did my bedroom. Because at the end of the day, for all his claims otherwise, that's the only way he knows how to do anything. Violence.

The knob rattles again, and then, to my annoyance, the lock clicks over.

"Decided to use a key this time?" I say as the door swings open.

Gideon glares at me from the doorway, so big and hulking that he nearly takes up the entire space, especially with the backlight from the hallway streaming around him.

"Stay the fuck away from Ivy," he says.

I blink and spread my hands through the air, feigning innocence. "Now, why would you say something like that?" I ask. "What do you think I'm going to do to her?"

"I know what you did to her house," he snaps. "There are fucking vines all over the back porch."

I laugh at that, genuinely startled—and pleased. My little back porch spell was more powerful than I realized, it seems. "All that tells me is the Shadow Thorn knows who she really belongs to." I lean back in my chair, tap my fingers on the armrests. "It's me, by the way."

Gideon's expression darkens, and I brace myself for him to throw himself at me. I can see the muscles bulging in his arms thanks to that stupid cut-off T-shirt he's wearing.

"She does not *belong* to you," he snaps. "I'm the one who claimed her properly. And anyway, she chose *me* when she came back. Not you." His eyes flash. "She thinks you're a creep, by the way."

"Does she?" I smile. "She didn't seem to think I was a creep when she was grinding that sweet pussy of hers against my thigh earlier today."

Anger flashes across Gideon's features, and he steps into the room, his hands curled into fists.

"Liar," he snarls. "She told me what happened. She didn't fucking want you. She *doesn't* fucking want you."

I don't say anything, just give him a cold, mocking smile.

"I mean it, Xavier." Gideon snorts like a bull. "You leave her alone while I'm gone."

"If you're so worried," I say lightly. "Why don't you take her with you?"

Oh, I got him there. A brief flicker of hurt passes through his eyes before he composes himself. "Because, unlike you," he says, "I don't force her to do something she doesn't want to do."

"Oh, so she doesn't want to go with you?"

"She has to work." The way he says it is too loud, too forceful. There's doubt there. Doubt because she wants to stay behind. "It's a long drive. And her class starts on Monday."

"Whatever you say." I lift my hands in false surrender. Gideon just keeps glaring at me. I know what he's doing, and I'm sure it's intimidating to the sacrifices who get corralled onto our property. But I'm not a sacrifice, and I know just how pathetic my brother can be. Especially when it comes to Ivy Myste.

"If I come back," he says with a slow, cold precision, "and I found you've done anything to her—if you've touched her again, if you've cast any more of your bullshit spells—" His eyes rage. "I'll kill you. I don't give a fuck about family tradition. I will cut out your heart and bury it in the garden next to all the rest of *my* sacrifices."

For a half second, I feel a quiver of real fear. Because he does sound serious. And I know how many hearts he's carved out in his lifetime.

But then I laugh. Maybe it's to cover up that fear. Maybe it's to mock him, to piss him off. To call his bluff.

"We're family." I rise to my feet. Gideon's eyes follow me, even though the rest of him doesn't move. "We're brothers, Gideon. And aren't brothers supposed to know how to share?"

Gideon's hand snaps and grabs my wrist, his grip like iron. Another jolt of fear quivers through me, and I fucking hate that he probably felt it.

"You don't want to share," he says in a low, growling voice. "You want her all to yourself so you can destroy her."

Then he shoves me, hard enough that I stumble backward and slam up against my desk.

"Touch her and I'll kill you," he says, right before he walks out of the room.

❦ 33 ❦

IVY

The next morning, someone knocks on my front door while I'm fixing breakfast in my eerie, green-tinted kitchen. I swear the bougainvillea is even thicker today, and I'm grateful that whoever it is came to the front, not the back.

When I answer, Gideon's waiting for me, his hair pulled back in a low ponytail and his face freshly-shaven. "Hey," he says. "Wanted to say goodbye before I head out."

I nearly melt on the spot. Last night, I had trouble sleeping—I kept tossing and turning in the creaking old bed, and I could hear the fucking bougainvillea scratching at the exterior wall like someone trying to claw their way inside. It was better when the sun came up, and it's even better now, with Gideon within arm's reach.

He won't be within arm's reach for long.

I shove the thought aside. I can't go with him. I have too much to do to get ready for my class on Monday. And the thought of leaving makes me queasy.

"I wish I could go with you," I say, pulling the door open so he can come inside. He does, sweeping me up in his arms and giving me one of those long, lingering kisses. Heat blooms in my core.

"Do you have time for that?" I murmur against his lips.

"No, unfortunately." He nuzzles against me. Kisses me again. "But I'm gonna take what I can get."

I blush; it's still strange for me, having a guy pay me this much attention.

Two guys, whispers a traitorous voice in the back of my head, one that I shove away immediately. Xavier absolutely does not count.

"You want some coffee for the road?" I ask. "Oh, and you should come look at those vines I told you about. I think they've gotten worse."

"I saw 'em already." Gideon brushes his hand over my hair. "Went around back to check them out." His eyes glitter strangely. "I'll cut them down when I get back, okay? I think you can hold out for the weekend."

There's something in his voice I can't place. A kind of forced cheeriness, maybe.

"I just don't want them to tear the porch down," I tell him.

"They won't."

Then he kisses me again, his hand curling up around the back of my head to pin me in place. And I'm not thinking about vines or about his brother or about anything else but him—his firm, strong body and the heat he sparks inside me.

"I don't need coffee," he says softly, brushing his lips against my ear. "Just this. A good luck kiss for the road." Then he nibbles against my neck, making me moan.

"You're getting me worked up. It's not fair."

"Getting myself worked up." He cups my cheek. "But it was worth it."

Then he pulls away, and his face is serious. Too serious, I think. "You still have my cell number, right?" he asks. "Because I'll have my phone turned on all weekend if you need me."

"Yeah, of course." I smile, trying to cut through the weird tension wrapping around us. "But I'll be fine, Gideon."

His mouth is tight, his eyes hard. "I told my brother to leave you alone," he says. "But if he doesn't, call me. Okay?"

As soon as he says *my brother*, my whole body tightens up. The memory-that-can't-be-a-memory flashes in my head, followed by an intense surge of guilt.

But why? It couldn't have possibly happened. And what did happen yesterday in the woods—that wasn't my fault.

"Okay?" Gideon prompts again.

"I promise," I tell him, squeezing his hands. "And I'll keep the deadbolt locked. Although it's not like he can come in through the back anyway, with the way the bougainvillea is blocking the door."

It's meant to be a joke, but it doesn't feel funny, not even to me. And Gideon certainly doesn't laugh.

"My match is on Saturday," he says. "Starts at 7:30 and will probably go until eleven or so. That's the only time I won't have my phone on me, okay?"

"Got it," I say, trying to hide the fact that his intensity makes me nervous.

And then, like that, he's gone. I stand on the porch and sip at my coffee long after he's jumped back in his car and roared down the dirt driveway, long after the dust has settled back into the grass.

He's gone, and I feel—strange.

I try to keep myself busy during the day. I focus on my class, working out of the living room with Gnocchi curled up beside me and the TV turned low, a reassuring background noise so I'm not jumping every time I think I hear someone stomping around outside.

Someone like Xavier.

But there's no sign of him. The summer's heat cocoons around the house, and I make it through half of my class prep by late afternoon. That's right around the time Gideon texts me, too, telling me he stopped in Jackson and he's thinking of me.

And that makes me think of him, and the way he marked me yesterday afternoon. That memory, at least, I can trust to be real, and I stretch myself out on the couch, sliding one finger up between my folds as I replay it in my head. But it keeps getting intercut with other images.

Like Xavier shoving me up against that tree in the woods.

Or someone fucking me from behind in that burned-down church while Gideon watches, grinning, stroking his beautiful cock.

I groan, arching my back, legs splayed wide. I imagine Gideon's between them. Then I imagine Xavier is.

I come with a deep, throaty yell, finger-fucking myself through the quakes. By that point, I'm not thinking of anything at all. Just a dark, twisted pleasure that twines around my heart like the thorny, bloody vines twining around my back porch.

I SHUDDER AWAKE, gasping at the fragments of the dream I just had.

Hartshorn. I dreamed of Hartshorn again. That hasn't happened since I came back.

I fight with the sweat-damp sheets, kicking them half off the bed. Then I slump down on the old mattress, breathing heavily as the fan circles overhead, dusting me with cool air. Gnocchi stirs at my feet and flicks his tail against my leg.

Something clicks against my window.

I freeze. It's not the vines, which are still scratching like fingers across the glass. This sounded like—

There's another click, loud and unmistakable. And I think that maybe it wasn't the dream that woke me up.

I fumble around on my bedside table for my phone. It lights up with the time. 2:55

Witching hour, I think vaguely.

Another click against my window. This time, I switch on the lamp, flooding the bedroom with light, and listen.

Nothing.

Well, not *nothing* nothing; I can still hear the vines scratching against the outer walls of the house. But I keep waiting for another click against the window that doesn't come.

I switch the light off again and slink over to the window, clutching my phone tight in one hand. At least I'm on the second floor. There's no way someone

Xavier

could be out there. Right?

I push the curtain aside and press my face to the glass. The moon is up, and it spreads soft, silvery light over the meadow and backyard.

No movement but the wind blowing through the grass.

I take a deep breath. *Stop psyching yourself out*, I tell myself, glancing down at the phone again. I know Gideon's in Huntsville—he called me earlier tonight when he arrived—but I don't want to wake him up. Not over some weird noises in my backyard.

Something creaks downstairs.

I freeze, eyes shooting over to the bed. Gnocchi blinks at me.

"It's the house settling," I tell him. Or tell myself.

Another creak. It sounds like it's coming from the stairs.

Gnocchi's ears flatten against his head, and panic surges up in my throat.

"Stay here," I whisper-hiss to him, but when there's another creak, this one long and ominous, he flies off the bed, a pale streak disappearing out into the hallway.

"Damn it!" I dart forward without thinking and stumble out into the hallway. Everything's just how I left it. Dark. Undisturbed. Gnocchi's nowhere to be seen.

I creep forward, my heart thudding. At least I still have my phone, and I pull up Gideon's number. But I don't press the call button. He's asleep, and I can't wake him over a bunch of weird noises in a hundred-year-old house and an easily spooked cat.

Another creak. I whirl around. All I can see are shadows and moonlight, which spills in from the window over the stairs. But those shadows seem to move, shifting and crawling over the walls.

"I'm going to call the cops!" I shout, feeling stupid.

And then I hear it: a low, rumbling chuckle.

"No, you're not, cicada."

Xavier steps out of the other guest bedroom, his hair the same color as the moonlight.

The phone slips out of my hand and lands with a crack on the hardwood floor.

"Get out of my house," I whisper. But there's no vehemence to it.

"No." Xavier ambles forward, his eyes never leaving mine. "No, darling. I don't think I will."

And then he lunges toward me, and I'm not quick enough to escape him.

34

XAVIER

Ivy smells like the woods right before a thunderstorm and like the honeysuckle that grows over the chapel hedge and blooms in the spring. She smells like fate.

I shove her up against the wall, hard enough that one of Gloria's photographs slides to the floor and cracks, the twinkling sound of broken glass filling up the space like starlight.

"Let me go!" Ivy shrieks, straining against my grip.

I bury my nose in her hair, chasing more of that scent. It shivers through me, making my whole body shudder. Ivy's squirming just makes the whole thing even more delicious.

"I'm going to call the cops!" she shouts.

I press the full weight of my body against her, grinding my throbbing cock into her thigh.

"With what phone?" I purr into her ear. "I believe you dropped yours."

Ivy glares at me with pure fiery heat. It's been a long time since I've seen that look in a woman's eyes. At Lethe, we negotiate everything beforehand, and I follow the contract to the letter.

But with Ivy, there's only one contract that matters: the one with the Shadow Thorn that Orpheus Hartshorn carved in blood and violence. By that contract, I claimed her fifteen years ago, and I have every right to steal her away from my brother.

I shove my leg between her thighs, and Ivy stiffens, just for a second. Then she pounds at my arms, trying to shove me away. I squeeze her throat in retaliation, and *that* gets her to go still. She stares at me with wide, frightened eyes, and my lust surges hot inside me. I tighten my fingers on her neck, making her lips part.

"Stop," she wheezes.

"If you can talk," I say, "you can breathe." I squeeze tighter, and Ivy drops her head back, scrabbling her bare feet against the wall. I saw my thigh back and forth, and even through the layers of fabric, I can feel the heat and moisture seeping out of her cunt.

"That's better," I say softly. Her eyes water and turn shiny in the moonlight from the window. "Now. Do you want to know why I'm here?"

Ivy doesn't move. I loosen my grip, and she sucks down a draft of air, her breasts heaving up against my arm.

"Do you?"

"No," she spits out. "How'd you even get in?"

I laugh. "You thought you were clever, changing the locks?"

She glares at me with those glassy, rage-filled eyes. God, she looks gorgeous like that. Angry and petulant. It takes every ounce of willpower not to spin her around and spank her for not welcoming me into her cunt the way she's supposed to.

"It's my house," she says, voice strained from my grip. "You —have no right—"

"I have every right, cicada." I slide my hand up from her throat to tangle up in her hair. The breaths she takes are short and panting, and I rub my leg against her clit again for good measure.

"No, you *don't*," she screams, jerking sideways. "And stop fucking calling me that!"

I drag her back into place by her hair, making her howl and reach up to grab at my arm. She kicks and squirms, and I shove my body against hers.

"All you're doing is turning me on more," I tell her, and that earns me another furious glare. "And I'll call you what you want, just like I'll come into this house when I want, since it's on Hartshorn property. You, my dear, might own the house, but you do not own the land." I jerk her up to me by the hair, brush my lips against her lips. She keeps them sealed shut. "I do."

"Your family does," she snarls. "Not *you*."

"It doesn't matter." I jerk her away from the wall, making her squeal and shriek. "I picked the locks to get inside, because, like I said, you have no right to keep me out."

She screams, clawing at me.

"I'm not my brother," I say. "I don't like to bleed."

I hurl her into the bedroom. The rose room, we always called it, because it has rose-patterned wallpaper and a dusty pink quilt on the bed—currently rumpled and twisted from Ivy sleeping in it. Or not sleeping.

"What do you *want*?" Ivy cries out, fear turning her voice tremulous. She stands crouched, hackles raised like a cornered animal. I smile sweetly at her.

"A kiss," I say.

Then I duck back out into the hallway and scoop up her cell phone. She tries to escape, darting out after me, but I expect it, and I catch her by the arm and shove her back into the room, this time throwing her hard on the bed.

"Nothing to say to that?" I ask lightly, kicking the door shut behind me.

Ivy lifts her gaze, her hair hanging in a tangle over her eyes. But I can see it. The hesitation. The confusion.

My little spell worked.

"Just like when we were thirteen," I add, ambling across the room toward the window where, ten minutes ago, I hurled stones at the glass. I wanted to make sure she was awake when I found her. I wanted to savor every tremor of fear and lust, which would be wasted if she were asleep.

"I didn't come here when I was thirteen," she says roughly.

I unlock the window latches and shove the glass up. The bougainvillea doesn't quite reach, although it's almost here, the thorny vines scraping against the sill.

Hot, damp wind blows in through the mosquito screen, and I can feel Him out there, witnessing our reunion.

"Oh, but you did," I say. "For three weeks in July. If I recall correctly, your mother had to travel to Chicago for work."

The expressions that flicker across Ivy's face are exquisite. From confidence to doubt to fear.

"We were inseparable that summer." I punch the mosquito screen, and it pops out of the frame and goes winnowing into the dark, caught by the gusts of the Shadow Thorn's wind. "Spent most of it down at the creek. The cicadas would always sing for you when we would sit on the rocks."

When I glance over at her, Ivy's eyes are wide with recognition. She remembers, I'm sure of it. The way the cicada song would swell so loud as to be unbearable. Dozens of them would come flitting down and sit on the rocks beside us, their emerald green bodies glinting like jewels in the sunlight.

I knew then she had been chosen by the Shadow Thorn, just like Orpheus Hartshorn a hundred years earlier.

"That's why you're my cicada," I say plainly. "Gran and Gloria might have buried you in the dirt like a cicada's nymph, but you clawed your way back up to me."

"That didn't happen," she snarls, lying to herself. "None of that fucking happened!"

"It did, I'm afraid." I smile thinly at her. "It happened because I love you."

"What?" Ivy blurts. "*Love* me? You don't even—No!"

That last word comes out as a scream as I hurl her cell phone out the window.

"Can't have you calling Gideon," I say, turning back to her. "The Harlan police won't do anything, but he sure as hell will."

Ivy stares at me with pure horror. When I step toward her, she scrambles back on the bed, and only for a second does she flick her eyes over to the closed door.

"Did you hurt Gnocchi?" she asks in a small, scared voice.

I have no idea what she's talking about. "Gnocchi?"

"My cat!" Her voice pitches upward. "Did you hurt him?"

I frown, briefly irritated that she thinks that's even a possibility. "I didn't even see your cat, darling. I wouldn't touch him regardless."

She sniffles, eyeing me cautiously. I move toward her almost like she's the cat in question—slow, careful. I don't want her bolting.

She doesn't. Good girl.

"Now that we're all settled," I say. "We can get started."

"What are you going to do?" Her voice is ragged.

"I told you." I crawl onto the bed, the old mattress creaking beneath my weight. Ivy scoots backward, and I snatch my hand out and grab her ankle so she doesn't run. "I want another kiss."

"I don't want to kiss you."

I draw my gaze up her leg, over the place where her little cotton nightgown has hiked up to reveal a sliver of underwear along her thigh. Then I keep going: Over her belly. Her breasts. And then I settle on her face, blazing with defiance.

My cock twitches. God, I love it when they fight back.

"You wanted to kiss me yesterday afternoon," I say calmly.

"I did *not*." She shrieks it too loudly.

"But you kissed me anyway." I move closer to her, running my hand over her calf, relishing her smooth, satiny skin. It feels waxed, and I ignore the twinge of jealousy over the fact that she almost certainly waxed her legs for my brother.

No matter. He's in Bumfuck, Alabama, and Ivy is here with me, the window open to let in the Shadow Thorn. I can hear Him: in the wind, in the soft music of the wind chime Gloria hung in His honor.

"You were quite enthusiastic, in fact," I add, shoving her nightgown up to her waist. Ivy gasps and tries to jerk it back down, but I grab her wrist and tackle her over so that she's on her back, and I'm the one pinning her there.

"Not even going to bother to deny it?" I say with a grin.

"Let me go," she tries to kick up her knee, aiming for my cock, but I catch the hook of her leg and shove it to the side, pressing my hips up against hers. A soft, scared whimper escapes her lips.

"I'm here to kiss you," I say softly, peeling down the straps of her nightgown so I can unwrap her breasts, my breath shuddering. I caught a glimpse of them yesterday, when Gideon was rutting on top of her, but seeing them for myself is nearly overwhelming. Especially the sight of her dark, rosy nipples standing at attention. "Like I did yesterday." I pull one of those nipples into my mouth, and her body goes stiff beneath me. I release it with a satisfied sigh. "And like I did when we were thirteen."

"That never happened," she snarls, jerking against me. "My first kiss was when I was fifteen—"

"That was your second kiss." I run my tongue along her neck, making her shudder and squirm beneath me. "I'm afraid you lost the memory of your first one. At least—" I stop, face to face with her, close enough that her breath blows against my lips. "At least I until I gave it back to you."

Her eyes widen, and the seismic waves of her fear ripple in the air around us. And then I take my third kiss, jamming her mouth open with my tongue. She makes a muffled noise of protest and does not, this time, return my kiss, just tries to fight back against me. I bite down hard on her lip in retaliation.

"Fuck you!" she screams, jerking her head away from me. There's a crimson swell of blood on her mouth. And in my mouth, too. I can taste it, salty and sharp. I haven't had blood in so long, and tasting hers stirs up the Shadow Thorn, who I can feel lurking outside the window, crouching in the bougainvillea that grew out of my obsession, watching us.

"Not tonight, cicada." Although it's so fucking tempting, especially with her warm, damp pussy straining up against my cock. She's wet, even if she doesn't want to admit it. And that's the problem—when I fuck her for the first time, I want her begging for my cock.

So I'll just have to satisfy myself with a kiss.

"Well, then what do you want?" she snaps. "You got your fucking kiss, didn't you?"

"I got *a* kiss. But I want another one." I peel away from her, reaching into my back pocket, where I slid a pair of handcuffs before I came to visit. I just touch them for now, preparing.

The wind pulses, bringing the scent of outside into the room. Ivy watches me warily.

"Then do it and leave," she says.

I grin. "If you say so."

I move quickly, before she can realize what's happening. I slap one handcuff onto her wrist and the other to the big wooden bedpost. It takes Ivy a heartbeat to realize she's trapped, but when she does, she starts screaming, a beautiful, melodious sound. I drop my head back, languishing in it.

"Let me go!" she screams, clinking the handcuff around. I drop my head back so I can watch her struggle, trying to squeeze her cuffed hand free.

"You'd have to break your hand to do that," I tell her, sliding back onto the bed. Ivy jerks her gaze over to me, eyes wild.

"Don't touch me," she snarls.

"I don't think you have much say in the matter."

She tries to squirm away from me, but I grab her legs and shove them wide. Then I press my nose up to her panty-covered pussy and breathe in the scent of her arousal: a sharp, unmistakable tang that makes the back of my jaw ache.

Ivy flops against my grip, but it's no use. I may not be as strong as Gideon, but I'm still stronger than her.

Strong enough to reach up one-handed and drag her underwear down.

"Stop!" she screams. "No!"

"I said I just wanted a kiss." I unwrap her cunt the way I did her tits, slow and methodical. This beauty I did *not* get to see yesterday, and the sight of it makes my cock ache with need. She waxed this, too, a gift for Gideon, no doubt. But without its soft fur, her pussy reveals all its secrets to me. It's plump with arousal, her pink lips glistening. I shove her legs wide again so she opens up for me, groaning deep in the back of my throat.

"Let me go!" she screams.

"Not until I've had my kiss."

And then I press my lips to hers, and I take what belongs to me.

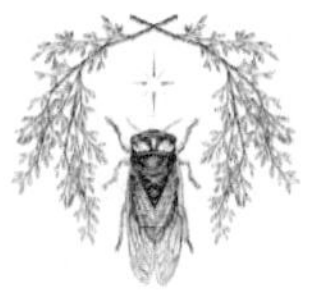

35

IVY

I can't believe this is happening. I can't believe Xavier broke into my house, that he handcuffed me to the fucking bed, that he's—

That he's eating me like I'm a last goddamn meal.

I struggle against him, or try to. He's stronger than his thin frame would suggest, and he has my legs spread wide across the bed as he plunges his tongue up into my cunt, kissing me with the same fervor that he did in the woods.

That he did when we thirteen—

No. That didn't happen.

But this *is* happening. This violation.

Xavier makes wet, sloppy noises as he shoves his tongue into my pussy and sucks on my lips. I'm vaguely aware that he's humping the bed, too, his hips rolling rhythmically against the mattress.

Just let him do it, I think wildly, although I'm still tugging on the handcuff. *So he doesn't hurt you.*

My phone. I think of my phone, somehow out in the field. It's the only way I have to call Gideon. I don't have his phone number written down anymore. Why would I?

"Fuck, you taste delicious," Xavier growls, the words blowing heat across my cunt. "I bet my brother can't keep his fucking mouth off you."

"Don't talk about him," I say weakly.

Xavier laughs and gives me a long, lingering lick against my slit that ends, finally, with a flutter against my clit. I clench my jaw to keep from crying out. I will not let him know this feels good. Just because he can activate my physical responses doesn't mean I want this.

Doesn't it?

"Gideon loves eating pussy," Xavier says, punctuating the words with hard, sucking kisses. "Anytime I find a girl that looks remotely like you, he's buried between her thighs before she's barely said hello."

My heart pounds. I don't want to hear about this.

Except I kind of do. *A girl who looks like you.*

Shameful pleasure quivers through my core. Fortunately, Xavier doesn't seem to notice as he suctions my pussy with his mouth, making more of those sloppy noises.

"It works out," he says, taking a break to nuzzle against my clit. I drop my head back and stare up at the moon-dappled ceiling. "He gets them so fucking wet." Another deep, sloppy kiss. "Almost as wet as you are now."

I squeeze my eyes shut. I know Xavier's just trying to upset me. There's no way he can know about his brother's sexual partners.

Except that Gideon admitted that they had shared women. *It's complicated,* he said, *but it's true.*

"He likes making them come," Xavier continues, alternating between speaking and tongue-fucking me. "I like making them suffer, although I'm not going to do that to you, cicada."

"I'm not going to come for you," I snarl.

"Yes, you will." He attacks me with his hot, devouring mouth. At first, he's just kissing my cunt, like he's been doing.

But then he moves upward and latches onto my clit, and I can't stop myself.

I cry out with a strangled groan of pleasure.

"There it is," Xavier laughs. "Go on, darling. I may not be doing this for you, but feel free to enjoy yourself."

I try to pull away from him, but it feels like his entire weight is pressed onto my body. Even if I weren't handcuffed to the bed, I don't think I could get away.

Xavier keeps licking me with long, unhurried strokes. And each one ends on my clit.

"Stop," I whisper, tears brimming on my eyelashes.

He doesn't. If anything, his licks become more forceful, and he doesn't stop to taunt me. I tug on my handcuffed arm, the cuff digging into my wrist, but I know it's pointless. He has me pinned.

And he keeps licking me. Kissing me. Devouring me.

I squeeze my eyes shut, my breath tight in my chest. The terrible truth is that it feels good. Almost as good as Gideon, and it's Gideon's face I see when I close my eyes. Gideon's naked body, his tattoos as bright as the Hartshorn garden. I imagine he's here in the room, but he's not trying to save me.

He's watching, standing over me, stroking his cock.

A groan escapes my lips, and I slap my free hand over my mouth. Xavier laughs against my pussy, then attacks it with more fervor, hoisting my hips up so I'm bent over at the waist.

You're going to come.

The voice reverberates in my head. It's not mine. It sort of sounds like Gideon.

You think we haven't shared women?

It's complicated, but it's true.

Xavier attacks my clit, sucking hard and eagerly, and I brace my jaw. I refuse to let him hear any sounds of pleasure. I hate that I'm even *feeling* pleasure, that it's quaking around in my belly. I hate that I keep seeing Gideon in my head, that I imagine him enjoying this as much as Xavier is. That I wish I had his massive cock in my mouth in this moment, my body linking the two brothers together—

My orgasm hits me like a thunderstorm. Every single one of my nerves lights up like a lightning flash. I scream and buck up against Xavier, but he slams me back down on the bed, his mouth still latched to my cunt. He doesn't slow his pace the way Gideon does, who nurtures me through the aftershocks, drawing out my pleasure without being overwhelming. Xavier clearly doesn't give a shit. He just keeps eating me out until it hurts.

"Stop!" I choke out. "Please! It's too much."

Xavier slides two fingers into my pussy, a sharp, unexpected violation that nonetheless gives my contracting muscles something to clamp down on. I shriek again, hating how good it feels.

"I decide when it's too much." Xavier fingerfucks me with quick, angry strokes. "Now, shut your mouth and don't interrupt my meal."

Then his mouth is on me again, as forceful as before. I pant and quake, my arm aching from being stretched overhead. And Xavier doesn't stop, just like he said. He keeps devouring me with firm, eager licks. Every now and then, he bites down, sharp stinging nips that make me cry out.

I hate that I like it, the sharpness of the pain contrasted with the wet, languorous heat of his tongue.

I slump against the mattress, too tired to try and fight back. For a long time, the only sound is from Xavier: his wet, slurping kisses and his throaty, satisfied moans. But then I start to hear my own quickened breaths and soft sighs.

You're going to come again.

I definitely hear it in Gideon's voice, and it's like I'm back in that motel shower with him as he wins his bet, his fingers working my clit. *I want you here*, I think tearfully, desperately, and the Gideon in my head smiles and kisses me, and I love it, being kissed in two places at once, and I come again, shaky and small.

And Xavier keeps going.

I whimper, my cheeks wet from overstimulation. Or fear. Or both. I focus my thoughts on Gideon, and something like calm washes through me. *I'm gonna mark you so my brother knows you belong to me*, he said, and I have the odd, spiky thought that he knew something like this might happen, and that's why he filled my pussy with his scent.

Is it wrong that I find solace in that thought? That it just adds to the heat between my legs?

Especially because Xavier gives no sign of slowing down, and I've given up on protesting. It's easier this way, to spread my legs for his hungry tongue, to let the intensity course through me like fire. It doesn't matter what Xavier does. Because Gideon marked me as his territory.

The window's still open, letting in hot, strange wind from outside, and it creates a contrast with the AC blasting out of the vents. Hot and cold. Fear and ecstasy. Arousal and disgust.

It all twines together until I'm nothing but quaking, shivering pleasure. I came again, I think; heat shoots through me and makes me jolt like I've been electrocuted. Xavier doesn't just stop; he scrapes his teeth against my oversensitive skin, making me scream and thrash against him. Then he plunges his tongue up inside my pussy, and it feels so good in contrast that I moan.

"That's it, cicada," he whispers, the first time he's spoken in a while. "Give me more of those tortured little noises."

"Go fuck yourself," I choke out.

Xavier's kisses slow, and fear twists in my chest. How the hell was *that* going too far?

"Oh, darling," he murmurs against me. "You have no idea, do you?"

"What the fuck," I gasp out, "are you talking about?"

And finally, *finally*, Xavier pulls away from me, peering up at me over the mound of my belly. His mouth and chin glisten in the moonlight, and I feel a terrible stab of shame that I could get so wet that he glistens.

"I already came, baby girl."

Baby girl. No. Those are Gideon's words.

"What are you talking about?" I snap.

Xavier grins wickedly, grabs my free hand, and slaps it on his crotch. It's wet and cold and sticky, and I yank my hand away in disgust.

"About ten minutes ago," he sighs. "But god, you're too delicious to let go."

Then, to my horror, he dives between my legs again. I scream as his mouth makes contact. I don't know how much more of this I can take. My pussy feels numb and raw under Xavier's mouth, especially after my brief respite.

But he doesn't care. He laps me up, pushing my legs wide so he can thrust his tongue up inside me. I weep, my thighs trembling. "Please stop," I whisper. "Please, it's too much."

Xavier's only response is to suck hard on my clit, making me yelp. I jerk against him, and the movement makes my body ache. Every part of me aches, actually, and the pleasure he's gnawing out of me feels more and more like suffering.

"Please," I whisper, my voice jagged. "Xavier, please stop. I can't take any more."

"I told you." He pauses, just long enough to peer up at me. "This is for my pleasure, not yours." Then his tongue is on me again, and I flop back, my handcuffed wrist burning.

But Xavier keeps licking and licking, over and over, until the world goes dark.

36

GIDEON

The phone jangles against my ear as I pace around the dark, empty corridor of a big community center in Huntsville. I haven't heard from Ivy since I checked in with her last night at the hotel, and I don't like this. I know she's got to get ready for her class, but it's weird not to have her call me back by now.

I never should have left her alone. Not with Xavier back at Hartshorn. Not with all his magic and fucking scheming.

The phone clicks over to voicemail. I hang up, not bothering to leave a message. I left one a few hours ago, plus there was this morning's text that went unanswered. Or unlooked at it, if the notification on my phone is anything to go by.

Music kicks in from the arena, thumping softly through the walls. A sound check—we still have a couple of hours to go until the doors open. But I can't go out there if I'm worried about Ivy. The promoter wants to see blood, and I can't deliver like that if I'm distracted.

Voices sound from down the hall. A couple of the local guys. The last thing I want is to talk to them, so I duck into a janitor's closet right before they come around the corner. I click on the light and lean up against the door, staring at the mops and cleaning supplies, listening to their laughter as they walk by.

Then I look down at my phone, my chest tight.

I dial up the house's landline again. I tried that earlier and didn't get an answer, but I'm going to try it one last time before I call Gran and see if she can go check on—

"Hello?"

Hearing Ivy's voice floods me with relief. "Ivy, thank god," I say. "Is everything all right?"

"Gideon?" Her voice brightens. "Oh, I'm so glad you called on the landline. My phone—" She stops, and for a moment, the phone just fills with static. "I dropped it when I went for a walk. It, um, shattered, and I couldn't get your number—"

Something's wrong. I sense it immediately: the way her voice catches, the hesitation in her words. "Ivy, are you okay?"

"I'm fine." Another long pause, and I squeeze the phone, my heart thumping. "I just—your brother came by."

My whole body goes cold

"Did he hurt you?" The question's out of my mouth before I can stop it. I don't want to skip out on the match, but if it means stopping whatever bullshit Xavier is up to, I'll do it.

But Ivy says, "No!" with enough conviction that I believe her. "No, I'm fine, Gideon, really. He—"

My blood lurches.

"He just came on to me again," she finishes. "I kicked him out. It's over. I'm fine."

Of course he fucking did. He thinks he owns her. But I'm the one with the claim. *Me.*

What the fuck is it going to take to get him to see that?

"I shouldn't have come out here," I tell her. "I'm sorry. I'll call Gran, okay? She'll make sure he doesn't bother you again."

"Don't say that," Ivy says quickly. "About not going to your match, I mean. You can call Judith if you think it'll help, but I just—" Her voice catches again. "I don't want you worried about me, okay? I was a little shaken up that I couldn't get a hold of you, but that's not a problem anymore." She laughs a little. "Just don't let me forget to write down your cell number."

"I'll give it to you now," I say, although my thoughts are racing. She's not telling me the whole truth, but she doesn't seem hurt or scared. *He came on to me*, she said, and I have a feeling that she may have given in.

For a half second, I see it. Xavier thrusting into her, his hands around her neck, Ivy moaning with pleasure.

My cock stiffens. I try to ignore it as I rattle off my cell number.

"Thanks," Ivy says brightly. "Can I call you tonight? After the show?"

"I'll call you at the house."

I know I should be seething with jealousy about it, about Xavier and Ivy. But I'm just so used to sharing women with him. He has all those connections at Lethe, and he knew how to use them to find women who looked like Ivy. Not just looked like her, but who moved like her. Spoke like her.

None were ever as good as the real thing, but they were close enough.

So, no. I'm not jealous. Not exactly. I know Ivy and I have a bond that Xavier can't shatter, no matter what magic he's brewing up in that third-floor bedroom.

But I am worried.

Worried that he'll hurt her, especially if it means keeping her close to him. I know what he likes, the way he chases cruelty. But if I'm being honest, that's not *all* I'm worried about.

Because I'm also worried that he'll tell her too much. About our family. About what we do. About what *I* do, and all the blood staining my hands.

"Gideon?" Ivy says, her voice small. "Are you still there?"

"Yeah," I say. "Yeah, I am." I hesitate, then add, "If he does anything—extreme, don't call the police, okay? Call the house. Tell Gran about it. Then call me."

Silence crackles on the other end. "Do you think he'll— what do you think he might do?"

Shit. I really didn't want to get her worried. "Probably nothing," I say. "I just don't want you to call the police. They won't do anything. But Gran won't let anything happen to you, okay?"

"Okay." Ivy sounds breathless. "Thanks, Gideon."

I squeeze my phone, heart pounding. Part of me wants to slam out of here and drive the ten hours back to Texas. But then Ivy says,

"Should I tell you to break a leg? Or is that worse luck in wrestling?"

Something about her question breaks the tension coiling up inside me. I laugh. "You know what? I'll take it."

"Good." She pauses, her breath filling up the phone line. "Gideon, I don't want you to worry about me, okay? Just focus on your match. I'll be here when you get back."

Fuck. I sure hope so.

I CALL Gran after I get off the phone with Ivy, and she gives me her word that she'll keep Xavier at home. It's the best I can ask for.

My match goes well enough. It's wild and furious and bloody, which is what the promoter wanted, but I have to force myself to pull back a couple of times. At one point, my opponent hisses out a sharp, "What the shit, dude?" when I go a little too hard on him. It jolts me out of the weird, hazy blood-lust I'm in, and we finish everything okay, and I apologize to him afterward. But it was just one sign out of a million that I shouldn't have come here without Ivy.

She sounds fine when I check in on her that night, her voice a soothing balm as I lie spread out on the bed. But I don't sleep much. The motel reminds me of the motel where I reconnected with Ivy this spring. Reminds me of how gorgeous she looked with her tits covered in my blood.

And then I start thinking about what she would look ike covered in her *own* blood, and I get all tight with anxiety.

Sometime around two in the morning, I can't stand it anymore, and I call Xavier. He doesn't pick up, so I text him.

> Don't fucking touch her.

That doesn't get a response, either. Not that I really expected one.

I doze off and on for a few hours, but what sleep I get is fitful and worthless. I finally give up around 4:30 and decide to just drive home early, my whole body seething with adrenaline. I'm used to long road trips, since traveling for matches is pretty much the only time I truly have to myself. Wrestling in general is the only thing I have for myself, the only thing that isn't all tied in with blood and magic and the Shadow Thorn. Normally, a match is a respite, a chance for me to pretend to be normal for a few days.

Not this weekend, though.

I tear across Mississippi and Arkansas, the sun rising behind me, casting long shadows on the highway. I barely stop, just keep driving well over the speed limit with my hands clenched tight around the steering wheel and death metal roaring through the speakers to help keep me awake.

It's hell, but it puts me back in Harlan a little after three in the afternoon. It's overcast here, the sky heavy with an impending storm, and the town looks sleepy, the way it always does. My family's money is the only thing keeping this place alive, and that's only barely.

Once I'm through Harlan, though, on the little two-lane highway that'll take me home, I'm torn between what to do. Check in on Ivy? She's not expecting me until Monday, and I'm so strung out from not sleeping that I'm not sure I'll make things better or worse.

That leaves my other option, which is to go straight to Hartshorn and beat the shit out of my brother until he tells me what he did.

That idea gets me excited. Fighting for real, spilling blood, always gets me excited. A gift from the Shadow Thorn, Dad told me when he was training me, although I always saw it as a curse. That's the real reason I got into pro wrestling—I wanted all my battles to be a performance. Wanted all my punches to be pulled. That's why wrestling makes me feel normal.

But Xavier fucked it all up this time.

In the end, I decide to go straight home. If Ivy's safe, I'll just look like a madman beating down her door a day early. But if she's not, it means Xavier did something, and she probably won't be in the house anyway.

Where she *would* be—that, I don't want to think about.

So I skip the turnoff to her house and keep going until I reach the entrance to Hartshorn, the big wrought iron gate that spells out the family name in curved, twisting letters. Vines have grown up around the sides of the gate.

No, not vines. Blood-red bougainvillea. My stomach clenches.

I'm certain that wasn't there when I left on Friday.

When I see Xavier's pricy BMW parked in the garage, I'm not sure if I should feel relieved or not. I pull in next to it and kill the engine, clenching and unclenching my fists. Taking deep, slow breaths. Trying to calm myself. I need to be calm, at least somewhat, to deal with Xavier properly.

When I think I'm ready, I step out of the car and into the thick, damp air. Everything feels sharp and electric, and dread twists in my belly. I saw the storm clouds when I was driving in and didn't think much of them; thunderstorms are normal this time of year.

But this isn't a normal thunderstorm. As soon as I step out into it, I know. This is the Shadow Thorn's doing.

A sacrifice is coming, Gran had said, but this doesn't feel like a sacrifice, either. This is something else. Something bigger.

Ivy.

"You can't take her," I mutter softly to the black-veined sky. Wind whips across the lawn, damp and ionized. The trees bow toward me. I know He's listening. "You can't have her!" I shout, and my voice catches on the wind.

It's not her blood I want.

I feel the voice more than I hear it, a deep, shuddering throb that makes my muscles quake and my cock stand at attention. I stumble forward, half-delirious from lack of sleep. But that message, at least, is reassuring. He doesn't want her blood. He doesn't want her death.

"She's mine," I whisper, and the woods rustle around me. I swear they whisper, *I know*.

37

XAVIER

I broke something open when I went to Ivy on Friday night. I can feel it buzzing through the house all day on Saturday, low and electric, a sense that something's coming.

It's intense enough that I don't even care that Ivy tattled on me to Gideon, which I only know because I get a visit from Gran after lunch, who comes into my room without knocking while I'm taking care of some business for my associates with the Five Courts. Boring shit, really. The whole thing is a glorified racketeering enterprise. Our five families might have been touched by an unfathomable darkness, but at the end of the day, we're just using it to control a bunch of low-level gangsters.

I sense Gran's presence before she announces herself, and I whirl around in my chair to find her staring at me with her arms crossed over her chest.

"Do not leave this house until Gideon gets back," she says.

"Oh, god. Are you taking orders from him now?"

"I'm very serious, Xavier." She is, as serious as she was after she found out that I had taken Ivy to the chapel. Not as angry, though.

"I don't care how old you are," she says. "I'll put the dreaming on you if I find out you were bothering Ivy again."

I bite back a smirk. As if that old childhood punishment scares me, especially now that the Shadow Thorn showed me how to do it to Ivy.

Granted, when Gran puts on the dreaming, she sends endless, visceral nightmares straight into your head. And I suppose there's some benefit in letting Ivy stew for a few days, especially since I have actual work to do.

"Fine," I say to Gran. "I won't go near her."

"I'll know," she says menacingly. I listen to her footsteps retreating down the stairs.

So I don't give Ivy an encore on Saturday, as much as I want to. On Friday, I could feel her relenting beneath my tongue, her groans low and hungry. I bet I could have her begging for my cock tonight.

I keep my promise to Gran, though. No nightmares for me, no orgasms for Ivy.

But when the storm clouds roll in on Sunday morning, heavy and ominous, I know something's happening. The weather app on my phone is predicting hot sunshine for the next ten days. Those storm clouds aren't about weather. I can feel it sparking in my blood.

That spark is what drives me to sneak out of the house. I don't break my promise, though. I don't go to Ivy's place. Instead, I hike across the damp, wind-swept garden to the chapel. It's Sunday morning, after all. Time for a church service.

When I get there, though, I see something that sends excitement flooding through my veins. I stop in the hedge entrance, staring at what can only be a sign from the Shadow Thorn:

Blood-red bougainvillea has grown up around the charred chapel walls, dotting it with the same crimson petals as the vines clawing apart Ivy's back porch.

"I knew it," I breathe. The Shadow Thorn watches me from the trees, His eyes scraping across my skin like knives. When I go into the chapel proper, thunder booms from someplace far away, and sheet lightning turns the world into a camera flash. But there's no rain.

Everything's held in. Denied release. Just like I'm going to do to Ivy when I get ahold of her.

I give the Shadow Thorn another small sacrifice, jerking off onto the ground and then cutting open my palm with a pocket knife. I squeeze my fist tight and watch the blood drip down in slow, steady drops. Each one is sucked into the soil.

"Tell me when to claim her," I say to the statue on the altar, who watches me with its flat, dark eyes. "Tell me, and I'll do it."

The wind gusts so strongly that the roof of the chapel creaks and moans, and the dampness beads across my skin. Somehow, the light in the chapel dims enough that, although it's nearly lunchtime, it feels like dusk.

"Tonight?" I say, excitement constricting in my chest.

Another violent gust of wind, and I know I have my answer.

I leave the chapel, stepping into an eerie darkness that makes all the insects go quiet. I consider peeking in on Ivy. Not to touch. I just want to look. But my phone buzzes, and it's Cullen Tyloch, who heads up the Court of Starlight, demanding to know my progress. By the time I finish texting back my reply, I'm at Hartshorn.

I go in through the front entrance without thinking, letting the door slam shut behind me.

"Gideon?" Gran calls out.

Fuck. I wasn't supposed to leave the house.

"I need to talk to you!" It sounds like she's in the study, and I don't think I can sneak my way upstairs.

"Gideon's not back until tomorrow!" I finally say, swinging around into the study doorway. Sure enough, she's sitting on that stiff, uncomfortable settee, one of our family's old leather-bound books in her lap. Behind her, she has the window curtains pulled back. It's so dark outside, though, that all I can really see are the ghosts of our reflections.

She looks up at me, frowning, and I brace for a tongue-lashing. But it doesn't come.

"Something's happening," she says. "We need your brother here."

"A sacrifice?" I say lightly, although I know damn well that's not it.

But Gran does, too. She shakes her head and squints down at the book through her elegant silver glasses. "Something bigger than that," she mutters. "Something—" She stops and looks up at me, pushing her glasses up on top of her head. "What were you doing outside? You didn't—"

"I went for a walk," I say. "I didn't go anywhere near Ivy's house."

Gran studies me for a long time, like she's sizing me up. I hold myself perfectly still, nervous that she sees something in me. Some trace of magic. If she finds out I unravelled the spell she and Gloria put on Ivy when she was thirteen, she'll do more than put the dreaming on me. She'll fucking kill me. Possibly literally.

Ivy was supposed to be off-limits. That's what they told me when I was thirteen. They said the same thing to Gideon when he fucked Ivy a few years later.

It's remarkable how *un*-off-limits she became for him, though, now that Gloria is gone.

"You didn't *do* anything, did you?" Gran finally asks.

Energy prickles over my skin. "I told you. I went for a walk."

"Not now," she snaps. "In the last month. All this back and forth between you and Gideon—"

"No, I didn't do anything," I say, keeping my voice smooth

to cover up the lie. "I've been dealing with Five Courts bullshit, that's what I've been doing."

Gran shakes her head and then looks out the window. "I need to call Jack," she says softly, and I think she's talking to herself more than me. "See what he says about all this." She snaps the book closed, releasing a cloud of dust, and looks at me with a sharp glint in her eye.

"You need to be careful," she says darkly. "Whatever it is you think you're doing."

"I told you, I'm not *doing* anything," I say, a little too loudly. "Gideon's the one fucking her."

Gran keeps her gaze steely. Not much fazes her, I'll give her that. "Not in the chapel," she says. "And he's being very careful about not bringing her to the house."

Yeah, he was so *careful* when he dragged Ivy into his living room in the old wing and cajoled her into fucking watersports. I keep my mouth shut, though. I know damn well he was mocking me, but that won't matter if I fuck her in the chapel tonight.

And it'll be easier to do that if Gran doesn't suspect anything.

"I gotta get some work done," I tell her. "Don't worry, okay? Nothing's going on."

A lie, and we both know it. Gran gives me a dark, suspicious look, but she doesn't say anything more. I'll take it.

I leave her to it, whatever she's doing with those old books, and go back up to the third floor.

The energy churning around outside with the incoming storm is churning around up here, too. I feel it as soon as I walk through the door, a faint crackling that dances across my skin. I slide down in my desk, pop open the laptop, and start following up with some of Tyloch's irritatingly banal contacts. It's relatively mindless work, and I let my thoughts drift while I do it.

To Ivy, locked away in her bougainvillea-wrapped farmhouse. Waiting for me, even if she doesn't know it.

I work through the dark afternoon. The storm still doesn't come, even though the wind howls viciously up here, rattling the old window frame around. "You as excited about tonight as I am?" I mutter, but the Shadow Thorn doesn't answer.

Or maybe the black storm clouds and damp winds and denied rains are the answer. An echo of what I'm going to do to Ivy.

Around three, I get up to stretch my legs, and I amble over to the window. The wind pounds against the glass, and I switch off the desk lamp so I can look out at the garden below. The storm, or whatever it is, feels closer. Even more present. Leaves and sticks and shredded flowers swirl around in a fury, but there's no rain even though I can smell it, dark and steely.

And then I see someone moving across the garden.

My heart freezes in my chest. No. It can't be.

I press against the cool glass, angry coiling around my heart. It *is*.

Gideon. I'd recognize his ape-like loping anywhere, even in the dark of a storm.

He's stalking toward the courtyard, his head bent down and his hair blowing into his eyes. What the fuck is he doing here already? He wasn't supposed to be back until Monday.

Ivy. He came back to protect Ivy from me.

My anger, just for a moment, flickers into fear. I step away from the window and switch the lamp back on, staring down at my open laptop. My work shit's still pulled up, but I can't think about that now. I've got more important concerns.

I slam the laptop closed just as I feel the walls rattle from downstairs. The house is too big for me to hear anything, but I can sense Gideon's presence nonetheless. His anger, lasered in on me like a weapon.

Acting on some self-preservation instinct, I dart out into the narrow, rickety hallway. Teenage Gideon didn't sneak around the way I did as a teenager—no one was inviting him to any pasture parties with the popular kids—so I'm not sure he knows the full extent of the servant stairs and tricky, windy little corridors in the house.

I bet I can get out and get to Ivy's before he finds me.

Assuming he hasn't been there first.

I shove the thought aside. She wasn't with him. He probably came straight home, harboring dreams of kicking my ass.

I dart down the hallway and slip into the servant's stairwell, moving lightly so he won't hear me in the walls. I hear him, though: his voice loud and booming and angry. I assume he's talking to Gran, although I can't quite hear her answers.

The stairs dump me out near the formal dining room, and I ease the door shut and press against the wall, still listening. It's quiet, save for the wind whistling around the house. But then—

"There you fucking are."

Gideon's hand squeezes my wrist before I can react. He whips me around, throwing me up against the far wall hard enough that a painting of my great-great-grandmother Evelyn, the first Hartshorn spouse, swings back and forth.

"What are you doing back so soon?" I ask, plastering on an expression of calm.

Gideon stalks toward me. He looks like a fucking madman, which is to say he looks like a classic Hartshorn. His hair is damp from the humidity and hangs into his eyes with a dark tangle. He didn't bother to shave this morning, and his scruff is already coming in, giving him that wild look my redneck cousins favor. To top it off, there's a big, angry cut across his forehead, probably from his stupid wrestling match.

Oh, and his eyes are twisted with fury.

I try to duck away, but he catches me, pinning me up against the wall by the throat.

"What'd you do to her?" he snarls.

I struggle against him, which is foolish, because it only makes him jam his forearm up under my chin, cutting off even more of my air.

"N-nothing," I choke out, gazing straight at him. "Calm the f-fuck down."

"You hurt her," he snarls, shoving his arm deeper into my throat.

I choke and sputter and try to pry his arm off. "You're c-cutting—" The words flounder around. "C-can't bre-breathe."

"Where is she?"

What the fuck does he think I did? I try to answer, but the words come out even more strangled. Gideon makes a noise of disgust and drops his arm. I'm too grateful to be able to breathe again that I don't try to run.

"Where is she?" he says again.

I look up at him—a raging beast of a man, the monster our father and uncle shaped him to be. The sacrifice-bringer. The Shadow Thorn's violent, cruel servant.

And he thinks Ivy would want *him?*

"I assume she's at home," I say coolly. "What the fuck are you doing back so early?"

Gideon lunges at me again, but this time I'm able to duck away. I take off running down the hallway, and he gives chase, just like when we were kids. I careen around the corner and dive into the dining room, which is black as pitch thanks to the heavy curtains and the unnatural darkness outside. I bang my thigh against one of the chairs and grab it, and throw it behind me. Gideon catches it.

"Did you just give me a chair?" he growls, hoisting it over his head. I whip around, fumbling my way toward the exit, but I'm not fast enough. The chair catches me on the back, and I fly forward, slamming my forehead into the wall. Pain blooms in my temples, and I stumble backward, dizzy from the impact.

Gideon's waiting. He grabs both of my arms, wrenching me into some painful wrestling hold. I fight against it as best I can, but there's no denying that, between the two of us, he's the stronger one.

"What'd you do?" he roars right into my ear. "I know you did something. What was it?"

I grit my jaw against the pain, trying to worm my way out of the hold. But I still feel a flutter of excitement—

Because Ivy didn't tell him everything.

Were you protecting me, my sweet cicada?

"Tell me!" Gideon roars, jamming his knee into the small of my back. I howl as my spine twists in a way it is definitely not supposed to twist, and Gideon digs his nails into my forearm, and—

And light floods the dining room.

"What in the *fuck* are you boys doing?"

Gideon drops me immediately. He's too well-behaved for his own good. I collapse to my knees beside the chair Gideon hurled at me, which is currently snapped in half.

"Ask him," Gideon snarls.

I lift my gaze to find Gran standing in the doorway. She's angry now. As angry as she was when I was thirteen. Angrier, possibly.

She looks at me.

"What did you do to Ivy?" she asks me in a cold, hard voice.

I grin, pushing myself up to standing even though my legs wobble unsteadily. "Nothing she didn't want."

"Liar!" Gideon roars, lunging at me again.

But he doesn't reach me. Because two things happen at once:

A clap of thunder rolls through the sky, so loud that it shakes our massive house at its foundation like an earthquake.

And the doorbell rings.

Gideon stiffens. Gran looks toward the front door, her face unreadable.

And I feel it deep in my chest.

That thing that's been coming all afternoon, riding on the wind of the Shadow Thorn's storm—

It's here.

38

IVY

I sleep in on Sunday morning, something I never do. When I finally do wake up, shuddering like I had a bad dream, the analog clock on the bedside table tells me it's nearly 10:30, but my room is dark even though I left the curtains drawn when I fell asleep last night.

It's raining, I think distractedly, although I don't hear any rain, just the soft buzz of the box fan.

I drag myself out of bed, my head fuzzy and thick. I can still sense snatches of my dream. A burned-down church. A patch of bluebonnets. River-green eyes watching me in the dark.

At least I actually got to sleep last night. At least Xavier didn't break in and—

Heat courses through my body at the memory. Heat and guilt. When he finally left me alone on Friday night, snapping the handcuffs off with a grin, all I could do was lie in the bed, my entire body shivering and aching. I was exhausted, but I couldn't fall asleep. I kept expecting Xavier to come slinking back in with his long, delicate fingers and eager tongue, and I wasn't sure if I wanted him to or not.

That made me feel guilty, too.

Eventually, Gnocchi trotted in and curled up beside me, and I drifted in and out of sleep. Yesterday was also a waste. My brand-new lock on the back door was broken—Xavier's doing, no doubt—and I wasted a good hour trying to figure out a way to keep the door jammed closed. I don't even know how he got through the vines. They're thicker than ever.

After that, I spent the rest of the morning looking for my phone in the grass. When I finally found it, it was cracked down the center and wouldn't turn on.

At least Gideon called me on the land line later that day. As soon as I heard his voice, all the muscles in my body relaxed, releasing a tension I barely realized I was carrying.

But I couldn't bear to tell him what really happened with his brother. Not over the *phone*.

At least, that's what I tell myself.

But because of all that, I spent yesterday knotted with anxiety, and my class isn't anywhere close to ready, even though it starts tomorrow.

I change out of my PJs and trudge over to the window, pushing the curtains aside to peer out at the meadow. It does look like a storm is coming in. The clouds are thick and heavy and black, and the grass ripples like the ocean. The wind chime spins around, and I can just make out the soft lilt of its low, bonging notes.

A dim, cozy day. Perfect for getting work done, assuming I can stay out of my head.

It works for a little while. I make breakfast, listening to that awful bougainvillea scraping against the window. After I eat, I brew some coffee and get to work on my class, and the quiet dark outside makes it easy to concentrate. So, by the time lunch rolls around, I feel like I've actually accomplished something. And that makes me feel good enough to call Gideon. If there's one thing that's nagged at the back of my thoughts while I worked, it's him. It's the thought of what he'll do when he finds out that Xavier—

Assaulted me, I tell myself. What Xavier did was assault, just like when he forced me to kiss him in the woods.

You liked it.

The voice is cold and cruel and makes my skin crawl.

"No," I whisper. "No, I did not."

The wind howls outside. It still hasn't rained.

After I put my lunch dishes away, I press the phone receiver to my ear. I've punched in the first two numbers when it hits me that there wasn't a dial tone.

I frown and punch in the rest of Gideon's number anyway. But nothing happens. The phone makes a kind of empty, hollow sound. No ringing. No voicemail message.

Fear knots in my chest. I hang up. Bring the receiver to my ear.

Silence.

I slide the receiver back into its cradle, my heart thudding. The truth is, I barely remember how landlines are supposed to work. I check the cord, and it's still nestled firmly in the wall.

The wind must have done something. Knocked something loose, maybe.

I grab my laptop off the kitchen table and move into the living room, telling myself I need a change of scenery, that maybe I'll put on the TV while I work. It's dark in here, especially with the curtains drawn tight over the windows. But something feels—off.

The storm, I tell myself. It's just the storm.

I switch the light on, but even the overhead lamp hardly seems enough to beat back the darkness. Still, I settle down on the couch, flip my laptop open, stare at my screen.

The wind is louder here. And I can hear something scratching against the walls. Sounds like it's coming from the chimney—

I glance over at the fireplace. And shriek.

Because there's bougainvillea growing into the house.

I leap to my feet, my laptop clattering to the ground. I barely notice, because my eyes are focused on the thick spray of bougainvillea blooms crawling out of the fireplace. It's the same thorny vines and blood-red blossoms as the bougainvillea on the porch.

I creep closer, my steps shaky. The vines have grown down the chimney, it looks like, and every time the wind gusts outside, they scrape against the brick, their leaves trembling.

This can't be possible. This was not here last night, when I sat in the living room watching YouTube videos on my laptop. I *know* it wasn't here.

But then Xavier broke in—

I stumble backward, tripping over my own feet. The vines crawl across the hearth, dusting it with the crimson petals.

A thunderclap cracks outside, so loud that I swear the house shudders. And then, a split second later, the lights go out.

All my coiled tension erupts in a scream. I bolt out of the living room and into the dining room and drag the curtain back to try to let some light in. Not that it does much good. I can't believe how dark it is outside. Like it's nighttime rather than the middle of the afternoon.

The house is deathly quiet without the hum of electricity, and the darkness seems to crawl around me, and for a minute, I think of Xavier, his body pressed against mine. And then I think of Gideon doing the same thing.

"Fuck!" I dart into the kitchen, where the bougainvillea is going wild against the window. Its insistent rattling and tapping sound like old bones. I throw open drawers until I find a flashlight. It doesn't provide much more than a small circle of white light, but it's something.

No electricity means no Internet, which means I can't do much for my class. I can't call Gideon. And I don't want to leave, not with such a massive storm heading our way. I can *feel* it, the way the air hums against my skin.

There's a bright flash of lightning that washes everything out. Then another furious thunderclap. The bougainvillea bangs against the window like it wants to get inside.

"Gnocchi!" I call out, moving into the hallway. I tell myself it's absurd to be scared: I'm an adult, and storms never even scared me when I was a kid. But *this* storm—

There's something weird about it. Something ominous. It's nothing like the desert storms back home, with the cloudbursts of dust that announce their arrival. This just feels heavy and oppressive. Like the sky is collapsing down on top of me.

"Gnocchi!" I shout, a little louder, panic weaving through my voice. I go into the hallway, my flashlight illuminating everything in patches. There's a group of framed photos of Golly and Judith. There's a vase of silk flowers. There's an old, folded-over rug.

I'm nearly to the base of the stairs when I hear one of Gnocchi's sharp, staticky hisses. I whip around, the flashlight a blur.

But then I hear something worse.

A snake's rattle.

"Gnocchi!" I scream, panic surging up in my chest. How the fuck did a rattlesnake get in the house? "Gnocchi, don't move!"

The rattle slows, and Gnocchi lets out a low, whining yowl, a sound that sends chills racing over my skin. I shine the flashlight up the stairs, my breath tight and panicked. No sign of him.

"Please," I whisper, tears threading through my lashes. I can't lose Gnocchi. Not my fluffy potato kitty, my best friend in the whole fucking world.

The rattle sounds again, louder this time, and I whip around, trying to calm myself. The flashlight dances across the floor, into the foyer—

That's when I see him. Gnocchi, his pale fur raised in a ridge on his back and his ears plastered against his head.

And he's staring down an enormous rattlesnake. Or what I assume is a rattlesnake. This snake is solid black, not like any rattlesnake I've seen before. But that rattle is unmistakable.

The rattlesnake is coiled, its head lifted and staring directly at my sweet Gnocchi, who lets out another low yowl. The snake's rattle vibrates against the floor, and it draws its head back. For a second, its eyes look like stars.

"No!" I scream, and I hurl the flashlight at the snake. It slams against the side of its head, sending it flying sideways. I dart forward and scoop Gnocchi up before he can jump on the snake, which it very much looked like he was about to do, and slam up against the front door.

Which is locked.

Worse, when I try to open it, the lock is jammed.

The snake rattles again, and I have no idea where it is, only that it's close. I swear I can feel it crawling on me—twining around my leg, wrapping around my hips. It's not, of course, but as I fumble with the lock, my fingers slippery with sweat, I keep slapping at myself.

Gnocchi squirms in my arms, his claws slicing across my skin. I squeeze him tighter and *finally* get the door unlocked. I drag it open and let the wind in, damp and hot and howling. Then I kick open the screened-in door and stumble out onto the porch.

Gnocchi yowls, his whole body tense with fear. "It's okay," I mutter to him, walking backwards across the porch. The screen door slams shut, but I can see the snake on the other side, rising up again, its eyes glittering.

That's not a normal snake. Rattlesnakes don't have solid black scales, and their eyes don't fucking glitter.

"I got you," I whisper, running my hand over Gnocchi's bristled fur. He clings to me, hooking his claws into my shirt, his tail tucking around my arm. I dart sideways, getting him out of view of the snake. It seems to calm him a little, but the wind is wild even here on the porch, whipping my hair around. Out in the front yard, debris blows around—leaves and twigs and those red bougainvillea blossoms, streaking the dark, shivery air like blood.

I take slow, deep breaths, trying to decide what to do next. I don't have my car keys, so I can't just drive somewhere else. And I don't want to open that front door again. Not with that rattlesnake coiled up in the foyer.

I still don't understand how it got inside. *Probably just the storm*, I tell myself, but it feels like an uneasy lie. There's something unnatural about that rattlesnake, even if I don't want to dwell on it.

I force myself to focus. I need to get inside.

The back door, I think, my belly twisting uneasily. I'll have to fight through the bougainvillea, but I never did find a way to really secure the door. I can go in through the back, lock Gnocchi up somewhere safe, and then deal with the snake.

I cradle Gnocchi closer to me as I duck off the porch. "It's all right, buddy," I whisper, squinting my eyes against the damp, whipping wind. There's no rain, at least, even though it looks like there should be with how dark the sky is. Just the howling, humid wind.

Gnocchi yowls and digs his claws deeper into my shoulder, but at least he doesn't try to squirm away or jump out. He buries his nose into my neck, and I stroke his fur as I go around the side of the house, trying not to think about the bougainvillea twisting over the siding. It's spread. There's no denying that, how it's wrapped halfway around the house like it's trying to consume it. But I can't think about that right now.

Until I *do* have to think about it, because I get to the back porch and it's a jungle of thorns of blood-red blossoms.

I stare at the bougainvillea in disbelief, the wind howling

around me. It's completely overtaken the porch, so much so that I can't even see the door. I can barely see the railing, and that's only because the wind pushes the bougainvillea aside, giving me flashes of white.

Fear knots so tight in my belly that I think I might throw up.

Gnocchi yowls and tries to wriggle his way free. I squeeze him tighter. "No," I say, more sharply than I mean to. "No, we're going to find a way in, okay?"

His tail thrashes against me as he claws his way up to my shoulders. I squeeze him as tight as I dare and take a stumbling step back, still gaping at the porch in horror. I was just out here yesterday, searching for my phone. It didn't look like this. It was overgrown, yes. But I could still see the porch.

I think of the vines crawling down my chimney, and chills ripple across my skin.

Gnocchi makes a sound I have never heard him make before, something like a growl crossed with a mountain lion's scream, and he tries to scramble out of my arms so desperately that he claws my skin and draws blood.

"Gnocchi, stop!" I cry as I wrangle with him, terrified he's going to escape and bolt into the woods, and I'll never see him again.

He twists around in my arms and growls again, ears flattened, as he stares at the nest of bougainvillea that used to be my porch.

Something moves in the vines.

I freeze, fear jolting through my chest. *It's just the wind*, I tell myself, but it's not just the wind, because I see it again. A tall, black shadow.

The vines rustle as it turns toward me and Gnocchi.

Its eyes glitter like stars.

I'm bolted in place. So is Gnocchi, who has stopped trying to escape and just trembles against my chest.

"Xavier?" I whisper hoarsely, even though I know it's not him. This person—this thing—is too tall. Too thin. I think its hands are tipped in claws.

It's not human.

It stares at me, too shadowed by the vines and the storm clouds for me to see anything but its starry eyes.

Then it grins. Or grimaces. Or says something, because I hear a voice echo in my head that is not my own and is not speaking a language I've ever heard before. Its teeth flash like knives.

Something hot and wet drips out of my nose. Blood. Gnocchi hisses.

The thing in the bougainvillea takes a single step toward us, and thunder rolls through the heavy clouds. Except it's not thunder, because there's no lightning, and the earth shakes.

It grins or grimaces or says something again. Pain throbs behind my left eye.

Gnocchi scrambles against me, tearing more cuts into my arms, and I get the sense that the thing in the bougainvillea likes it, the scent of my blood.

It takes another enormous, thundering step—

And I finally find the courage to run.

39

IVY

I run to Hartshorn. Where else can I go?

I tear through the woods, pressing Gnocchi as close as I can against my chest, ducking as the trees and vines and scrub brush tear at my body. I don't look back. I don't check on Gnocchi, who is still trembling in my arms, because that would require me to stop.

I just keep running.

By the time I burst out of the woods and see the massive grey wall of the Hartshorn mansion, my lungs are burning for air. But I don't stop. I cut across the open field, ducking the flying debris that's whipping around in the wind. I don't even know where to go—there are so many entrances, so many doors, so many windows—and so I just run around to the front entrance of what Gideon calls the new wing, with its big carved double doors. I always thought the carvings showed the surrounding woods, but now I think they look like bougainvillea vines.

"It's okay," I gasp out to Gnocchi, who stirs against me, yowling softly. "We'll be okay here."

I press the doorbell, and the chime echoes hollowly inside.

Then I suck down deep drafts of air and try to decide what I'm going to say when Xavier answers. Or Judith. God, I hope it's Judith.

The wind howls. Silent lightning cracks the sky. And then I hear the lock turn.

When the door opens, it's Judith. I've never been so grateful to see her face, even though her expression is strange. Almost like—

Almost like she's expecting me.

"Ivy," she says, her shoulders hitching a little. "Of course."

I don't know what to say to that. So I ignore it. Because I can't be out here anymore. "I'm sorry to bother you," I say shakily. "I—" I take a deep breath before I spill out something too crazy. "There's a rattlesnake in my house."

"Come in." Judith pulls the door open wider. I step through the threshold, and the stillness in the foyer is sudden and surprising. They didn't lose power here; a lamp glows softly in the corner.

Gnocchi stirs and lifts his head, looking around with huge eyes.

"And who's this?" Judith says with a smile, holding her fingers out for him to sniff.

"Gn-gnocchi," I stammer out. "I'm sorry, I couldn't leave him. The snake almost—"

"It's fine." Judith looks at me, her eyes pale and hard. *Like stars*, I think distantly, then shudder. "Poor thing has been through a lot. How about we set him up in one of the bedrooms so he can calm down?" She smiles and strokes his forehead, and Gnocchi doesn't try to squirm away. "I have some food I put out for the strays that he can have."

I nod, feeling numb. Now that I'm inside, out of that fierce, eerie wind, my terror is starting to subside, although I still feel shaky and uncertain. The thing I saw in the bougainvillea—it couldn't have been real.

Could it?

Footsteps echo off the walls, and my chest clenches up. But it's not Xavier who steps into the light of the foyer.

It's Gideon.

"Ivy!" he cries when he sees me, and all I can do is gape at him. Gnocchi leaps out of my arms, and Judith sweeps him up, which he doesn't seem to mind. Gideon throws his arms around my shoulders, pulling me up against his firm chest, and I can't help it. I melt into him.

"Gideon," I breathe. "I thought you weren't back until tomorrow—"

It nags at me that he's here.

"I came home early," he says into my hair, squeezing me up tight. "I was going to come by, but I had to—"

The floor creaks, and I look over Gideon's shoulder.

Xavier.

His eyes bore into mine, but his expression is dark. Jealous. He looks rumpled, with mussed hair and disheveled clothes.

Guilt twists hard in my chest. I can still feel the ghost of his tongue between my legs, licking furiously at my clit even as I begged him to stop.

Gideon senses him, too, because he lets go of me and turns around and then steps between me and his brother.

"Boys," Judith says sharply. I'd almost forgotten she was here. She steps up between the two brothers. Gnocchi's draped over her shoulder and looking perfectly content, which is at least one less thing for me to worry about.

"Don't let this go on," she says softly, switching her gaze back and forth between them. "I told you something was coming. Well, it's here."

That brief sense of relief fades, and fear blooms in its place, sharp and bright. Judith looks over at me, and I swear her expression is almost apologetic.

"Don't be afraid," she says.

Before I can respond to that, she sweeps out of the hallway with Gnocchi, leaving me alone with Gideon and Xavier.

For a moment, none of us moves. The wind howls outside, although it sounds further away in the fortress of Hartshorn than it does Golly's old farmhouse.

"Why are you here?" Xavier says, still staring me down.

Gideon bristles. "Leave her alone," he says. "You've done enough fucking damage."

He knows, I think suddenly. Xavier's expression gives nothing away.

"Why'd you come here?" Xavier asks me. "What made you run out in the middle of a storm with your fucking cat?"

"It's not raining," I say stupidly.

"It's a windstorm," Xavier replies. "Why are you here?"

"Leave her *alone*," Gideon snaps, and I hear something like desperation in his voice.

"No." Xavier strides closer. "You heard Gran. Something's here." He stares at me. "You saw Him, didn't you? It wasn't a snake. It was Him."

"Don't," Gideon says, but he sounds defeated.

"Who?" I say weakly, but I know exactly what Xavier is talking about. The shadow in the bougainvillea.

Xavier grins, and it's the grin of a madman, of a killer in a movie. "The Shadow Thorn," he says.

Those words cut right through me. I stagger backward, feeling that sudden stabbing pain behind my eye. Gideon calls out my name, although it sounds far away, and when he wraps his arm around my waist, his touch feels distant, too. Like my body has gone numb.

"You did see Him," Xavier says softly. "I knew it. I knew you were meant for me."

"Shut the fuck up," Gideon snarls, pulling me closer to him. The vehemence in his voice startles me. "Give it up, Xave. You don't have a claim on her."

"What are you talking about?" I wrench out of Gideon's grasp and whirl around so I can face both of them. The two brothers—light and dark, slim and strong, cruel and kind. "A claim? What?"

"It's a tradition in our family," Xavier says, and Gideon shushes him.

"What is?" I look at Gideon. "What don't you want to tell me?"

"You don't want to know about it," Gideon says quietly. "Trust me."

There's another terrible, shaking thunderclap, and my heart leaps in my chest.

I told you something was coming.

A monstrous shadow with stars for eyes takes a single, earth-shaking step toward me.

Well, it's here.

"There was something on my back porch." The words come out in a blur. "I don't know—I couldn't really see—"

"The Shadow Thorn," Xavier says, although he's looking at Gideon. "Because He approves my claim. That's why He was in the bougainvillea."

"He approves mine," Gideon snarls, and there's that vehemence again. I feel it down in the marrow of my bones, feel the strength of him as he glares at his brother. I still have no idea what they're talking about, not really. But something—

Something flashes in my memory. The burnt-down chapel where Xavier kissed me.

But so did Gideon. No. That can't be right.

"Who is the Shadow Thorn?" I finally say, and both brothers look over at me.

Xavier looks as he did two nights ago, feral and cruel.

Gideon looks tired.

"He's something very old," Xavier says. "And very powerful. And a hundred years ago, He gave our family a gift."

Numbness washes over me. This is crazy.

As crazy as bougainvillea covering my house overnight. As crazy as a shadow with a step that can shake the earth.

"He wants us to be together," Xavier says softly. "You and me. Because when I was thirteen, I kissed you in His chapel—"

When Gideon hits him, the sound rings out as loud as those thunderclaps. Xavier slams up against the wall and grins. I turn to Gideon in disbelief.

"Why did you—" But I falter, because Gideon doesn't look himself. Fury twists his face, and the muscles cord in his arms.

"That was fifteen goddamn years ago," Gideon growls at Xavier. "And it didn't mean shit."

"It couldn't have even happened," I say weakly, and both of them look at me. "I didn't come here when I was thirteen. My sister—"

"Your sister doesn't remember, either," Xavier says.

"Stop *lying* to me." I glare at him. "Just—tell me what's going on. Tell me why I saw that monster on my fucking back porch, why—"

"I did tell you," Xavier snarls. "Gideon's too chickenshit to explain it, so I will. My family worships a god older than time itself, and He wants you to be part of the family, too."

I whip my gaze back and forth between them. The wind outside seems louder, like it's trying to claw its way inside.

And although what Xavier is saying is absurd, it also feels—

It feels *right*.

"Gideon," I whisper. "I trust you. Is Xavier—"

"He's not lying," Gideon says softly.

Dizziness sweeps over me. For a moment, the dark foyer seems to spin.

"But don't listen to him about him claiming you." Gideon's voice is firmer now. "That's a choice you ma—you get to make."

Xavier scoffs.

Gideon cups my face with both hands, tilting my gaze

upward so that I'm looking straight into his eyes, which, in this moment, feel as dark as the storm churning around outside. "You saw Him, didn't you?" he asks quietly. "The Shadow Thorn?"

I tremble. I can't say yes, even though I can feel that dark, terrifying presence. Its starlight eyes are peering at me through Gideon.

So I just nod.

Gideon pulls me up to him, his nose buried in my hair. "I know it's scary," he murmurs. "But you get to decide, okay? Not us." He nuzzles against me, then takes a deep breath. "But if the Shadow Thorn wants you here, then—then you're supposed to be here."

I cling to him, trying to sort out what it means. What's true. What's not.

"Did I really come here when I was thirteen?" I whisper against Gideon's chest, his warm, cedar scent wrapping around me. "And kiss Xavier?"

Gideon hesitates, his muscles stiffening. "Yes."

The world whirls around again, but at least Gideon's here to hold me upright.

"You don't remember it because—" He stops and squeezes me a little tighter. "It's complicated. Your mother didn't want you to. So Gran and Gloria—"

He doesn't want to go on, and I'm shaking with all of this knowledge, not sure what to make of it. If there can be shadowy gods, why wouldn't there be magic and witchcraft? Why wouldn't there be even more terrible things?

"Why didn't she want me to remember?" I whisper, and Gideon strokes my hair.

"We're not supposed to talk about this," he finally says. "It could make you sick."

"Enough." Xavier's voice cuts through the foyer, and I pull away from Gideon to find him glaring at us, his arms crossed over his chest. "Forget what happened in the past," he says. "You can decide again."

I press closer to Gideon, and he wraps his arm protectively around my waist. Xavier still looks feral in the shadowed light, his smile cold and calculating.

"You want me to—what?" My voice trembles. "Choose between you? I choose Gideon."

As soon as I say it, doubt surges through me, and I don't know why. Of *course* I would choose Gideon. He's sweet and handsome and has never done anything to me against my will, even though he fucks like a monster.

But something tugs me toward Xavier, something dark and terrifying. A tether I wish I could snap.

And Xavier doesn't waver, as if he can sense it, too.

"I was actually thinking we could do something more interesting than that." Xavier moves toward us, and I feel Gideon tensing again.

"Stop," he says in a low, warning tone.

"I'm not talking to you." Xavier stares at me. "I'm talking to Ivy."

I watch him, cautious and wary and also faintly curious. I shouldn't, but I want to hear what he's going to say.

"Let's make it a game," Xavier says. "The Shadow Thorn loves games."

That name sends another sharp, violent shudder through me. But I cling to Gideon's arm and wait for the rest of Xavier's proposal.

"You technically chose both of us," Xavier says. "Me, fifteen summers ago. And Gideon—"

Gideon makes a warning noise in the back of his throat. Xavier's eyes flicker over to him. Back to me. I don't know what it means.

"Gideon, you choose this summer," he says with a smile.

My heart flutters. "I don't remember choosing you," I say to Xavier, doubt prickling in the back of my throat.

He rolls his eyes. "Yes, you do. I gave you the memory back."

"I remember *kissing* you," I say darkly.

Xavier sighs. "It doesn't matter," he says. "I'm talking about a do-over. But we'll let the Shadow Thorn guide your choice this time."

"How?" Gideon asks, voice low.

"A game, like I said." Xavier tilts his head, studying me. "Ivy, you'll run. Me and Gideon will chase you. Whoever catches you first—that's the winner."

Lightning floods the foyer in a sudden flash, and in that blinding brightness, I swear I see a too-tall shadow standing behind Xavier, its mouth split open into a toothy grin.

Then the dark floods around us again, and thunder booms overhead.

"We'll do it in the old wing," Xavier says. "Gran never goes in there."

"You don't have to do this," Gideon says, but even I hear the doubt in his voice. He doesn't believe what he says.

I turn around in his arms and gaze up at him, his brow creased with worry. A game of hide and seek. All I have to do is make sure Gideon's the one who finds me.

"What if I want to?" I whisper.

Gideon's eyes widen a little. And I feel something harden against my thigh.

"You want to, too," I murmur.

"Of course he does," Xavier laughs. "I'll bet he'll even put on that mask of his, if you want it."

We both look over at Xavier, leaning up against the wall with his arms crossed. He frightens me, but that fear just sends heat flooding between my legs. Just like the idea of Gideon chasing me through the dark in his leather wrestling mask.

"He's not even trying to deny it," Xavier says with a laugh.

Gideon's arms tighten around me. "I would," he says, softly, into my ear. "If you want."

I can feel his cock digging into my thigh. Feel just how much he likes the idea.

And I wonder, briefly and absurdly, if Xavier's cock is hard, too.

Something slams around in the wind outside. Lightning flickers again, and this time I don't see anything until the light fades, and two stars glimmer over Xavier's shoulder.

"We'll give you a head start," Xavier says, but I'm looking at those two stars, and I know Gideon was wrong.

This isn't my choice.

It's the Shadow Thorn's.

But I'm not going to fight it.

✥ 40 ✥

IVY

The old wing of the house is even darker than the new wing. All the lights are off, and thick, velvet curtains block what little light might seep in from outside.

Behind me, the lock in the door clicks over, shutting me into the wing. Xavier said they would give me a five-minute head start. Gideon told me to be brave.

For a second, I just stand there by the door, taking deep breaths, half-expecting to see a pair of starlight eyes in the dark. I can't believe I'm doing this.

But I also can't believe how fucking *right* it feels.

I take off down the hallway, feeling my way along the walls so I don't trip over anything. My fingers comb over a light switch, and I flick it up and down. Nothing happens.

Fuck. The lights were still on in the new wing. Is this Xavier's doing? Or something else?

I don't think about it right now. I need to focus on finding a place to hide so I can wait and watch for Gideon, then pop out at the last minute so he can catch me. That's my conscious thought, anyway.

Because something else lingers beneath the surface. Something that wants to play the game for real. To give up the choice that Gideon says is mine to make, and to let the darkness decide for me.

No. This is just a game, and I only agreed as a way to get Xavier to leave me alone.

Didn't I?

My fingers fumble over a doorknob, and I pull it open, blinking in the darkness to try and discern what room this is. I think it might be a closet, although it seems empty. There's certainly enough space for me to fit comfortably inside.

That's when I hear the thump of footsteps from somewhere nearby, heavy and male.

I dart through the doorway and ease the door shut, taking deep, careful breaths. I press my ear to the door and listen.

Nothing. Just the ceaseless howling of the wind. Then—

"Where are you, cicada? I can hear you scurrying around in the walls."

I gasp and jerk back, then slap my hand over my mouth. The footsteps thud heavier, and I step back, hoping to find clothes or boxes or something I can hide behind. But the closet keeps going.

It's not a closet, I realize. It's a hallway.

Footsteps pound overhead, and I press my back to the wall and move sideways. One of the servant's hallways, I think, hazy memories flashing through my thoughts. Xavier and I used them that summer when we were kids, sneaking from one side of the house to the other.

Both summers we were kids.

I've got to get out of here. This is one of the first places he'll look.

I move more quickly until I arrive, finally, at another door, which I crack open. Grey, eerie light filters in. It's a kitchen, although one that looks like it hasn't been used in years. The stove is boxy and out of date, and cobwebs drape from the light fixture. The refrigerator hums, though, which means there has to be electricity.

I try the light switch. Still nothing.

The storm pounds against the kitchen windows, mostly branches and leaves and a few thin streaks of rain. I creep into the next room. I assume it was a dining room once, although it's empty now, save for an antique china cabinet full of pale plates practically glowing in the darkness.

I press against the wall and listen. Nothing but that howling wind. I need a hiding spot, a real one. Someplace to wait for Gideon.

So I move forward, stepping into some kind of parlor or sitting room, the antique furniture lurking like monsters in the dark. This room leads into a foyer with a flight of stairs. And another door.

I dart over to the door and drag it open and am immediately met with a torrent of wind and cold, misting rain. I shriek and try to slam it shut, but the wind pours inside, too strong for me to fight. It rips the door out of my hands, and it slams up against the far wall with a loud, echoing bang.

"You want to take this outside, cicada?"

I scream and whirl around as Xavier swings around the stairs. But for a moment, I don't think it's Xavier, because he's wearing a mask. Not a dark leather muzzle like Gideon's, but a pale skull that covers half his face, leaving his mouth free and his eyes two dark pits.

"Get away from me!" I shriek

Xavier laughs and saunters toward me. "Looks like I won."

No. No, I won't let him.

And so I dive out into the storm.

It's a panicked, stupid move—Gideon will be looking for me inside. But I won't let Xavier win this stupid game. I *won't*.

The wind is even more furious now than it was earlier. It feels like long, sharp claws that want to shred the skin from my bones, but I don't care. I duck my head and run as hard as I can across the rain-slick grass. It's not raining much; just a damp, chilly mist that glazes over my hair and leaves a chill in its wake.

Xavier's laughter follows me on the wind, and when I glance behind my shoulder, he's following me at a leisurely pace. In his dark clothes, all I can really see of him is his mask.

Fear spikes through my chest, and something else sparks through my core. Something I don't want to think about.

I veer to the left, trying to get around to another entrance of the house, to find some way back inside and into Gideon's arms. But the wind and the darkness both seem to batter me around, and suddenly I'm running between rows of shredded rose bushes, the blossoms scattered across the grass like fallen leaves.

The garden. How did I end up in the garden?

I twist around to look over my shoulder. There's no sign of Xavier, but Hartshorn rises in the distance, wreathed in grey mist and crowned by dark trees.

I turn again, trying to make a wide arc back to the house. But then a figure darts in front of me. A shadow with a pale face.

"Got you," Xavier snarls, grasping out to me. I scream and spiral away from him.

"What'd you do with Gideon?" I shriek, flying through the wind toward the thick wall of trees, their branches thrashing back and forth in the storm. Xavier laughs behind me.

"Nothing!" he calls out, his voice dangerously close. "He's looking for his little rabbit, same as me."

I dive into the trees, straight into a thicket of underbrush that claws and scrapes at my skin. Behind me, Xavier curses, and the brush rustles as I shove my way through, not caring about the thin lines of blood forming all over my bare skin. I have one focus. One thought.

Get away from Xavier.

And I do. I burst out of the brush and into a narrow clearing. The trees block the worst of the wind, although their leaves rustle wildly overhead, and debris rains down on me and sticks to my damp skin. I surge forward through the woods, batting away vines and wayward branches. The rain has picked up a little, weaving through the trees and soaking my hair and T-shirt. But I keep running, wildly and without purpose, until I'm certain I've lost Xavier.

Only then do I slow down, first to a jog, then to a walk, then to a complete standstill, leaning up against a nearby pine, the bark sharp against my back. I suck down shuddery breaths and try to ignore the ache in my legs. I'm not much of a runner, and I can't believe I ran as far as I did.

While I try to catch my breath, I also listen. The forest is full of sounds: the thrashing tree branches, the howl of wind, the patter of rain, the occasional rumble of thunder. None of the furious thunderclaps that shook the whole world, thank god. Just a soft, throaty mumbling.

I peel myself away from the tree and stagger forward, my legs stiff. I weave through the trees, my panic at being caught by Xavier melting into a more primal fear—

That I'm lost.

I can barely see in front of me. The rain drips into my eyes. My clothes cling to my skin. I'm wet and breathless and uncomfortable.

They said I'd run until one of them caught me. But what if neither catches me? What if I die out here? What if—

What if that dark shadow takes me instead?

Something cracks behind me, loud as a gun blast. I whirl around, eyes scanning the shadows. The woods are full of movement from the wind, but one shadow moves differently from the others. Slower. More calculating.

I take a step backward, and the thought of running feels like a nightmare. Maybe this is what Xavier wanted. To wear me down into submission.

But then the figure steps out from behind the trees, and it's too tall, too big, to be Xavier.

"Gideon," I breathe in relief.

He stops a few feet away from me, his face hidden by the leather straps of his mask. All I can see is the wet tangle of his hair and the glint of his eyes.

Like stars.

"You caught me," I say.

"Not yet," he answers, and fear twists around my heart. It also drips down between my legs. I squeeze my thighs together, waiting for him to come to me and fuck me in the wet dirt.

Then lightning blinds the sky and illuminates the forest, and for a split second, I see everything: The spindly background of trees, the leaf-soaked ground, and Gideon, hulking and swaying like a monster, his eyes boring into me.

And behind him, with a too-long hand on his shoulder, is the creature that was in my bougainvillea, grinning at me with its rows of furious teeth.

I scream, a sound that tears out above the storm.

And then I run.

It feels delirious to be running from Gideon. But it also feels bright and exciting, especially when I hear the heavy thud of his boots behind me. I surge forward, giving him chase, anticipation pricking over my skin.

"Run faster, darling," Gideon calls out, his voice low and growly in a way that makes heat pulse in my core. "I'll catch you eventually."

I know he will, because I'll let him. I'll slow down or trip on purpose. But not yet.

I burst out of the forest and back into the beating rain and howling wind. It tears at my hair and clothes as I race forward, Gideon pounding behind me. The cemetery is up ahead; even in the dark, I can make out the pale statues, glowing as if they're suffused with moonlight. My feet slip over the wet grass, and I can feel Gideon surging closer, his steps heavier.

"Ivy," he gasps out. "Keep going."

It's not what I expect him to say, but I listen. I tear through the cemetery. When lightning flashes again, accompanied by that terrible thunder, and I see something up ahead.

A burned-down church surrounded by a thick hedge of flowers and vines and shrubs.

My heart shudders in my chest, and suddenly all I want is to be in that church, on my back, with Gideon thrusting between my legs.

So even though my entire body is screaming at me to stop, I keep racing through the wind and rain until I reach the hedge. And I dive straight into it, screaming as the branches claw at my face. But it's only for a second. Then I'm on the other side, and the burned-down church rises before me, shrouded in grey misting rain.

I stop and breathe, licking the rainwater away from my lips. I can hear Gideon's thudding footsteps coming from my left, and when I glance over, I see him, racing toward me in the shadows.

But there's another sound, too. A sharp, hysterical laughter. Another set of footsteps.

And then suddenly Xavier's running at me from the right, his skull mask as pale and glowing as the statues in the cemetery.

I scream when I see him and wrench around toward Gideon, who barrels toward me like a bull. I lunge forward, my arms outstretched, and Gideon grabs my hand, knotting our fingers together—

At the exact moment that Xavier's arms wrap around my waist.

41

IVY

Gideon's hand is warm against mine, and for a moment, we're not out in the cold, damp rain. It's warm and sunny, and there are so many bluebonnets growing around our feet that the air smells like honey.

But then Xavier's arm tightens around my waist, and I'm plunged back into the shivering darkness.

"I got her," he pants, gripping me so hard it's like he's drowning and I'm his life preserver. "I won."

"No, you didn't." I stare down at the place where my hand is linked in Gideon's. "I grabbed Gideon's hand. I— We—"

I look up at Gideon like he might have an explanation. But he just stares down at me from above his mask, and I can't deny it. I know exactly what happened.

"We caught you at the same time," Gideon says softly. He looks past me to Xavier. "It's a tie."

Xavier howls and tries to jerk me backward. But Gideon doesn't let me go. He moves with me as I squeeze down hard on his hand, and in a flash, I'm wedged between the two of them so that my breasts press against Gideon's chest and my ass notches into Xavier's pelvis.

In this position, there's no denying how hard both of them are.

"It's a tie," Gideon says again, this time looking at me. Then he unlinks our hands to cup my cheek. All I can do is stare up at him as the rain streaks over us, cooling the heat of my body.

A tie. A tie I let happen when I ran from Gideon.

This is what you wanted.

The thought hits me like a thunderclap, and I sag backward into Xavier, who runs his hands over my hip, slow and seductive.

"A tie," he breathes into my ear, the cool surface of his mask pressing against my cheek. "Do you know what that means?"

"No," I whisper, still staring at Gideon's masked face, monstrous in the grey filtered light.

"We both won." Gideon runs his thumb over my bottom lip, his eyes boring into mine. For a second, I don't know what to do. I'm trapped between them. I can feel Xavier's warm, shuddery breath on my neck, like he's about to kiss me.

And I want him to. I want them both to kiss me.

Before I can stop myself, I draw Gideon's thumb into my mouth and suck on it, keeping eye contact with him the entire time.

His breath hitches, and his cock jumps against my thigh. He glances over my shoulder again. At Xavier.

"What do you want to do about it?" Xavier growls, the words warming my skin.

I don't know if he's talking to Gideon or to me. But I do know that Gideon can't answer. Only I can.

This was a game. But the three of us weren't the only ones playing. And I'm certain this is the outcome that the fourth player wanted.

It's the outcome you wanted, too.

I slide my mouth off Gideon's thumb and turn my head

toward Xavier. He lifts his masked face, and all I can see of him are his parted lips.

"You both won," I murmur, feeling dazed. "You both—"

Xavier kisses me, and he makes it feel like an act of violence, grabbing my head and yanking me sideways away from his brother. But as soon as our lips touch, I know this is right. They both won.

And they can both have me.

I moan into Xavier's mouth as our tongues grapple together, like we're fighting each other. But at the same time, I snake my hand up Gideon's chest so I can curl it around his neck, holding him in place. I do not want to let him go.

Xavier growls into our kiss, grinding his cock up against my ass. I jerk away from him, breathing hard, and turn back to Gideon.

"Take it off," I say roughly, reaching up to pluck at his mask's straps. "I want to kiss you, too."

For a moment, Gideon just stares at me, rainwater dripping off his hair.

"You fucking chose me," Xavier says, trying to drag me backward. I brace my body, though, and keep my gaze fixed on Gideon.

"No, I fucking did not." I look at Gideon as I talk. "You both told me you've shared women before." I glance over my shoulder at Xavier, his eyes barely visible from behind that skull. "So share me."

For a moment, none of us moves. But the forest comes alive as wind gusts through the trees, blowing the rain across us.

"Fuuuuuck," Xavier groans, the one word dripping with lust.

I look over at Gideon, my breath tight in my chest.

Then he reaches up, unlatches his mask, and throws it on the ground. When he kisses me, he does it just as roughly as Xavier. Rougher, even.

"Inside," Xavier snaps. He wraps his fingers up in my hair

and drags me away from Gideon's devouring mouth and over to his. When he breaks the kiss, he growls against my lips. "We're claiming you properly. In the chapel, in front of the Shadow Thorn."

This time, when he yanks me away from Gideon, Gideon lets me go, and I don't fight it either. Xavier drags me forward through the misting rain, the painful tug on my scalp blooming heat between my legs.

The church's blackened doors yawn open ahead of us, wreathed in red bougainvillea.

For a moment, I'm nearly overwhelmed by that dark presence watching us from the trees, and panic surges up in me. I hear Juniper's voice echoing in my head, telling me that this place drives people crazy.

No, I realize, stumbling up the steps after Xavier. No, it drove her crazy. But I'm meant to be here.

Xavier heaves me into the church, his grin savage beneath his skull mask. Somehow, it's lighter in here than it is outside, everything gleaming like it's drenched in moonlight instead of rainwater. I stumble out of Xavier's grip and down the overgrown aisle, drinking in the strangeness of this place. I can tell it was a church once, a long time ago, with the broken-down pews and the rotting altar up ahead.

But the statue sitting on that altar was never in any church that I've seen. It leers at me, like it's a living thing, like it's excited for the depravity that I know is about to unfold because I can sense it thick in the air, radiating off of Xavier and Gideon both.

I turn away from the statue to face the two brothers, who stand side by side. Xavier still has his mask on, although he watches me with a skeleton's grin. Gideon looks like he wants to devour me.

"Strip," Xavier orders.

"Make me," I counter.

Gideon smiles at that, although it makes Xavier scowl. I hold my hands out at my sides.

"I'm waiting," I call out, taunting.

It's Gideon who moves first, launching himself at me, grabbing me by the hips and guiding me to the thick, leaf-covered ground. He shoves my soaked shirt over my head and throws it aside. Wrenches my bra up so my breasts spill free. When he pulls one of my hard nipples into his mouth, I groan and squirm against the ground, rolling my hips to fuck the air. His tongue is scorching hot compared to the chill from the rain.

"We're supposed to share, *brother*." Xavier drops down beside me and pulls his mask off. Then he bends over and bites down hard on my free nipple.

I shriek and jolt at the contrast: Gideon's wet mouth, Xavier's sharp teeth.

"She likes pain," Xavier purrs, massaging my breast. "Did you know that, Gideon?"

Gideon stops sucking on my tit long enough to say, "Shut the fuck up." Then he latches onto me again, and I wind my fingers through his hair to hold him in place.

Xavier watches with a dark gleam in his eye. "I need you," I tell him, the desperation making my voice pant. "Both of you. Now."

Xavier arches an eyebrow. "You hear that, Gideon? *Both* of us."

I groan in frustration and grab at Xavier to pull him toward me. I want him to bite my tit again, but he sweeps up instead and kisses me on the mouth, harsh and forceful, and honestly, that's just as good.

For a long time, we stay like that, Gideon sucking on my breast and Xavier sucking on my mouth, and all I can do is hump the air, my cunt desperate to be filled.

But then Gideon pulls away and moves between my legs. Xavier breaks our kiss and smirks over at him as Gideon yanks my shorts down and then my panties, flinging both over his shoulder.

I'm naked, completely at the mercy of the two Hartshorn brothers.

"Told you," Xavier says, moving down to suck and bite at my neck. "He loves eating pussy."

Gideon only grunts once in response before his mouth is on me. I cry out, opening my legs wider for him as he licks the full length of my slit with a slow, agonizing stroke that makes me moan and shudder. Xavier moves to my bare shoulder, scraping his teeth over my skin. I flail my arms, not sure who to grab onto, and eventually I grab both of them by the hair, like I can pull them into me and keep them there.

Gideon keeps licking my pussy, sliding his tongue up between my lips and flicking it over my aching clit. Xavier wraps his mouth around my nipple and sucks hard. All I can do is make small, whimpering noises as a hot, swollen pressure builds in my belly. Gideon wraps his arms around my thighs, holding me down while he eats me. Xavier's mouth is a sharp, constant tugging on my sensitive nipple. I buck with the first quivering tremor of an orgasm.

Xavier chuckles softly. Then he bites down. Hard.

I scream and jerk up. Xavier shoves me back down by the throat, his eyes gleaming.

Gideon never stops devouring me.

"I want to play another game," Xavier purrs, pressing his fingers against the side of my throat. "Gideon knows it."

That's the first thing Xavier's done that gives Gideon pause. He stops his feasting, although I can still feel his breath on my throbbing clit.

"W-what game?" I whisper.

Xavier rubs his thumb over the hollow of my throat. "A game we play at Lethe."

"Lethe?" The river of oblivion from Greek mythology. I'm halfway to oblivion now.

"A sex club," Gideon says, and I drop my gaze to find him still hunched between my legs, his mouth glossy with my arousal. "In Houston. That's where we..." He looks at Xavier, who grins wickedly.

"Where we fuck women who look like you."

Pleasure jolts through my body at Xavier's words. No, not just his words—Gideon's rubbing my pussy, slow and teasing. I can feel his eyes burning into me.

"Do you want to know how to play?" Xavier asks softly.

Between Gideon's fingers on my pussy and Xavier's hand around my neck, I can barely breathe. When I look up, all I see is a web of dark trees, the grey sky, the shattered roof of this terrible church.

This church, where I know, without a single doubt, that I'm going to sell my soul.

Gideon slides a finger into my cunt, making me jolt again. I look down at him, and he's watching me with an intense gaze.

Then he gives me one small, reassuring nod. I turn to Xavier.

"Tell me," I say.

He smiles cruelly, his eyes glittering. "The rules are simple," he says. "Gideon will try his hardest to make you come."

On cue, Gideon slides another finger into my pussy and strokes both against my G-spot, making me jump and cry out with pleasure.

"But I don't want you to come." Xavier squeezes my neck a little harder, his fingers spread out wide. "And I will punish you for not following my orders. Do you understand?"

Gideon brushes his thumb across my clit, and I know I'm going to lose this game.

"Let's play," I breathe.

42

XAVIER

I vy's going to come fast. I can tell by how violently her legs shake as my brother dives into her cunt again. Friday night showed me exactly how she looks before she unravels.

"Don't disappoint me," I warn her, sliding my hand away from her neck to squeeze one of those gloriously full breasts. Ivy gasps and bites down on her lip, and I know she's trying so, so hard not to come. But from the sounds Gideon's currently making between her legs, I know he's using his mouth again. And I know she's not going to last long.

"Don't do it," I growl, bending over to draw her other nipple into my mouth. She tenses beneath me, but I don't bite her. At least not yet. Instead, I tease her nipple with my tongue, rolling it around in my mouth like a pebble while I tug and pull on her other breast. Giving her those little sparks of pain I know she likes so much.

Ivy makes a low keening noise, her whole body quaking against the floor. I release her tit and look up to find her face twisted with pleasure—head thrown back, eyes squeezed shut, cheeks flushed red.

The shadow of the Shadow Thorn gazes at us from its place on the altar, and for a second, I swear I can see the air shimmering around it like an oil slick.

Ivy's keening turns to a frantic, staccato panting—a countdown to an orgasm if I ever heard one. I glance down at Gideon, who has his face buried in her pussy so deep that all I can really see of him is his rain-damp hair.

I look back at Ivy, and her eyes flutter open, her pupils blown out so that her irises look almost black.

"Don't fucking do it," I say.

"Gideon— I can't— I—"

I laugh and grab big handfuls of her tits. "You hear that, Gideon? All the blood has flown out of her brain and into her clit."

He grunts and keeps on with his meal. Ivy stares at me with desperation in her eyes, her pants growing faster.

"You won't like it when I punish you," I tell her, leaning over to suck on her tits again. "I've been nice so far. But if you disobey—"

Her whole body bucks up. Gideon presses her back down.

"Don't do it," I purr, scraping my teeth over her nipple. "Don't you dare."

Then I pull her tit into my mouth and bite down even harder than I did before. And it has the exact effect I want. Ivy erupts into a long, wailing scream, her body rippling with the force of her orgasm. I lean back so I can watch her fall apart on the filthy ground. Gideon, of course, drags the whole thing out, and part of me wants to be jealous that he's the first to make her come.

But I can feel the Shadow Thorn watching us, and I know I'm going to give her something even better.

"You little slut." I wrap my hand around her neck again to force her to look over at me. "What did I fucking tell you?"

She pants out a few words of protest, or something. They aren't really intelligible.

"Gideon, stop being a greedy asshole." I'm not looking at him, though. I'm looking at her. My Ivy. "This whore disobeyed me. You know what I do to disobedient whores?"

I tighten my grip, and Ivy's eyes go wide and glossy. Out of the corner of my eye, I see Gideon sit up, lumbering like a beast.

"Gideon can tell you, can't he?" I glance over at him, and his expression is as lust-drunk as hers. The entire half of his face is wet from her orgasm, too, and I bite back a flare of jealousy. "Tell her, big brother. Tell her what I do to disobedient whores."

Gideon gives me the same withering look he always does when I talk like this. "She's not a whore," he says.

I roll my eyes and turn back to Ivy, who's still shaking beneath my grip. I let her go, but only so I can slap her lightly on the cheek. She cries out a little, more in surprise than pain. We'll change that.

"Don't listen to him," I say. "You're exactly like the whores my brother and I have shared before. Now get up and go kneel in front of the statue."

I slap Ivy again, harder, and this time she moans softly and arches her back, her legs still flopped open, giving Gideon a perfect view of her cunt. Fucking asshole.

"Move!" I bark, and Ivy actually does what I say, scrambling back across the ground. I rise to my feet, distractedly rubbing my cock over my clothes as I watch her crawl up the altar, her movements shaky and uncertain.

"She's afraid of Him," Gideon murmurs, right next to my ear. I jump; I hadn't heard him move over to me.

"She'll be afraid of me soon enough," I growl, although I know he's right. I can sense her uncertainty as she looks up at the statue. The little quiver of fear. She can sense Him, I think.

His presence flooding the chapel, watching over this heady, dark ritual.

Ivy looks over her shoulder at me. At us. "What now?" she asks, and there's a touch of defiance in her voice that makes my cock jolt.

"Put your hands on the altar," I say.

Oh, she doesn't like that. Her eyes flick over to Gideon.

"Don't look at him," I snarl. "You disobeyed *me*, cicada. Now stay on your knees, put your hands on the altar, and wait for your punishment."

Ivy's eyes flash again: with defiance, with irritation, with lust.

And then she actually does what I ask. She twists back around, takes a deep breath, and presses her hands to the edge of the old stone altar. The statue rises above her, the ugly leer on its face deepening. But I'm not worried about the Shadow Thorn right now. All I care about is the sight of Ivy's smooth, shapely back, the way the soft line of her spine flows into the swell of her ass.

I'm going to put my cock in that ass by the time we're through. I'm going to make her scream with pain and pleasure both.

But not yet. I step toward her, my hand slowly unbuckling my belt. She hears it; I can see the way her shoulders bunch with tension. But I wait until I'm right beside her before I slide the belt out of its loops. I want her to hear every sound, every promise of what I'm about to do to her.

Ivy takes a sharp, shuddery breath. She's gripping the altar hard enough that her knuckles whiten, and her damp hair hangs in her face. She already looks wrecked.

Not wrecked enough, though.

I whip the belt through the air, making it crack. Ivy jumps at the sound.

"You're gonna hurt, baby girl." I run my hand down her

back, relishing the silkiness of her unbroken skin. "And you know why?"

She doesn't say anything, just stares at the altar. The Shadow Thorn's gaze is a weight on both of us.

I snap the belt across the fleshy part of her upper back. It's nothing. A warning shot. But Ivy still gasps softly.

"Good whores answer when they're spoken to," I say. "Now, let's try again. Why are you going to hurt?"

Ivy takes a deep breath and lifts her gaze to the base of the statue. Her whole body trembles. Her voice trembles, too, when she answers. "Because I came."

"Because you came," I sigh, glancing back at Gideon. His expression is unreadable. I hope he's fucking jealous.

Then I heave my arm back and bring the leather part of the belt down across her back as hard as I can.

Ivy screams. It's not the scream she made when she came. It's a scream of real, true pain, and the sound goes straight to my cock and makes my balls tighten up against my body. I whip her again, just as hard, for nearly making me come in my pants. And she screams again, then makes a kind of sobbing sound. Two red welts bloom across her back like flowers.

The Shadow Thorn's statue grins, showing a row of carved teeth.

I kneel beside Ivy and press my lip to her ear. She stiffens, her breath shuddery.

"That was nothing," I purr. "The price for disobeying me is blood."

Her breath catches.

I stand up. Take a step back. I need plenty of clearing room.

"You watching this?" I call out to Gideon, although I don't take my eyes off Ivy's beautifully marred back.

"You know I am," he growls.

I grin. Then I swing the belt down again. The wet *thwap* it makes across Ivy's skin sounds like music, especially since she keeps herself silent save for a muffled grunt of pain.

I wind the belt around my fist, slow and calculated. And then I unleash on her.

It's a fucking symphony. The air sings around the belt's leather as I bring it down to her, a soft melody punctuated by the percussive smack across her skin. And then, of course, there are the sounds Ivy makes: those muffled grunts as she holds back, and then the more soaring, sweeping screams as she gives way beneath the leather. I'm unrelenting, swinging the belt over and over until her skin finally splits open.

I smell it, just for a second, that sweet coppery tang. And only then do I let the belt drop to my side. I want to admire my handiwork. I want Gideon to admire it, too.

"Get over here." I finally look over at him; he's sitting on the front pew, watching us with a black, intense expression. "I want you to see what I've been doing to her."

"I can see from here," he says sullenly.

"Jealous?" I grin at him, and his expression gets even darker. Oh, he *is* jealous, although I know him well enough to know that he's not jealous of me or of what I'm doing.

He's jealous of Ivy. He wants to suffer as much as she is right now.

"Come on," I say. "Come look at our whore."

"Don't fucking call her that," he snaps. He also jumps to his feet, although he has to shift his oversized erection around when he does, so it ruins any attempt at being threatening.

Before I can make fun of him, though, Ivy speaks.

"Gideon." She says his name like it's a healing spell, like it soothes her pain. She tilts her head, and through the tangle of her drying hair, I can see tear tracks on her cheeks. She looks past me, though. To Gideon. "I want— want you to see. I want —come help—help him."

And for a moment, it's like the whole chapel fills with electricity.

Gideon doesn't hesitate. He's such a goddamn simp that he rushes over to her and kneels down and cups her chin in his hand. She stares up at him, eyes glittering, and I see something there I really don't like.

I think it's love.

"Gideon doesn't know how to do this," I say sourly. Then I hit her again, angling the belt so it hits the cut on her back. Ivy howls in agony, and red blood smears across her pale skin.

Gideon jumps up, glaring at me. "What the fuck," he snaps. "Be careful."

"Cicada," I say. "Look at Gideon's cock."

Gideon gives me an annoyed, weary look, but Ivy obeys. It helps that she's perfectly in line with it.

"You see how hard he is?" I hit her again, although without the fervor of earlier. I need her to register what I'm saying.

"Yes," she whispers.

Gideon glares at me.

"He wants to be in your place." I swing the belt down, making her jump. "But he doesn't want me to be the one beating him." Another hit. More blood. Ivy moans. "He wants you to do it."

This time, I don't hit her, although I see her tense in expectation. I drop the belt and turn to Gideon. "Isn't that true, big brother? You want our whore to split your back open?"

Gideon's chest heaves. His eyes glitter. "What the fuck do you care?"

"We're sharing her." I reach over her and tangle my fingers up in Ivy's hair so I can jerk her head back. Her eyes drink us both in. "Cicada, tell my brother how much you want to make him bleed."

Ivy runs her tongue over her swollen lips. Gideon breathes

roughly beside me, probably pissed that I clocked him so well. He can thank me later.

"Do you want that?" she says softly, looking at Gideon.

He nods. My brother is nothing if not predictable.

"Then so do I," she says.

I drag her up the hair, vaguely nauseated by the sweetness these two assholes are injecting into the proceedings. As soon as she's on her feet, Ivy yanks the belt out of my hand.

"I ought to whip you," she says.

I grin. "Please. You loved every second of that. I know a pain slut when I see one."

Her sulky silence is all the proof I need that I'm right. I wrap my arm around her bare waist and jerk her up to me so her blood soaks into my shirt, and the pressure of my body makes her wounds hurt.

"I want you to look at this slut," I say to Gideon, sliding my hand down until it's nestled between her legs—which she helpfully parts for me, leaning her bloody back against my chest and letting the belt dangle from her hands. I rub my palm against her dripping pussy. "Look how wet she is from me whipping her."

I draw her pussy open to show him. Ivy whimpers softly. Gideon licks his lips.

"That's how you know she's made for me," I purr, keeping my gaze fixed on Gideon. "Why the Shadow Thorn sent her to me."

"Sent her to *us*," he growls, stalking forward. I cup her cunt with my hand, relishing the damp heat of it. Gideon stops, his eyes dropping to the belt.

And then Ivy cracks it through the air.

My cock leaps at that, at the forcefulness of the movement, at the way her clit flutters against my hand.

Fuck me. Ivy's a pain slut in more ways than one. How did I

not see it? A masochist and a sadist, all rolled into one perfect toy for the two of us to share.

Too bad I don't like sharing.

"Let her go," Gideon says hungrily. "It's my turn."

I tighten my grip on Ivy's cunt. "To do what?"

But it's not Gideon who answers. It's Ivy.

"He wants me to hurt him." Her chest rises against my arm. "And I want to do it. Let me go, Xavier."

My cock jumps at the eagerness in her voice, at the dark cruelty straining against her breathlessness.

And I'm surprised by my own eagerness. Not to hurt her, but to see what cruelty she's capable of.

"Are you sure you're ready for that?" I murmur into Ivy's ear, puncturing the question with a sharp nip at her neck.

"You have no idea what I'm ready for." She tries to pull away from me, but I yank her back, hard enough that she sucks air through her teeth when her wounds slam against my back.

"You're right," I growl into her ear. "I don't. And you *did* disappoint me earlier, when you came so quickly."

Gideon's eyes flash. He steps forward, once again adjusting his enormous erection. From the look of that mountain in his pants, he's as hard as I am.

"But now's your chance to redeem yourself," I continue, sliding my free hand up around Ivy's neck so I've got her pinned by the throat and the cunt. She squirms against me, wriggling her ass against my cock. *In time, darling,* I think. I want to see what she can do first.

"Xavier, let her go," Gideon says darkly.

I ignore him and tilt Ivy's head toward me. Make her look me right in the eye.

"Do you want to come again?" I ask her, grinding the heel of my hand up into her pussy. Ivy cries out, then bites down on her lip. When she doesn't give me a real answer, I slap her cunt. "Tell me, you little pain slut. Do you want to come again?"

"Yes!" She squirms, and I squeeze her tight, holding her in place.

"Then hurt my brother," I order. "Make him bleed."

Ivy's flushed lips part. Her eyes gleam with desire.

"And if you impress me—" I stop, glance over at my brother. He's rubbing himself over his pants. "If you impress *both* of us, then I'll make you come so hard you won't be able to walk. Do you understand, whore?"

Ivy nods, her whole body trembling. She tries to pull away. I don't let her.

"But if you disappoint me again," I say, pressing my forehead to hers so each of my words becomes a kiss. "I'll hurt you more than you ever imagined. Do you understand?"

Ivy nods. I squeeze her throat.

"Say it. Out loud. Do you understand?"

"Yes!" she croaks out, and I shove her toward Gideon, sending her stumbling over the plant-strewn ground. Gideon catches her before she can fall, though, and gazes down at her, eyes searching like he wants to make sure she's okay. She nods at him, one of those silent gestures of affirmation.

Sickening.

But then she turns toward me, and she's an absolute vision: naked, her back streaked with welts and blood, and clutching the belt that did it to her.

"Now," I say, sinking down into the pew. "Let's see how cruel you can be."

43

GIDEON

I grab Ivy's chin and force to look at me. She's breathing hard, her pupils huge. And there are so many things I want to tell her. Like how beautiful she looked, kneeling in front of the Shadow Thorn's statue. Or how good she tasted while she came on my tongue. But right now, I have a desperate need for blood. For pain. I think the Shadow Thorn wants it, too.

"Don't let Xavier intimidate you," I finally say. "You're doing so good, baby girl. But I need to feel it, okay?"

Ivy takes a soft, shuddery breath. "I understand," she whispers, and I feel the muscles in her arm tense as she squeezes the belt.

I kiss her, slow and deep and romantic. Mostly because I want to, but also because I want Xavier to see it. I want him to watch as she melts in my arms. He needs to remember she doesn't belong only to him.

"Get on with it!" he bellows from the pew. "This shit is boring."

"Ignore him," I whisper to Ivy, taking her free hand in mine. Then I lead her back over to the altar.

The Shadow Thorn watches us through His statue, its mouth twisted into a grimace of delight, its eyes glittering like stars. Ivy stares up at it, her breath shuddery like she's afraid. I wonder if she felt Him while she knelt at His feet and Xavier split her open.

I wonder if she'll feel Him now.

"It's watching us," she murmurs.

"*He* is," I correct her. "And yes. Because He wants this."

I peel my shirt away and drag Ivy up for one more kiss, even though the gentleness of a kiss isn't remotely what I crave right now.

Then I kneel in front of my god.

I put my hands on the altar, just as Ivy did. I give her the canvas of my back.

"Don't forget!" Xavier calls out mockingly. "If I'm not impressed, I'll make you hurt so bad, *baby gi*—"

The whistle of the belt drowns out his voice, and a split second later, pain lances across my back. I grunt. Press against the altar.

"Harder," I rasp. "Put your whole back in it, baby."

I hear Ivy take a deep breath. Then I hear the whip-crack of the belt, and then I don't hear anything because I'm overtaken by the hot, glorious sting of my suffering.

"That's it," I gasp, staring at the base of the statue. "Just like that."

She unleashes on me then, each lash of the belt hotter and sharper than the one before. I moan through each strike, thrusting my hips into the air, wishing I could be inside her while she hurts me, like the night we fucked in the motel. It doesn't help that I can hear her quickened breath between strikes, and it reminds me of how she sounds before she comes.

"Harder!" I shout, still gripping the altar. My back burns like it's on fire, and I can feel the blood, too, dripping down my back in long, warm trails. It splatters across the ground and steams a little. An offering to Shadow Thorn.

Ivy shrieks and brings the belt down with enough force that I arch my spine, roaring through my pain. My cock throbs, and it takes every ounce of willpower not to pull it out and start stroking. Because if I do that, I'll come, and I can't have that. I have to come inside Ivy, have to shoot my seed into her womb while she's convulsing with her own pleasure.

I squeeze my eyes shut, thinking of it as Ivy beats me with the belt. The pain is starting to soften at the edges. It's starting to become that dark, heady pleasure that only blood can bring.

If I'm not careful, I'm going to come without even touching myself.

"Fuck," I gasp out, humping the air. That only seems to spurn Ivy on, and in the middle of her torrent, I twist around to get a glimpse of her—

She's a fucking goddess. Her hair's wild from the humidity. Her skin's gleaming with sweat. Her eyes burn with lust.

Cum surges into my cock.

"Stop!" I shout, slumping forward onto the altar. "Stop, baby. I'm gonna come."

Xavier's mocking chuckle fills up the chapel, but it's easy to ignore, especially when Ivy kneels beside me and puts her warm, soothing hand on my shoulder.

"Are you all right?" she whispers.

I turn to her, looking at her through the veil of my sweat-damp hair. She's so pretty like this, a naked plaything who gives me exactly what I need.

"I'm going to fuck you so good," I say. "You won't be able to think straight."

Ivy blushes.

I slump forward, pressing my forehead against the altar. "Give me a minute," I mutter. "I need to—to calm down."

Ivy brushes her fingers through my hair, her touch making

me shiver. Then she stands, her feet shuffling softly over the grass. I can hear Xavier stirring around behind me, too. He's probably as anxious to be inside her as I am. That's how the binding works, after all. We have to fuck her. We have to come together.

My whole body's shaking as I come down from the high of the pain. Slowly, I roll myself over until I'm sitting at the base of the altar. For a moment, all I can see is the chapel, green and hazy in the filtered light of the storm.

Then I see Ivy, her hand snaked between her legs, her fingers moving in slow, lazy circles.

I grin. "You liked that as much as I did, huh?"

She nods shyly and flutters her eyes closed—

And then Xavier's there to ruin things. He slaps her hand away and grabs her by the throat, grinning wickedly.

"For fuck's sake," I groan. "Let her come. She more than earned it."

"Oh, on that we agree," Xavier jerks Ivy up to him, and I notice the way she melts against his back, submitting to him as easily as she submits to me. It ought to make me jealous, but it doesn't.

This is what the Shadow Thorn wants. I can't pretend to understand it, why we have to share her. But His desire is clear. And if it's His desire, then I guess it's my desire, too. If it means I get to be with Ivy for the rest of our lives, it's worth it.

"But here's the thing." Xavier's voice jerks me back from my drifting thoughts. I force myself to focus on the two of them again, the way he holds her in place so casually, a doll to be used. *Our* doll to be used. "I don't want her doing it herself. *I'm* going to do it, and you're going to watch, big brother."

Ivy moans with anticipatory pleasure, a sound that makes my cock ache.

"I want you to keep your hands out in the open." Xavier

drags her backward, over to the front row pew. "The last thing we need is for you to come early and fuck everything up."

"Speak for yourself," I snap. "I'm the one who's actually done this ritual before."

Xavier shoots me a death glare before tossing Ivy onto the pew. She settles into it, spreading her legs and reaching down to rub her clit behind Xavier's back. I grin. There's my good girl.

Of course, when Xavier notices, he launches himself at her, jerking her arm away. "What did I tell you?" he growls.

"You said I could come," Ivy responds sweetly, which just makes me laugh.

"She's got you there," I tell him. "You keep fucking around."

Xavier scowls at me before settling down on the pew. He arranges Ivy on his lap, working in his usual methodical way: making sure she's on her back and her legs are spread, with one resting on the back of the pew and the other grazing the floor. Then he slides his fingers along her pussy.

Ivy cries out, jerking beneath his touch. He might not know her body as well as I do, but he knows how to make a woman come when he wants. He settles back in the pew, fingerfucking our Ivy without any real urgency. It's driving her wild, though. She groans and whimpers and rolls her hips. I doubt he's going to give her an easy release.

"I don't know about you," Xavier says. "But I think we need a game plan." He trails his free hand along the side of Ivy's neck, although he looks at me and talks like we're discussing some shared chores we need to take care of and not claiming Ivy Myste once and for all in the chapel.

"A game plan?" I say, arching an eyebrow. My cock throbs, still too sensitive for me to risk doing anything but sit here.

"Yeah. We've got to fuck her at the same time, don't we?"

I tighten my jaw. That's the only thing that makes sense, with the way the ritual works. The only thing that feels fair. I'm genuinely surprised Xavier is willing to admit it. I guess this really is what the Shadow Thorn wants.

Ivy moans and squirms on Xavier's lap as he keeps plying between her legs. I wonder if she's even registering what we're saying.

The idea that she doesn't is... incredibly fucking hot, actually.

"Well," Xavier continues. "This is what I think. You've already—"

My whole body stiffens, and I jerk my head no. Ivy still doesn't remember when I claimed her for the first time. That spell is still in place. What we do in here—it'll break it, probably. But I don't want her to find out before that happens.

I don't want to risk hurting her any more than I have to.

Xavier does cut himself off, though, curling his lips up in his cruel, mocking smile. "You've already fucked her," he says, and I know what he means. Here. I've already fucked her here. "I want something new. Something virginal."

Ivy moans and says something that sounds like, "What?" Xavier just chuckles and twists his wrist in a way that makes her whole body shudder.

"You heard that, did you, cicada?" He makes her shudder and scream again.

"What are you getting at?" I ask, impatient.

But Xavier ignores me. "Cicada," he says sharply. "Ivy. Look at me."

She does. Lust and jealousy twine through my core, each one heightening the other.

"Have you ever been fucked in the ass?" he says.

Ivy whimpers and shakes her head. He gives me a mocking grin, which I return with a glare.

"Never went that far, big brother?" he asks. Ivy pants and shakes. Xavier touches her like giving her an orgasm is a second thought, a thing to check off a to-do list. Like the sight of her naked, trembling body isn't the most beautiful fucking thing he's ever seen.

"Didn't want to hurt her," I say sullenly.

Ivy cries out, arching her back. I'm really not sure she's registering this conversation.

"Well, it works out for me," Xavier says, his hand moving faster over Ivy's pussy. She's on the verge of coming, and I have to use every ounce of my willpower not to reach down and stroke my cock. "Because I'm going to fuck her virgin ass while you take her used-up cunt."

I bristle at his words, but Ivy doesn't. She comes with a loud, throaty scream, the sound ricocheting around the chapel and making the air hum with a hot, crackling energy. Behind me, the statue seems to throb, the same way my cock is throbbing.

"On your knees," Xavier snarls to Ivy, tossing her down to the ground so she lands hard on all fours. I jump at that, warring emotions tearing through me. I don't want him hurting her. But I can't deny that the way she submits to him —the way she submits to *us*—has me dizzy with something like magic.

Ivy peers up at me through the tangled mat of her hair, her hands digging into the thick layer of leaves and plant matter. She arches her back, sticking her ass out at Xavier, who slides lazily off the pew and pushes her legs a little further apart.

"What are you doing?" I step toward them, horny and wary all at once.

"Getting her virgin asshole ready," Xavier says.

"Gideon," Ivy gasps. "Come here. Help him."

The words make me shudder with need. And how the fuck can I say no to her?

As I get closer, I can see better what Xavier's doing: teasing her asshole, probably smearing it with all the liquid arousal from her orgasm.

"She's fucking tight," he says to me. "No wonder you didn't bother."

I glare at him, but Ivy's looking up at me, her eyes pleading. "Please," she whispers. "I need both of you, Gideon."

"And what do you need from me?" I ask her, moving closer, fumbling with the fly on my jeans. Ivy watches me hungrily. "My cock? Do you want my cock in your pretty mouth while Xavier gets you ready?"

Ivy nods, biting down hard on her lip. I pull my erection out and bat it gently against her cheek, which makes her sigh.

"Please," she whispers.

"Hold it in your mouth," I tell her. "If you suck me off the way you usually do, I'm gonna come too early."

That earns me an irritated glare from Gideon, who's still fingering her asshole.

"Missed your chance to have you dick sucked," I tell him as I press my cockhead to Ivy's wet lips. She parts them for me and draws me into her mouth, which might as well be heaven. Not that my family gives a shit about heaven.

Not that I do, either. Not when I have this angel of a woman on her knees for me.

She swallows me inch by inch until almost my entire length is resting along her tongue and down the hollow of her throat. Then she holds me there, just like I said, and I wrap my fingers up in her hair and enjoy the sensation of being held by her. It doesn't hurt that every now and then she moans from Gideon's assplay, sending seismic waves rippling over my dick.

"Is she close?" I ask him.

"I told you, she's as tight as a goddamn drum." Xavier gives her a soft smack on her ass, which makes her jump around my dick. "But I've got two fingers in there. She's like all good little sluts, isn't she? Knows her place."

I don't say anything, just stroke her hair and relish the

warm, silky sensation of her tongue on the underside of my cock.

"Putting your dick in her mouth was a good call," Xavier adds, then spits into his hand and rubs it up against her asshole. "Gets her nice and wet."

Ivy moans a little, pushes her hip back. "Yeah," I say, still stroking her hair. "Sucking *my* cock always gets her wet."

That earns me another annoyed glance from Xavier, but he doesn't say anything, although I see him gathering up that aforementioned wetness to slick her asshole. I'm honestly glad he suggested we do it this way. I'd rather spill my seed in her womb.

Ivy makes a wet, choking sound around my dick, and Xavier chuckles. "Three fingers," he announces, working his arm back and forth. "Oh, she's taking me now, the slut. Almost as good as she's taking that ugly-ass python of yours."

"You want to see her take me?" I taunt back, twisting my hands up in Ivy's hair. To her, I say, "Let's show him, baby. Open up wide."

Ivy moans her delight and stretches her mouth open. Then I slide halfway out of her, keeping eye contact with my brother the whole time. He frowns, clearly irritated.

I thrust back into her mouth, making her whole body jump. The test round, and she definitely passed. I start thrusting, although I keep each movement slow and measured, careful not to bump too hard against the back of her throat. Ivy, of course, takes me like a queen. Drool slides out of the corners of her stretched mouth, and she gazes drunkenly up at me, her fingers digging into the dirt. She's never been more beautiful.

I slam my full length inside her, groaning in pleasure. Then I start face-fucking her in earnest, which earns me little desperate noises out of the back of Ivy's throat.

"Don't come," Xavier says warningly.

"Hurry the fuck up." I rock into Ivy's face, grunting at the sweet pleasure of her mouth. "I'm ready to share my claim."

❧ 44 ❧

IVY

I'm floating. I'm on my hands and knees, drifting up from the wet, cold ground. Only two things keep me from drifting away entirely:

Gideon's rock-solid cock slamming into my throat, and Xavier's agile fingers spreading my asshole open wide.

I give myself over to it: all that overwhelming sensation. All that overwhelming *pleasure*. My back still stings from where Xavier whipped me, and my arms still ache from when I whipped Gideon. My pussy is throbbing to be filled. Two mind-blowing orgasms and I still haven't been filled properly.

And I need it. If I don't get plugged tight, I think I might die.

Suddenly, strong hands tangle up in my hair and jerk me away from the comforting choke of Gideon's cock. I cry out, spit spilling over my chin, and get whirled around to face Xavier.

He has his cock out now, too.

It's not as big as Gideon's, but that's not saying much. Xavier's still bigger than other men I've been with, and he squeezes his rigid cock at the base and then slaps me across the face with it.

"Swallow me," he orders. "I need you to lube my dick up."

He doesn't give me any choice but to obey. The second my mouth opens, he slams into me. After Gideon, Xavier is easy to swallow. Still, he goes just as deep, slamming his pelvis into my face until my nose is buried in the musky damp of his pubic hair.

"Fuck," he gasps. "She *is* good at sucking cock." He pulls hard on my hair. "But sorry, cicada. I'm gonna need you to choke."

Then he shifts his angle so his cockhead rams up against an overly sensitive spot in the back of my throat, and I gag around, my eyes streaming tears.

Footsteps. I feel Gideon's hand brush against my bare shoulder, a soft and reassuring touch. "You've got this baby. Just breathe."

"Stay out of it, Gideon." Xavier thrusts into me again, and this time, when I gag, I feel something rising up through my throat. "Oh, fuck, there it is."

Xavier drags me off him as thick, clear spit gushes over his cock, making him gleam in the dim light. I gasp for air, nearly choking on my own spit. But I hardly have time to collect myself before they're both heaving me to my feet. I can hardly stand, my body is so weak from all the pleasure.

Fortunately, Gideon's there to hold me upright as Xavier strips off his pants and then settles onto the pew, his legs spread wide so his cock juts straight up, glossy with my spit.

"Get that tight ass over here," Xavier orders.

I take trembling steps over to the pew, Gideon holding my hand the whole time. When I get to Xavier, he grabs my waist and jerks me away from his brother, then whips me around so I'm facing away from him.

Facing the statue.

Its terrible, leering grin has grown since I looked at it last, and the fear that ripples through me is indistinguishable from my lust.

Xavier presses his cockhead against my asshole. I push back on him, needing him inside me. I need *both* of them inside me.

But Xavier slaps me hard on the ass, making me yelp.

"You think you can just shove yourself down on me like that?" he mocks. "No, darling. I don't just give my cock to greedy whores. You need to beg if you want me to fuck you."

"Oh, for fuck's sake," Gideon mutters.

"Shut the hell up," Xavier snaps. "Ivy. Beg."

"You don't have to do this," Gideon starts, but I shake my head.

"I want it," I tell him, rolling my hips against Xavier's cock. And here in the heady, strange space of the chapel, it's not a lie, either. I've never said anything truer. "I want both of you so fucking bad." I glance over my shoulder so I can see Xavier staring at me from beneath the fringe of his blond hair. "Please put your cock inside me," I whimper to him, feeling weak and servile and utterly sexy. "Please, Xavier. I can't stand it anymore. I need to be filled. I need—"

Xavier slams his cock into my asshole with no warning and no real preparation. Beautiful, exquisite pain tears my body in half, and I scream through it, my hands flailing out to grab at Gideon. And Gideon, of course, is there for me, lets me wrap my arms around his waist so that his cock slides between my tits.

"Fucking hell," he says. "You didn't have to do it like that."

"She likes it," Xavier says, easing me back into him. "Don't you, slut? You like the pain?"

I look up at Gideon through tear-glazed eyes. "Yes," I whisper, which is another truth. "And I need you, too. Gideon. Please." I shift back on Xavier, crying out as his cock presses up into me, alien and unfamiliar. But I want to spread my pussy wide for Gideon. I want to show him how wet I am for him.

And he sees it, too, his eyes dropping down to drink in my swollen pussy. I fall back against Xavier's chest, breathing hard, thumbing my clit. "Please," I whimper. "Please, Gideon. Fill me up completely."

The air sparks. The shadows swirl around us, wriggling like snakes.

"Claim me," I gasp. "Both of you. Claim me."

Gideon steps up to me, clutching his cock, and rubs it along my slit. I groan, spreading my legs wider for him, but he takes his time, slowly easing himself inside me.

"You're doing so good," he whispers, cupping my face with his hand, his eyes boring into mine. "You're taking us so well."

"Don't tell her that," Xavier snaps. "You aren't even halfway in yet."

"Ignore him," Gideon tells me, running his thumb over my lip. He pushes deeper into my cunt, and I suck in sharply at the pressure of both of them. It's overwhelming, being so full. "You're doing beautifully, baby girl."

Then he thrusts his hips, sparking me with pleasure. I cry out, and Gideon hooks his arms under my legs and says, "Stand." I think he's talking to me at first, but then I hear Xavier's chuckle.

"You want to lift her?" he says.

"I want to fuck her," Gideon says. "And it'll be easier like this."

Then, in one dizzying movement, the two Hartshorn brothers hoist me up. I cling to Gideon's shoulders as he and Xavier start fucking me in earnest, their cocks sliding in and out of me in a staggered, pounding rhythm. It's unlike anything I've ever felt, all that pleasure building so deeply inside me. All that sense of being filled to the brim.

I squeeze my eyes shut, panting through their thrusts. I'm

squeezed between their two bodies, trapped in a place that feels like the exact place I'm supposed to be.

"You feel so fucking good," Gideon pants against my lips before dragging me into a deep, sensual kiss. Heat shudders up from my core.

"You're a tight little whore, I'll give you," Xavier rasps behind me, his mouth on my shoulder. "A tight, needy slut. You've been waiting your whole life to have two cocks inside you, haven't you?"

I moan into Gideon's mouth. Because all of Xavier's cruel degradation is true, isn't it? This is what I've always needed—to be speared by two Hartshorn cocks at once, balanced between them in an overgrown church while something in the darkness watches on.

They carry me backward, taking me toward the altar with that awful, leering statue. Their movements are fluid and choreographed, and they don't even have to speak as Gideon pulls me with him to the ground so that he's on his back and I'm riding his cock, rolling my hips against him so each thrust sparks my clit. Xavier keeps ramming into me from behind, fucking me with a sharp, painful cruelty.

The three of us fall into a rhythm there in front of the altar. Gideon's cock in my pussy is liquid pleasure, and Xavier's cock in my asshole is a sharp, burning pain, and the sensations braid together until I know I'm going to come. It's building up like a fire deep inside my core, and I scream against Gideon's tattooed chest, wild and hysterical.

"You feel that?" Xavier rasps. To me, to Gideon, I don't know. "You fucking feel that?"

"Yes," Gideon groans, right before he catches my mouth in a kiss.

Xavier sinks his teeth into my shoulder.

And the pleasure tears through me like an invading army. I

quake between them as my orgasm explodes outward in rippling, frantic surges.

At the exact moment I spill over, Xavier shouts, slamming himself all the way to the hilt. Gideon roars, arching his back. Somehow, through the haze of my pleasure, I feel the hot spurts of their cum erupting inside me. Two places at once, just like my orgasm.

Something happens, then. Something more than coming, although it feels kind of the same—a whole-body quake that makes me gasp and jerk between the two brothers. The air seems to shift and tighten, like invisible ribbons are winding between the three of us, tying us together.

I lift my gaze, panting and gasping, and I see that dark shadow rising behind the altar, its eyes like stars.

It smiles at me. At us. For a moment, all I can see are teeth. And then it says something that sends another pleasurable jolt through my core, something that makes my head ache. It's in that strange, terrible language, but this time, I can understand it.

Welcome home.

And then it's gone. Only the statue remains. I slump forward, draping myself over Gideon's chest so I can ride the swell of his breath. He slides his hands around my waist, pulling me into him, and I don't want to separate. Not from Gideon. Not even from Xavier.

In the end, Xavier's the first to detach from the tangle. He slides out of my ass with a grunt. "God damn," he mutters, and I listen to his footsteps on the soft, overgrown ground.

Then I'm being lifted, cradled between two strong, familiar arms. Gideon carries me away from the altar, and I watch the statue watching us, waiting for the shadow to reappear. But it doesn't.

"Are you okay?" he murmurs into my hair. "Tell me you're okay, baby."

And I keep staring at the statue. At its terrible grin, its hideous features. I'm not okay. Not because of what we did, not because I feel regret.

But there's something deeper. Something cracking open inside me.

I really did sell my soul.

"Ivy?" Gideon lowers me to the ground and grabs my shoulders so he can look down at me, his eyes searching over my face. "Talk to me."

I can feel Xavier lurking nearby, watching us. I lift my gaze to the lattice work of trees overhead, the branches dripping with diamonds.

No. Raindrops.

And then the world around me flickers. I'm with Gideon, here in these ruins or this chapel or whatever it is, but it's not dark and rainy. It's sunny. There are flowers everywhere.

He's younger, his hair shorter, his face clean-shaven. He only has a handful of tattoos, all of them wrapping around his left arm.

I swoon a little, staggering backward, and I'm in the damp, rain-soaked chapel again. I collapse onto the rotting pew where Xavier made me come.

"Ivy?" Gideon's voice is bright with alarm. "Ivy, talk to me."

More images flash through my head, rapid fire, one after another.

I'm strapped to a table in a dark, hot shed, dots of sunlight slicing through tiny holes in the ceiling. Golly is there with Judith. They're chanting. I'm screaming out protests, tears streaming down my cheeks. I'm thirteen, and they're doing this because I kissed Xavier.

Then I'm older, my hair the bright blue I dyed it when I was eighteen. I'm out of college for spring break. I never came here in college. Except I *remember* it, the way I remember kissing Xavier. I'm walking across a field of wildflowers toward a wrestling ring where Gideon is hurling himself against the mat, over and over, creating a steady drumbeat that matches the blood pumping in my veins. When he stops, he looks at me over the ropes and smiles, and my heart flutters.

I'm in his bedroom, moaning as he devours my pussy. Moaning as he fucks me while I lie on my belly. Moaning as I wrap my lips around his cock.

I'm holding his hand as he guides me through a gap in the hedge. Here, to this place.

He's fucking me in front of the altar, me on all fours while he grips my hips to thrust into me, both of us panting in unison.

I'm in the shed again, strapped down, screaming.

You shouldn't have come back here, Golly says, brushing her hand over my hair. *You should have stayed in New Mexico.*

And then I'm back in the wet, dark chapel. I shriek and yank away from Gideon, staring up at him in confusion. Xavier creeps closer, a dark curiosity threading through his features.

"What do you remember now?" he asks me in a soft sing-song.

"Shut up," I snap, still staring at Gideon, who watches me with a kind of wariness. A kind of sadness. A kind of under-standing.

"We—" My voice lodges in my throat. "We've done this before, haven't we? You and I."

Gideon closes his eyes, and that's all the answer I need.

He fucked me here when I was eighteen, and he never fucking told me.

"Both of you." I stumble backward, the chapel swirling around me, the air so thick with humidity that it's hard to breathe. "They took away my memories of what happened with both of you—"

Xavier scowls. But Gideon only gazes at me with the most

mournful, apologetic expression I could imagine on a man, eyes brimming with sorrow.

"It was Gloria," he says hoarsely. "She didn't—she didn't want you to be part of all this. She made Gran do it."

"Why?" I shout, confusion pounding in my head as more memories flood through it. Most of them are about Gideon. A week. I was here for a week during my freshman year of college. I couldn't stop thinking about Hartshorn, and I came back during spring break, and Gideon was waiting for me.

I didn't remember the kiss then, either.

"Because our family is really, really fucked up," Xavier says with a smirk. "Isn't that right, *brother?*"

The glare that Gideon gives him is terrifying. A warning.

"Why didn't—why didn't she want me to—" They didn't explain anything to me before, either. I can remember being thirteen and Golly taking me and Juniper to Hartshorn right before we were supposed to leave for the airport. *We just have to take care of something*, she told me, and we walked through the woods to a shed that smelled like rotten flowers. I can remember it, that smell, the way it clung to the back of my throat. I remember the bones on the floor, the weapons on the wall. Judith in a black veil that hid her eyes.

Golly wore one too.

I scream, and there's something about this space that swallows the sound up. I remember the magic, how it felt like razor blades carving my brain into pieces.

Golly did that to me. She was so desperate for me to forget Xavier and Gideon that she and her wife tortured me twice.

"Why didn't you tell me?" I scream at Gideon, and he blinks like he's trying not to cry.

"I couldn't," he says shakily. "Gran said it would hurt you. Xavier did something to make you remember, but I can't—I don't know how to do magic, and I didn't want to—" He spreads his hands out hopelessly. "I just wanted to start over," he says weakly. "Me and you. Without the Shadow Thorn. But that wasn't possible."

The Shadow Thorn. The words thrum in my head, and I stagger backward, sweeping my gaze around. It was watching us, that shadow-cloaked monster. Watching Gideon and Xavier destroy me.

It's gone now. I know that as surely as I remember what happened to me. Not just the horrible torture in the shed or the sunny days spent in Gideon's arms or Xavier's awkward, thirteen-year-old-boy kiss, but the fact that my *mother* demanded I forget it all. That she ordered that torture, for me and Juniper both. And she lied about it.

"My mom," I gasp out, trying to work out my confusion. "She—"

"I think she asked Gloria to do it," Gideon says, very quietly. "I don't think Gloria wanted to."

It hits me like a slap. He's right. I'm certain he's right.

I look up at him again, him and Xavier, wrapped in the soft, post-storm sunlight. The darkness is diluting away. The storm served its purpose.

It brought us together, once and for all.

"I have to go." I spin away from the pew and gather up my clothes, still drenched in rainwater. I put on my shirt, my shorts. Leave my underwear. "I have to—I have to find out why."

"Ivy!" Gideon calls out, but I ignore him and race out of the chapel, back toward Golly's house.

Back toward home.

45

IVY

I press the phone receiver to my ear, the ringing tinny and distant. I punched in Mom's phone number without thinking that the call might not even go through—it's a long-distance number, can you even call long distance on a land-line?—but it seems it does.

Whether she'll answer is another matter.

Another jangling ring, then a click. Then Mom's voice, low and cautious.

"Who is this?" she says. "Judith, you better not be—"

"Mom?"

There's a beat of silence, and all I can do is stand there in the kitchen, shivering wildly, my thoughts cobwebbed from what happened earlier in the chapel. I ran blindly through the shredded woods and the debris-strewn meadow, all those long-forgotten memories flashing wildly through my head.

I needed answers.

Especially when I stumbled up to the back porch and found that all the bougainvillea was gone. Every single vine—vanished. The leaves and red blossoms clung to the porch, wet and papery from the rain. I knew then that the rattlesnake would be gone, too. It had served its purpose. It had gotten me to Hartshorn.

And I had given myself up to that family's madness.

"Ivy?" Mom says. "Ivy, is that you? Why are you calling from Gloria's number?"

Her voice drags me back into the now-sunny kitchen. I squeeze the receiver, my palm slick with sweat. Now that I have her on the line, I realize I don't know how to ask what I need to ask.

"I lost my phone," I say.

"Are you all right?" Mom sounds worried. But suspicious, too. "You know I don't like being in that house. In that *place*."

I know she means Gloria's farmhouse, but I think of the chapel, wreathed in grey mist and downy light. The burned walls and the forest forming a cathedral roof overhead. The ecstasy that ripped me to shreds.

The memories.

"I have some questions for you," I spit out, not knowing what else to say.

The line buzzes.

"Is that why you didn't call me back?" Mom's voice suddenly sounds thin and fearful. "Your sister and I were worried sick that you were just ignoring—"

"I have questions for you," I say again, louder. More firmly. I decide to rip it off like a Band-Aid. "Did Juniper and I come here when I was thirteen?"

This time, there's a clatter on the other end. Shuffling. When Mom answers again, she sounds breathless.

"Why would you say that?" she asks, much too lightly.

I clench my jaw. "We did, didn't we?" I lay out the details as I remember them. "You had to go to some training for work. You had gotten a new job, I think. We flew into Houston. Golly picked us up at the airport, just me and Juniper, because you had to catch a connecting flight to Chicago. Did that happen or not?"

Mom gives a soft, hiccuping sob. "How—"

"How do I remember?" It comes out louder than I expect, and there's a harsh, petty part of me that wants to tell her exactly what I did to bring the memories back. *All* of them.

But I know that if I do that, I won't get the answer I need. "I don't know, Mom. I'm curious why I *forgot*."

She sobs again. "Ivy, you never should have gone back th—"

"What did you do?" I yell so loud I hear my own voice recycled back to me through the phone. "What did *Golly* do? And Judith? Because I remember—"

"Don't say it!" Mom shrieks. "I can't stand to hear it!"

Anger surges through my chest. "But you asked them to do it?"

"Of course I did!" she screams. "Because that place had its claws in you! And I had to do it to poor Junie even though she was safe because I couldn't have her saying anything, but He wanted you—"

She cuts herself off, and my skin prickles at the word *He*, and I can picture him, the shadowed god with stars for eyes. The leering statue that presided over me and Gideon and Xavier, our bodies bleeding and tangled in the dirt.

"Who is He?" I say softly.

"The devil," Mom answers in a shaky, tremulous voice.

This is the absolute last thing I expected her to say. We were never a religious family. "You're an atheist."

"I don't believe in God," Mom says sharply. "But I've *seen* Him. So it's not a matter of belief."

Dread coils around me, dark and thick.

"I grew up with it. Your grandmother didn't involve me, but that *family*—" Mom spits out the word like poison. "They were always there, with their rituals and their—" Mom's voice cracks. "I didn't want that for you. I knew it was a mistake to send you girls there, but I didn't have a choice either time. And when that boy kissed you—"

I freeze. There it is. The proof that my memories are real.

"I couldn't stand the thought of you being part of that. So I asked your grandmother to do something about it." Mom's voice is flat. "And she did."

"Magic?" I whisper, feeling absurd.

Mom doesn't answer, although I can hear her breathing on the line. In the silence, memories flare to life. Memories of that dark shed, and the chanting, the pinpricks of sunlight in the darkness, the knives in my brain.

"She *tortured* me," I gasp. "Twice."

Mom goes quiet on the other end of the line. "It didn't take the first time," she says after a long time. "You kept... talking about that place. Dreaming about it. And then your first year in college, you told me you were going to stay on campus during spring break, and instead you went *there*."

Where I fucked Gideon. I remember Hartshorn in the spring, the grounds flooded with wildflowers. Gideon's eager, groping hands.

And then Golly dragging me to the shed again.

Anger scorches over my skin. "And you asked her to do it then, too. To torture me again."

"I begged her to do it," Mom shouts. "Because I couldn't lose you to that place! Once you fall in, you can never get out!"

I scream wordlessly and slam the phone down in the cradle, loud enough that it jangles through the kitchen. My eyes itch like I want to cry, but there are no tears, just a hot, surging rage.

The phone rings, and I scream again and yank out the connecting cable so silence falls over the house.

Then I stumble into the living room, switching on the lights as I go, even though I'm even more certain now that there's no snake in this house. I'm not sure it was even a snake before. It was—

It was Him.

The vines are gone from the fireplace, although the evidence that they were there has not. The stone is still littered with dried-out leaves and red petals, and I sink down in front of it, staring at them, my body buzzing.

I've been so wrapped up in remembering what happened in the past that I've barely thought about what just happened in the present.

This memory sends pleasure jolting through my body. A different kind of heat washes over me as I fall backward into the chapel: the agonizing cut of Xavier's belt, its marks still burning my flesh. Gideon's mouth on my cunt. The confusing tangle of their hands and their tongues and their teeth on my body. The way they lifted me between them, balancing me on their thick, hard cocks, and worshipped me until I was a ruin.

I wrap my arms around myself, chilly in my damp clothes, even as my lust burns me alive. Syrupy golden-hour sunlight pours in around the thick curtains. The black storm has completely evaporated now. My wet hair and clammy shirt are the only evidence that it happened at all.

Once you fall in, you can never get out.

Except I didn't fall in, did I? I ran straight to that chapel, and I willingly gave myself up to two priests of the devil.

46

GIDEON

"You can't go."

I stop in the doorway to the kitchen, where Gran is shuffling around, making dinner. Gnocchi trots along beside her, his fluffy tail lifted in a friendly question mark. It's my first time really seeing him, since he had been hidden away the night I spent at Ivy's house. But he blinks up at me now, his eyes big and green.

"You didn't know what I was going to say," I tell Gran sullenly, even though she's correct. For the last hour, I haven't been able to stop thinking about Ivy, about how she spread herself open for me—

and for Xavier

—in the chapel, offering her body up to the Shadow Thorn without spilling a drop of blood. Her scent is everywhere on me, as sweet as honeysuckle. Every time I brush my hair out of my eyes, I smell her on my fingers.

"I didn't need you to say it." Gran sets a big cast-iron skillet on the stove and looks over at me, her gaze clear. "I can feel it radiating off you. You're worried about Ivy."

"The phone line's disconnected!" I stalk into the kitchen,

where Gnocchi sniffs at my ankles. "She ran out of the chapel when she remembered everything, and I'm afraid she's hurt. You *said* it would hurt her, remembering everything at once."

Gran calmly pulls ingredients out of the refrigerator. Heavy cream. Sharp cheddar. A bulb of garlic.

"I understand, but *you* can't go." Gran turns to face me, and I stiffen at the way she stresses the word. "You don't feel it, do you? You're head's still back at the chapel."

Dread knots around in my stomach, especially when Gran goes to the pantry and pulls out a bag of potatoes and a big white onion.

"What are you making?" I ask, my mouth suddenly dry. Because I know. I have been distracted, too caught up in claiming Ivy with my brother to realize the change in the air.

A sacrifice is coming.

Gran just looks at me. "We'll be feasting tonight."

"No!" I shake my head, curl my hands up into fists. "No, I can't do it. We'll have to wait for the next one."

Gran gives me a long, reproachful look.

"Please!" My thoughts are wild. This is the last fucking thing I want to deal with. What I *want* is to take Gnocchi back to Ivy and curl up with her on the bed, his fluffy body nestled between us, and explain everything she needs to know.

Like how Uncle Jack had to lock me in one of the house's bedrooms when Gran and Gloria went to erase Ivy's memory after our first time together in the chapel because they knew damn well I'd try to stop it. Or how Gloria told me after that she only did it because she was afraid she would lose Ivy for good if she didn't.

Or how I haven't been able to stop loving Ivy for the last decade because she's *mine,* and this afternoon only proved that once and for all.

Even if she's also Xavier's.

"Gideon," Gran says sharply. "The Shadow Thorn just

offered you and Xavier a tremendous gift. You know damn well how these things work. And you know damn well you can't just *skip* a sacrifice tonight."

"But she remembered," I say weakly. "She could be hurting right now."

Gran turns to her cutting board. "We can send Xavier to take care of her."

"Xavier?" Anger bristles down my spine. "Absolutely not. He'll make things worse."

Gran sighs, lining a potato up on the cutting board. "You boys are going to have to learn to share."

"It's not about sharing," I snap. "It's about him being a goddamn asshole."

"I'll make sure he's on his best behavior." She punctuates the sentence with the *whisk-thud* of the knife slicing the potato into paper-thin discs. She's making scalloped potatoes to go with the meat.

The meat that I have to provide.

"And how are you going to do that?" I shake my head. "No, no. Make him kill the sacrifice."

Gran sighs again. "Gideon, if that was remotely a possibility, I would do it. I understand your concern. But you do these things much cleaner, and you have much more experience, and—"

"I only have the experience because you forced me to have the experience!" I shout. "You and Dad and everyone else! Why the *fuck* couldn't Xavier have—"

Gran slams the knife down and whirls to face me. "Gideon, you aren't fifteen years old anymore. You know damn well why your father did things the way he did. Now, go get ready. I'll send Xavier over with some mother's milk to help Ivy relax."

I tremble with rage. Sharing her in the chapel had been one thing. That was a ritual, an act of worship, a claiming.

But I don't want to share her like this. I want to be the one to take care of her, to kiss her worries away. Xavier can fuck her if she wants to fuck him. But he's not a good person. He's not a good *boyfriend*.

"He's going to make things worse," I growl.

"He's going to do exactly what I tell him," Gran says, "or else he'll get a week of the dreaming. Does that make you feel better?"

I frown. The dreaming is a punishment, an old one in our family. Nightmares, basically. The most vivid, most horrific nightmares you can imagine. And they don't fade after you wake up.

"What are you going to tell him to do?" I say.

Gran smiles at that and turns back to the potatoes. "She's lucky to have you watching out for her," she says as she slices. "I told you. I'll give him a pitcher of mother's milk and tell him he's not to touch her inappropriately. The girl needs to rest anyway." Gran glances at me over her shoulder. "And when you're done, while I'm preparing the meat, you can go check on her. If anything's wrong, he gets the dreaming."

I scowl, still irritated. But I can also feel it, the sacrifice. There are two of them, winding their way through the back-country roads. A man and a woman, I think. Pulsing with life.

But more than that, I can feel the Shadow Thorn's hunger. He's ravenous after what happened this afternoon. The storm. The ritual. The claiming. That's how things have always worked in this family: He gives us gifts, and we repay him with blood.

And he did give me the biggest gift of my life.

"Promise me," I say. Then, after a moment of consideration. "No. *Swear* it."

Gran looks over at me again, amusement sparkling in her eyes. "You really are serious about her."

"Do it. Or I'm letting those sacrifices go."

Gran doesn't believe me, and I don't know if I believe myself. But she does nod.

"I swear on the Shadow Thorn," she says, her eyes meeting mine. "I will not let your brother harm Ivy Myste."

She stabs the point of the knife into her thumb until blood beads up, bright beneath the kitchen lights. Then she smears it on her forehead, the way Catholics do ashes at the start of Lent. Never once do her eyes leave mine.

"May this blood burn me if I break my oath," she says, before turning back to the potatoes.

I take a deep breath, the air crackling with the energy of her spell.

"Thank you," I say stiffly.

"Go," Gran says. "Get ready. If you weren't so fucking besotted, you'd know they're almost here."

"I do know," I snap, and Gran just shoos me away. Gnocchi looks up at me and meows, his eyes big and round. I give him a pat on the head before I go over to the old wing to prepare.

I CROUCH IN THE UNDERBRUSH, the leaves still dripping from the storm earlier. Every drop of water reminds me of Ivy— chasing her through the wind and rain, the searing warmth of her naked body against mine, the sharp cruelty of her lashes with the belt, the hot sheath of her cunt.

I close my eyes and let out a long breath. No. I have to concentrate on the task at hand. Gran's right. Fifteen years of doing this shit means I can do it quickly and cleanly. The quicker I can take care of it now, the faster I can check on Ivy and make sure she's okay.

And make sure my sadistic younger brother hasn't made things worse.

The sound of a car engine cuts through the soft, rustling

woods. I shift in the underbrush so I have a better view of the little two-lane highway that cuts through our property. In Harlan, they call it Satan's Ramble because so many travelers disappear along this stretch of road.

Everyone knows why. But they don't talk about it. The Shadow Thorn's doing.

The sun is setting, and the light is purplish and soft. When the tidy little Honda comes around the bend in the road, they already have their headlights on, bright LED lamps that look like twin suns. I readjust my rifle so I can shoot a little earlier, before the headlights blind me.

I can't see the sacrifices in the car, but I know these are the right ones. The forest changes: the wind blows harder, the cicadas scream louder. I can feel the Shadow Thorn pressing down on me, guiding my movements as I lower my eye to the scope and lift my finger to the trigger.

The *bang* of the rifle echoes through the forest, and it only takes one shot. The rear driver's side tire on the Honda explodes into ribbons, and the car careens across the road, spinning in circles across the asphalt. I set the rifle down and pick up the hunting knife Dad gifted me on my tenth birthday, the year my training started.

All my movements are easy. Practiced. I've done this a thousand times before. I've done this more times than I've fake-fought in a wrestling ring.

The car slams into one of the pine trees in a cascade of metal and glass. I rise, clutching the knife in one hand, and stick to the shadows as I move toward the accident. The first of the sacrifices climbs out of the driver's side door—the woman. There's a cut on her forehead, blood trailing down between her eyes, and she runs around to the passenger side, calling out, "Bryan! Bryan!" in a frantic voice.

I'm numb to it. This is my real job. Not keeping up the Hartshorn estate. Not wrestling on the indie circuit. At the end of the day, those are just my covers. This is what I'm destined to do with my life.

I think of Ivy, flushed and panting, her nails digging into my arms, and I don't know how she's going to react to any of this. I don't want to tell her, although I suppose, if the Shadow Thorn really does want her to be a Hartshorn, she'll have to find out eventually.

Just like Gloria did. Just like Mom did. And she'll have to make the same choice they did, too.

I put the thought aside. I need to concentrate, especially now that the other sacrifice has staggered out of the car. He's a pretty big guy, but he's also hurt, his face completely covered in blood. The woman clings to him, pressing her hand up against her head, her voice high-pitched and panicky.

They haven't called anyone yet. Not that it matters. The Harlan County sheriff's department knows to leave us alone.

I slip close, moving in that quick, silent way Dad and Uncle Jack taught me. The sacrifices still haven't noticed that anything's wrong. They're too focused on their injuries.

Quick and clean. In and out. I fix Ivy's face in my mind so I don't get carried away.

Then I attack. I go for the man first, barreling out of the woods and tackling him out of the woman's arms. She screams, a sound that blends in with the screams of the cicadas.

The man struggles back against me, acting on instinct. His arm swings up to catch me in the jaw, but I duck and slide the knife into the side of the throat. Quick. Clean.

When I yank it out, blood sprays like a fan, glistening in the falling sunlight. And the whole forest breathes out, like the Shadow Thorn is sighing with delight.

"What did you do?" the woman screams, shrill and panicky. "What did you do?"

I stand up and turn toward her. She's young; they both are. College age. Something pulled them onto the East Texas back roads and away from the interstates. Maybe a wrong turn, maybe a sense of adventure. It doesn't matter. The Shadow Thorn willed it to happen, and here they are, ready to be prepared into a thank-you gift. An exchange. The Shadow Thorn gives my family what we want, and we gift Him blood in return.

These two college kids are the price for claiming Ivy.

"Why did you do that?" the woman screams, the question dissolving into a sob. She sags, and for a moment I think she might faint—which, honestly, I would prefer. But then some survival instinct kicks in, and she turns and runs down the road, back the way the car came.

I chase her. It's nothing like chasing Ivy. It doesn't give me a thrill. It's work.

It's work when I catch her, too, grabbing her by the waist so that her feet lift off the ground in frantic, terrified kicking. "Don't!" she screams. "Please!"

I don't say anything. I have no doubt that if Xavier were doing this, he would toy with her. Toy with both of them, actually. Injure them and force them to entertain him while he jerked off with their blood. He'd taint the sacrifice. Taint the meat.

Dad sensed that sadism in him young and didn't sense it in me, and that's why I'm here and Xavier is not.

"Why?" the woman begs, tears streaming down her cheeks. "Why are you doing this?"

"Because my god wills it," I answer, right before I drag the knife over her throat.

47

XAVIER

My bougainvillea is gone.

I stop in the backyard of Ivy's house and gaze up at the now-cleared porch, feeling rankled. That was proof of my claim, and now it's gone.

You don't need proof anymore, whispers a voice on the wind, speaking with the sound of the trees and the insects and the earth tumbling beneath my feet. I scowl. Yes, I got to fuck her. But I didn't exactly get what I wanted.

I stalk forward, clutching the thermos of mother's milk that Gran shoved in my hand, her threat whipping around in my head. "Do not harm that girl or I will give you a week's worth of the dreaming," she said, stirring a pot of greens on the stove. A sacrifice meal. I haven't had one in ages, but I figured we'd get one after the chapel this afternoon.

I knew the threat was serious. I saw the blood oath on her forehead.

"Did Gideon make you do that?" I asked, arms crossed. She just looked at me.

"Be back by midnight," she said. "I expect you to participate."

Participate in the meal, she means. The ritual. I figured as much, and I'm inclined to do it without protest. I mean, I *did* finally get to fuck Ivy after a fifteen-year wait, and I can only thank the Shadow Thorn for that, even if—

Even if it came with some strings attached.

Gideon. I saw the way Ivy looked at him in the chapel, her eyes big and adoring. She bared her back for me, choked on my cock, let me ravage her virgin asshole. But she never once looked at me the way she looked at Gideon.

I step up onto Ivy's porch, consider knocking, decide against it. If Ivy decides she doesn't want to let me in, I don't want to get saddled with a week of nightmares for my trouble.

Fortunately, the lock's still broken from when I snapped it a few days ago, so all I have to do is ease the door open. It's easier this time, without that bougainvillea, but I don't have the hot, fluttery anticipation in my chest. *Do not hurt her*, Gran said, and I knew what she meant even if she didn't say it.

Don't do anything Ivy doesn't agree to.

The house is dark and quiet and cool. I slide the door shut behind me, then stand and listen. The house seems to breathe, slow and steady. I almost think Ivy might not be here—it's not like I checked to see if her car was in the drive—when I hear a scraping upstairs.

She's in her bedroom, then. My dick stirs at the thought.

I make my way to the stairs, then up to the second floor. There's a triangle of light spilling into the hallway, the soft hum of TV voices. I move along silently and then step into the doorway.

She doesn't see me. She's sitting at the desk, her legs tucked up in the big office chair, watching something on her laptop. Some old rom-com from the looks of it, a pretty brunette with glasses arguing with her gay friend.

"Knock, knock," I say with a smile, and Ivy screams and

nearly falls out of her seat. She catches herself on the desk and twists around to look at me, her eyes wide with fear.

"What the fuck are you doing here?" she demands.

I tsk softly. "Is that any way to talk to your partner?"

"You're not my *partner*." She stands up and presses her spine into the desk like she's preparing for me to attack. The movie plays softly in the background. "Where's Gideon?"

Hearing his name sends a burning jolt of jealousy straight through my chest. Even after all that happened this afternoon, *he's* the first one she asked about?

We both chased her.

We both came with her.

We both *claimed* her.

"Busy," I say tightly, although something sparks in my head. A rather naughty idea.

But one that might be worth a week of the dreaming.

Ivy glares at me. "Why are you here?" she says softly. "And why didn't you knock like a normal person?"

"Like Gideon?" I say mockingly, stepping into her room.

"Yes, like Gideon."

I ignore the second stab of jealousy. "Well, Gideon's not here," he says. "I do things my way." I hold up the thermos. "Gran asked me to bring this to you."

Ivy keeps watching me, as wary as her cat. "What is it?"

"Mother's milk." I unscrew the lid and pour out a little of the pale, creamy concoction. "She said to tell you that you've had it before. When you passed out." I peer up at her. "That's a story I'd like to hear, by the way. Did Gideon fuck you out of consciousness?"

I hadn't meant to say that last part, but it comes out anyway, hard and bitter.

Ivy doesn't answer. But she does grab the lid out of my hand and inspects the mother's milk. "I remember this," she says softly. "They told me it was horchata."

"They taste the same," I say, sitting down on the edge of her bed. The same bed, of course, where I handcuffed her and devoured her sweet pussy while she begged me to stop. "But no, this is not horchata. It's magic."

Ivy looks at me from over the lid, her face unreadable.

"Gran's a witch," I say easily. "In case you haven't figured that out yet. Gloria was, too." I grin. "So am I, I suppose you could say."

"Is Gideon?" he asks.

Fuck, I wish I could slap his name out of her mouth.

"That's not really Gideon's skillset," I say. "Thinking, you know."

Ivy rolls her eyes. "It's a bad look," she says. "Being so jealous of him."

Then she knocks back the mother's milk like she's shooting whiskey, and her words burn just as bad, making my skin prickle with something like embarrassment.

"There's nothing to be jealous of," I snap, even though it's a lie and we both know it. "You came just as hard on my dick earlier as you did his."

Now it's Ivy's turn to burn up, and her pale skin shows all of it, a pretty pink flush to her cheeks. The same pretty pink flush as when she was coming, actually.

"How much of this can I drink?" she asks.

"All of it," I answer. "It helps with the aftereffects from the chapel. From the Shadow Thorn's presence. And from—" I grin at her. "From getting your memories back."

Ivy sits down in her chair and pours out another lid's worth of mother's milk. Me and Gideon and our cousins used to drink it all the time as kids. Every time Dad or Uncle Jack or Gran showed us something new, something about the truth of our family, they would serve up a big glass of the stuff. I haven't had it in ages. I don't need it anymore. But I can smell it, those milky notes brimming with almond and cinnamon, and I think of summer afternoons with my hands covered in blood.

Gideon's hands are probably covered in blood right now. I bet Ivy wouldn't be so quick to defend him if she saw that.

The idea shudders through me, taking form. We both claimed her, yes. But if she rejects Gideon, his claim won't matter. Gideon's *far* too much of a gentleman to force himself on her.

I'm not, though. It would be a delight to grind down her hesitations until she's my bride and mine alone.

Ivy sips on the mother's milk, watching me over the lid. "Does Judith still have Gnocchi?" she says suddenly.

"Of course she does," I tell her. "He won't stop following her around the kitchen."

A smile flickers across her lips, just for a second. I think it's the first time she's ever smiled at me.

"I can come get him," she says. "I'll get his carrier and—"

"He can stay with us until tomorrow. Gran won't mind." In truth, I think Gideon's going to bring him over after he finishes carving up the sacrifices. He'll have time while Gran's cooking them for the feast. He's so fucking predictable. I know he's thinking he'll bring over the little fluff ball so Ivy can bat her eyes at him and tell him what a hero he is for being nice to her cat, not knowing he was elbow deep in human intestines an hour or so earlier.

If only she could see it. Now, when she's still shaky and trembling from the effects of being in the Shadow Thorn's presence. When she's uncertain about what she offered up on the floor of the chapel. I know she's not going to talk about it with me—I can sense it, her guardedness, her distrust. She's afraid of me.

Afraid of me when she should be afraid of Gideon.

"You know," I say, crossing my legs, leaning forward. "I think I ought to come clean about something."

Ivy jerks her gaze up and watches me warily.

"I read your dissertation," I say smugly.

"Excuse me?"

"Well, a draft of it." I keep my eyes fixed on her. "I've been keeping an eye on you for a long, long time, Ivy Myste. Particularly your academic career."

Ivy scoffs, but I can sense she's trying to hide her fear, too. "If that were true," she says darkly. "Then you would know I never submitted my dissertation." She pauses, then adds, somewhat defensively, "I'm still working on it."

I grin. "Yes, I know," I say. "You emailed the most recent version to a Dr. Rebecca Muñoz at The University of New Mexico—what was it? Last fall?"

The thermos slides out of Ivy's hand and cracks across the floor, spilling the last of the mother's milk.

"How do you possibly know that?" she hisses.

I smile and spread my hands wide. "I work for an organization," I say. "That has access to those kinds of things."

That is one perk of being the family liaison for the glorified mob that is the Five Courts. It wasn't hard to bring in a little black hat computer nerd from one of the minor families to hack into UNM's email database.

"Don't you want to know what I thought of it?" I ask. "Your dissertation?"

"You didn't read it," Ivy snarls.

"Oh, I did." I printed out the whole fucking thing, in fact, scouring for clues as to how I might bring Ivy back to Hartshorn. I don't tell her that, though. It's not relevant to what I want right now.

"You wrote about the Bluebeard motif in twentieth-century American Gothic fiction." I stand up, keeping my eyes fixed on Ivy. She braces against her desk. "You argued, if I was reading it correctly, that such stories show a yearning for the transgressive." I stare at her, feeling my skin prickle. "For the violent. For the desire to be *chased*."

Ivy winds back her arm to slap me, but I catch her by the wrist and squeeze her bones together, my eyes never leaving hers.

"I know Bluebeard wasn't the focus," I say. "But that section stood out to me the most. All those clueless brides searching for knowledge and finding death instead."

Ivy jerks her hand away from me.

"I think you should leave," she says stiffly. "Thank you for bringing me the mother's milk. It did help. Please tell Gideon—"

"Don't you want to know what Gideon is doing?" Anger coils around in my belly. She's treating me like nothing happened three hours ago. This woman worshipped my cock like it was her god. Now she won't even look me in the eye.

But she'll ask for my brother.

"What does that have to do with anything?" she snaps. "You're the one hacking my private emails. Now get the hell out of my house."

"Gideon has *everything* to do with it, darling." I sink to my knees in front of her, trying not to rage when she twists away from me. *Patience*, I tell myself, gazing up at her like I'm about to propose. And I suppose this is a proposal of sorts. It's certainly the first step in making her mine for good. "Have you ever thought about why you might be so fascinated by the story of Bluebeard and his hapless wives that you built an entire academic career around it?"

"I would not say I did that."

I run my hand along her bare thigh, relishing the way she stiffens beneath my touch. She might not *like* me, but she'll let me touch her. She'll let me do more than that, too.

I step at the hem of her shorts and keep my hand there. Her pulse pumps beneath her skin.

"I beg to differ, having read your dissertation." I peer up at her and smile when I see the way she's biting her lip. "So answer me, cicada. Why do you think you were so fascinated?"

"I don't understand what you're getting at," she says shakily. "Does this have something to do with…"

Her voice trails off, and I hear a gust of wind outside.

"The Shadow Thorn? I suppose so." I slide my hand further between her thighs until I'm cupping her pussy, her damp warmth more than evident. "Thinking about this afternoon?"

It's too much. She snaps her legs shut and then whips herself away with enough force that she almost breaks my wrist. I grin. "I'll take that as a yes."

"Xavier, please get out of my house." She stumbles backward, moving toward the door. "I appreciate you bringing this drink, whatever it is. It is helping. But you need to leave."

I rise up slowly. Her eyes drop down to my crotch, just for a second. I make a show of adjusting my erection for her, which turns those pretty pale cheeks red again.

"You want to see my brother," I say softly, striding toward her. "Even after everything, he's still the one you want."

She doesn't move away as I approach. Nor does she protest when I wrap my fingers lightly around her throat. No, that excites her. I see the flare of lust in her eyes, hear the sharp intake of her breath.

"He's behind the door you shouldn't open," I murmur, tilting my mouth against her ear. God, the tremble of her body against mine is intoxicating. Any amount of punishment will be worth what I'm about to do if it means I get to feel this every day for the rest of my life. "There's a little shack on the edge of our property. Behind the chapel. You've been there before. Twice."

She swallows hard.

"That's where he is, darling. Behind a door he desperately doesn't want you to open right now."

I release her and step back, admiring my handiwork.

"Go fuck yourself," she snarls.

"Oh, I will." I grin. "And I'll be thinking about your sweet cunt while I do."

Ivy slaps me. The sting of her palm sends fire shooting straight to my cock, and it takes every ounce of willpower not to bend her over the bed, shove down those shorts, and slam my dick into her ass without any preparation. Any other woman, I'd punish her insolence.

But with Ivy, I'm playing a long game.

"You won't be slapping me when you find out what he's doing," I say in a sing-song, stepping backward toward the door. "I know you're curious, cicada. Just like Bluebeard's transgressive little wife."

"Get out!" Ivy shouts.

And this time, I do.

48

IVY

I listen to Xavier's retreat through my house, his footsteps heavy and stomping. Only when I hear the slam of the back door do I slump down in my chair, shaking with adrenaline.

I hate the way my body reacts to him. Hate that I feel the slick of my own arousal, all because he held me by the throat and whispered roughly in my ear. Hate that, as hard as I try, I still think about how good it felt to have him buried in my ass, especially with Gideon stretching my pussy to its limits.

My head swoons. I wish I hadn't spilled the rest of the horchata-that's-not-horchata all over the floor. Maybe I shouldn't have drunk it—I'm sure Mom would say it's poison. But it did soothe the desperate chatter in my head. At least until Xavier filled it up with something new.

A shack in the woods. A door you shouldn't unlock.

I shake my head, trying to put the thought away. I know damn well what Xavier's doing: trying to drive a wedge between me and Gideon. Because, despite this afternoon, despite all this talk about *claiming* me and dark rituals and whatever the fuck else that happened—

Gideon's the one I want. The one I choose.

You won't be slapping me when you find out what he's doing.

I stand up and pace around the room, trying to work off my energy. It's unnerving—to say that least—that Xavier read my unfinished dissertation. Because he definitely did. The part about Bluebeard is minor, but it's in there. And only someone who's read the stupid thing would know that.

I don't want to think about what organization he could possibly be working for that would allow him to access my advisor's email. Or what it means that Gideon didn't tell me the truth about it. What did he say Xavier did? Consulting work?

It wouldn't be the first lie of omission Gideon's guilty of. He never mentioned fucking me when I was eighteen, either.

I go over to the window, the gloam of twilight lying thick across the woods. Xavier is a dark shadow moving toward the trees, and I feel something tugging in my chest, wanting to follow him.

A shack in the woods.

It rankles me that Gideon kept secrets. I realize they weren't exactly lies. But they were hollows in our conversations. A changed topic here, a glossing over there.

And he did the same with his work at Hartshorn, didn't he? "I have chores to do," he'd say, kissing me on the cheek. "Some work to take care of around the estate."

But this is a strange time to be doing chores. And what could be so important that he sent *Xavier* to check on me? Even after what happened? *Especially* after what happened, when my memories came flooding back and Gideon was at the center of them?

A cold sliver of fear cuts through my chest, and I think, suddenly and inexplicably, of those photographs I found on Golly's laptop. The piles of bleached white bones.

Then the skull that Xavier wore as he chased me through

the rain. It hadn't felt like plastic, had it, when it brushed against my cheek?

I jerk away from the window and stalk out of my room, my hands shaking. I try to tell myself to calm down, that Xavier's playing some cruel, jealous game, that Gideon will be here when he's done—

Doing what? What is Gideon doing?

I couldn't lose you to that place! Once you fall in, you can never get out!

I'm in the kitchen before I know it. Xavier left the light on and the door hanging open, just an inch. Without the vines, it's easy to step out on the porch.

I stand on the top step, a warm, familiar wind pushing my hair away from my face. For a moment, I think I hear a rough, raspy whispering in a thorny language. And then that's gone, too.

Xavier's nowhere to be seen. I know that there is a good chance this is some kind of trap, that when I step onto the path to Hartshorn, he'll be waiting for me, and he'll shove me up against a tree or tackle me into the ferns and take what he wants—

what you want

—but I can't stop working over what he said. About Bluebeard. About doors and secrets. About Gideon.

And I can't stop thinking about the bones on Golly's computer.

I suck in my breath and step out into the grass, plunging forward through the gloam. After the pitch of the storm earlier, the twilight is easy to navigate without a flashlight, especially with the moon hanging full and heavy in the sky, bigger than it ought to be and bright enough to cast very thin shadows from the trees. When I step into the woods proper, fireflies swarm out. It feels like there are millions of them.

Just like with Gideon, back in April.

My chest tightens. The fireflies surge forward in a ribbon of light, compelling me to follow. And I do. I plunge forward, taking the same path that I took that night with Gideon—right at the fork instead of left, until the creek glimmers silver through the trees, like it's filled with starlight. I listen to its soft, quiet babbling and follow the swarm of fireflies along the path until I come to the cemetery where Gideon kissed me for the first time.

No. Not the first time. The first time this summer.

I can sense the presence of the chapel, heavy and dark. But that's not where I'm meant to go, is it? Not now.

The fireflies swirl around like falling stars, as if they're waiting for me to decide what to do. *No sign of Xavier*, I think distantly, and that just makes the knot in my chest even tighter.

Because it means this isn't a trap. This is—something else.

The wind picks up, blowing around scraps of leaves and flowers from the storm earlier. They cling to my bare skin, damp from the humidity.

I step forward into the cloud of fireflies. The drift forward, and I follow them with shaky steps, trying not to think about how magical they felt that night in April, and how sinister they feel right now.

They veer me away from the chapel and deeper into the forest, into a part of the woods I barely recognize. There's a path here, too, narrow but clear. The trees creak overhead, their branches braiding together. My footsteps are a soft, pattering sound against the pine needles, and it's almost too dark to see. Almost.

A light appears up ahead, wavering and yellow. I stop, fear spiking down my spine.

The wind gusts hard, and the fireflies disperse, carrying their tiny blinking lanterns out into the dark thicket.

A little shack on the edge of their property, Xavier said.

I move forward, slow and cautious. This could still be a trap.

There could be a shack, but it's Xavier waiting inside, not Gideon. Because what evil could Gideon do? Yes, he wasn't honest about the past. But he did have a reason. He said he did it to protect me.

The path twists to the left, and the woods clear out, and there's the shack. Seeing it jolts me like lightning, because this was where Golly and Judith brought me when they took my memories away. I remember it—Golly dragging me by the wrist through the hot woods, sweat already making my shirt stick to my back. It had been mid-afternoon, the hottest part of the day. *I'm sorry, Ivy, but I don't have a choice. Your mother doesn't want this for you.*

Something surges in me. Golly did have a choice. But I didn't. That option was taken away from me—by my mother, by Golly, by Judith.

They did it when I chose Xavier, when I was too young to know what he was.

But they did it when I chose Gideon, too, when I was eighteen and *did* know what I wanted. I remember it, how badly I wanted him. How badly I still want him.

If he's in there, I'll choose him, no matter what. And if Xavier's in there—

Heat buzzes across my skin. I remember his teeth on my nipple, his belt on my back, his cock in my ass. I remember how hard I came beneath his fingers.

I slam forward into the clearing, up to the door to the shack. I can see someone moving inside, blocking the light spilling through the gaps in the boards. My breath is caught in my throat, and my heart races like a hummingbird's, and when I pull on the door, I expect it to be locked, just like the door in the Bluebeard story.

But it's not locked. It swings open, and warm yellow light spills into the darkness—

Along with a hot, coppery stink.

The first thing I see is Gideon, and I feel an immediate burst of relief. But then he looks up from the table, and his face twists into an expression that is either horror or despair. Or both.

"Ivy, no!"

But by then, I've seen it. The body lying on the workbench where Golly and Judith carved out my memories.

A woman, her blond hair draping like a curtain over the side of the table, and her chest split open. Her cracked rib cage looks like roots jutting up out of the swamp of her organs, wet and red and glistening.

And Gideon—

Gideon's hands are drenched in blood up to his elbows, and he's wearing a white apron splattered with blood. Everything's splattered with blood. The table. The walls. The big cooler sitting on the floor next to—

I gag and stumble backward. There's another body, a man, his head tilted to the side, a jagged red line across his throat, empty eyes staring at me.

Gideon says something, but his voice sounds muffled and far away, like he's underwater. I'm aware of him moving toward me, his bloody hands outstretched. But it's not *his* blood. It's—

Meat. There's meat hanging from the ceiling, red and gleaming.

"Ivy," Gideon says, and my name rings out clearly. He sets something down as he steps around the table. A butcher's cleaver. "Ivy, please, just breathe."

A scream erupts from my lungs. Gideon reaches out to me again and then freezes, as if he's seeing his hand for the first time.

"What are you?" I shriek, backing out of the shack, the smell of blood still thick in my nostrils. I don't understand what I'm looking at. But I also understand completely.

I understand, suddenly, why my mother hates this place.

"Ivy," Gideon says softly, but I turn and run, wild, into the woods, where I'm caught by a tangle of brambles that scrape and drag on my skin. I scream and thrash, trying desperately to get through them and failing. When I whirl around again, Gideon is standing in the doorway, pulling the bloody apron over his head. "Ivy, just breathe. I'm not going to hurt you, okay? I would never hurt you."

"You're a *murderer*!" I scream, the word hanging in the air between us.

Gideon shakes his head sadly. "I'm so much worse than that," he murmurs.

I burst out of the bramble and run sideways, looking for the path in the sallow light of the shack. I have to get away from Hartshorn. I have to get Gnocchi somehow, and I have to get in my car and drive as far from here as I can—

Footsteps sound behind me, soft and crackling.

"Get away from me!" I shriek, whirling around.

But it's not Gideon. It's Xavier, his face carved up with a wicked grin.

"What did I tell you?" he says mockingly. "You really are Bluebeard's poor, curious wife."

"Fuck you!" I scream, and then I run away from him, tearing off down the path.

But I don't get far. Because a pale figure steps in front of me. A woman with hair the color of freshly fallen snow.

Judith.

I stumble to a stop. I can barely see her face in the darkness, and I have a single, wild thought—that she's in danger, that she has to get away from here.

"I'm sorry about this, sweetheart," she says softly. "May Gloria forgive me."

And then she jams a needle into my arm. The prick of it feels like a bee sting.

And then I don't feel anything but a heavy, thick numbness that pours through my limbs.

And then I can't stand. I can barely think. I topple around and fall hard on my side, blinking up at the dappled, moonlit woods

The last thing I see is Xavier and Gideon, standing side by side, and the black, starry-eyed shadow rising behind them.

TO BE CONTINUED

Thank you for reading A Dream of the Forest! I hope you enjoyed it.

I know that's a big cliffhanger, but don't worry: the series continues with A Nightmare in Her Heart, which will be released in early 2026.

To make sure you don't miss it—or any of my other releases—sign up for my newsletter at rosebitterly.com/newsletter. When you do, you'll have access to several freebies, including a prequel story about Judith and Gloria and a bonus spicy scene between Ivy and Gideon!

ABOUT THE AUTHOR

Rose Bitterly is a hopeless romantic who has been reading and writing scary stories since elementary school—imagine her excitement when she learned you could blend the two! Today, she writes dark, immersive horror romances featuring slashers and other monsters, all shot through with a hint of the occult. Visit her online at rosebitterly.com.

Never miss a new book! Sign up for Rose's mailing list and receive free bonus stories: https://www.rosebitterly.com/news letter.